**Boswell wrestled with the Angel of Death
and suddenly realized
that everybody dies . . .**

With that realization he begins an odyssey of the
ego, searching out VIP's and prostrating himself
before them. He seeks out the world's richest man,
history's first international revolutionist, a Nobel
prize-winning anthropologist, an Italian *principessa*.
Although he has embarked upon a journey that cannot help but disillusion, it is his destiny!

BOSWELL

A picaresque novel
by the man of whom
New York Times Book Review
would write

"no serious funny writer in this country
can match him."
STANLEY ELKIN

Novels by Stanley Elkin

A Bad Man
Boswell
Criers and Kibitzers, Kibitzers and Criers
The Dick Gibson Show
The Living End

Published by
WARNER BOOKS

Stanley Elkin

BOSWELL

A Modern Comedy

WARNER BOOKS

A Warner Communications Company

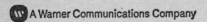

For Joan, for Philip, for Zelda, and Diane
And for my father

Part One

I

Everybody dies, everybody. Sure. And there's neither heaven nor hell. Parker says hell is six inches below the ground and four above the head. So we walk between, never quite managing to touch either, but reassured anyway because heaven is by two inches the closer. That Parker! What difference does it make? Everybody dies and that's that. But no one really believes it. They read the papers. They see the newsreels. They drive past the graveyards on the outskirts of town. Do you think that makes any difference? It does not! No one believes in death.

Except me. Boswell. I believe in it. I believe in everything. My metaphysics is people, the living and the dead. Ladloc, the historian, says that history is the record of all the births and deaths for which there is a record. History is dates. John Burgoyne was born in 1722 and died in 1792. Louis XVI: 1754–1793. (Do you suppose Louis knew of Burgoyne's death? Do you suppose he said, "Ah, he's gone now, the old campaigner"? Do you suppose he suspected he'd be dead in a year himself?) Shakespeare: 1564(?)–1616. Caesar: 102 (or 100)–44 B.C. History. But do you notice how as one goes back the birthdays become less certain while the year of death is always absolute, fixed? Do you think that's an accident? Listen, death is realer than life. I saw a sign on U.S. 40 in Kentucky. It said REMEMBER YOU MUST DIE. I remember. But I never needed the sign. I had my own father. My father was a healthy man. Content, vigorous,

9

powerful, well. But when he died, he died of everything. The cancer, the blindness, the swollen heart, the failed markets. But even that, the death of one's father in a hospital room, the kiss goodbye inside the oxygen tent, isn't enough for some people. Even if they stretch a point and come to believe in the death of others, they refuse to believe in their own.

I remember reading in the *St. Louis Globe-Democrat* an interview with the murderer, Braddock, when I was a kid. Braddock, waiting in the deathhouse, told Edward Renfrue, the reporter, "When they pull that switch, they'll be pulling it on the whole world. Nobody will outlive me. Nobody. The warden. The president. You. My girlfriends. Nobody. Everybody dies when I die." He could believe in a fantastic short circuit that would end the world, but not in his own mortality. Do you suppose only a murderer thinks that way? Go on, it wasn't until they pulled the switch that Braddock understood what it was like to *be* a murderer. Then he murdered everybody, all of us, the born and the unborn. And don't you think he didn't close his eyes two seconds before he had to just to make sure? Just so as not to be proved wrong? Listen, even my father, my own father, when I kneeled beside his bed in that white white stinking room, looked at me and there was blood in his eyes. Why, he's angry, I thought. He's mad at me.

I'm different. I remember I must die. It explains everything. People who do not know me well—people who don't keep files on me, as I do on them (5 by 9 cards with the person's name and dates and a brief identifying phrase)—think my interest in them is faked, self-interested, that I'm a social climber on the make for everybody. The truth is I've a sort of chronic infidelity. It's not that I have a disappointment threshold lower than most, or a higher hope. It's just what I said: congenital infidelity. I am not a lover but I am like one. I am a strategist, an arranger, a schemer, but there is nothing sinister about me, nothing sinister even about my plans. It's as though I had devoted my life to arranging surprise parties, and, indeed, there is something celebrational in

10

many of my contacts. I have in my files an engraved invitation in a raised, wonderfully ornate script:

Mr. & Mrs. Richard Montrose Shepley
Would Take Infinite Pleasure in Your
Attendance at the Marriage
Ceremony of their Daughter,
Celia Rochelle,
To Mr. Leon Randolph Wesley,
The Son of Mr. & Mrs.
Mark Hawthorne Wesley . . .

All those parents, still living, that striking girl, that marvelous young man, all those beautiful flowers, that sunny Sunday, that handsome church, those honoored guests. That is precisely the note *I* aim for.

But who keeps Boswell's file? Persons in institutional relationships to me? Government agencies? Department stores? Junk mailers? My book clubs? What do *they* know—a name, an address, a vague notion of my income? I at least have seen most of the people in my files, have been in their neighborhoods, have tasted the cuts of their meats.

Who has been in my neighborhood, who has tasted my meat? I have. I have. Who keeps Boswell's file? Boswell does. I do.

In a way I have never been sure who my first celebrity really was. It depends, as do most things, upon what one is willing to count. I can remember, for example, going to radio programs to see the announcers, men in shirtsleeves, their watches handsome on their wrists. One of these could have been the first, then. Von Zell or Norman Brokenshire or Alec Drysdale or Dell Sharbard or Bill Goodman or Westbrook Van Voorhies. Fame was quantitative, disembodied, in direct proportion to how many heard the voice, bought the product, listened to the name. It had to do with the number of thousands of watts of a given station, with fortuitous time-slots, the ability to overcome static. (Even so, it was what they did *before* airtime that fascinated me—their deep-decibeled, low-throated "damns," their nervous coughs, the occasional, luckily glimpsed, shiny spit that sprayed off their expensive lips.) I took the Radio City tour five times before I realized it was a failure. To see Harry Von Zell five times was, finally, redundant. I was jaded. I had climbed that mountain, been in that state capital, seen that wonder of the world. Even at first, then, experience was horizontal. What does a kid know? Everything, everything.

I stopped the tours. For me the *scheduled* appearance of a famous man was of no more account than the scheduled appearance of a famous planet. If it were available, it was of no use to me. You couldn't buy a ticket of admission. It was of no use to go to theaters, concerts, ball games. Experience was something oblique, not crept up upon so much as come across. When I read *Moby Dick* I at last had a name for it. The *gam*. Two ships meeting accidentally in the middle of the ocean.

What opportunities, then, for the landlocked, for a child? For the time being I made do with the crank, the exotic, with people who, self-scarred by characters which were forever too much for them, were perpetual butts and trailed their shameful fame like cans tied to dogs.

But the first really famous man I ever met was Dr. Leon Herlitz, B.Pg., Berlin; M.Pd., Baghdad University; Ph.D., Lucerne. He's dead now, of course. He leaves no survivors (none of us do), so I suppose I'm free to tell what I know. I have a feeling, however, that many already know his secret, that he instilled confidence by placing himself at our mercy, by making himself repeatedly vulnerable, exposing his heart, so that after a while it became merely a gesture, too automatic to be real superstition, a physicist touching wood. It was endearing though, no matter how many times he must have done it and despite the disparate personalities to whom he must have exposed himself. It was a testimony to—no, more —an endorsement of the really gentle needs of human beings that no one has ever used the information until now—saving only Dr. Herlitz, of course, whose information it really was and so who was entitled to use it.

He was an amazing man, Herlitz. I'm not being sentimental. Of course he was my first famous man; of course we all have an unreasonable loyalty toward our first celebrity, what Randolph calls "the hypnostatic effect of the primal evening star." I realize all this. Nevertheless, Herlitz was a truly remarkable man. (I pay for having had Herlitz as my first great man, I pay for that. What expectations he created in me about great men!) Wasn't he already an old man in 1922? When I first met him years later he was ancient. Who could count his years? I remember Ebbard Dutton's article in *Sports Illustrated* on how Roger Maris got into baseball. Dutton referred to Herlitz as "the Satchel Paige of Psychologists." It is awesome to think of the stages of the man's career, the active influence he's had on our culture from the last quarter of the nineteenth century up through the development of the hydrogen bomb. One doesn't know whether to call him an historical or a contemporary figure. Why, he must already have been an adult when he put Freud into psychiatry in the last century; a man well past middle age when during World War I he acted as Chief of Personnel for the German army, personally assigning, on the basis of intricate tests and interviews, each German officer above the rank of lieutenant to his particular army, sector, regiment, battalion, even company. Bhangra, the Indian war historian, says that Herlitz, single-handed, "was responsible for the long duration of the war. The Germany army was, in essence, the most signally ill-equipped, ill-prepared, anachronistic army ever to fight a major war. Only the circumspect appointments and assignments of officers made by Dr. Leon Herlitz can account for the effective participation of the Germany army in the First World War. Herlitz raised the Department of Officer Personnel into a deadly instrument of warfare. It is not to be doubted that with even a mediocre army supported by even mediocre equipment Leon Herlitz could have conquered the world." So he was already old when he talked Lindbergh into flying the Atlantic and ancient when he counseled the French Existentialists.

In truth, of course, Herlitz was not really a "place-

13

ment counselor." His official title at Harvard during the last years when he developed the famous classes of 1937 through 1945 (what an official Department of Health, Education and Welfare survey calls "collectively the most successful group of college graduates ever to enter the fields of Science, Finance, Government and the Arts"), was "Psychological Placement Officer." Herlitz didn't counsel. Herlitz commanded. When he was through with you your life was fixed, charted. He raged through your ideas about yourself like a violent wind. He was a kind of scientific gypsy, reading your fortune, your future. Like no other man who ever lived *he knew what was best for people.*

I encountered Dr. Herlitz during the famous "last phase." It was after he voluntarily left Harvard in 1945. A man of great age, of extraordinary age, he who suspected and knew so much must have suspected his death. The old forget their deaths as easily as men forget old debts (we think we are forever quits with the world, all obligations canceled or unincurred). They have lived so long that they have developed a kind of hubris which even age and infirmity cannot defy. That's why they seem so serene; it's pride. But not Herlitz. It is my belief that a terrific anxiety overcame him and that this anxiety was less for himself than for his world. How could he be sure that the most promising men of their generation would continue to pour into Harvard where he could counsel, command, shape what might otherwise have been their unfulfilled lives? He hit upon the idea of a world tour. (Leonard Zeiss, the geriatrician, is convinced that for a man of his extraordinary years, Leon Herlitz was remarkably sound physically, but that in subjecting himself to "the Tour" he made himself prematurely vulnerable to the ravages of old age. It is a genuine tribute to Herlitz's humanity that he was so loved by the scientific community. After all, to Leonard Zeiss, the geriatrician, Herlitz could easily have been just another old man. What was it, if not love, which guided Zeiss' hand when he concluded his report in *The Journal of the American Medical Association* on "Herlitz As An Old Man": "It was the Tour

14

which took him. He might be alive today had he stayed on at Harvard. Leaving there must have been for Herlitz like her journey with Conway beyond the valley of Shangri-La was for Lo-Tsen"?)

On his tour he went chiefly to the high schools, sometimes notifying them only hours before his arrival. In that last phase he ranged all over the world, hitting each continent except Africa, where he hoped finally to spend the most time but which he never reached due to his tragic death. (Lane, the sociologist, is just *one* scientist who directly attributes the generally backward condition of Africa to the fact that Herlitz did not get there in time to guide its potentially great men.) At any rate, Herlitz ranged the world. In each country the government itself put its most rapid transportation at Herlitz's disposal. Within the borders of a given country he was flown gratis at top speed wherever he wished to go. (Indeed, in the last days he became something of a political football. Governments looked upon Herlitz as a sort of natural resource, and, jealous that other countries might use his services to their disadvantage, did all they could to delay his departures. I make no charges, but it is well within the bounds of reason that Western Civilization may have been in rare accord when it caused these delays. Motivated by the white man's traditional fear of the black man, there may have been a gentlemen's agreement to "Keep Herlitz out of Africa!")

To whatever city or town or hamlet Herlitz came, there would be assembled its children. These he would pass before, looking into their faces for some sign which only he could recognize. Before some individual child he would stop, scrutinizing the face carefully, and, still operating on some principle which only he understood (it was not brilliance; often quite ordinary people were singled out by Herlitz for special attention), he might point toward the child and say something to an aide who walked beside him with a clipboard. In this way he managed before he died to look into the faces of many of the world's children. Frequently, if he found no individual "subjects" (Herlitz's term), he might categorize an entire

15

group before he went off. "These kids, farmers!" he might say, or, "Barbers." "Realtors," he might say, "the rest, salesmen."

So I met Herlitz when I was still young and he was, perhaps, the oldest man I had ever seen.

Why did he pick me? There was no question about it, not even the hesitation and the staring I had heard about. I was not even standing in the front row. There were five lines of us stretched across the outside entrance to the assembly hall. I stood in the fourth—to the side. Yet that man picked me out as though no one else were there. Had what really happened been that I had picked *him* out, trapped him with my eyes? What does that mean? A seventeen-year-old with seventeen-year-old empty eyes to hold the eyes of a man like that? Impossible! What was it in my face? What sign of intelligence or hint of destiny that had escaped teachers, relatives, friends, that had slipped by even myself who looked for it, who peered nightly into the bathroom mirror as one looks into a microscope, had he seen as clear and there as a light in a window? What hint of character, gleam of heroism, finger to plug dikes, nose to sniff smoke, eye to see flame, mouth to shape warnings, had that man come upon when I, conscious but careless of finger, nose, eye and mouth, had, in the awful anonymity of my youth, signed my raffle tickets academically, with no thought to win? I felt like the thief on the Cross, shaken by an unuttered "Who, me?", my very unlikeliness (but not *that* unlikely) suddenly the stamp of my identity. My first thought as Herlitz stepped, no, pressed, through the ranks, shouldering aside in his ruthless, old man's way the more and most likely in order to reach me, was, Why, he's a fraud.

But then, of course, he couldn't be. After all, even if picking me were a stunt, the ultimate act of arbitrary power, transmogrification of frog into prince, why, at least he could *see* prince somewhere within the rolls and folds of frog flap. Anyway, this is what I thought then, when I still lived behind my adolescent pimples and worried (even after I had fathered a child) whether girls would kiss me. But in a way, that kind of skill still

16

amazes me. Any sort of insight does. I am mystified, too, by music coming from portable radios, and by the novelist's induction of character through a description of his hero's bone structure. I remember one book I read where everyone in a family was against a proposed daughter-in-law because when they met her they all felt she looked sickly. I can never tell when someone looks sickly. Broken bones, yes, because that's surface. Blindness, arthritis, mumps and measles. Beyond that I cannot go. Some can. I can't. Maybe that's why I must talk to people, ask them leading questions, put them in contrived situations, turn the pressure on. I want to hear them yell for help. That I can understand. I suppose Herlitz saw all this. That Herlitz!

What else could he see? My clothes? I dress like a sergeant in civvies—seven-ninety-five slacks in *Webster's New Collegiate Dictionary*-cover blue, wastepaper-basket green, woodwork brown; two-ninety-five white short-sleeve shirts, or white short-sleeve shirts with speckles of color; brown Toby Tyler shoes. That I was an only child? Really, this is embarrassing. It is not my method to speak of myself—or rather, of my past. I find I can barely remember it. At any rate, since I cannot speak uncritically if I speak at length, I will speak briefly.

My name is James Boswell. My parents are dead. My mother, poor woman, died when I was seven and left me to be raised by my father until I was ten. Then he died. My father left me his taste in clothes and his sister with whom I lived until I was fourteen, when she died. A sister of my mother brought me along until I was sixteen. She died and I reverted back to my father's side, where a bachelor uncle took me the rest of the way.

I am thirty-five years old, but I have a son twenty. He was born out of wedlock to a fifteen-year-old girl who died bearing him. Her parents took my child in exchange for their own. He knows me and who I am.

That kind of childhood gives a kid a pretty solid taste in funerals, but not much else. Of course, a real knowledge of funerals is no small thing. In a way, it qualifies one for life. It gives one, too, a certain sense of transience. Maybe that helps to explain my fascination with

17

famous men. The famous are not transients at all, and this is odd. They spend so much time being guests one might think there would be something impermanent about them, but it's not so. Of course they die, but I don't mean that. Everybody dies. And all this wailing about Ozymandias is a pile of crap. They remember his name, yes? They get it right in the papers, no?

Herlitz shouldered the others aside and came right toward me. "Him," he said, pointing at me with his cane. "Come," he said. "Come, come." He turned to Kohler, the principal. "We can be alone, where?"

I trailed behind the two of them, and every so often Kohler would pause, turn around, and look at me. I knew he was trying to remember my name, who played no piano, who made no speeches in the assembly hall, who shot no baskets. "Come. Come," Hertlitz said, although Kohler led us. He seemed to say it as much to himself as to Kohler or me, as though he were dissatisfied with a merely implicit urgency. The great, I remember thinking, are articulate. I followed Herlitz, his checkered jacket in the heavily dated Clark Gable style, his white, widely belled trousers, his old man's white shoes. From behind, his impatience manifest in the angry taps of his cane, he suggested something strongly imperial, a cousin of the prince, an arch archduke. The high school corridor might have been the czar's green lawn, Herlitz's cane, a croquet mallet.

Kohler stopped. "You may use Mr. Fossier's office." He opened the door and Herlitz went in. I stood clumsily just inside the threshold, feeling as I have in doctors' examining rooms when faced with more than one chair to sit in. Herlitz was as alien in that office as I was myself, of course—more, presumably, since I had been there before and he had not. But the great, as I say, are used to being guests, used to using other people's facilities. He took command easily behind Fossier's desk, placing his cane carefully across the faces of Fossier's children beaming ceilingward beneath the desk's glass top.

"Come," Herlitz said angrily. I sat across the room from him primly, feeling queerly like a woman.

Herlitz glared at me without speaking.

18

It's a test, I thought, afraid even of shifting in the chair. Look, my life was on the line. I knew his reputation. Suppose I made a mistake. Suppose I accidentally sat down as an actor would sit down, or maybe even as the secretary I felt like. Suppose Herlitz wasn't that good. Suppose he couldn't see that it wasn't really me sitting there. I had to trust him, had to trust his test. I thought of the examining room again, remembering the seemingly dissociated questions of doctors who had quizzed me. You have a pain in your back. "Do you like bananas?" the doctor asks. Your elbow tingles. "Have you ever been sued by a Frenchman?" he wants to know. We don't see how, but they're able to tell a great deal from our answers.

Herlitz continued to stare at me. "Do you know Freud?" he asked finally, speaking so softly I could barely hear him.

"The psychiatrist," I said.

"One of the five greatest Jews," Herlitz said.

I nodded agreeably.

"Name them," he said.

I could not seem to speak. I looked at Herlitz guiltily, shaking my head. This man who before had struck me as so impatient suddenly seemed content, massively placid and serene. We might have been passengers together in an open car, riding smoothly at dusk past beautiful fields.

"Moses," he said. He seemed to exhale the word.

"Moses, yes," I said.

"Christ," he said.

"Christ."

"Marx," he said.

"Marx."

"Einstein," he said.

"Einstein."

"And Freud."

I nodded again, but not just agreeably this time. I could not tell what had come over me.

"Only Freud and Einstein I knew," he said. "I just missed Marx."

"You know Einstein?" I said.

"Einstein only twelve people in the world under-

19

stand. I know ten of them." He leaned forward. "Listen," he said. "We can't waste time. I killed a man."

I stared at him.

"Okay," he said, "here's how it happened. It was in connection with Schmerler."

"Schmerler."

"That's what I said."

"You killed him?"

"Killed Schmerler? What are you talking about? I loved Schmerler." He sighed. "I did him early. There have been many great men since but I'm proudest of him, I think." He coughed. "He was my baby," he said shyly.

"I don't know Schmerler," I said.

"Who knew Schmerler? I told him a million times, 'Schmerler, you're an enigma, Schmerler.' It was a shame he didn't make himself understood better. He could have been the biggest name in the Zionist Movement. But no, *he* had to insist upon making the Jewish Homeland in Northern Ireland. He used to argue with Weizmann night and day. 'Weizmann,' he says, 'your Jew isn't basically a desert-oriented guy.' That was Schmerler for you. If you say you don't know him, there's your clue. He was always correct in principle, in theory. Mao used to call him 'The On-Paper Tiger.' "

Herlitz looked at me. "Oh, I see. You mean you don't *know* him. Well, *incipience*. He was an inventor of political movements—that was his specialty. Groundfloorism. A familiar figure in every important basement in Europe. He was in on everything. Oh boy, what wasn't he in on! Communism, Fascism, the Fourteen Points.

"Well, it was tragic. A very sweet man. He used to emphasize that it was life, *life* which was important, my kindness to you here, now, which counts; your politeness to me in this place at this moment which is all-important. He believed only in surfaces, Schmerler. Oh boy, was he deep! 'Herlitz,' he'd say, 'the most important thing is to live with yourself. We do terrible things. Remember, whatever you do in this world you've got to forgive it. You've got to remind yourself and remind yourself, it's not your fault.' Well, everybody took advantage. Moses

20

had Pharaoh, Christ, Judas. Marx, of course, nobody liked. But *Schmerler*—it was painful to see it.

"Heinmacher—it disgusts me even to say his name —and that other one, Perflidowitz. All right, everyone knew he was a gangster, when he betrayed, nobody could be surprised. And Reuss. Hmm, that such a father could have such a lovely boy! I did him in Berlin in the old days. He's in monorails, the great monorail developer."

He waved his finger at me. He took his cane from the desk and touched my chest with it. "All right, now I have something to tell you. Listen. Wait." He got up and went to the door and opened it. He looked for a moment up and down the corridor and then closed the door, locking it. He motioned for me to pull my chair closer to his. He was not satisfied until we were both sitting behind Fossier's desk. Then he put his elbow on the desk, and carefully fitting his yellow head into his white cupped palm, he slid the elbow three or four inches forward along the smooth glass top. In this position he turned to me, looking not so much conspiratorial as despairing, his old, baggy skin upwardly taut, like a younger man's.

"I was the last man on the Continent to remain faithful to Schmerler. Did *I* remain faithful to him! He would have been the loneliest man in Europe if it weren't for me. Sure. What did *they* care, Heinmacher and that gang?

"Do you understand the wickedness, the elaborate trap? They helped him with the grand design. Well, *grand*. That was the irony, it *wasn't* grand—just a very minor experimental Slavic revolution, that's all, just to keep his hand in. That whole part about the disposition of the Magyar royal family was Heinmacher's idea. I never said Heinmacher wasn't clever; of course he's clever. Imagine. Making shotgun weddings between the royal family and its servants! It would have fouled the blood lines for generations! And then to fail to come forward like that when the gunboats were already in the harbor, not to have prepared the people, the underground press, not even to have told the leaders—Schmerler never suspected the conspiracy against him, *the jealousy*. To his dying day he thought that anybody who opposed him

21

opposed him on principle. Principle! I'll give them principle! What a scene. Terrible. They disclaimed everything, everything. He looked like a fool. I'll never forget that laughter. All right. I admit it. I was there. What could I do? As it was I did what I could. We stood there—together—outside the summer palace, waiting for the tanks.

"I will tell you a lesson. Look for the power. The power is always responsible. Well, it was simple. Who had the power in 1923? Perflidowitz and Heinmacher and Reuss, of course. Their sellout was all that was needed to undermine Europe's confidence in Schmerler. What, finally, do *people* know about things? These men were professionals. They *wanted* to ruin him. And I know for a fact that it was Perflidowitz himself who started that shameful name going around—'*Basement Schmerler!*'

"I'll tell you something. History is the record of great men's jealousies. That's all.

"You see, don't you, they had forgiven themselves. It's ironic. They took the one thing he stressed again and again and used it against him. They had forgiven themselves in advance for all the evil they would ever do. It gave them their strength.

"What could I do? Could I let this happen? What were my obligations to Schmerler whom I had made—and, through him, to Europe, which he had made? Of course. I murdered Reuss. I killed him. Well, what else could I do? These were civilized men, Europeans. Reason they could cope with; emotion they could cope with. Only barbarity they could not cope with."

He took his palm away from his head, and the skin dropped slowly into place. "Understand," he said, "I am not speaking metaphorically. This was no symbolic slaughter. I killed *him*, stopped his heart, spilled real blood." He paused, and then, looking down at Fossier's oldest boy, appeared to study him momentarily. "Chicken plucker," he said absently.

"So they knew," he said, turning to me again. "Heinmacher knew, Perflidowitz knew, that one man in Europe anyway was still loyal to Schmerler and would kill to prevent him harm. *That* took the sting from their jealousy.

22

"But I betrayed Schmerler, too. My confession is not that I murdered Reuss, but that I have never forgiven myself for murdering Reuss." He touched my arm. Painfully, it seemed to me, he shook his head, the loose skin and pouches of ancient flesh subtly readjusting themselves. Then I noticed that his right eye, the one he had hidden in his palm, was fluttering involuntarily, the pupil itself seemed to vibrate wildly, while his great, old, almost colorless left eye continued to stare at me. He pushed himself back from the desk.

"It was the clothes," he said.

He seemed bored, perhaps only tired. The hell with what the papers say, *The Reader's Digest*. It takes Barney Baruch longer now to make those millions. And Frost is nobody's Bobby. He's beyond even Robert. No financier, no poet, no placement officer ever screwed around with time and got away with it. Herlitz still had the stuff, but it was the old stuff. And if that was the source of awe, it was the source of pity, too. However, I was wrong. He was only waiting until I understood.

"The clothes," he said. "Your clothes. You dress like a pensioner. You're—what?"

"James Boswell."

"No, no, your age. Fifteen? Sixteen?"

"Seventeen."

"Oh," he said. "Already seventeen."

Clearly he was disappointed. Perhaps I had first struck him as precocious. It was as if whatever there had still been time for if I were fifteen or sixteen, was out of the question now at seventeen. I was not precocious after all. I was retarded.

"All right," he said, suddenly energetic. "What do you want?"

Again I didn't understand.

"From life. From life. Those clothes, those wonderful clothes, that sort of effacement at, what is it, seventeen —all right, even seventeen. Remarkable! You almost prove Hibbler. If he were alive to see you he would dance. Do you know that? Of course not, my baby, how could you know that? Hibbler was the great interpreter of myth. A brilliant man. Pointed out that the animal's

23

threat to eat a child alive in fairy tales is a euphemism for the sex act. Children have understood that for years. Well, that's beside the point. You know of course the story of the Emperor's clothes?

"There was once a proud and foolish Emperor. One day the Emperor had to consult with his tailor regarding his costume for a very special state occasion. Now, in the past the Emperor had been unkind to the little tailor, and the tailor, annoyed at the Emperor's tyrannies, decided to play a trick on him. 'Sire,' the tailor said, 'I knew you would need them and so I have been working on these for nine months. Wear them, your Highness.' With that the tailor held out to the Emperor—nothing. Absolutely nothing. The Emperor was confused, but the tailor hastened to reassure him. 'They are woven of magic thread, your Grace. To fools they appear like rags, or less than rags, but to the genteel eye they have the magnificence that only an Emperor would dare to appear in.'

"Well, you have imagination, you've already guessed the end of the tale. The Emperor walks naked through the streets, all his subjects laugh at him, and the Emperor thinks, 'What a lot of damned fools the people are.' Well, of course, two things are to be seen in the story—a secular rebellion against authority, and what Hibbler called the 'humorous ghetto defense.' You were certainly aware that the trickster was *a little tailor*. But what interests me is the use you've put the story to, your interesting reversal of it. It *was* the clothes, *of course. You* have managed to become invisible inside *them!*

"What are you, a *voyeur?* Do you ride piggyback past the girls' bathouse? You don't even blush. Invisible again. Marvelous. Use it. Use it. I see your deference to me. Any other lad your age would already begin to be restless, uneasy at my words. Not you. You hang on each one. I knew I wasn't wrong about you. What do you get out of it, I wonder? Ah, never mind, you won't tell me. You couldn't. Yet I think I can find a way to use you. You see, James Boswell Voyeur, we have a perfect relationship. You bite your lips and stare and I bite my lips and am an exhibitionist. Marvelous. There are things you

24

could *do*, Boswell. You could be, for example, a great biographer. Magnificent. No, no, I see not. That would put you in the game. Nothing must ruin your splendid non-intervention. How did you get so wise at only seventeen? Ah, you're a devil, Boswell.

"All right, why not? I have made doctors, scientists, bankers, artists, presidents. Why not a bum? Why not a great bum?"

He was making fun of me, I thought. All his confessions, his disappointment at my age, his talk about what life was all about and about my clothes were his way of deriding me. He was a sport, this old fellow. And he had known his man, all right. He had picked him from the fourth row—to the side. And why? Because he knew that was where I would be standing, would have to be standing. Oh, the great, the great, the wanton great, they kill for their sport. Then I thought, Do you think it's easy to thrust someone's fate at him? Do you think all you do is go up to a person and whisper, "Get thee to a nunnery," "Pull that sword from that rock," and that's all there is to it? The boys in the back room know: none of us choose to run. So if they push a little bit, what then? It's psychology, Boswell, psychology.

"What," Herlitz said. "What did you say?"

"Nothing."

"Louder."

"Nothing. I didn't say anything."

He looked at me suspiciously. "Am I wrong about you? Am I?"

"I don't know," I said.

"It could be. I'm a man. Only a man. Men make mistakes. Let me look closer. You had something else in mind, then? Something better? Softer? More luxurious? Tell."

"I don't know," I said. "I'm all alone. My mother, father—I have a baby already," I said.

"Wealth, huh? A dynasty? You want to found a swimming pool and teach your child water safety? Never to point a rifle unless he means to kill? Remount horses which have thrown him? What to do with pits? To make

25

a code of the smaller sanities? Well, Boswell, go some-where else. I do not make men wealthy. I do not even make them happy. I only make them great."

"Make me," I said very quietly.

"Louder. Speak up. You are already invisible. Do not be inaudible too. Leave clues."

"Make me. Make me great."

"No," he said. "I can't because you are not great. I am no little tailor. There is no magic thread. I can't make you great because you are *not* great. Perhaps you are not even very different. You are only a little interesting. You are Sancho Panza, Boswell. The second team. That's not so bad, hagh?"

"Is that what you mean by a great bum?"

"Stop it. *Voyeur!* We both know what you are. Stop it! You're trying to anger me. You're too young and I'm too old. Boswell, you're an *utzer*. You egg people on, hold their coats. I've already confessed a murder to you. Don't be greedy. Now, now, it's not a bad life. Really."

It was as though he were trying to talk me into going into some sort of institution.

"Come," he said. "Hand me my cane."

I picked up the cane and gave it to him. "Is that all?" I asked.

Some reflex caused him to shudder. Then he straightened, and with the cane began to trace gentle, invisible rings. "Boswell," he said, "you will grow hand-some and straight and tall. You will please many hosts. Rooms will be aired against your arrival, towels fluffed and set across the foot of many beds. Train schedules will be checked, planes met, chauffeurs given instructions." He advanced toward me, making passes with his cane. "You will sit, my friend, at the captain's table."

I could not watch the cane. I was afraid he was going to strike me with it. I looked down and closed my eyes. I could feel the cane stir the tops of my hairs as Dr. Herlitz waved it over me. "You will make a fourth," he said, "hold rings, kiss brides, name children, have pass-ports, hear confessions, drink saved wines. You will sit beside kings in the concert hall. Boswell. *Voyeur*, Eye, Ear, you will pull your chair beside the roaring fire.

Boswell, Boswell, Go-between, Welcome Guest, Reliable Source, Persona Grata. I weep for you."

He stopped. I opened my eyes. "What will I do?" I asked.

Herlitz stood before me. He seemed not to have heard me. Stiffly, awkwardly, he looked like someone who had just come out of a trance. He didn't recognize me. "What will I do with my life?" I asked again.

Suddenly he dropped his cane. It rolled under the desk.

"What shall I do to live?" I pushed the desk out of the way and stooped and retrieved his cane.

"Oh, that," he said. "Become a strong man."

II

It was like a room inside a jungle. We moved with steamy abandon inside our glazy bodies, our muscles smoothly piling and meshing like tumblers in a lock. There was in the atmosphere a sort of spermy power, but a power queerly delicate, controlled, something not virginal but prudish, held back. Everywhere the taped wrist, the hygienically bandaged knee joint, the puckered, cottony whiteness of jockstrap gently balancing our straining balls. Even coming to the gym regularly I could never breathe that acidy air, moistened by the body's poisons, without being struck by the fact that I was in a place of conservation, of a cautious, planned development of the body part, a sort of TVA of the flesh.

A gymnasium is not unlike a church, a bank. It has the same sense of dedication, of a giving over, a surrender to an over-riding principle. It's not God or money—it may not even be health, finally. Probably it's just the development of the muscle itself, the aggrandizement of limbs and flesh, a cultivation as real and grand and impractical as the raising of any hothouse bulb. I had come to think of my fellows in the gym as one thinks of the members of some spiritual order. Even though I was one of them (you could not distinguish me from them; Herlitz was right), I felt the same mixture of admiration and fear I have felt about young priests.

And if they were like monks, brothers, like monks and brothers, too, they each had their special saints, their favorite parts. Malley doing knee bends on a dimpled mat wanted powerful thighs. Sisley on the rings wanted his thick shoulders, his great round arms. Levine, lonelily bouncing a basketball in small circles beneath a suspended backboard (I never saw him take a shot), was a wrist man. Lacey running, blowing out his breath in deep wet grunts like a steam engine, his sneakered feet stamping the gym's white-lined floor, was passionately interested in his wind, his big lungs. Flambeau, patiently centering the broad wheel-based poles of the volley ball net, longed for some total development. Not for him the broad forearm if it meant the spindly leg. His was the big picture, some wider, more elusive ideal.

I had been coming to the gym for two years and was a regular myself (Oh, there are no buddies like locker room buddies. Each day we see each other's behinds, groins, penises. I have worn Malley's jock; he has worn mine. What is left but for us to like each other?) although I had no specialty. I did everything, developed everything (not like Flambeau, whose exercise led to a sort of delimiting or self-containment): chest, legs, back, arms, hands, neck, jaw, watching with a kind of pride my companions' pride in the steady ballooning of my parts, growing, as Herlitz said, taller, but wider, too, expanding, blooming, becoming. I was big now, big, and to strangers watching, my great huge body might have seemed a threat (ah, but they couldn't see my heart; that grew too—that love limb). I worked steadily, somewhat absently, without either sorrow or joy. In the locker room, for two years, I had been taking my towel from Baby Joe, who pushed it toward me sullenly from behind his wire cage. For two years I had weighed myself each night on the tall, free scale (each time, I mean it, pleased to be getting something for nothing), recording the steady accretion of pounds. For two years sitting naked and wet on the low, peeling bench by my locker, feeling beneath me in the vapory room something like a thin coil of excrement, hearing behind the iron double-deck lockers the rhythmed smack-thwump of Peterson, the handball player. (Peterson is very interested in the development of

29

hands. He no longer wears a glove. I've felt the hard, smooth calluses of his upper palm; I've seen him hold a match against the unprotected skin.)

And if I had not yet sat at the captain's table, I had at the coach's, making with others the rude, brutal shop talk of athletes. The brutality is spurious. There is a real camaraderie here, the intense group feeling of amateurs. We are like crew members of a bomber. The camaraderie shines sportily down even from the walls in the gym's corridors where hang the framed pictures of the teams: basketball players in trim, incredible shorts, in thick-numbered undershirts; football teams in their intricate, hyperbolic gear; baseball teams in puffy knickers, starchy hose, the players' brows lost in the shadows of their caps so that they seem faceless. Somehow all seem faceless and—oddly, since these are athletes—bodiless too. Only their uniforms bulge clear. When the pictures are large enough to reveal their features, the men, for all their fellowship, seem sedate, serious, like men getting married.

Often I have come to the gym alone at night (I have a key, and though there is no heat the exercise soon warms me). Sometimes I have been startled to come upon Singleman, the gymnast. He comes alone too and sets up his bar and makes giant circles in the dim light of the caged ceiling bulb. (Everything in the gym is caged, barred, protected from our raw force. It is the architect's detail, the mind's contempt for the body.) It is something, to be there straining at the weights and hear Singleman whirling behind me, to hear the snap-whrr-snap as he soars, falls, soars in the dark. It isn't all camaraderie. On a deeper level we are self-absorbed. Like the monks. It's a question, finally, of our own soul, our own body. We dry ourselves with the intense absorption of men cleaning weapons. We rub each part with a selfish vigor, reach up inside our bodies with the towels. We toss them without seeing into the big canvas hamper.

There is a bulletin board near the mirror where we comb our hair. (Like any athletes we try to hide our bodies when we are in the streets. We hide them inside ordinary clothes, beneath carefully combed hair.) A post-

30

er admonishes us to drink more milk, to beware of sunburn. Tacked to the board is a clipping from the sports' page which tells of the training habits of Bob Wormer, the Olympic decathlonist. "Every morning Big Bob runs up Mile High Mountain near Lago, Colorado, where he lives. 'Believe me, I'm not starting from sea level either. They call it Mile High Mountain because it sticks up a mile higher than any of the mountains surrounding it. I figure I must be pretty near ten thousand feet up when I get to the top, Bob claims. He's done it, when he's felt he's needed the additional challenge, with a knapsack filled with rocks on his back. "There's no telling what the body can do if it's pushed," Big Bob says. Well, that may be, but it is this reporter's guess that there aren't many men around who would be willing to push Big Bob's body." I read the clipping to cheer me up. I am feeling down. Believe me, I haven't started from sea level either.

It had been occurring to me all day that nothing had happened, that everything was the same as it was when Herlitz had spoken to me. Only I am stronger, bigger. Tonight my uncle will challenge me again and I will be tempted to leave him. He will hold me to the smallest promises, remind me of things casually said. My uncle loves me. This is a new thing in my life. But he is only an uncle, and he is sick. I have been thinking lately that my life is off-center. In all this world I am closest to an uncle. *I* am father to a child I have seen only once. I am a kind of widower at twenty. Every few years I am freshly made an orphan. My friends are the men in this gym, off-center themselves.

Baby Joe watches us dress with his fevered, jealous eyes. Malley. Peterson. Levine. Singleman. Flambeau. Marty Penner. Lyman Necchi. Perry Lacey, the runner, sings a bawdy song in the shower, ever cheerful, ever big-lunged. I see him in the mirror as he steps out. He is smiling and I wonder if he has just jerked off. He likes to do it in the shower, he says, because then the water washes the scum down the drain. Perry is very neat. This is true. There is no scum on his shorts, no hair on his comb, no lint in his pockets. Perry is pristine. A pristine horse's ass. He comes out of the shower and claps his hands and Baby Joe tosses him a towel. He pats himself all over his body with it as though he were applauding. He shakes his head like a dog and water spritzes onto Flambeau's white duck trousers. (Only Flambeau dresses like an athlete. In street clothes, he looks as though he were on his way to the tennis courts.) Lacey shakes his head again; more water comes off his hair.

"Come on, Lacey, you're doing that on purpose," Flambeau says.

"Kiss mine," Lacey answers neatly. He takes his towel by two corners and twirls it around rapidly. It is now a terry-cloth whip and Perry is Lonesome Lacey, the Nude Cowboy. Before I know what is happening he has come up behind me and flicked my ass murderously with his towel.

"Take that, and that, and that," he says.

"Lacey, go run some laps."

He squares himself off to face me, bouncing up and down alertly on his legs. The springs, he calls them. The springs. He hits me with the towel again. I try to move aside, but Lacey is a fast man.

"Lacey, I'm going to hit you with a bar bell."

"Pals," he says and extends his hand.

I take it and crush it a little, which makes Lacey sore. He flings his towel down and comes toward me, but Lyman Necchi hips him aside. "Lacey, go get dressed. Jimmy would kill you."

Lacey is reasonable. He knows it's true. "You guys make me sick," he says. He says it cheerfully and I am convinced it is his big lungs. "I mean it. You make me absolutely sick. You think all a runner is is fast. You don't think a runner's strong." When he goes to bars Lacey talks about good little men. "Well, a runner's very strong. He's got endurance as well as speed. Endurance counts. Persistence pays."

I go back to my locker and start getting dressed.

"Big. Big. That's all you know. It makes me sore. It really does. I mean, for Christ's sake, they've got laws, official laws about a boxer's hands. Did you know that? It's actually illegal for a boxer to hit somebody with his hands. They're 'lethal instruments' in the eyes of the law. Weapons. It's as if he took a gun and shot you."

"So?" Malley asks.

"So? So what's so special about a boxer? Why just a boxer? The public don't know nothing. Do you mean to tell me you don't think a runner's springs ain't just as lethal?"

"Or his breath?" I say, thinking of Lacey's lungs.

"Wise guy," Lacey says with cheery contempt.

"A golfer's club, that's lethal too. That's a weapon," Flambeau says.

"A forward's set shot," Levine contributes.

"A wrestler's sweat suit," Malley says.

"A jockey's horse," says Peterson.

"Kiss mine," Lacey says.

"Oh, come on, Lacey," Lyman Necchi says. "Do you think that if a golfer clubbed somebody with his number nine iron he wouldn't be arrested? Is that what you think? What's the matter with you?"

"That's not the point. It specifically mentions a boxer's hands in the law books, and it don't say nothing about a golfer's number nine iron."

"Lacey's right," Flambeau says.

" 'Lacey's right, Lacey's right,' " Marty Penner mimics. Penner is my friend—at least I think he would be if we ever saw each other outside the gym. He lifts weights, too, but he has contempt for it. He does it, he has told me, because, like me, he is afraid of death. He feels he must keep in shape. But he does not come to the gym every day; he is not really a regular. Often he watches me as I press the bar bells. I know he hears me as I pull at the weights and murmur the little incantation which helps me to raise them: "Because my heart is pure. Because my heart is pure."

The others finish dressing and one by one drift off to their homes, their bowling alleys, their pool parlors. But I move slowly. I remain behind lacing my shoes, and Penner paces his dressing to match mine.

Lacey works on a spit curl in front of the mirror and then turns to us. "See you guys tomorrow," he says.

"Good night, Lacey."

Lacey nods to me and walks off.

"Hey, Lacey," Penner calls.

Lacey turns and looks back down the row of lockers. "Yeah?"

"You're a prick. Good night."

Lacey waves.

Penner sits down. "Have you heard anything about a job?" he asks.

"No."

"What are you going to do?"

"I don't know. It's winter. I guess all the action is down in Sarasota at the winter quarters."

"You going down?"

"I don't think so. I'd feel like a jerk. How do you apply to be a strong man? What do you do? A routine? I can just see some guy watching me in a tent someplace while I audition. 'Yeah, kid. You're strong but you ain't *powerful*, you know what I mean?' It's nutty. Who needs it?"

Penner smiled.

"The Great Sandusky is in town," I said.

"Sure," Penner said "Call *him.*"

I shrugged. "I guess."

Penner buttoned the big walnut buttons on his car coat. "Let me know what happens," he said and went out.

"Sure," I said. I gave a final tug at my lace and it broke. (I am always breaking my shoelaces.) I took a lace from one of my gym shoes and put it in the street shoe. When I got up to go I turned to Baby Joe, who was locking up his towel cage. "Hey, Baby Joe," I said.

"Yeah?"

"How long do you think that cage would last if a big strong guy like me went to work on it?"

"You horse, I'll know who done it," he called after me.

I don't mean to give a false impression. There are men who in the presence of madness become polite, sedate. Men who hear old ladies out, who listen to their fixed and mad ideas—sunspots. Hitler living on some

34

Brazilian beach, the end of the world—and stand back, uncommitted but very polite. Of course you know where their hearts are and what they think of those old girls. The politeness is just aloof contempt. Not with me. I am listening. My mind is open, my contempt is not aloof. If it turns out that she is mad after all, I may not argue her out of it. There is too little time and too many old ladies. With me it's a question of conservation, of human economy. There will be other old ladies I have to answer. In a girl's arms and the girl has pimples and her breath is foul and the room is hot and the sheets are sticky and I'm tired anyway and the girl looks up and asks, "Jimmy, do you love me?", I would not just say "Yes" or "Sure thing," or, prizing my crummy little integrity, tell her "No" and list the reasons. I would make a pitch. And that's *my* crummy little integrity, my Boswellness. What I mean is, I horse around when I have the chance. For an idolator I am no respector of persons save my own.

Uncle Myles was a bachelor and a lawyer and a Mason and a delegate to the Republican Convention and a deacon in the church and an honorary member of the Fire Department and a Friend of the Museum. He had charge accounts in all the department stores in our city and one in Weber and Heilbroner in New York and in Marshall Field in Chicago and Neiman-Marcus in Dallas and I. Magnin in San Francisco and Kauffman's in Pittsburgh. Were he alive today he would carry in his wallet credit cards from all the major oil companies. It goes without saying that he would be a member of the Diner's Club and Carte Blanche and all the rest. What he did not have was a season ticket to the ballpark and a subscribed box at the symphony and a book-club membership. He did not have them because they cost money, and my uncle did not have that either. He held the charge accounts because his credit was so good, and his credit was good because he never bought anything. He would have liked to—and that helped me to love him. Really, my uncle was not so different from myself. With me it was men; with him it was institutions. So I guess in an odd, collective way that made him a men man too.

As I have said, my uncle was a lawyer. A defending and defending attorney. He never made very much from it, though. Not that he defended lecherous old Negroes in Mississippi for winking at some passing white lady, or spun stately theories to night-school classes. No, he did not do very well because he was convulsive and trembled before the jury at the wrong time, and because he was a sort of civil-rights lawyer in reverse. He took the side of the Establishment in all things; indeed, he took the side of all Establishments. The Establishment rarely needs legal defending, and when it does it has the services of lawyers who do not shake. So my uncle, who was a regular himself, and an honorary member of the Fire Department and a Friend of the Museum, was left with the irregulars —defending, as it were, lecherous whites who winked at passing Negresses.

But my uncle was no fool. His arguments were better than mine, and I was afraid of them. I had lied to Marty Penner: I hadn't gone to Sarasota because I couldn't make up my mind to leave my uncle. Actually, I had become so accustomed to my guardians dying out from under me that I wasn't prepared to do the leaving myself.

I went home on the bus. From the street I could tell that the apartment was dark, and I was grateful. My uncle sometimes went out alone at night. He had friends, I suppose. Everyone does. When I entered the apartment the house was quiet, and again I was relieved. I notice I frequently feel relief when people I am supposed to love leave me to myself. Bonner is right. Such a weight is the burden of love that the human being, even a strong man like myself, must put it down every so often. Women do not understand this; they are hurt when you hint it, and I suppose it is because they do not love as much or as strenuously as we do.

I went into my room and lay down. I had exercised heavily that day and I was tired. I was almost asleep when I heard a noise coming from my uncle's room. It sounded like someone making violent love. The bedsprings were squawking in a steady passion. Could my uncle have a woman in his room? The idea saddened me, as other people's lovemaking always does. When after about ten minutes the sounds still hadn't stopped, I began to worry; I was certain it was a woman and that my uncle was humiliating himself on her. Then, of course, I realized how stupid I was. He was sick. I got out of bed and raced into his room. I snapped on the light.

My uncle was in bed alone, his body convulsed, his arms flung behind him on the headboard. He had smashed his watch crystal, and there was blood on his wrist. His left leg, arched, banged against his groin. Dreadfully, he had an erection. I leaned over his face.

"Can I help you? Uncle Myles. Can I help you?"

Below me my uncle's body whipped and snapped. He might have been a dancer.

"Can I help you?"

"Sure," he said. "Sing something."

What did he want from me? What did he think a human being was, anyway?

"Come on, strong man," my uncle said. "Pull my arms down." Inside that turbulent body, his voice was steady, almost calm. "Hurry, hurry before my bones break."

I reached out for his wrist, but was helpless to hold it. I tried again, and it twisted crazily out of my grip. "Both hands, Samson. Both hands."

I took my uncles's wrist in both my hands and pulled it toward the bed. The other hand, still free, punched the side of my head, but I wrestled his right arm down and kneeled on it. It continued to jerk, but finally my weight was too great for even those powerful convulsions. Then I tried to take his other arm, but it moved wildly away from me. Even after I managed to trap it I could not pull it down—I had no leverage. I had to straddle my uncle's chest. Careful not to lose the arm I had already imprisoned, I pressed down on it with my knee. Then I reached toward his bleeding left wrist. It spun away from me, and for a moment I thought my uncle might be controlling it. (*"There's no telling what the body can do if it's pushed"*—Big Bob.) I took the arm at last and pulled at it as one pulls at an oar to turn a boat. The arm rattled and jerked, at one time taut and

37

resisting, at another suddenly relaxed, pulling me off balance. Finally I mounted it with my knee as I had the other. I was now straddling my uncle's chest, my knees dug into the hollow where the elbow bends. His face was white, wet. I looked down at him and he avoided my eyes. "The leg," he said into the sheet. "Please, the leg." His leg, out of control behind me, was like something loose.

"I'll have to lie on you."

I maneuvered the two arms, pinning them next to his body, and then slowly I reached around my uncle's sides and locked my hands behind his back. Oh, the sad, sad uses of strength, I thought. I leaned down over him, my face sliding across his shoulder and into position against his turned head. My ear was next to his throat, and I could feel the heavy pulsings of his jugular. At my back his leg slapped against his groin. When the leg relaxed for a moment I thrust my legs between his, but instantly his legs contracted and crashed against me. I waited for the leg to go slack and then tried to slip one foot through his knee's arch. I missed and kicked his calf, but the second time I managed to push my leg under his. His leg came up again and for a moment we rolled dreamily. Then I was able to hook his errant leg between mine, and by pushing backwards with all my strength force it down. I lay now entirely on top of him, hugging him. I could feel his erection against my stomach. We lay like lovers. He was sobbing.

"It's all right," I said. "It can't be helped."

His body stiffened and relaxed, stiffened and relaxed, but gradually his convulsions subsided. I continued to hold him. His sobs shuddered through his body, and then, slowly, they subsided too. I relaxed my grip but did not get off immediately. Then I rolled over and stood up.

My uncle could not look at me.

"I'm sorry," he said finally. "Oh, James, I'm so sorry."

"I thought you were with a woman," I said.

"Damn a man's body," he said. *"Damn* it," he said angrily.

38

"It's all right," I said. "Really. Please, Uncle Myles."

"You'd better change," he said. "Your pajamas are damp."

"I will," I said. "It's all right."

"Damn a man's body," he said.

"I guess I'll go change."

When I came back my uncle was sitting on the edge of my bed.

"I brought you some tea," he said.

"Oh," I said. "Thank you."

"Let's drink it in the living room."

"All right." I carried the cup into the living room and sat down on my uncle's sofa.

He took a seat across the room from me. "It's not cold, is it?" he asked.

"No," I said, "it's fine."

"Lipton's is an old house," he said. He was trying to get back his composure, to win back whatever he thought he had lost to me. His body had just shown him what he was, what we all are, and now he had to forget it.

"An old house," he said, snug in his faith in the established firm.

"Sure," I said. "That's why the tea's hot."

"What?" he said. "Oh. Yes, of course."

I wished he would get another hard-on right there in front of me, that he would vomit in his Lipton's. But all he did was sigh, extending his palms along the hard wooden arms of his chair. He crossed his legs and one pajamaed leg swung smartly out from beneath his silk robe. I could see his white heel where the slipper hung slackly.

"I think we'd better talk seriously," he said.

He seemed to be studying me. What he said next surprised me. "How much do you weigh?" he asked.

"Two thirty."

He shuddered.

"James, people are frightened of you. Do you know that?"

I stared down at my feet like a damned kid.

39

"It's true. You are actually frightening to people. Can you blame them? Two hundred and thirty pounds and barely twenty years old. What are you trying to prove? Do you want people to look at a man and see a horse? I don't understand it. Look at that hand. It's as murderous as a butcher's cleaver. Your legs are like trees. You've the chest of a draft horse. It's disgusting. It's not attractive. Do you think girls would find it attractive? People are frightened."

"Are you frightened?"

"I'm your uncle."

"Are *you* frightened?"

"I would be. I know what you're like, however. I'm your uncle. I . . . Yes. I'm frightened. Yes, I'm very much frightened. I think of the strength in you and I'm terrified that you won't always control it."

"Aren't you afraid I might lose a little control over it right now?"

"We're civilized," he said. Sure we are, I thought. He was himself again: my uncle. Back in the saddle. I told you we weren't very different. All right, my horseness was outside, visible. He kept his in stables of his own devising. What was the difference? His blood was on my hip, for Christ's sake. Right now my pajamas were stiffening in the sink.

"I mean to talk seriously to you and I will," he said. "What do you intend to do with your life?"

"I'd like to lift elephants, Uncle Myles. Tear phone books."

"A strong man," my uncle snorted. "In a circus. A side show, not even a circus. Strength is humiliating to a man, do you know that?"

"Is it?"

"Physical strength is humiliating to a man," my uncle shouted. "Listen, do you know what distinguishes human beings from animals? Love? Law? Reason? The ability to walk upright? None of those things. None of them. Any lioness loves its cub. Every herd has rules. A fox has cunning. A horse can rear. No. Only one thing distinguishes men from beasts: respectability. I'm not talking about self-respect. That's just ego. A cat has that.

Respectability is grander. Do you know what it is? Do you? Respectability is the decision of the private man that the powers of this world are right. The decision of the private man to be one with those powers. Decency is nothing more than the condition that what he considers valuable, *you* consider valuable, *I* consider valuable.

"There is a universal assumption, James, that man has intrinsic worth. He has. If he has worth then his products have worth. If his products have worth then they should be conserved. If they should be conserved then it is a privilege to have as many of those products as one can. I'll go further. It is the *duty* of the private man to have those products. He must get all he can. Not to do so is waste. Waste is sin. If waste is sin, hoarding is virtue. Put money in your purse, Boswell. Put things on your shelves, in your closets, your banks, your vaults. How much closet space is there in a circus trailer?"

"This is ridiculous."

"No. Conserve. Conserve. Man is basically a collector."

"A squirrel can do that."

"That's the squirrel's decency then, that it can save. Conserve. Collect. Accumulate. Receive. Get. Take."

"Have you?"

"Well, I've failed," he said. "But I've tried. It's not a sin to be poor, Boswell—no one says that. It's only a sin to accept one's poverty. Where are you going?"

"I have to make a call."

"To one of your freaks?"

"Sure."

"Not from my phone. I forbid it."

"All right. I'll go downstairs."

I went into my bedroom and flung clothes on my body. I started out. "A strong man," my uncle laughed, coming after me. "Is that what you want? To be gaped at? A respectable man doesn't call attention to himself. His life is quiet, sedate."

Kiss mine, Uncle Myles, I thought. He almost had me, the little bastard. He could make me ashamed of my size, all right, any time he wanted. But at the last moment I remembered *his* size. I remembered, of all things, my

41

Uncle Myles' erection and the weird spontaneity of everybody's life. Why fight it? We're all of us strong men. We taste like big game, I bet. We're gamy. We taste like tiger and ape and zebra.

"So long, Uncle Myles," I called back to him. "You throw a very sedate convulsion, do you know that? Clean that wound, Uncle Myles. Close up that skin. Put on a Band-Aid. Johnson and Johnson is a very old house."

"Where are you going? James, where are you going?"

"To the freak show. That's where."

I knew I would not be back until I had seen it.

So I was out in the street. I was twenty years old and out in the winter street, and what I had were the clothes on my back and the back itself and a key to the gymnasium. That's savings, right? That's conservation and collection and accumulation. That's getting, isn't it? I had cornered the market. Boswelfare!

There are getters and there are spenders, Uncle Myles, I thought, and we both know what I am.

I thought of Penner, the man who was my friend, or who would have been my friend if I had had a friend. (Uncle Myles once told me that I didn't make friends. He was right.) I would call Penner. It seemed very important. I went into a drug store and squeezed into a booth. I looked his name up in the book. Only just then something went wrong. The collection was temporarily embarrassed. I had no dime in the accumulation.

It is virtually impossible for a healthy but despondent two-hundred-thirty-pound twenty-year-old, with nothing but the clothes on his back and the key in his pocket and friendless and oldly orphaned and newly de-uncled and no dime to make a phone call and no visible prospects, to die in a phone booth. Something happens. It's a life principle. Wheels turn. Conditions ripen. It isn't much, you think? Lover, it is all I have. Don't forget it and you will be happy and you will go far.

I went outside. The movies were letting out. Right in front of me people were coming out of the theater and heading for their cars. I ducked down a side street and looked for a car with no snow on it. When I spotted one I went around to the trunk and, stooping, lifted it by its frame. I moved carefully sideways toward the curb and settled the rear of the car into as fluffy a snow bank as you ever saw. Then I stepped into a doorway to wait.

In five minutes there they were—some fat-throated, deep-voiced guy and his juicy wife. I swear I could see the wild sports coat beneath his overcoat, his wife's blond hair under the babushka. They had just seen David Niven and she was telling him what a cute picture it was. They were laughing and he opened the car for her and then went around to the driver's side. He got in and started the motor. It was a beautiful thing to hear. It purred like a dream and David Niven was a good actor and Detroit made swell cars and in a few minutes the heater would be blowing out hot air like a blast furnace and when he got home he was going to thump Blondie. Only—only the bottom fell out of his world. The rear wheels were spinning nine hundred miles an hour. The car was a slush-maker, an ice machine. He got out to see what was wrong, then came around behind the car and moved his fedora professionally back on his brow.

"What is it? Let's go, I'm cold," his wife said.

"Yeah, well, I'm in a damned snowdrift."

"Well, get out of it. I don't want to freeze to death out here."

"I'll have to rock it."

He got back into the car and heaved it forward an inch and backwards an inch. The car settled down into the snow until spring. He gave it more gas and stalled the motor. He tried it in first, in second, in high, in reverse. In neutral. He got out of the car again.

"Will you have to call the motor club?"

"Shut up."

"Maybe if you rocked it some more," she said.

"It needs traction. It's got no damned traction."

"That's too bad," she said. "It's so cold."

"It needs more traction." He stooped down and patted some snow into the ruts.

43

"You'll get a heart attack," his wife said.

"Get behind the wheel and put it in first. I'll push."

"Call the motor club already."

"Just put it in first, will you!"

"It's so cold," she said. She lowered her voice. "It's not a safe neighborhood."

They tried it once his way and then she came out of the car. "You'll get a heart attack and freeze to death in the street," she said. "Let me push."

"Get back in the car," he shouted. "Get back in the god-damned car."

It was time. I came out of the doorway and walked past them. The man looked at me and his wife whispered something to him. "Maybe if two people push," he said loudly.

"Are you having car trouble, sir?" I asked.

"Yes," he said. "I seem to be stuck in a drift. I figured if we both pushed while my wife tried to drive we might get out."

I walked over to the car. "It's in pretty deep, isn't it?"

"One solid shove and I think we could move it," he said hopefully.

"That's a two-dollar shove," I said.

He looked at me. He hated me, but he understood me. I think he may even have admired me.

"All right," he said. "You get me out of here and I'll give you two dollars."

"Get in the car," I said.

"You can't do it by yourself."

"Get in the car and turn off the motor."

"Turn it off?"

"I'm going to lift your car."

I bent down over the car and pressed my face against the cold trunk. I placed my hands underneath the frame and lifted. "Because my heart is pure," I said, and heaved the car out of the snow bank.

The wife gasped.

The husband coughed nervously.

"Two dollars," I said.

"Certainly," he said. He turned his back to take his wallet out, then handed me two dollars. "You're pretty strong," he said.

"Thank you."

"Well, I guess I'll be going," he said, backing into the car.

"Watch the way you park it from now on," I advised him.

I went around to the wife's side. I could see her push the little button down that locks the door. She was looking up at me as her husband drove off. I winked at her and waved. I tried to let her know in that wink, and I think she may have understood, that there are forces in the world against which even David Niven is helpless, against which cuteness is about as effective as snow piled against a tire for traction.

I put the two dollars in my pocket next to my key and walked off whistling. It was the first time I had ever turned my strength to account. My uncle would have thought I was crazy, but Herlitz, Herlitz would have been proud!

I called Penner.

"Penner?"

"Yes. Who is this?"

"Boswell."

"Who?"

"James Boswell. From the gym."

"Oh. Sure."

"Listen—Penner? I wonder if you could put me up for a few days. I've had some trouble with my uncle."

"Oh."

He put his hand over the receiver. There was somebody there. I knew what he was feeling. You just hate to turn people down if they don't mean anything to you.

"I'm still here," he said. "You need a place for tonight, is that it?"

"Well, for a few nights. Until I decide what to do."

"This place is awfully small. Just a room."

"Oh. Well, that's all right. Thanks anyway."

"Have you got much luggage? I mean there aren't any bar bells or anything, are there? I've got limited closet space."

I remembered what my uncle had said about circus trailers. "I haven't any luggage."

"Well, come on over. We'll work something out."

"That's all right, if the room's that small, I'm not offended if—"

"No, it's all right. Come on over. I'm glad you called."

"You're sure it will be all right."

"Sure I'm sure. Certainly. It's okay. Listen—" He lowered his voice. "I'm glad you called."

"Well, if it's all right. I'm leaving now."

I took a taxi to Penner's and gave the driver the rest of my two dollars. A spender spends. What's $1.90? This was all in the old days, you understand. I wasn't established and I was more or less innocent and everybody's secrets were important to me. I had no discrimination, no taste in these things. If a man clapped a hand over a receiver he had something to hide. If he turned around two minutes later and lowered his voice and told you he was glad you called, he had two things to hide and maybe more. He was a good person to put up with. Who knew? Penner could turn out to be a queer, an embezzler, somebody into the mob for a few thou. I needed an intimacy badly. What innocence!

I've been going over some of my notes. What can I do with this stuff? I feel nasty tonight. From the old days: Boris Schlockin, the professor, joined the Communist Party *after* the Depression. Noel and Elizabeth Sarrow's baby, Eileen, was adopted. The girl is 17 and doesn't know. Philip Paris wrote his wife's doctoral dissertation. Dr. Fernan Bidwell, who lobbies for the AMA against socialized medicine, does illegal operations. Herman Ote, the Boy Scout official, is a homosexual. Cardinal Fellupo was a suicide. Murray Butcher, the famous racer, drinks while driving. These are people I don't even know, you understand, just that I've heard about. Usually I do not spread gossip. I use it to trade with, of course, but I am no gossipmonger. It is just that I must know it. I can't help myself.

The driver let me out in front of Marty Penner's rooming house. (It has just occurred to me that Penner must have been my first host.) There was a directory in the hall, a blue slate with the roomers' names and room numbers written in chalk. (Later I copied some of the names down on file cards and asked Penner about them casually.) Penner lived on the first floor all the way in the back. I knocked.

"It's Boswell."

"Come in. The door's not locked."

Penner was frying eggs on a hote plate. The coil looked barely warm. "It takes a half hour," he said, "but they're usually delicious."

I nodded. There was only one bed and we were both big men. I wondered where I would sleep.

"Did he throw you out?" Penner asked.

"What?"

"Your uncle. Did he throw you out?"

"No. I think I left on my own. Maybe it was both."

Penner took the pan off the hot plate and stuck a fork into the eggs. He ate them out of the pan. "Out of the frying pan into my mouth," he said with his mouth full of yellow egg. "Sorry I haven't got any more or I'd offer you something. You've probably eaten, though. It's pretty late."

As a matter of fact I hadn't, but it *was* pretty late. I made allowances, as I always do for my hosts. Whatever it was that had been upsetting Penner when I spoke to him on the phone, he seemed pretty jaunty now. "How long do you think you'll need the place?" he said.

I told him it would be a terrific favor if he could let me stay three days. I hadn't the slightest idea where I would go after that, but things happen.

"Three days," he said as though that were what he was chewing in his mouth. "Three days. Well, we'll see."

This was some Penner, I thought. Well, we'll see, indeed. He was pretty sprightly about other people's troubles. I am not a rude man. I decided to let him control

47

the moods in that small room. I told him about the car lift. I made it very funny, but Penner didn't laugh. I resented his indifference, but then I wondered where I got it, my resentment, my expectations of how people ought to act, to me and to each other. What was I? A booted-around guy who since age seven had never managed to run up more than four years in any one place. A guest in my own family, for God's sake. How would I know anything about these things?

But I knew, all right. Penner was being lousy. And I knew this because whatever else I am or am not, I am a social person. I came into the world knowing.

I let Penner finish his eggs. They took as long to eat as they did to make. When he finished he went over to a tiny washstand in the corner of the room and rinsed out his pan. Then he took a coffee pot from behind a green-cloth covered apple crate and put in some water and a single tablespoon of coffee. "There's only the coil," he said, "so if I make eggs I have to eat them before I make the coffee."

"I see."

"It makes for a long meal. Aids digestion."

"It would."

"Just one coil, one cup of coffee, one room, one closet, one bed, one faucet in the sink. And me, I'm single," he said. "Simplicity. Functional, right?"

"Listen," I said, "you could have told me on the phone. I don't want to put you to any trouble. I've got a key to the gym. I'll sleep there."

"No, no," Penner said. "Don't be silly. Are you putting me to any trouble?"

I had to admit that I didn't seem to be.

"Look," he said, "this is a rooming house. There's always an empty room. I'll find you one when it's time to go to sleep."

"What about the landlady?"

"Deaf."

Penner picked up a newspaper. He read for a while and then remembered that I was sitting there on his one chair. "Have you seen the paper?"

"No," I said.

"Here." He handed me the classified section.

"Have you got the society section there?" I asked.

"Oh. Sure. Here."

I read every word. I usually do, but tonight I was compulsive about it; I was damned if I would say another word to Penner until he spoke to me. I stared at the sons of, the daughters of, the announcements of, and read the character lines in the faces of important-looking bankers at their winter homes in Florida, and the character lines in the butts of their nieces on the white sand beaches. What was he thinking of? Was everyone crazy? What did he mean with his *sotto voce* "I'm glad you called"? Was he a master ironist? Who had been in the room with the rude bastard? If I'd had any brains I would have stood up and gotten the hell out of there. At least I could be silent.

"I've finished this section," I said. "Would you like to see it?"

I know, I know. But I'm a spender. A spender spends. It doesn't make much difference what other people do. He picks up checks. He picks up checks and picks up checks.

"No," he said. "I'm pretty tired. I'll find you a place to sleep. You stay here. It wouldn't do for both of us to be prowling around the halls."

When Penner went out I was tempted to look around his room to see if I could find out anything about him. But I didn't know when he would be back, so I sat perfectly still and looked over the society section some more. Maybe he was testing me; maybe the son of a bitch was right outside the door and just waiting for me to make a move.

In a few minutes he was back.

"Four-L," he said. "You don't need a key."

It was obvious by the way he sat down on the bed that he didn't mean to escort me. One coil, one cup of coffee, one room, one bed, one trip to 4-L.

"Well," I said, hating my lousy character, "good-night, and thanks."

"That's all right."

I found the stairs and went up. It was dark and I

49

had to light matches in front of each doorway to read the room number. The numbers and letters were thin tin cutouts and I wondered abstractedly just who made them. What kind of market was there for 4-D, 3-M, 2-R? It was a strange world I was alive in, and everybody had seemed to find a place in it for himself. By the time I found 4-L I was pretty sorry for myself. I turned the handle gently, found a light switch and looked around. There were no sheets on the bed but there was a blanket in the closet. I turned on the tiny radiator, and rolled down the mattress and went to sleep.

When I woke in the morning I had to go to the bathroom very badly. It's all those eggs I didn't eat, I thought. All that coffee I didn't drink. For some reason I felt it would be trespassing to use any toilet but the one on Penner's floor. Downstairs there was a line of people waiting to get in. Penner wasn't in the line and somehow I knew that it was he in the bathroom. The others looked at me suspiciously.

"Where's Schwartz's room?" I asked a man at the back of the line.

"I don't know no Schwartz," he said. "There a Schwartz here?" he asked an old man in front of him.

"Maybe that's the new guy up on three," he said. "Look on the board in the hall."

I thanked him and went toward the front. Nobody was watching me, but I looked at the board anyway. I couldn't go back, so I went outside. It was cold and I had left my coat in 4-L and I still had to pee but I would have to stay outside until they had all cleared out. I thought of going into Penner's room, but that crowd in the hall would think it suspicious. In about ten minutes I walked back anyway. There were still a few people in line. The old man looked at me. "Did you find Schwartz?" he asked.

"Yes," I said. "He's up in 4-L."

"Fine," he said.

"Where's Penner's room?" I asked.

"Oh, Penner. Penner's in 1-M."

"Thank you," I said and walked down to Penner's room. I knocked.

50

"Boswell?"

"Yes."

"Come on in. Door's open."

Penner was making himself more eggs. He was already dressed.

"I had a pretty good sleep," I said.

He looked at his watch, and then began spooning eggs out of the pan into his mouth. I was pretty hungry, but I didn't have any illusions.

"You're dressed," I said. "Do you work far?"

"Not far."

"Uh huh. Listen, Penner, would it be all right if I hung around the place today until it's time to go to the gym?"

"Sure," he said. "Perfectly okay. There's a little restaurant on the corner where you can grab some breakfast."

Hadn't he listened when I told him about the two dollars? Penner was a rat. As soon as he was gone I would pee, and then I would come back and steal his eggs.

"Will you be coming to the gym tonight?" I asked.

"I don't know," he said. "I've got to get out now."

"Goodbye."

He closed the door without answering and I heard him go down the hall.

When I came back from the bathroom I looked around for Penner's eggs. I couldn't find them anywhere and decided that I would make some coffee. Inside the coffee can were three eggs. I broke them into the pan and scrambled them with Penner's one spoon. It took a long time and I couldn't wait. I ate the wet, loose eggs and then washed the pan and the spoon in warm water from Penner's single faucet. Then I put on six cups of coffee and lay down on Penner's bed to wait.

I fell asleep and woke to the smell of strong, burning coffee. I drank about two cups and poured the rest down Penner's one sink.

Now I was through. There was nothing more for me to do. I looked for something to read, but all I could find were a Bible and last night's newspaper. I read the Bible for about forty minutes but it only made me sleepy. I was still curious about Penner, of course, but there was nothing in the room that told me very much. It was true about the simplicity of his life. He wasn't a getter either. He had only two shirts in his drawer, two pairs of slacks and a couple of ties in his closet. It was like a wardrobe one takes somewhere for the weekend. Why I realized suddenly, that was what my wardrobe was like, too. Were Penner and I somehow alike? Had he spent himself down to this? Now I was very curious about Penner. I had been kidding around before. Now I went to the door and locked it. I turned back and looked suspiciously at everything—for letters, a diary, anything. There was nothing. I pulled back the blanket and investigated Penner's sheets. In the closet I found his laundry bag. I took it out and emptied it on the floor. I stooped down and picked out his underwear and looked inside. I thought I heard someone coming and I shoved everything back into the bag and put it in the closet. Whoever it was came up to the door and shuffled around outside it for a few minutes and then turned and left. It was a light step, either a woman's or a very small man's. I wondered about it for a while, then went back to Penner's bed, picked up the Bible once more and soon I was asleep again.

Sometime in the middle of the afternoon I opened my eyes. I was laying on the bed like an ox, the radiator bubbling and hissing in the overheated room. I turned on my side and scraped against the Bible. I moved my feet off the bed and pushed myself upright with my arm. My feet were so heavy I couldn't move them from their position on the floor. I had the impression they would grow there, rooting downward through the thin flooring, spreading outward toward the walls, through them. I felt massively doughy, unconsolidated. Probably it was time to go to the gym, but who needed it? It was absurd to exercise, to make myself larger than I already was. As I sat heaped like bedding on Penner's mattress, it occurred to me that I was larger than anything in that room— perhaps larger than anything in that house. Certainly I was bigger than anything up in 4-L, but what did that mean? Four-L was a little room, practically unfurnished. I seemed almost architectural to myself, something in the landscape. Not a mountain or a building or even a tree— a bog, the weed row along a railroad track in summer.

I was not meant for afternoons, I could see that. What had I been doing with my afternoons before I came here? There had been the gym, of course, and a couple of years in a junior college. I had filled my days, I suppose, as a careless man covers a wall with paint. There were great gaps.

I stood up. It was a major effort. Like lifting a car. Penner's room bored me. Penner bored me.

When I thought of Penner I remembered the eggs. There were the shells, still on the side of the hot plate. I tried to imagine what he would say. He would, I decided, be disappointed in me; I would be the proof of his queer theories of hospitality. Screw him. I could break his back. I could cripple him.

I started to cry. Break his back. I was some guest. The host doesn't like it when his guest steals his food? Break his back. Blind him with a punch. The Social Boswell. Bosill. Bosbad. I had to replace the eggs, put back the Bible, make the bed.

I straightened the room and went out into the street. Penner hadn't said anything about a key so I left the door slightly ajar. Nobody breaks into an open room. What if one did? Penner's room would break a thief's heart. It had broken mine, Boswell, the Egg Stealer's.

I cursed myself for the cab and the flamboyant tip. Bosbad the Show-Oaf. I would have to get some money, but I knew even as I walked around looking for likely cars that I wasn't up to the car-lift. It was light out and there were people on the street and how could I be sure of picking the right car and even if I did what if it belonged to some housewife with a lot of packages? She'd either give me a dime or call a cop. I walked down the unfamiliar street, cold and desperate but certain nevertheless that something would happen simply because I needed something to happen. I had been outside for about twenty minutes when I realized that it was all

53

pretty ridiculous. I was forced to a revision of my theory. Things happen all right, but they are unexpected things. No prayer is answered.

It was too cold just to walk. I went into a bar where about half a dozen men sat drinking and talking. The bartender looked up at me and nodded. I stood just inside the bar and smiled back at him, trying to convey that I was neither a drinking man nor a talker, just a guy trying to warm up, neighbor. I exaggerated my discomfort by giving myself great hearty whacks with my palms. I embraced my shoulders, I shook my head, I brr-rr-rrr-ed through my lips, I clonked imaginary snow from my imaginary boots. "I'm back, Martha," I called to myself, "the colt's foaled, the sow's pigged, the hen's chickened." "You come in here, Sam," I called to myself from the kitchen, "and take some hot cocoa."

"Cold are you, big fella?" the bartender said.

"Witch's tit weather, mister," I said.

"Have a shot. Warm yourself."

"Too cold yet," I said.

A couple of men looked around at me, then turned back to their drinks. One of them whispered something into the ear of an old man who sat beside him. With painful jerks the old man turned on his stool to look at me.

"He's big. He's big," he said in a loud voice.

"Shh. *Daddy*," the man who had whispered said.

"All I said is he's big. He *is* big," the old man said again.

"My father is impressed with your size, sir," the man explained.

"I'm big," I said agreeably.

All the good little men in the bar looked around at me.

"You think he's a Polack?" the old man asked his son.

"Shh. Daddy!"

"Your Polacks are big men," the old man said. He turned to look at me again. "Are you a Polack, sir?" he said.

"No, sir," I said. "I'm so big because I work out in a gym."

"How's that?" he asked.

"I lift the weights," I said.

"Oh," he said, disappointed, "a weight lifter. All those fellows are muscle-bound." He turned to his son. "Some wiry fella could kick shit out of him."

"Just a moment, sir," I said, inspired.

"How's that?"

"That's the biggest fallacy in the world," I said.

I walked over to the old man, took my coat off and rolled up my sleeves. I turned around slowly in front of the old man. Everybody in the bar was watching me. "Do I look muscle-bound?" I appealed. "It's the biggest fallacy in the world. 'Intelligent lifting creates strength without giving the appearance of crippling, freakish muscular definition,'" I said as if I were quoting.

"Just look how cold he was," someone down the bar said. "Sluggish blood. Muscle-bound blood. It don't circulate fast enough."

I looked at the man sternly. "Do you say I'm not strong?" I asked him.

"No. My God, anybody could look at you and tell you're strong. Hell yes, you're strong. Sure you're strong. I'd never say you wasn't strong. I'm just thinking about what my cousin told me who's a doctor. He once proved to me scientifically that pound for pound the strongest human being is a kid. If a kid was as big as a man he'd be dangerous he'd be so strong."

"Well, how come they ain't dangerous when they grow up?" the old man's son said. "Kids grow up, don't they?"

"Ah," the man down the bar said, "there's where you miss the point. It's a question of ratio. My only point is it's not just size."

The old man asked if he could buy me a drink.

"Thank you, sir," I said, "but I'm in training for the Olympics."

"Going to beat the Russkies, hey?"

"I'm sure going to try, sir," I said.

55

"I still say it stands to reason if a man is bigger than another man he's got more power," the old man's son said.

A couple of others agreed with him and I sensed my opening. "No, the doctor's right," I said, indicating the man at the other end of the bar.

"How's that?" the old man's son said, hurt because he had been defending me and I had abandoned him.

"Well, power has nothing to do with size," I explained. "Size is just weight. Look, there are several men here. Now it stands to reason that all you men taken together have more size than I do, isn't that so?" I asked this of a man who had as yet taken no part in the conversation.

"You're bigger than any man here," the man said.

"Taken together, I said."

"Oh, yeah, taken *together*."

I turned to the old man's son. "Well, if you have more size than I do, then if your argument is right you ought to have more power than I do, too. But I say you don't. I say that even though you have more size you don't have more power. We'll arm wrestle. I'll bet I can beat any two of you at once."

"How you going to do that?" the bartender asked.

"Well, I'll sit here with my elbow up on the bar and two of you try to pull it down so that my arm touches the bar. If you can't do it, I win. How about that, Doctor?" I asked the man down the bar. "Is that a fair test?"

A man on the other side of the old man's son looked at me. "You want to bet us, is that right?"

"I believe in my strength," I said.

"How much are you betting?" the man said.

"You say."

He got off his stool and stood by the bowling machine. He signaled for the other men to collect around him. They had a conference, and then the man stepped from the group and came toward me. "We bet ten dollars," he said, "but you've got to whip four of us."

"One against four?" I said. "Aren't you ashamed to come up against me with four helpers?"

"Oh, come on, fella," the man said. "You're a hus-

56

tler. Do I look like a jerk? A guy comes in and says he bets he can beat two men he *knows* he can beat two men. It's a trick."

"It's no trick," I said. "It's strength."

"Strength or trick, what difference does it make? If you suggest the bet it's because you know you can win it. All I want to do is even up the odds. I'd say if you're prepared to take on two of us you're probably prepared to take on three of us, in a re-match. What I'm saying is let's save us all some time and start with four right away. You might even be able to do it against four, but that's where the bet comes in. I don't think you're that strong."

There is such a thing in this world as counter-hustling. This man was a counter-hustler.

I didn't know if I could beat them. There was no trick. I needed the money. Penner needed eggs.

"Well?" the man said.

"One of the four has to be the old man," I said.

"Crap," the man said, "even if it didn't kill him, he'd be in the way. There's going to be a lot of guys pulling at that arm."

I hesitated.

"You pick the four you want to go against," the man said generously.

I stood considering. "All right," I said at last. "The bartender. The doctor. The old man's son. And you." That left three men out of it, the old man and a couple of truck drivers sitting in a booth.

"He's afraid of you, Pop," the bartender said to the old man.

"All right," the counter-hustler said, "you set it up. What do you want us to do?"

I got up and slipped into an empty booth. I motioned two of the men to sit facing me. The doctor and the bartender sat down. "The old man's son stands next to the doctor," I said. "You stand next to him."

"You've got all the room," the counter-hustler said.

"You arrange it," I said.

He shrugged. "Okay, we'd be crowded any way we did it. Your way is all right."

"There has to be a time limit," I said.

"No time limit," the counter-hustler said.

"Don't be ridiculous. We could be here all night. Shouldn't there be a time limit, Doctor?"

"I should think so," the doctor said professionally.

"Five minutes?" I said.

"Ten," said the counter-hustler.

"Seven," I said.

"All right," he said, "done." He turned to his team. "Okay. Now for Christ's sake, let's not pull against each other. Doctor, you and Leroy push at his wrists. Me and Tommy will be pulling at him. Don't any of you let go. If I see a spot open that needs some additional pressure I'll get on it. The rest of you: *Don't let go!* Now, we can use both hands. He can only use one. That's eight hands to his one. We'll have him down in no time."

"Wait a minute," I said. "Who's got a watch?"

"I do," the old man said.

"All right, you start us. If my arm is still up after seven minutes, blow the whistle."

The truck drivers came out of their booth to watch. "I seen a fella do this once against seven guys in Dallas," one of them said.

"Horse shit," I said. "I'm the strongest man in the world." I let my elbow come down sharply on the table. I made a fist. Four pairs of hands grabbed my wrist. I clenched my fist hard and the wrist swelled. The muscles in my forearm jumped. The forearm thickened. No hand could go all the way around my wrist. "Start us off," I said to the old man.

"One for the money," the old man said, "two for the show, three to get ready, and four to go!"

I braced myself. When the old man said go, seven hundred pounds of force shoved suddenly against my arm. Pain shot through it, but I held. At first I simply resisted but gradually I began to pull against them. Although it made the pain worse, I pulled against them viciously. I knew I was discouraging them. It was what I wanted. They were thinking, If his arm did not come crashing down after that first thrust it will never come down. I felt their pressure slacken individually. If they didn't work together I could beat them.

58

"Come on," the counter-hustler said suddenly, "all together. When I count three, pushers push and pullers pull with all your might. Your biggest effort."

Their pressure relaxed almost completely while he counted.

"One," he said.

"Two," he said.

"THREE!"

"Because my heart is pure," I yelled.

I felt strength surge into my arm. It drained from my legs, my chest, my back, my free arm, and spilled like water seeking its own level into the besieged arm. "Because *my* heart is pure," I hissed at them. Their effort collapsed, their attack came to nothing. They began to push and pull against each other, coughing and panting.

"It's no use," the old man's son said.

"He's just one guy, God damn it," my enemy said. "His arm gave a few inches that time. Come on. One. Two. Three." They weren't ready for him. The doctor lost his grip and his hand fell uselessly to the table.

"Don't let go, don't let go!" my enemy screamed. The doctor rushed his arm back into the contest but he grabbed the hand of the old man's son. "No," the counter-hustler said in despair, "that's your own man." He released his grip on me and guided the doctor's hand to a vacant area on my arm. "All right," he pleaded, "another shove. We can rock him down if we swing our guts into it. Are you ready for me to count?"

The men grunted.

"One," he counted, "two—all right, thureee!"

This time they came against me together. They shoved and pulled at my arm like men hauling down a flag. It was their lives' most serious effort. My arm began to give. I thought they had broken it. A great pain, like something loose, slammed and tore through me. Pain came up my elbow like fire. I groaned. I could see tears on my fist. "No." I screamed. "No. No. *No!* I will not be beaten. I will not be beaten. Because my heart *is* pure. Because my heart *is* pure!" Inches away from the table I was able to check the arm's descent. They tried by sheer weight to force the arm the rest of the way down, but they had lost their rhythm again. Whatever it was that had brought them together, that had decided them to come to that bar in the first place—whatever mutuality of fate or luck or just plain taste that had caused each of them to accept my challenge, something monolithic in their lives which charted, categorized, classified them as though they were so many similar though perhaps not identical pieces of fruit—was gone. I hated them after all, my victims, because they could permit themselves to *be* my victims, because my victims were not great men, because my arm hurt. My arm went up easily, smoothly.

They hung on for the rest of the seven minutes, clinging to my arm indifferently, as they would in emergency to some piece of baggage they could not quite decide to abandon. They were dispirited, each in some particular stage of despair, routed, finally, as all men *are* finally routed, as individuals.

The old man called time and the hands came off my arm like so many birds quitting a branch.

The bartender handed me my ten dollars.

"No hard feelings," my enemy said. "You were getting pretty sore there."

"No," I said, "of course not." I rubbed my arm, holding it up, offering it to them. "It hurts," I said.

"It was a good fight," he said.

"It certainly was," I said.

Was it? Was it? These particular victims didn't think David Niven was cute—they thought he was a fag. These particular victims didn't get spooked in bad neighborhoods. But these particular victims were victims, too. One didn't do battle with them, one didn't fight the good fight against them. Not the *good* fight. I was miserable. Where's my life, huh, Herlitz? *Herlitz?*

They wanted to buy me a drink. No, I said. They wanted to challenge me with five guys, with six. With seven. Like the guy in Dallas. With eight. Better than the guy in Dallas. No, I said, though I knew now I could win. No. They offered to empty all the bars, to flag down trucks, to call cops in off their beat. They offered money. They would sponsor me; I would be their boy, their champion. Who needed it? No, I said. No.

I had forgotten first principles. I didn't mean to be a character in a bar. All right, a strong man is not a bank president, but if he's on a stage there's some distance at least. People don't know anything about him. They don't even know his name. What was the name of the last magician you saw? Immortality is works—I insist on that. If people remember *me* I'll be embarrassed. Damn a man's body anyhow, as my Uncle Myles, the convulsive, says.

I went back to Penner's room, straightened it, then went to the market and bought eggs. I got a paper and read the gossip columns. I looked longingly at a picture of a presidential dinner party; the Belgian Ambassador was smiling, his ear cocked aristocratically toward the lips of the woman next to him, the wife of the British Prime Minister. Prime Ministers are prime, I thought.

I crumpled the paper and shoved it away from me. What time was it? There was no clock in Penner's furnitureless, wardrobeless, eggless world. I had forgotten to look when I was in the street. My arm ached. When would Penner be back? I didn't even know where he worked. He was "not far." Yeah, me too.

I went to the window. A lady was passing in the street with a green laundry bundle under her arm. I opened the window. "Lady, what time is it?" I called.

She passed by without answering, without stopping, without even looking around, as though strangers shouting to her from windows for the time of day were one of the hazards of city life she had been prepared for. Meet overtures with silence. Better than judo.

"Thank you, lady, and the same to you."

I thought I might go out and spend some more of my ten dollars, buy some elegant little something for the man who has nothing, but my heart wasn't in it. Or I might pretend to rent a room someplace. I had heard that landladies were supposed to be talkative. My heart wasn't in that, either. Where was my heart, anyway, I wondered. Let Penner come back. We young men could talk over our plans.

I heard the same light footstep in the hall I had heard earlier. It came right up to Penner's door. Then

61

someone was saying words into Penner's woodwork. "Marty? Marty? Are you there? It's me."

"Come on in, it's not locked," I said, using Penner's favorite ploy—a lie, incidentally, as I discovered at feeding time.

A girl came in. A pretty little thing, but pale and frail looking, whose passion brought on asthma attacks.

"Where's Marty?" she asked, surprised.

"Not far," I said.

"Are you his friend?"

"Like a brother," I said.

"Is Marty coming back soon?"

"Have a seat," I said. "We'll wait for him together."

"Who are you?"

"Jim Boswell."

"I don't remember Marty talking about you."

"I don't remember Marty's talking about *you.*"

"Oh," she said, "I'm Alice. I'm Marty's friend." I didn't believe that one, I can tell you.

"Listen," she said, "are you very close to Marty?"

"Not far."

"Tell him not to do it."

"He wants to do it," I said. "His heart's set on doing it. You know how Marty is."

"It will ruin his life," she said.

"He doesn't think so," I said curtly.

"You sound like you think it's a good idea," she said sadly.

I shrugged.

"I don't understand how a friend of Marty's could feel that way," she said.

"Marty thinks it will be fun," I explained.

She looked at me curiously. I had probably made a mistake.

"Does Marty know you're here?" she said suspiciously. "I could call him," she threatened. "Who are you?"

"Alice, I told you. I'm Jim Boswell."

"I'll come back later," she said, "when Marty's here." She moved toward the door uneasily.

"Alice," I said sharply, "please sit down. I want to talk to you."

"I think I'd better come back later, Mr. Boswell."

"All right," I said, "but it's silly to be shy. I know about last night. It was me who called. Didn't Marty tell you that?"

She turned, troubled and unconfident.

"I don't think it was very nice—what Marty did."

"What did he do?" she asked in a dry voice.

I remembered the hand over the mouthpiece. "He threw you out," I said.

Alice came back to the chair and sat down. "I thought it was a woman," she said quietly. She started to cry.

"Oh, don't do that. Alice? Please don't cry."

I moved over to her chair. One hand was across her eyes. I leaned down toward her. "Please, Alice," I said. "I'm sorry." There were carbon smudges on her fingers, little bits of eraser rubber under her nails.

"Did you come here from work?" I asked as gently as I could.

She nodded. "Where's Marty? Where is he?"

"Were you here earlier this afternoon?"

"On my lunch hour," she sobbed. "I had to take a cab."

Everybody was always coming up to Penner's place in a cab. It might have been the Ritz.

"Please don't cry," I said. "Please don't." I wanted to touch her, to hold her like a little girl in my lap, to squeeze her behind. I wanted to change her life, to cure her asthma, to give her talent and lovers and irony and wealth. I have always had an unreasonable sympathy for certain unmarried working girls. Not waitresses, not stewardesses, not even girls who work in stores—but office girls, girls out of high school who become clerks and typists, girls who file things. (Frequently I am sorry for people without realizing that my own circumstances are substantially the same as theirs; the thought of people having to live in apartment buildings depresses me, yet I have lived in them and they aren't bad.) When I see such girls on a bus or overhear them on their lunch hour in a cafeteria they make me sad. Where will they meet the fellows, I wonder. Do church functions really work? Who will mix with them at mixers? How about stamp clubs? Pen pals? Travelers Aid?

Alice continued to cry, her sobs coming in dry little wheezes. Her nose was running. I thought of the man in the bar whose hand had to be guided to my arm. I thought of my muscles. Who had given them to me? I had. Free enterprise had. Let Alice lift weights. Didn't Weinbuhr himself say that compassion is the retreat of the impotent?

"Alice," I said, "suppose Marty comes in? You don't want him to see you like this." Now I was speaking her language. She stopped sobbing and looked up at me gratefully. I helped her to her feet. "Don't chase him, Alice," I said. "A man doesn't respect a woman who chases him."

"That's right," she said.

"Of course," I said. "And a girl's got to look attractive for her friend. Nobody looks good with puffy red eyes and a runny old nose."

"That's for sure," she said.

"Now you go on home and when Marty comes in I'll talk to him."

"Yes," she said.

"That's better," I said. I opened the door for her. "Go on home now." I winked at her as she went out. "And, Alice—"

"Yes?"

"Wash those fingernails, sweetie."

Penner came in about ten minutes after Alice went out.

"You're not at the gym," he said for a greeting.

"No."

He took off his coat and immediately began to prepare his dinner. When he pulled out the coffee can he saw the eggs I had bought. Without a word he put one egg in the pan.

Alice, I thought, you don't know how lucky you are.

64

I let Penner scramble his egg in peace. When it was ready he took the pan and sat down on the bed. "Father," he said, "for that which I am about to receive I thank Thee." He chewed the egg solemnly, and when he had finished he brought the pan to the sink, scraped some bits of egg into a small bag, and washed out the pan. Then he took the bag and went to the window. "When you came last night, I forgot about the birds," he said. He emptied the egg onto the ledge, then returned to the bed. Seeing the newspaper I had crumpled, he picked it up, smoothed it out and turned the pages.

"Where's the classified section?"

"It's all there," I said.

"Oh yes, I missed it before." He opened it up and went down a few columns with his finger. "Nothing tonight," he said, as if to himself. He looked relieved.

"Are you looking for a job?"

"No."

"A new place? Look, Penner, if I'm making you uncomfortable I'll get out."

"No, of course not," he said.

I must have looked skeptical.

"No," he told me, "I like having you. Really." He lowered his voice as though he were embarrassed. "Sometimes—in the ads—there are people in trouble. Perhaps I can help them."

"Oh," I said.

Penner went back to the paper. What was he all about anyway? Birds? Ads? Alices? Oh yes, Alices.

"You had a visitor today, Penner."

He hadn't heard me.

"I say you had a visitor today."

"A visitor," he repeated.

"A girl."

That worried him. He looked like someone who had been told he had mice.

"Alice was here," I said.

Now he just looked disappointed, but there was shock in it, too, as though coming to his room were a vicious weakness he thought he had cured her of. "Oh,"

65

he said, "I'm sorry to hear that." He put the paper aside.
"Did she want anything?" he asked wearily.

"To see you. She said she'd come back."

"I don't know what to do," he said.

"Penner, she told me she was with you last night and
that you threw her out."

"No," he said. "That's not true. I told her she could
stay. I did."

"But *I* was coming."

"Please," he said, "you don't understand."

"Well, Penner," I said, getting up, "I've still got my
key to the gym. I'm sorry I inconvenienced you, or if not
you, Alice. After I leave she'll come back and you can
work something out."

"No," he said, looking genuinely frightened, "you
can't go. You asked to stay. You have to stay."

"What are you talking about? Come on, Penner."

"Oh, Boswell. Boswell, you're pushing me into hell."

"Penner, *please*. What is it with you?"

"Nothing. Just stay."

"Goodbye, Penner."

"A vow," he said.

"What's that?"

"I've taken a vow. That's all."

"What are you talking about?"

"A vow. I took a vow never to refuse anyone anything. It's so hard."

"A *vow?*"

"I want to be a saint."

"Then share your eggs," I said.

He looked about to cry. First me, then Alice, now
Penner. There was something tragic loose in that room.
The heart's raw onions.

"God forgive me," he said. "I am not a naturally
virtuous man. It's harder for me. I have a terrible sen-
suality, Boswell. When Alice was here last night we did
awful things. She's in love with me. She wants me to
marry her. I can't do that."

"Of course not," I said. "Saints are all single men.
Penner, stop this crap. What are you giving me?"

"For nine years I have never refused a human being anything. That is the vow I made to our Lord."

"All right, why?"

"I am in love with Jesus."

"Okay, Penner."

"I'm going into the Church."

"You? A priest?"

"If He will have me."

"Okay, Penner."

"Why are you scorning me? Is *your* soul saved?"

"Who knows, Penner?"

"Do you want me to pray with you?"

"Play with me?"

"*Pray* with you."

"No."

"If you stay we can go to church together."

"Is that where you go in the daytime?"

"Yes. I'm there all day."

"Penner, I don't know if you're conning me or what, but you put on a terrific show."

"It's because I'm not innately virtuous that you don't believe me. I saw the eggs you bought. I pretended to ignore them because I was jealous of your generosity."

A weight-lifting saint. A sound soul in a sound body. Why not? Didn't the Virgin herself like tumblers? Penner was an athlete of God like the old ascetics. He played it too close to the chest, though. His room, his conversation when he wasn't being baited, his hospitality, his days in church. If he never refused you he made it awfully hard for you to ask. He gave you the classified section, put you up on the fourth floor. He kept his eggs in coffee cans.

"Penner," I said, "I wish you a happy journey to God. I hope you go Pullman, but personally I can't stay with a man who is not innately virtuous. So goodbye and eat plenty of eggs."

"You asked to be my guest," he said pathetically.

"I'm releasing you, Penner. It's okay. Hey, God, did you hear that? I'm releasing your servant Penner. I don't want to stay in his room any more. How's that, Penner? All right?"

"You son of a bitch," he said. "You mother fucker."

"You've got a lot of class, Penner. Tell Alice good-bye and give her a little pinch for me, Saint."

"Boswell, forgive me. Please," he said. "I'm so sorry. Let me pray for you."

"Okay, Penner, pray this. Pray I stop crapping around."

III

Perhaps there are men in the world's counting houses with larger fortunes than Midas'. Perhaps there are anonymous fourths sitting around the world's tables who have played better bridge than Hoyle. But it doesn't make much difference. Midas has had fortunes named for him; the Earl of Sandwich, lunches. So it's not quantity alone. One speaks, too, of the quality of a fortune, the quality of a love affair. My heroes don't give only their time or their lives to their works. They give their names as well. They know what they're doing. They cast their names upon the waters and they come back tenfold, a hundred, a million. It is the Christianity of Fame.

You can imagine, then, what the Hercules/strength equation must have meant to a man like The Great Sandusky. He could afford it, you say. Yes, but it hurt.

"He was a strong guy, sure, but could he have had better developed lumbar lats than that?" Sandusky has asked, his feet a careful nineteen inches apart, his hands locked in impossible tug-of-war behind his neck. He couldn't have. In his prime Felix Sandusky had the biggest lumbar lats in the business. According to Sandusky, "Hercules got a good press only because the rest of your Greeks were little men. Sure, vitamins have killed the strong-man game. People are taller now, bigger in the arms, the legs, the chest. You hear a lot of talk about longevity, statistics about the average man living thirty or forty years longer than his great-grandfather, but that's only half the story. Your trunks are vaster now. Look, it's like anything else. It's all contrast. Everybody has force." (Sandusky liked to call his strength force.) "But if a guy has only a little force then a guy with just average or a little better than average force is a big deal. Hercules could probably take care of himself, but your general run-of-the-mill Greek was a guy with lousy force. So don't tell me about Hercules! What with health foods and wonder drugs and vitamins and scientific weight training it takes a real man to stand out today. Every Tom, Dick and Harry has force today."

Getting to meet The Great Sandusky was my first campaign.

I left Penner's as elated as I had ever felt. Twenty-four hours before I had been broke. Since then I had earned twelve dollars and still had more than eight, which meant that I was *getting,* including expenditures, at a rate of better than seven-hundred-fifty per cent. That was very high-grade *getting* for me and quality *keeping* for anyone. Furthermore, I had made a decision which would change my life: a decision not to mess around. Herlitz helps him who helps himself.

In the gymnasium, daydreaming, just before sleep on the tumblers' mats I had pulled down from the wall, the idea came to me: The Great Sandusky. The very name was a revelation. The Great Sandusky. We were both strong men of the world. He would help me. That he was in the city was common knowledge to all the regulars in the gym. It was Penner who had shown me the feature article on him in the paper. It said he lived now in a hotel near the river. I would write him. The Great Sandusky. Of course!

I let myself into the gymnasium office, took three sheets of stationery, and wrote:

The Great Sandusky
Riverside Hotel
2nd and Steamboat Streets
St. Louis, Missouri

Dear Sir,
     I am an admirer of yours. Not simply because of your feats (which no man could gainsay), but because I am a strong man myself and know what effort was involved in the accomplishment of those feats. I should like very much to meet with you in order to discuss your achievements and to talk over with an expert certain plans of my own. Please arrange whatever appointment would be convenient to you. May I close by saluting a pioneer in strength and by remaining yours very truly, etc., etc.

     I wrote it several times until it was awkward and stiff enough. Then I signed the letter and addressed the envelope. At the last moment I had an idea that would demonstrate my earnestness. I hunted around in the office until I found a couple of nails. These I bent and put into the envelope with the letter.
     I supposed I would hear from him within two days. What the hell, an old man, out of condition, in a lousy water-front hotel—he would answer as soon as he got the letter. He would go downstairs and beg a few sheets of hotel stationery from the night clerk and painstakingly scratch out a reply. He didn't. I heard nothing. On the fourth day I wrote again:

Dear Sandusky,
Perhaps you thought my last letter insincere, the work of a crank, or the teasing joke of a jealous man. I assure you neither assumption fits the case. I have the greatest respect for your feats. I know of your fabulous cow lift. A picture of you pulling the locomotive is in my wallet at this moment next to my mother's own [with my crummy eight dollars, buddy] and I should like to assure myself that a life given over to the cultivation of strength reaps rewards in later age commensurate with the Spartan, with the *Herculean* [knew what I was doing] efforts necessary to develop that strength.

71

Remembering what I had read in the papers I crossed out "strength" and wrote "force." "I am a professional myself, sir," I finished, and signed the letter.

Instead of two nails I enclosed a half-inch spike which I paid a professional machinist to heat and bend for me. This time Sandusky would certainly answer. When he didn't I was more surprised than hurt. Then it occurred to me that, after all, he was now an old man. Perhaps he was dead. I called his hotel.

"May I speak to The Great Sandusky?"

"He ain't in."

"Please, it's important."

"There's no phone in the room."

"I don't care what you give the cops to keep your license. I'll see to it that Fire Chief Lesbeth hears about every one of those violations. You'll be out of there so fast your head will spin. Get Sandusky."

"Who is this?"

"It's Jimmy Boswell, that's who it is."

"Just a minute. I'll see if he's back."

He went away.

"Hey, Boswell. The old man won't speak to you. Says to tell you the spike is a cheap trick, that any jackass with reasonable force could bend a friggin' spike."

He hung up.

So, I thought. He had hubris, the old man. So much the better. The great are touchy folk. They are goosey. The goosey great. I give them every credit. It's a free history, right?

I wrote a third letter:

> My dear Sandusky [I began] I appreciate your reluctance to meet with outsiders, with the jackals who feed off the greatness of others. Let me be frank. I read the feature about you in the papers. It was disgusting. If I were a lawyer I would advise a suit. It made your efforts appear comical. The reporter's insistence on your emphasis on the sub-scale of ordinary Greeks was a deliberate attempt to offset scientific observations by making them

72

appear hobby-horsey. To provide amusement for weak, fat-ridden office workers. What does an outsider know? Has he sweated under the strain of a bench-lift; has he felt the pull of the jerk-and-press; the thrill of the curl; the back-hoist; the arm wrenching, shoulder wrecking agony of the dead lift? I am a strong man, Sandusky, and I have a legitimate historical interest in your training. If bending half-inch spikes is labor for a child then what is this?

I enclosed a twisted one-inch spike.

I received no reply, but in the mail three days later was a package for me. In it was the spike. Sandusky had straightened it.

In a hardware store I bought two pounds of iron filings. I put them in a box and sent them to Sandusky.

Two days later there was a post card addressed to me in the gym office. On the front was a picture of a sunset over some southern resort hotel. On the back was one word: "Come."

I went to Sandusky's hotel that same night. It was very ratty. The numerals on the control buttons in the single narrow elevator were smudges. Behind a clouded glass at the rear of the elevator was a faded picture of a rooster. "Good Morning!" it crowed. "Have Breakfast in the Wake-Up Room!" Beneath it a sign warned, "Room service is dis-continued after midnight." Another sign said, "Laneur Hospitality Is World Famous. A Laneur Guest Is an Important Person. Under this someone had written "Fuck you." I read the inspection certificate. There was some very tiny print and seals and stamps and then the legend: "This elevator is authorized to carry no more than nine hundred (900) lbs. This elevator was last inspected on *April 10, 1939.*" It was signed illegibly. I looked at the heavy, raised brass OTIS medallion on the clumsy control at the front of the elevator. The control itself looked like something you drove a trolley with. I pulled the handle back and forth but nothing happened. The thick, important-looking handle slid uselessly to and fro in the wide slot.

73

The elevator moved slowly up to Sandusky's floor. The cock crowed good morning. Room service warned. Laneur boasted. Guests retaliated. Authority regulated. It was a babble of silent, hopeless, irrelevancy. Inauspicious, I thought, inauspicious. The corridors on Sandusky's floor smelled like a men's room in a railroad station. What a masculine smell, I thought. I knocked on the door. There was something like a nervous, surprised little movement behind it, but no one answered. I knocked again.

"Who's that?" a voice said.

I knocked.

"Who's that, I said."

"It's Big Boswell," I answered powerfully.

"No," the voice said, "go away."

"Sandusky, is that you?"

"Go away, I said."

"I was invited. It's Giant Jim. I must see you."

"No," the voice said. "Go away. Leave me alone."

"You invited me, Sandusky. It's Giant Jim Big Boswell. I have to talk to you."

"Leave me alone, I said. **Go** away."

"Is that you, Great?"

"No."

"It is. I've come miles. From Idaho where I train. Where I carry trees up mountains to train. Let me in."

"No, I said."

"All right, Sandusky, I've had enough. You saw what I did to that spike. How much easier it would be for me to do the same thing to this door! I warn you."

"Listen, you get out of here. I don't have to see anybody."

"All right, Sandusky. I warned you. Now I'm going to break your door. I'll make wood shavings out of it. You could put them on a floor in a butcher shop."

"Stop," the voice said. "I'll open the door."

It opened. "Sandusky?"

"Come inside."

"The Great Sandusky?"

"Don't make bad jokes. Come inside."

There was a mistake. In his pictures Sandusky was a

74

huge man with a great shining massive skull, the famous "battering ram." He was bulky rather than muscular, meaty, red-fleshed, faintly Tartar, a circus poster strong man in leopard-skinned dishabille, one furred strap tight across a wide and straining shoulder. He was fearful even in the photographs, like some strange wet animal. On a circus poster the man before me might have looked like the company's advance man, nothing more. He was shorter than Sandusky could possibly have been, and if his appearance suggested that he had ever been in athletics it was because he looked so much like a vaguely seedy high school basketball coach who had known his share of point shavers, gamblers and hoods. A baggy sharkskin business suit gave him the careless, spilled-soup look of the insider, the man who breaks training. His fingers had the mustardy nicotine blotches of the revolutionary, and indeed, against the background of his hotel he looked like some out-of-date anarchist.

We looked at each other narrowly for a moment and then the man, smiling, offered me his hand. It's a trick, I thought immediately. This was a hand which had crushed rocks. For all its shabby appearance of disuse and even disease, it would attempt to crush my own. He would break my fingers, would he? All right, I thought, we'll see. Trying to appear as casual as he I let him have my hand. As soon as we touched I braced and squeezed first; there was no resistance, and I pressed the hand as I would a sponge. As he pulled his arm away I saw that I had made a mistake.

"Do you want to kill me? Is that the way you show your respect?"

"I'm sorry," I said awkwardly. "I was trying to impress you."

"You would impress me better if you behaved yourself."

"I'm sorry," I said. "Forgive me."

It was my flaw. If I met a great athlete I tried to crush his hand; a great banker, I cashed a check. Herlitz, that magician, was right again. I was a fourth—Boswell, the world's sad fourth, who played other people's games by other people's rules. A reader of labels, of directions, a consumer on the most human of levels. Vampire. Sancho. Jerk.

Sandusky, if the little man *was* Sandusky, was backing away from me and rubbing his hand. I apologized again. He sat on the edge of his unmade bed.

"I made a mistake," I said.

"All right," he said, "forget it."

"It was supid of me. I'm sorry." I apologized some more. I saw it gave him courage.

"Three years ago," he said at last, "I would have thrown you through the wall for that."

"Yes."

"I would have torn off your head."

"Yes," I said. "Certainly you would have."

"I had a terrible temper."

"I heard that."

"I was a wild man of Borneo in a side show when I was a young man and they had to let me go I was so realistic."

"I read that somewhere," I said.

"I once broke a man's back who got too close to my cage."

"Didn't the police—"

"The rube called me a fake and threw peanuts. What police? What could they do, put handcuffs on me? *Handcuffs?*"

"They would have been like so much string," I said.

"Yeah, string," he said. "Crap, what does it mean? You see what happens to a man?" He held up his hand.

"I'm sorry," I said again.

He ignored me.

"Did you think Sandusky would be like this?" he asked. "I was hiding out. I don't know how that reporter found me. How do they know those things? He used old pictures. I made him do that. You know what surprises me most?" He looked up at me. "Sit down." I looked around for the first time, and noticed that except for the bed and a chest of drawers there was no furniture in the room. I had to perch on the edge of the bed with Sandusky. I sat carefully, prissily. Only roommates plop down on each other's beds. A gentleman uses another man's bed as he would another man's car; it is highly personal machinery. Still, I thought, remembering my feelings when I had sat in the office with Herlitz, there is something deeply feminine in me. I thought absently of all the thank-you notes I would one day write.

"What surprises me most is the pain," Sandusky said. "As an athlete yourself, you know that training is an accommodation to pain. That's all. A champion is a man who has mastered pain. You'd think my training would have accustomed me to it." He lowered his voice. "They want to throw me out of the hotel. I holler. At night. I holler."

"Have you been sick?" I said.

"Sick? Hah, what would you know about it?"

"I'm sorry."

"It's my fucking constitution. With my trouble any other man would have been dead in eight months. Me? Three years now and God knows how long to go."

I could not really believe in Sandusky's illness. "Why don't you kill yourself?" I suggestd.

"Don't be fresh," he snapped. "Say, you got a lot of nerve going around telling people to kill themselves." He considered me for a moment. "Did you really do that?" he asked.

"Do what?"

"That thing. The spike. Or was it a trick?" He meant the filings.

"It wasn't a trick," I said.

He shook his head in soft, sad wonder. "You're the strongest," he said. "You got any money for an old champion?" he asked plaintively. He pronounced it "champeen." He was mocking me.

"Have you got any scrapbooks?" I asked.

"What's that?"

"Scrapbooks. Pictures of yourself—from the old days."

"Say, what's the matter with you? Are you straight?"

"Please," I said. "I'd like you to show me your scrapbooks."

Sandusky laughed crudely. "Why?"

"I'm a professional," I said. "It's scientific."

I'd had the idea when he told me about making the reporter use old photographs. There must be a scrapbook. That would be the thing—a guided tour. History is rare. It happens once. Who sits under the apple tree with Newton? For the sake of argument, you're Moses' closest friend. But when he climbs Mt. Sinai he climbs alone. A tourist sees the mountain, and some raggedy Arab leads him up and shows him a piece of broken stone. But it's not the same thing. What do *places* mean? *Tombs? Relics?* What counts is people in the moment before history happens. So if Sandusky had a scrapbook it was not enough just to see it. I had to sit by while *he* turned the pages. Ersatz? Certainly, who says no? But I must always go as close as I can go, sidling up to the fearful edge of someone else like a man with vertigo. I tell you there is a sort of shame for me in not being one of the Trinity, such absolute chagrin in not being important that I can hardly look anyone in the eye. I am just Boswell the Big. What a burden for a strong man. In the presence even of Sandusky I felt a sort of awe; even an old success, a past, provocative as a scent, could hold me.

"So you're a pro, what difference does that make? What can you learn from photographs?" Sandusky asked.

"That's not it," I said. *"Please."*

He threw up his hands. Under his sleeves, I knew, the flesh around his upper arms hung slackly, like an old woman's on a bus. "I keep a few pictures," he said. He seemed apologetic. "Loose," he explained. "There's nothing you could call a scrapbook." He went to the chest of drawers and bent down.

He keeps them in the bottom drawer, I thought, where it's uncomfortable for him to get at them. He's humble. Not like Herlitz.

Having to stoop like that was obviously uncomfortable for Sandusky, and I stood to help him. He heard me move and looked back over his shoulder impatiently. "I can still pull out a damned drawer," he said.

"Of course. I was just stretching."

He scooped out a pile of pictures from beneath some

78

papers—certificates and documents—and ran his hand over them rapidly, like a man in a gin rummy game looking through the discard pile. He picked out some pictures and pushed the rest back into a dark corner of the drawer. I saw the face of a woman on some of them—in my business one learns to look quickly—and wished that I might be able to look at these. (History is gossip, too, right? What stocks did Sandusky buy? Who was the beneficiary of those policies?) He picked up what was left and brought them back to the bed.

"These are just some poses," he said shyly. "They're corny, but you can get an idea." I took the photographs from him and looked at them carefully and slowly. "Of course I was pretty young when these were taken. A kid. Younger than you are, probably," he said. "I was sort of a model in those days. That's how I broke into the game." As I looked at the pictures of Sandusky in his prime, of a near-nude Sandusky in postures of incredible stress, I was struck not so much by the contrast between the vigorous body of the young man and the collapsing presence sitting next to me, as by the complete lack of self-consciousness in the face on the photographs. There was an absorption so intense it might almost have been indifference. The young man wallowed in the sense of his body. A professional indeed. He was like a stage magician feigning surprise at the bunch of flowers suddenly appearing in his hand. I stared at the pictures, trying to get inside not his body, but the *achievement* of his body, the historic *occasion* of his body.

I must have embarrassed Sandusky. "They're poses," he said again.

"Yes," I said hoarsely, "I know. Poses."

I looked still more closely at the pictures. I examined them like a detective looking for clues. That's what I was, a detective. I searched for the essence of Sandusky's greatness, the achievement of man into meat. He had been like Christ, Sandusky. I saw that his shyness now was no swift accident, no result of the mere, though sudden, confrontation of the discrepancy between youth and age, wholeness and infirmity. It was there *then,* in the photographs. What I had mistaken for self-absorption, for

79

pride, was a thorough selflessness. Sandusky, if he had ever existed, had disappeared behind that body, behind those eyes. His achievement was a self-sacrifice, not like my petty push-ups in the gym, a means to an end. Sandusky's exercises were a means to *the* end. Remember, you must die. The corpse. The body. Sandusky remembered.

There was one photograph of Sandusky's great, flexed right arm. In profile he gazed down at the bicep, transfixed. In another he stood with his fists on his hips. Where the elbows crooked, meaty slabs of muscle seemed to spill from the Niagara of his upper arms down into his forearms. His thumbs shoved against his rib cage, swelling his chest. In another he posed flatfooted, his toes lost, melted together in the overexposed photograph that washed his body in a frightening light like the brightness of a saint in a vision, the fingers of one hand splayed, rigid as steel tubes. His other hand grappled his wrist. I had the odd feeling that were he to let go he would have flown apart, the muscles flying outward from the center like shrapnel. This same quality of desperate containment pervaded all the photographs. Even in the pictures that showed Sandusky lifting heavy weights, he seemed not so much to be lifting them as burdened by them. In one his arms thrust defensively upward toward a huge bar bell. He squatted beneath the heavy weight obscenely, his knees spread wide and as high as his chest. His face was an agony, a passion of tears and pain, his breath heavy balls that threatened to pierce his cheeks, like the representation of Zephyrus in classic paintings. Lifting the weight, he seemed caught in some final humiliation. There were many such pictures. Another showed him upright, the weight high over his head. He almost seemed suspended from it. In the last photograph he actually *was* suspended. He hung in a device, his arms flung back across a horizontal bar, his shoulders wide as planks under the tremendous pressure. Wound about his entire body were thick chains from which, pendulant as gigantic metal fruit, were suspended huge weights like railroad wheels. Ah, I thought. Ah.

Sandusky looked over my shoulder. I heard his thick breath. "They're poses," he said. "When I was a kid."

"Of course."

"The weights came later. Stunts," he said scornfully.

"Heroic feats."

"Stunts. Lousy stunts. I liked the body-building, the training—that was good. You can see in the pictures. After I started doing the stunts I got fat, thick. I lost my definition."

You never had any, Sandusky, I thought. That was your triumph. "That's what made you The Great Sandusky," I said.

"Oh, that. You want a laugh? Here, look at these." He handed me two photographs I had not seen. One was of the lower part of his body, his waist and legs; the other was of everything above the waist.

I looked at the photographs and then at Sandusky. "They're nice," I said.

"Don't you get it?" he said. "Don't you get it?"

I shrugged.

"Lower Sandusky," he said, pointing to the picture of his legs. Then, touching the other photograph, "*Upper* Sandusky! The town in Ohio! Get it?"

He handed me a full-length portrait of himself. "Greater Sandusky?" I said.

"Yeah," he laughed, "yeah, yeah. *Greater Sandusky!*" He clapped me on the back. He laughed and laughed. "*Greater Sandusky,*" he wheezed through his laughter.

"Greater Sandusky." I laughed with him. "Greater Sandusky! Greater Sandusky! Yeah. Yeah."

"Yeah," he said.

"*Greatest* Sandusky!" I roared, putting all three pictures in a pile.

"Yeah," he laughed, "*Greatest* Sandusky!"

He fell back on the bed, one arm flung heavily across his forehead. The other he raised weakly to his lips, trying to contain his laughter. He looked like someone who knew he would be sick, and the sight of him beside me, beneath me, the strong man wrestled to his bed by laughter, made me laugh more. You'd have had to have been there, I kept thinking, already trying to explain to someone else afterwards what it had been like. You'd have had to have been there. I tried to say "Greatest Sandusky" again to keep the joke going. Sandusky saw me and shook his head in warning. He took his hand away from his lips long enough to say, "Do-o-n't. Doannt. Don't. No. D-dd-doonnt."

I was made ruthless by my laughter. *"Greatest* Sandusky," I said.

He giggled.

"Greatest *Sandusky,"* I said.

Sandusky roared.

"Greatest Sandusky!" I yelled at him.

He collapsed in laughter, the water rushing from his eyes. Startled, I saw that he looked like the Sandusky of old, the Sandusky of the photographs, his cheeks blown out in a rage of pain, his eyes drowned in his effort's flood. Sandusky beneath the Bar Bell, beneath the world's gross weight, who held that weight from the ground, who was all we had between it and us. Sandusky's face, its urgent effort, angered me. The heroic effort, the bald look of strain. There it was, the history I pursued and pursued, the moment I chased to see George do it. I gazed down at the straining Sandusky and wondered if it was possible to kill a man by making him laugh.

"Sandusky," I yelled, screaming to make him hear me, "Sandusky, why does a strong man wear a jock?"

"D-d-do-on-nnt. Doannt."

"To hold his bells up."

"D-o-o-n't. Ple-plee—leeze."

"Mr. Sandusky, how is a strong man like a man who serves food in a restaurant?"

"D-on't."

"They're both *weight*ers!"

He laughed, strangling, but I saw that he was regaining control. It was too bad, I thought. "If you can't join 'em, kill 'em." The new Boswell: Boswell the Bad. Aesthetically it was a pity. I could imagine Sandusky dead, and calling the police myself to report it, and their coming and finding Sandusky's corpse. The Corpse of Sandusky, the heroic mold, all muscles and laughs. "Of course, gentlemen, he died out of his prime, but the essential materials are still there," I would tell them, lifting a loose flap of skin and pulling it taut. "We could take him to a taxidermist and have him stuffed. It's what *he* would want." I would explain to the Inspector that I had told him a joke and he had died. But it was too late; already Sandusky was sitting up, his feet over the edge of the bed. He looked like someone who might wake with a hangover. He was disreputable, torn, and seemed as seedy as he had when I first came in.

"That was a good laugh," he said stupidly. He smiled, remembering it.

"Yes."

"It's been years since I had a laugh like that."

"It's good for you to laugh like that once in a while. It clears the system."

"Well, sure," he said, "I know. When I was developing the body I used to make it a habit to read the joke books. It's a very good lung exercise."

"Is that a fact?" I said. When he said *"the* body" I felt another twinge of anger. He had confirmed again the selflessness of his life's effort.

"I'm a little tired now," he said apologetically.

"Sure," I said, "I'll get out of here."

"Maybe you could come back another time. I enjoyed talking to you."

"Sure," I said, and got up.

"Wait a minute," he said. He came over to me. "You might as well take one of these." He handed me one of his poses.

"Oh, I couldn't."

"Sure," he said. "What the hell." He looked at me carefully. Then, to my surprise, he reached out and touched me. He put his hands on my arms, and stooping, slid his palm down my thighs. On his hands and knees he held my calf muscle, molding it, almost. "Say," he said, looking up at me, "that's all right." He straightened up. "You got any pictures of the body? I'd like to see those calves."

"Gee, I'm sorry, Mr. Sandusky, my photographer

83

promised he'd have some ready for me yesterday, but he ran out of the high-gloss paper we use."

"Oh," he said, "I see."

"Some should be coming in soon, though," I said. "I could let you have a chest and legs and thighs, of course, and a neck that I'm very proud of. I saw the neck proofs yesterday when I went to the shop, and I think they're terrific."

"I'd like to see them," he said. "The neck was always one of my weak spots, as you probably saw."

"No," I said, "you had a distinguished neck."

"Well, it was *scrawny*," he said, lowering his voice. "I was susceptible to sore throats and I could never exercise it the way I should have."

"The way it deserved."

"Yeah," he said, "the way it deserved."

"Well," I said, shoving out my hand, "thanks for everything."

"My pleasure," he said.

I held up the photograph he had given me and grinned.

"Forget it," he said, "my pleasure."

Pleasure, I thought, leaving him, what would you great men know about pleasure?

IV

I still have in my files the photograph Sandusky gave me.
A picture of a serious young man (like one of those
figures you see in a tableau—can it move, does it breathe,
is it real?) in a loin cloth. His arms (of course, that is
merely a convenience, a convention of language; they are
no more *his* than mine) fluid with muscle, his chest . . .
It's in my files. A cornerstone!

Herlitz, you comedian, you clown, you had some
Old World fun with Boswell, hey? That Herlitz! He
played a joke. Not just on me—on Freud, on the German
generals, on the man with the monorails. He gave us
projects. What, you think greatness is fun? Laughs? You
think it's all honors and international congresses and
dressing for dinner? No, I tell you. Everybody dies. We're
all lashed to the mast. The man goes down beneath his
cause like the soldier beneath his flag. Only his achievement, his *thing*, lingers. Men leave us their lousy things,
that's what. Vaccine or the patents or a greasy wallet with
fourteen dollars and change and sixty dollars in uncashed
traveler's checks—it's all the same. (They take it out of
the hospital safe and send it to you in the mail. "Here are
your father's effects," the letter says, not unkindly. They
call them that, *effects*. Who needs his effects? I want
him.)

So it was his selflessness I couldn't stand in Sandusky, his heatless heart. Reckless! Let's not kid ourselves, we all have to vacate the premises. But the *great*?
They receive their eviction notices and—poof—it's into

the street at once with their furniture and effects. It's stupid. Stupid? It's immoral, what Forbush calls "The Mad Scientist Motif of Modern Life." You think that's an exaggeration? When the professor takes out the young girl's brain and wires it up to the ape, you think maybe he's got something against that girl? Like hell. The product at any price. So they go on pumping yellow jack into their veins, feeding themselves plague in the afternoon tea, dropping the bomb first on each other to see if it will work later on us. Like Sandusky, they build the body and scorn the soul. Maybe, at bottom, that's good Christianity —maybe, at bottom, that's what makes saints—but it's immoral, damn it. Give me the self-centered who don't make anything. Give me, by God, the raptless.

I came away shaken from my interview with Sandusky. Well, it was a disappointment, you see, a revelation. After Sandusky I would always know where I stood. It was I who had betrayed Herlitz after all. I had ignored what he had told me, that I was not a great man myself. Boswell, the sneak hero.

So I went on the wagon. I made resolutions. Lay off the great, I told myself, stay away from them. Swear off. You are not up to even the over-the-hill great, their frigid Decembers of achievement.

Ah, it was conscious though. I couldn't help my *feelings*.

What I was really doing was lying low.

An excerpt from my journal:

May 14, 1948. Los Angeles.

A curious thing. Perhaps I *am* a man of destiny—of sorts. At least one of those people to whom things happen. Like two weeks ago when I slept with the whore. I didn't have anything with me. But in my excitement I couldn't wait, and since then I've been worried about syphilis. It's really amazing. I know absolutely nothing about syphilis. Ignorant as a bird. I had meant to go to the library to look it up, but I never got around to it. It was really preying on my mind when a few days ago *Time*

86

magazine devoted two pages to it in the Medicine section. A coincidence, I suppose, one I must make nothing of, but that sort of thing happens too frequently for me to brush it aside. I *am* special, unique. Not, I'm afraid, in any way that will ever do me any good, but I won't be bored, I think. Do others feel their uniqueness as much as I do? Mine is sometimes staggeringly oppressive.

That's not the reason for this entry, however. (See? Now I have "reasons," though when I first started this journal it was only because I felt I needed some device to stop time, a sort of spiritual Brownie. I made entries like those phrases travelers put down in guestbooks: "Awe inspiring." "I am thunderstruck." "It makes one feel insignificant." But the truth is, nothing makes me feel insignificant. Hell, big as it is, couldn't make me feel insignificant.

I came to Los Angeles to wrestle. I've been here almost three days. I must be particularly careful in Los Angeles. My resolution. And the temptation is great in a city like this. If one doesn't absolutely shut his eyes the possibilities that he will run into the great are enormous. Washington, D.C., is the same way; so is Manhattan. So I must be very careful when I'm there, too. In Washington the great are too busy, and in New York they are frequently strangers in town themselves, but in Los Angeles they're at home. Instead of this relaxing them, as one might think it would, it makes them even more self-conscious. This is their territory, but somehow they expect to be spotted. Perhaps they are even eager for it. Even in slacks and sandals they seem to throw out hints of their presence as sure and solid as a scent. Of course I am particularly vulnerable to this, and the temptation is always to forget what I learned from my encounter with Sandusky, to throw it all up and devote myself to some strategy which will engage their attentions. Also, there is the fact that I wrestle. I am, after all, something of a public figure myself—though, strangely, I am not really colorful or flashy enough to be a feature attraction, or even, for that matter, a contender in the more important preliminaries. I start the evening, or end it, or am the other guy on unimportant tag-teams. Nevertheless, I have often spotted stars in the audience. They flock to exhibitions of this sort. They sit there, their collars opened, their hats high on the backs of their heads, and scream obscenities at us. The women are even worse than the men. They come in furs or evening dress and study us darkly. We athletes are sort of American bullfighters. They admire us for what they think is our simplicity, our animality—which is only surface, after all, while their own is buried and therefore more urgent. Before the ballplayer, the wrestler, the boxer, the bullfighter, there was the gladiator, before that the Christian martyr, before that some shepherd on a slope of the Apennines.

So whenever I am here I must exercise my full will. It's a real test of the resolution I made over a year ago. (In Cedar Rapids what danger am I in? Some obscure millionaire? A governor, perhaps, if I'm lucky? *Lucky?* What am I talking about? Which side am I on?) And then one doesn't simply fly into Los Angeles two hours before a match and then out on a late plane two hours afterwards. Bogolub, the big promoter out here, insists on the wrestlers having at least two sessions in the gym before they go on—even sub-eventers like myself. I once complained to him that I thought the act got stale if it was rehearsed too often. "I don't think so," Bogolub said. He's a tiny man, white-faced, like someone with a heart condition. He goes in a limousine which he drives himself to all the gyms in the city to watch his wrestlers. "I don't think so," he said. "I think practice makes perfect." "I can't agree," I told him. "That's what makes horseracing," he said, pointing vaguely toward the ring. I shrugged and went off to work out on the mat—my kind doesn't even get to use the practice ring—with the ox I had been matched with. About ten minutes later the guy had pinned me according to plan and I was lying there underneath him, thinking absently of my Uncle Myles and how I had been either on top or underneath more men in my life than girls, when I saw Bogolub watching me carefully. It was almost a quarter of an hour after our talk, but he continued as if there had been no interruption. "In addition," he said, "you're just a tanker. The biggest men, the *biggest,* work out the routine in the gym before a match." He's an interesting man. He's invented most of the famous wrestling personalities—a Herlitz of the Mat World, as it were. (There I go. Since I resolved not to chase the great I find that more and more of my time is taken up with the parochially important or the simply unusual. Why, for that matter, did I even challenge Bogolub? What am I? A dumb tanker. If I want to wrestle in Los Angeles I have to play by his rules.)

So in Los Angeles the question of how I can spend my time is very serious. I could stay in my room, I suppose, but what's the point? Somehow I keep forgetting that I am still a very young man. In another context, with parents or perhaps just friends, I might even be considered a kid. Loneliness makes for precocity, but there is a danger that it makes for world weariness, too, if you let it. What right have I got to be world weary? A dumb tanker! There will be no drinking myself unconscious in hotel rooms for me, yet, no going down to some all-night cafeteria for a two-o'clock cup of coffee and a quick shot of human companionship. Just because one is resigned does not mean one is through. I promise you at least that much, Boswell. You are not through, in no sense washed up, you and your middle-aged heart. Just because you have it figured about life—*everybody dies*—there's still no reason to turn yourself inside out, to go through the world skeleton first, to make every morning shave a *memento mori*. I try to keep myself presentable, like some old lady in a home for the aged with eau de cologne up her smelly crotch. That's the ticket. Appearances, the heart's red hair ribbon. *That's* what makes horseracing! So I force myself.

Well, that's not accurate. It's true that sometimes I have to force myself—but not last night. Last night I was feeling pretty good about things. I wanted to see a motion picture. But in Los Angeles you can't go to a first-run movie without running the risk of bumping into some damned movie star. They're crawling all over the lobbies on some crazy busman's holiday. Do I need that kind of aggravation? I figured it would be best to get out of town, so I bought a paper to see what was playing in the suburbs. In Chilanthica there was a revival of *Plenty of*

Daddies with Edward Arnold and S.G. "Cuddles" Sackell and Eugene Pallette. Carmen Miranda and José Iturbi are in it, too, and Margaret O'Brien and Sabu, the Elephant Boy, in his first non-jungle picture. It introduces little Dickie Dobber, whom I've never seen in anything else. I see this film whenever I have the chance. One day I'm going to buy my own print, just to have it around.

I called the theater and asked when the last feature started; then I called the public service people and found out exactly how to get there. (Just like the old days. In certain ways I am still a planner, an arranger. My movements are a series of carefully plotted steps, like the directions on how to assemble a child's toy. It never rains on my picnics.)

The name of the movie house in Chilanthica is the Orpheum. At first this was very satisfying. Nothing had ever happened to me in an Orpheum. It would be like being bitten by a dog named Rover. But then I thought, Chilanthica is a very small town, there's only one movie here. "Orpheum" is always the *other* movie in a small town, practically a brand name, the manager's choice after "The Chilanthica" has been spoken for. It was disquieting. (I'm not that sensitive, but as I say, Los Angeles makes me nervous.) There was only the Orpheum, I kept telling myself, *only* the Orpheum. It was fishy. It was too much like being reduced to primal things. It didn't make me any easier to note that the movie was on Elm Street. And sure enough there was an ice cream *parlor* (not a shoppe) across the street. Had the town been called Centerville or Maplewood I might have bolted, but "Chilanthica" was enough like the real world. So, like a jerk I bought my ticket and went in. It was, as I say, primal—like walking out onto a bare stage. I needn't have called; there was only one showing. At 8:30, of course. I stood in the lobby watching some of the others coming in. It was pleasant at first, like the experience with the name, to see their anonymity, to exult in it as one can sometimes revel in muddy river water. A GP; the man who owned the filling station; the druggist; Mother Hubbard from the restaurant; the couple that ran what must surely have been "The Emporium" (he, vaguely big-time, well-dressed, sporty; she, almost but not quite chic). And people. Respectable, safely unimportant. Had I my wits I would have realized how pat it all was, they all were, these maskers, these phony Republicans.

Indeed, as a stranger, I had *their* attention. I saw the man from the Emporium eying me. Too big for a traveling salesman, he was thinking. Maybe a lettuce farmer. Has money for a movie. Maybe the talk about drought is premature. It might be a better year than they say. Have to talk to Margot about the fall line.

I walked off and bought some popcorn from the high school girl at the candy counter. She was a thin little thing with no makeup except for some heavily applied Johnson's Baby Powder over her pimples. She handed me the popcorn and smiled nervously. She lays, I thought triumphantly. I breathed in deeply, smelling the popcorn, the butter, the salt, the waxy paper around the candy, the spilled soda bubbling down the drain of the Coca-Cola machine, the rust around the handle of the water fountain. Filling my lungs with the pleasant mediocrity of the place, I could settle down here, I thought. A nice place to raise children, hey, Herlitz? They would let me play in the band, go to the dances in the community center. (It was all center, this place, for the inner man.) Just forty-five minutes from Broadway, oompa, oompa pa. I actually whistled it and Mrs. Emporium, Margot herself, looked up and smiled at me. Mother Hubbard smiled at me. They don't whistle songs like that any more, I thought. Who eats real home cooking these days? I winked at her and she blushed. *Blushed!* Fool, idiot, fall guy, I should have thought. A setup. A shill. The whole town's a shill. They *don't* eat home cooking any more! Main Street's a novel, not a place. They've money in the bank, kids on Fulbrights. In the summer they go to Rome and have audiences with the Pope. Some guy in New York writes copy for Mother Hubbard's soup. The factory is behind the shoppe (not the parlor). It's served in Rosenthal bowls in executive suits from here to London. There are no people any more. Everybody's a personage. Interview them, interview them all!

I went into the auditorium and sat down. (I sit

toward the front. There's nothing wrong with my eyes. I want to see everything. *Everything!*) The place was filling up rapidly. I was breathing heavily. At last it was sinking in that I wasn't safe. But then the house darkened and Pathé News came on. It was safe, after all, I thought. The newsreel was two weeks old; I had seen it ten days before in a town in Nebraska. That's right, drown me, ye backwaters!

Blissfully I watched for the second time some floods in the Ohio Valley. It was cute the way the narrator described it. (When no one is killed in a disaster the narrator is cute, though he gets serious when there's a lot of property damage.) I saw a demonstration in Frankfurt, Germany, of a new kind of roller skate. The shoe part of the skate was about two feet off the ground. The wheels were attached by powerful springs to the shoes and every time the skater made a stride he'd bounce up high in the air. Then some girls tried it and of course they couldn't do it very well and they fell down and you could see their underwear. Then there was a Press Club luncheon in Washington for President Truman. (Some people behind me applauded. A bad sign—in the real small town, in Nebraska, there had been boos.) A reporter asked the President about his plans for November and Truman smiled and was coy. "That would be telling, wouldn't it?" he said and everybody laughed. (I could find out. *I* could.)

There was a Bugs Bunny at which I laughed contentedly. (The only time I am really at ease in a movie is during the cartoon. There *is* no Bugs Bunny. There *is* no Mickey Mouse.) And then, the worst time for me, the coming attractions, all those stars to look at. I stuck it out, and actually it didn't go too badly. Science fiction and second-rate westerns and I hadn't heard of many of the actors.

Then, at last, the picture came on.

It was just as grand as I remembered. It's about three old bachelors who own different department stores and have to live together in the same Manhattan apartment because each distrusts the other. It shows how their lives are changed when Sabu, the Elephant Boy, comes to live with them. Sabu is an orphan whose parents have

92

been eaten by tigers back in his native India and Edward Arnold hears about it and brings him to the States for Christmas. He's got it worked out that this will help his sales figures, and Eugene Pallette and S. G. "Cuddles" Sackell have to go along with him because if they don't they think it will hurt *their* sales figures. Of course none of them is really thinking about Sabu, and everything is so strange and new for him that he gets a little nervous and has to run off from time to time to the Bronx Zoo and climb in with the elephants and talk it over. But if it gets out that Sabu isn't happy it will hurt *everybody*'s sales figures, so the three old men make up amongst themselves that they've got to be better to Sabu. Well, it's a wonderful movie. Edward Arnold was never suaver, Eugene Pallette was never fatter, nor his voice more husky. They play curmudgeons, even S. G. "Cuddles" Sackell. The three of them are very shrewd, very stuffy—all anybody could want in a father.

After a while, though, although they don't dare let the others see it, they really begin to like Sabu for himself, and then they start to outbid each other for his affection. They know he likes animals and there's a scene where Edward Arnold sneaks out during the night and brings back a baby elephant for Sabu. When Eugene Pallette sees it the next morning all he can say is "Hmph, you call that an elephant?" and that night he goes out and brings back a bigger one. S. G. "Cuddles" gets it all mixed up and brings Sabu a beautiful pair of matched tigers. This bothers Sabu because of what tigers have done to his parents, but he doesn't let on. As a matter of fact he gradually begins to forgive the tigers. Listen, why not? These old men can't do enough for him. I've never seen anything like it. They turn on the love. They pour it all over him. What don't they give that nut-brown orphan! Pajamas, robes, electric trains, radios! They have three different department stores to choose from! And at night Sackell sings Rumanian folk songs to him and Edward Arnold recites poetry. Even Eugene Pallette comes in and croaks out something at bedtime. They tuck him in all night long.

It's marvelous—all those people breaking their

necks for him, the economy of the City of New York contingent on Sabu's happiness—all those daddies. He even has a kind of kid sister in Margaret O'Brien, who lives next door and comes in mornings to teach Sabu manners and how to be a good American. Actually, the only person not taken with Sabu is Margaret O'Brien's cousin (and this I resented, seeing it as a deflection from the real meaning of the picture), played by Dickie Dobber. This was a snotty kid, a *real* curmudgeon. That sort of thing doesn't look good on a child and I was glad when Sabu's elephants turned on him.

Then comes the best part of all: the scene where they give Sabu the marvelous birthday party on the day he's legally adopted by the three magnates and becomes an American citizen. This is where José Iturbi (playing himself) is one of the entertainers and Carmen Miranda (playing Margaret O'Brien's maid, but really more like Sabu's aunt than hired help) tries to get him to play some snappy rumba. Everyone is shocked, of course, because José Iturbi is an irascible Latin genius and believes only in serious music, but in the middle of the concerto that he's composed for Sabu's birthday he gives a sly wink and goes into a jazzy riff that leads into the rumba. Dickie Dobber unbends and nods at Carmen Miranda as if to say, "Hey, José Iturbi's all right!" but of course Carmen Miranda knew it all along. (After all, José Iturbi really *is* a Latin. Like Carmen Miranda herself.)

Well, it was marvelous, and pretty soon I had forgotten it was really Edward Arnold up there, and Eugene Pallette, and, oddly, even José Iturbi, but just then—just when Edward Arnold is starting to tap his foot to José Iturbi's music and the elephants are beginning to sway their trunks—the film snapped. You could actually hear it tear and go around flap-flap on the reel. Everybody groaned.

In the darkness, before the lights came on, I heard a voice next to me.

"Damn it, it's the best scene in this turkey. You know old Kuperman, what a stickler he is for realism? He had the property man use VO in Eugene's glass. Well, you saw it yourself. When the barman pours Edward's drinks it's from the bottle to his left. Eugene's shots come out of the one next to it."

"You're kidding," someone on the other side said.

"You know old Kuperman."

"Was Pallette really loaded?"

"Loaded? There were a dozen and a half takes, Elizabeth."

I knew. Even before the lights came on, I knew. It was Sabu, the Elephant Boy! It was Elizabeth Languor, the film soprano!

A man runs and runs. He does his push-ups, lifts his weights, builds his body, wrestles his wrestlers, pins, is pinned. It's the old one-two. The old give-and-take. He gives and gives; they take and take. It's not like in the old days when there were guarantees. That wop Aeneas had a belt, a spear. As long as he wore the one and threw the other they couldn't touch him. Even the gods couldn't touch him. Me they can touch. I do my best. I go on a bus thirty-five miles out of my way to a town nobody ever heard of, to a "Chilanthica," a place to raise kids, where it's fun to be a citizen, where when you vote you come away feeling clean all over. I pick a picture nine years old—and look what happens.

Once I was waiting to buy rolls in a bakery when a man rushed in carrying a package. He was *mad*. "See here," he screams, shoving this package onto the counter, opening it as one might open a newspaper full of garbage. "See here, damn it," he yells at the old lady who owns the bakery. "I warned you about the nuts. My wife is a sick woman she can't eat nuts it gives her gas. And what do I see? Nuts! *Nuts!* I particularly didn't want nuts!" That's right. I know how he feels. You get what you don't ask for.

When the lights came up I glanced to my left. Not despondently to see if I was right, or even hopefully to see if I was wrong, but—here's the sickness, you see; here's me all over—*instinctively*, to see what they were wearing. Sabu had on white trousers, a rope belt, a tailored black shirt. Wound round his head was a turban with a glittering black jewel in the center. I was surprised to see that he wore glasses. My first thought was of this journal. "Sabu, the Elephant Boy and Hollywood star, has to wear glasses when he goes to the pictures." I glanced hastily at Elizabeth Languor. Gold brocade slacks, a gold belt, a soft pale sweater over a tight black T-shirt. There was a scarf around her neck. Hmm, I thought, a scarf, maybe to protect that throat. They caught me staring at them—did they think they had been recognized? Did they expect me to ask for an autograph?—and I turned away.

What should I do? Leave? Change my seat? Ignore it?

I couldn't leave. The picture had been ruined for me, but I couldn't leave. I couldn't change my seat. Indeed, had they changed theirs I would have followed. Ignore them? Hah!

Instantly, you see, I was off the wagon. I tried to rationalize. You've never done an elephant boy before, I told myself, conscious that I had used Herlitz' word. After all, it's not as if you went looking for it. It fell in your lap. My lap, indeed. The gods have laps, not men.

Then my struggle was over. I leaned toward Sabu and listened.

"Have you ever done anything else with Kuperman?" Elizabeth asked.

"Not yet. Irv Teller thinks I'm just right for the Arab who goes over to the Jewish side in *Storm in the Desert*. Koop starts shooting it in the fall, but I'm a little reluctant."

"Oh?"

"I've never worked with camels," he said.

Elizabeth and I laughed. Sabu looked at me severely.

The lights went out again. "Vun-two, vun-two," S. G. "Cuddles" Sackell said. "Loook, loook at ze elements, vat zey do ze roomboom."

"Iss prununce *chr*oomba," Carmen Miranda said, snapping her fingers and grabbing his hips.

"Hmph," Eugene Pallette growled huskily, something funny happening to his eyes, "you call *that* shaking? I'll show you shaking." He began moving his hips violently and caught little Dickie Dobber full in the chest, jamming him helplessly between the two elephants.

"That's not in the script," Sabu said to Elizabeth Languor. "He did that on his own."

Real VO, I thought. Real Eugene Pallette drinking real VO.

The camera moved in jerkily to expose Dickie Dobber's white, panic-struck face. The elephants rumbaed menacingly. Only Sabu could call them off.

"Koop left this in?" Elizabeth asked.

"Yes, isn't it marvelous?"

When everything was calm, Edward Arnold went up to Eugene Pallette and pulled his sleeve. "Better stay away from the bar," Edward Arnold whispered. He said "bah."

"He's wonderful, isn't he?" Elizabeth Languor said.

"He certainly is," Sabu said.

"I was with him in *Latin Holiday*," Elizabeth said.

Was that you, I wondered to myself. I thought it was Jane Powell.

"Honestly," Elizabeth said, "he's so paternal and dignified. He had little Jane Powell thinking he really *was* her father."

That's right, I thought, you were the one who went to school in Switzerland, the daughter of the big industrialist.

Eugene Pallette looked up at Edward Arnold. "What bar?" he asked. He was panting heavily.

"By the wall," Edward Arnold hissed.

"Hmph," Eugene Pallette rasped, "you call *that* a wall?"

Sabu put his arm around Elizabeth Languor's shoulder. " 'And let there be no moaning at the bar when I put out to sea,' " he whispered. He said "see."

I squirmed in my seat; I bit my lips; I pinched myself to see if I was dreaming. I had never been happier. There he was—Sabu, fourteen feet tall up there on the screen. A Star. Only not a star up *there*—up there only Rama, triply adopted son of department store magnates, Down here, beside me. I could smell elephant on him. Fourteen feet tall down here. It was a wonder he could even fit into the seat. And Elizabeth Languor thrown in! Could there be greater happiness in this world? I forgot my guilt and uneasiness. What guilt, what uneasiness?

Suddenly it wasn't enough just to sit there—I had to impress them in some way. But if I spoke they would change their seats. They would call the usher, and I might be arrested. The law is made to protect the great. That's civics—the folks in Chilanthica would know about that. I could explain to them who I was. "Perhaps you've seen me wrestle, Sabu and Elizabeth. On television. On the TV. Perhaps you saw me break the Mad Magruder's ass." I could lower my voice. I could wink, blow my fingernails; "it's all *fixed!*" I would say precisely. Then later, over a tall drink, I would tell them the secrets of my trade, and in a little while, after confidence had been developed, I would pounce. "Is Hollywood fixed?" I would say. "Is *Holly*wood *ffixsed?*"

Idiot! You think they don't have jails in Chilanthica? (I saw it, a single jail, like the town's single movie. The "pokey," they would call it.)

I tried to control myself, to concentrate on *Plenty of Daddies,* but I couldn't even understand it any more. The temptation was simply to turn in my seat and stare at them. Every so often that's just what I did. I would turn my head an inch and glance at them out of the corner of my eyes. I was sure they noticed it. I was sure, in fact, that while they pretended to watch the picture they were staring at me in the same way, and that if I had nerve enough I could say just the right thing to engage them. The chat over a drink wasn't such a wild notion after all. I wasn't an idiot; I am an interesting human being. Surely they could respond to *that*. That was the pitch, of course, but how would I make it?

Nothing happened. The movie was almost over, and soon the lights would go up and we would all shuffle out to our cars, our houses, our buses, our hotel rooms. Surely it was too much to expect that Sabu and Elizabeth would go across the street to the ice cream parlor.

Act, I thought. Act!

I looked to my right. I was on the aisle. I looked to

my left. Sabu. Elizabeth. A filled row. I made my decision. I stood up.

I turned to Sabu, the Elephant Boy. "Excuse me," I said gravely.

He looked up at me, confused.

"I have to get by," I explained.

Instinctively he pulled in his legs, but then, glancing significantly toward the aisle to my right, he frowned. I moved against his legs heavily.

"Ouch," he said softly.

"Excuse me," I said. "I'm sorry if I hurt you."

"Oh, wait a minute," he said, and stood to let me pass.

I halted in front of Elizabeth Languor. She glanced up at me and stood without a word. I moved quickly past the rest of the people in the row and out into the aisle. I went to the lobby and put a dime in the Coca-Cola machine.

"They stood up for me," I croaked. "They stood up for me. Sabu and Elizabeth Languor."

I threw the Coke away untasted and rushed back into the theater. I haven't been gone long enough, I thought. It'll look funny.

The big production number was on the screen. Edward Arnold and Eugene Pallette and S. G. "Cuddles" Sackell had their arms around each other. They had just merged their three department stores. Sabu was on one elephant and Margaret O'Brien was on the other. They all seemed to be coming through the big Manhattan apartment right into the audience. José Iturbi's piano was following them. Everybody was singing Sabu's concerto. I was coming down the aisle while they seemed to be coming up it. It was thrilling.

I moved into my row. Already people were getting up to leave, but I pushed past them to get to my seat. They looked at me, annoyed, but made timid by my size.

When I got to Sabu's and Elizabeth's seats, they were unoccupied.

Boswell, I thought, mover of men!

The journal entry closes there. I was up most of the night writing it, and Felix Bush, the Schenectady Stalwart, beat me the next evening in a match I was supposed to win. Bogolub came into the locker room afterwards while I was still in the shower.

"Boswell!" I pretended not to hear him.

"Boswell?"

"Boswell, you in there? You hear me? You in there? Well, I hope you're in there because that's where you wash up and that's what you are, you understand? Washed up! No more in LA do you wrestle for me in my gardens with the television and the hook-ups to San Francisco and all the way up to Portland, Oregon. That's all finished, tanker. A guy that can't win a fixed fight! Wash up good, you hear me? I'm paying for the soap and I say to you you are welcome because you are washed up in Los Angeles, do you understand me?"

"Yes. Beat it."

"Beat it? Beat it? Do you threaten me, phony? I better not understand you to threaten me because I got guys who sell popcorn for me in this place who can whip your ass. You're finished."

I came out of the shower and went over to my locker. Bogolub followed and stared at me while I dried myself. It always makes me nervous when people look at me when I'm naked. Even girls. I turned my back.

"Dry up good, do you understand me?" Bogolub said.

"Please," I said wearily. "Mr. Bogolub."

"No no, my boy," Bogolub said gently, "you miss my meaning. You shouldn't catch cold. You missed a spot on your back. Where the yellow streak is, *that's still wet!*"

I turned to face him. "Look," I said.

"Show me your ass again. I can't stand to look at your face," Bogolub said.

I shrugged.

"Why did Felix Bush beat you?" Bogolub demanded.

"I guess I was just bushed," I said.

"Schmuck," he said. "Pig-fart."

"Get out of here, Mr. Bogolub."

"Get out of here, Mr. Bogolub," he mimicked. "Get out of here, Mr. Bogolub." And then, in his own voice, "No tanker tells me to get out of my own place. You get out. You get dressed and get out. And that reminds me, I meant to tell you before. Why do you wear those crummy clothes? You look like something in a playground. I pay you. Wrestlers make good money. Ain't you proud of your profession?"

"Wrestling is not my profession," I yelled.

"That's right. Not no more. Not in Los Angeles it ain't."

"Okay."

"Okay! Yóu *bet* okay! A tanker who can't win a fight that I go to the trouble to fix it for him. With rehearsals yet. Let me tell you something, Mr. America, let me tell you something about the economics of this profession."

I looked up at once. There was fixing beyond fixing, and I was going to hear about it. It was all I could do to keep from putting my arm around Bogolub, from offering him a swallow of the mineral water that was in all locker rooms.

"You don't know yet the damage you done tonight, do you, tanker?"

Better remain sullen, I thought. He explains because he thinks you're sullen. Even in retreat, I thought, even in retreat I pursue. Even when I avoid them I embrace insiders, their silly trade secrets, their lousy shop talk.

"Contracts have been made, do you understand that? How am I going to juggle all those contracts? Bush was supposed to fight Fat Smith here next month. Maybe he won't. Maybe you ruined it for him, too. It's something I got to figure it out. How can Smith go up against him now? He was on the card right here last week and lost to the Chink. Maybe you don't remember the terrific beating you give to the Chink yourself last time you was here, but the public remembers. So right away, it's an overmatch. A winner against a loser. It's inconsistent. Where's the interest? A guy like Bush is supposed to lose in Los Angeles. All of a sudden he beats a contender."

"Me?"

"Yes, you. In the long-range geometry I had plans for you. Clean-cut. A Mr. Universe type."

"I didn't know about that," I said.

"Big shot. Vigilante. Take things into his own hands and doesn't know what he's doing."

"What difference does it make? So Bush wins one fight. Who's going to think about it that way?"

"*Think* about it? *Think* about it? Who said anything about anyone thinking about it? It's the *feeling* of the thing. The balance. That's what makes a good card. You queered that. Now I'll have to readjust outcomes all the way up the line to get the balance back. And who pays for all that? *I* pay for it. It means new routines, new choreography, new identities, new costumes."

"I'm sorry."

Bogolub wasn't listening. He wasn't even mad any more; he was just thinking out loud. "Maybe I could mask somebody. Maybe some old tanker could come in masked. A new personality. That might fix things."

"I could go against Fat Smith if I wore a mask," I said. "Bush could fight my man."

Bogolub was silent.

"That would restore the balance," I said.

"Who you supposed to be fighting?" he asked finally. "The Grim Reaper, ain't it?"

"Yes."

"We'll see. I won't make promises. You're still on my shit list."

"I'm really sorry about tonight," I said. "I was sick."

He looked at me. He didn't believe my excuse, but was grateful that I made one. "You'd have to change your style," he said.

"Yes," I said. "I'd *have* to change my style."

It was because of Sandusky that I was wrestling. After our interview I returned to the only home I had, the gym. I stayed there, working out desultorily in the afternoons, sleeping there in the evenings. For about a week I simply drifted like that, knowing, I think, that sooner or

later I would have to go back to my Uncle Myles. I was
running out of money, I was getting bored. But mostly I
was running out of money, since there is always something vaguely exciting about being on the bum. There
wasn't much I could do to make money. I couldn't
continue to throw cars into the snow and then pull them
out—the work was seasonal. I stayed away from Uncle
Myles because I believed, as I still do, that things happen.
But lying on the tumblers' mats at night, my only covers a
half dozen volley ball nets (so that I felt oddly like a
captured fish and dreamt of the sea), I knew that whatever was going to happen had better happen soon.

Then a week after I had seen Sandusky I got a letter
from him. It was odd to think that the only being in the
world who knew my address was The Great Sandusky. I
opened the envelope.

My dear Boswell,
    I have been thinking over your problem. I
think it's better to face things right off then to
deceive yourself for a while only to find out
when it's already too late that you've just been
kidding yourself along. I don't know what's going to happen in the future but I can tell you
that right now and for a long time to come
probably the strong man game is dead. Now I
say that speaking from a background of experience which covers I don't like to think how
many years. The facts are this: 1) That Vaudeville is dead and that let's face it it was in
Vaudeville that the real muscle money was
made. It isn't only strong men of course. Acro-
bats, animal trainers, all that crowd I used to
tour the circuits with are in the same sinking
boat. 2) There are still circuses and while it's
true that circuses have absorbed a certain number of the acts there was never any real demand
for a strong man in a circus. Now I know, I
know you always hear the term "Circus Strong
Man," but think about that for a minute. Did
you ever see a strong man put on an act in the

big ring? If you're honest with yourself you'll have to admit you did not. His apparatus is too costly and clumsy (and anyway who could set it up unless it was another strong man). No, your "Circus Strong Man" if the term means anything at all was a guy in a side show in a tiger suit, a freak with a bald head and a phony mustache. His size came more from good German beer than it did from training. You don't want any part of that. 3) The carnival or "carny" as it is called *does* still use a strong man act, but more often than not it is faked and as with the side show it is not a good life. It is not clean and the traveling is not interesting. All towns you never heard of in N. Minnesota and etc.

So all the old showcases for a strong man act are gone, Vaudeville being the main one. (Now some of my friends think that television may bring new inroads but, frankly, I cannot agree and I think they are just kidding themselves and whistling in the dark. What would be more ridiculous than a guy claiming to have force lifting weights on a little tiny television screen? Those weights would look like six-ounce balls. No, definitely not. Besides, in an act like mine was there had to be audience contact and on television you couldn't have that.) Now there's one other thing to think about as you probably know yourself. I am referring to the so-called "physical fitness magazine." Well go ahead if you want to but if I had my way they wouldn't be allowed to sell them. That world is just inhabited by a bunch of queers and fags. How would you like to have it on your conscience that some nut is using your picture in a magazine to jerk off in front of? It's worse than the carny and more filthy and I wouldn't think you'd want to touch it.

Well, you must be asking yourself, what does all this mean for me? Where does all this leave *me?* Well frankly, and I say it right out because I don't like to see you break your heart, it means *that there's no place for you in the strong man game!* Face it now, Boswell, I tell you like a father.

However, I have been thinking that there's one area left that I haven't mentioned and that's wrestling. A lot of the boys go into that and make good money and a famous name and it's not a bad life. I know what you're going to say, that wrestling is fixed. Well it is and it isn't. What I mean is that there *are* clean wrestlers and even those that are fake have to demonstrate a mastery of the different holds and etc. And don't think it doesn't hurt when you get slammed around like that! Of course you know how to fall but plenty of bones are still broken. So don't kid yourself about that! After all, they're really *wrestling.* Only the winner is fixed. And what does an artist care about that, right? It's the form of the thing. The same as in weightlifting or anything else.

Now I don't know whether this sounds like good advice to you or not. Maybe like most young men you would prefer to beat your head against the wall than learn from an older person's experience, but I think you're more sensible than that and so I took the liberty after you left me of writing to an old friend of mine who actually used to manage me at one time, maybe you heard of him—Mr. Frank Alconi—about you who now handles wrestlers and promotes matches in Jersey City. He wrote back saying that he is always looking for big strong boys like yourself for the ring world and that if you are interested he will forward train fare, coach of course. His address is Frank Alconi, 9 Water Street, Jersey City in New Jersey.

Do as you please, but I think this is the best thing. Whatever happens good luck to you. I sign as I used to in the old days when it meant something.

Yours in Force,
Felix Sandusky

P.S. Where are the poses you promised? I want to see that neck.

I wrote Frank Alconi for the money, and he sent it, and I went to Jersey City and became a wrestler.

I became a wrestler, I suppose, because, resolutions or no resolutions, it is an integral part of my character to take advice from the great. A reflex action. Go with the experts, I always say. There's no father-figure crap about it. *My* father is dead.

I never sent Sandusky a picture. He had to be made to understand that it was my neck and I did not intend to do any better by it than I did by myself. There would be no silk shirts around it; I would not flatter it with ties. I wrote Sandusky once thanking him for his interest because that is good sportsmanship. Otherwise, when I was in St. Louis I sent him passes to the matches and that was the end of it. If he was so in love with my neck he might want to be around when it was strangled.

Frank Alconi put me to work at once. I was already strong, of course, and Alconi said I was a natural and anybody Felix had faith in by Jesus he had faith in too. But for a long time I didn't know what I was doing. I went wearily up and down the East Coast between Jersey City and Raleigh, North Carolina, precariously ambulatory, describing my sensations to myself in a kind of hospital shorthand—restive, critical, grave. Indeed, my memories of those first weeks are chiefly memories of liniment. My body was like some great northern forest, one part of which was always on fire. The other wrestlers kept telling me what a good sport I was and visited me at the rubbing table afterwards. Beating me up made them feel young again. They seemed to like to feel my muscles. I can remember more than once, lying on the rubbing table near unconsciousness and death in the unheated basement of a civic auditorium, looking up into the loveless smiles of ancient apes, having them stare down at me lost in wonder, and then, tracing their prehensile fingers over the bumps and hollows of my flesh, pointing with inverted pride at their own tough and lumpy bodies, which looked, from the angle at which I saw them, like great hairy mounds of red meat. Then these fellows would shrug, pull on their pin-striped businessmen's suits, snap their *Wall Street Journals* smartly under their armpits, and go off with a wave to lose themselves among the traveling salesmen in the hotel lobby. In those days druggists went blind mixing special liniments to keep me alive.

When I got back to Jersey City I told Alconi I would have to have more training.

He grinned. "Tough. Felix said you was tough."

I rubbed my neck sentimentally.

"Rough, huh? Trip's been rough?"

"A cob, Mr. Alconi."

"Sure. It's the gym does it. All the time developing yourself against instruments, against metal, when what you need's contact with human beings. Where's the fight in a bar bell?"

"That must be it."

"Sure," Alconi said. "You need the old smash." He ground his fist against his palm. "The old kaboom. The old grrr-rr-agh." He pulled some air down out of the sky, cradled it in the crook of his right elbow, and strangled it. "The old splat cratch." He kneed an invisible back. "The old fffapp!" He grabbed handfuls of invisible hair and gouged invisible holes in invisible eye sockets.

"With all due respect, Mr. Alconi, that's not what I need," I said. "That's what I've been getting. What I need is to learn to protect myself against that."

"Sure," he said. "I understand, kid. Only I'm not your trainer, you realize. As your manager I get thirty-four per cent of your purses. As your trainer I'd be entitled to another"—he considered my bruises—"fifteen per cent."

"Sure," I said.

"That would still leave you with fifty-one per cent of yourself. You'd be in command."

"Chairman of the Board, as it were," I said.

"Yeah," Alconi laughed. "That's right, Chairman of the Board."

I slept on it. The next day I went up to Alconi again. "Who'd pay expenses?" I asked. I had been paying my own.

Alconi frowned. "What the hell," he said, "we'll take the railroad expenses off the top, the gross. We'll split."

"Okay," I said.

We signed a new contract and I went back to my hotel and renewed auld lang syne with a pharmacist I had been keeping.

In the morning Alconi called me over to his office in the gym. "Boswell," he said, "Jimmy, you lucked out. I got a class of ladies starting Monday and I'm registering you."

"Ladies!"

"*Girls. F*emale wrestlers."

"You want me to train with girls," I said.

"Jimmy," he said, winking evilly, "it's better than bar bells."

"Sure."

"The coming thing," he said expansively. "Lady wrestlers. The wave of the future, Jimmy. I can foresee the time when they'll be girl tag teams, girl midgets, interracial girl wrestling, mixed matches with men."

"*Interracial* mixed matches with men," I said.

"Let's go slow, Jimmy," he said.

At first I was shy. After all, it's an odd feeling to see the world strapped across the thick, broad shoulders of some nubile young lady, an extraordinary concept to be struggling for air nuzzled against the breast of some matronly female giant. But I got used to it, and soon began even to enjoy myself. This was frequently and embarrassingly apparent even to the young ladies. Ultimately, for everyone's protection, Alconi's male instructor had to put me on a private crash program. It wasn't the same.

Training with ladies, however, even for as brief a period as I did, had an oblique side effect on my style.

108

For a long time I was reluctant around the area of my opponent's chest. Understanding the cause, I attributed this to some innate though grossly misdirected sense of decency on my part, but it was noticed by the fans and their explanations leaked back to me. "He's a chicken," some said. "No," said the others, "he killed a man once in Canada with a bear-hug and he's afraid he might do it again."

I emerged from my training somewhat better pre-pared for the professional knockabout I had engaged for. I had learned, as Sandusky put it, to fall. This is useful knowledge, as everyone knows.

.For a year I wrestled everywhere—earning, curi-ously, different reputations in different parts of the coun-try. I was too small-time, you see, for it to matter much. In the Southeast, for example—the Memphis–Nash-ville–Mobile–Birmingham–Little Rock–Jackson–Biloxi–Jacksonville–Tampa–Savannah–Atlanta circuit—I nearly always won. (Alconi explained why. I was, as Bogolub was to tell me later, clean-cut, a Protestant, Mr. Universe type, Anglo-Saxon all the way.) But in the coal mining Middle Atlantic states I always lost, for the same reasons that I was let win in the South. Elsewhere it was the same pattern. Here a winner, there a loser. I was earning a little more money now, though the fact that the instructor had to give me private lessons upped Alconi's take a couple of per cent and I was no longer Chairman of the Board.

It went like that, as I say, for about a year. But at about the time I had the row with Bogolub in Los Angeles, Alconi suddenly died. He left no heirs, abso-lutely none, and my contract reverted back to myself. It was like having my salary doubled, and when Bogolub threatened to cut me off in Los Angeles, and perhaps wherever he had influence in the West, I stood to lose something for the first time in my life.

That's why I had apologized.

Bogolub explained that if I assumed a new identity I could no longer wrestle on the West Coast as myself.

"That's all right," I said.

He looked at me narrowly.

"What's wrong?" I asked.

109

"Nothing," he said. "Some guys mind."

He wanted me to stay over in Los Angeles a few more days to talk over plans, line up new matches (most of them with men I was already scheduled to meet), and sign new contracts. I had to cancel matches in Sacramento and Berkeley. Bogolub was so excited about launching a new career for somebody that he agreed to split the forfeit fee with me. When I saw him two days later he asked me if I had any ideas.

"About what?"

"About what? About the costume!"

I hadn't thought about it, but I remembered something Sandusky once told me about his Wild Man of Borneo days. I used that as a base and made up the rest as I went along. I tried to seem enthusiastic. I would paint my body green, I told Bogolub, and wear a monster mask. There would be fangs, and saliva could drip down from them like stuff coming off stalactites. I could call myself "The Wolf Man" and explain my complexion by the fact that I was raised in a cave in Bavaria until I was eighteen.

Bogolub listened to me and seemed to be considering it thoughtfully, but after a while he frowned.

"It's no good," he said at last. "It's too corny."

"Gee, I liked it," I told him.

"Nah," Bogolub said, "what'd happen when you sweat? The green paint. It's no good."

"How about an executioner's mask? I could wear an executioner's mask that goes all the way down to my shoulders. With big holes for the eyes and the nostrils."

"You ain't got the body for it," he said professionally. "You got a young body. That's what we've got to start with."

I nodded gravely.

"Sure," he said. "We got to work on that angle of it. We can't make you into something horrible when you ain't."

"You can't make a sow's ear out of a silk purse," I said brightly.

Bogolub didn't answer; he was lost in thought. After a while he smiled and patted his stomach affectionately.

"Have you got an idea?"

"I think so, I *think* so. How would this be? We put you in a white silk mask—like The Lone Ranger's, only white. And you wear white trunks and a beautiful white silk cape. And white shoes. Nothing else. Very simple. You're The Masked Playboy. You wear the mask because you're really a millionaire's kid and you don't want your parents to know that you're wrestling professional because it would break their hearts. 'THE HIGH SOCIETY WRESTLER! WHO IS HE?' How's that?"

So I became The Masked Playboy. I remembered the reaction in the picture when José Iturbi played boog-ie-woogie. It was our instinct to applaud such acts, to wink at Carmen Miranda with Dickie Dobber when the time came. The secret handshake of the eye. Classical was only fancy, but popular was good. And when we said good we *meant* good, God's good. Little was big and weak was strong and poor was rich. The ultimate, the crowning glory, was what I was to stand for, to demonstrate behind my silk mask—like The Lone Ranger's, only white—that rich was poor, that alive will one day be dead. Applause. Cheers. Winks.

This was in the early days of the baroque wrestler and Bogolub's maneuver was very successful. Now it was arranged for me to win fairly regularly. Bogolub explained the motivation. Why, after all, would a millionaire playboy like myself continue to wrestle if he lost? He would *have* to be a pretty good wrestler. Bogolub was pleased with his invention, and I began to have more and more dates on the West Coast. Once Bogolub explained to me that my masquerade was actually helping free enterprise and capitalism. There was far too much crap going around about the working classes, he said; if Americans were made to see how tough and down to earth a rich man's son could be they would sit up and take notice and it would be good for business.

For five months I toured, climbing the country in busy, sooty eastern and central tours, a wrestler in industrial towns, a loser, comic relief for the day shift. Making the more leisurely long, low southern lope, a whipper of Wops, a Spic scourger, Hebe hitter, Polack pounder—the

111

White Hope of God Knows What. Then the western trip. Quick—off with the horn-rimmed glasses, into the cape, the mask, the white shoes. The Capitalist's Friend, Free Enterprise's Prize. A Masked Playboy who didn't need the money but beat up guys to show he was regular. Like Christ, really—who couldn't use the death but died anyway to show he was regular.

All this was in the preliminaries, of course. Alarums and excursions without. In the anteroom of history, as it were—the man who fights the man who fights the man who fights the man who one day saves or kills the king.

Then one evening, six months after putting on the silk mask in Los Angeles, I was having dinner with a promoter in Columbus, Ohio.

"I was out with Barry Bogolub a couple of weeks ago. He came East on a scouting tour. You work for him, don't you?"

"Yes."

"Yeah, he was telling me. Seems you got this gimmick going for you in LA. Mystery Playboy or something."

"The Masked Playboy."

"Yeah, that's right, he was telling me."

"What about it?"

"Nothing. It sounds good. Next time you're in Columbus, bring your mask."

So, gradually, the real Boswell began to fade. Long live Boswell. I wrestled increasingly as "The Masked Playboy." In hick towns there were write-ups in the paper. I gave out interviews. I'd sit in my hotel room drinking expensive Scotch, a silken ascot around my neck, my legs crossed, staring democratically at the reporter across from me.

"Yes, that's right. Educated at Cambridge. But I told Father at the time that I shouldn't be content with a sedentary rich man's life. He thought it a youth's threat, of course, and meanwhile I developed my body to what you see now."

"Were you actually in the Four Hundred?"

"Well, not actually. There was some nasty business some years ago about an uncle in trade. If I had to place the family, I'd put it somewhere in the low Five Hundreds."

"I see," the reporter would say, tiredly. Then, "You're not supporting the family now, of course—it hasn't . . ."

"Fallen on harder days? No, I should think not. Otherwise I might be able to take off this damnable mask. No, no, the Van Bl— whoops, I mean the *family,* the family is monied."

"They've got a lot of money," he'd say, writing it down.

"Oh, Lord yes, I should say so. But a fellow likes to earn a bit of his own, you know."

"Of course."

Of course.

Articles began to appear about me in the magazines. There was an editorial in *Ring;* my sort of "showmanship" might proliferate, it warned, and bring about the further vulgarization of a once noble sport. Other magazines, the body-building books and that sort, took the story—or pretended to take it—at face value, passing it on to their readers (who *were* those people anyway? more boogie-woogie winkers, I suppose) so that it actually gained in translation. I wrestled, they said, only in those towns where I had factories or brokerage offices or banks.

I was bigger now, more important than I had ever been as myself, and the lesson was not lost on me. For the first time I began to take the wrestling seriously. As the months went by I gathered more and more of a reputation; there was even talk that one day I would be a serious contender for the championship. Which brings me back to St. Louis and my first appearance in a main event.

Bogolub had told me on the night he wanted to throw me out of wrestling that I might one day have been a contender, that he'd had his eye on me. Perhaps it was true, I doubt it, but perhaps it was. Probably he said it to add a fillip to my loss, to start in the young man's mind the old man's myth, "I could have been the champion—" We are instinctively ironists, tricky tragedians. But if it was not true when Bogolub said it, a year later it was.

113

I got a call from Bogolub one night when I was in Fargo, North Dakota.

"Boswell? Barry."

"Yes, Mr. Bogolub?"

"Peter Laneer broke his leg in Philly last night. He was supposed to go against John Sallow in a main event in St. Louis Friday but there's no chance of his making it. I want you to go down and take his place."

"I can't do it," I said. "I'm fighting in Des Moines Friday."

"Called off, Jimmy."

"What about the forfeit fee?"

"Jimmy, you're talking about peanuts. This is a main event in St. Louis I'm talking about. You're big time now, Jimmy. Give me a call when you get to LA." He started to hang up.

"Mr. Bogolub. Mr. Bogolub?"

"Come on, Jimmy, this is long distance. Fargo ain't Fresno."

"What about the arrangements?"

"Oh, yeah, in my excitement I forgot to tell you. You lose."

"What's that?"

"You lose. Routine number thirty-eight. Give them a show, you understand, you're an important wrestler, but you lose. I can trust you."

"Mr. Bogolub, the last time I was scheduled to meet him I was supposed to win."

"He's the next champion, Jimmy. Be a little patient, please. Give me a ring as soon as you get to LA."

"Mr. Bogolub, I don't want to fight him. I don't want to fight him Friday." I was talking to myself. Bogolub had hung up.

I went down to the National Guard Armory. I don't remember who I wrestled—which is odd for me; I never forget a name. I stumbled through the routine and it was a lousy show, even though I won. The crowd was booing me. "Hey, Masked Man, go get Tonto," someone shouted. "Hey, Keemosavee, you stink." "Take off the mask, Prince. The ball is over."

114

In the locker room, afterward, the fellow I beat sat down next to me. "What's wrong, Jim?" (The wrestlers, of course, knew who I was. In a way the wrestlers were wonderful. They always played to the other fellow's costume.) "Don't you feel good?"

"Ah, Bogolub called before the match. I fight The Reaper Friday in St. Louis."

"That's terrific," he said. "That's really great. Main eventer?"

"Yes."

"That's marvelous, Jim. That's really terrific."

"I lose."

"Oh," he said. "Oh, that's different. That's too bad. That's a tough piece of luck, Jimmy.

He thought I felt bad because I was supposed to lose. I was a comer, a contender. One day I was supposed to be strictly a main eventer. The Reaper already was. If I was scheduled to lose to him in my first appearance in a main event it probably meant that Bogolub was narrowing the field, was dumping me. I was better off winning the little matches, better off even losing some of them, than losing the big ones. It was too soon for me to go against Reaper and lose.

But I hadn't been thinking of my career at all. This was personal. I was thinking about John Sallow. John Sallow, The Grim Reaper, was the wrestler I had been scheduled to fight in LA just before I disappeared out there as Boswell. Sallow had been fighting under one name or another for years. He had been a wrestler before I was even born. He had wrestled when the sport *was* a sport, before it had become an "exhibition." At one time in his career he had beaten Strangler Lewis, had beaten The Angel, had beaten all the champions. He had fought everywhere—Europe, Asia, Africa, Australia, the Americas, everywhere. It was impossible to know how many fights he'd actually had, partly because many were in days and towns when and where they did not keep records, and partly because of his many changes of name.

Sallow wasn't very active in the thirties, though he fought some during the Depression, but he came out of his semi-retirement during World War II when many of the younger wrestlers were in the service. One day he would beat them, too, just as he had defeated the older champions. It was phenomenal to see the old man work. The crowds loved to watch him, loved to gape, fascinated, at his wily, ancient movements. He was curiously lithe; watching him, you had the impression that he was detached, that the body which moved so gracefully before you was somehow something which he merely inhabited, oddly like clothes which move always a split second after the agent inside them has already moved. This gave the impression of an almost ruthless discipline of his limbs. His face carried this even further. It was impassive, totally without expression, without the familiar landmarks of either love or hate. Nor did he fit conveniently into the traditional role of hero or villain in his matches. True, he never employed the obvious techniques, the blatant eye gougings, hair pullings, finger bendings, chokeholds, which sooner or later could bring even the most sophisticated crowd to its feet, but there was latent in his movements, always slow, always oddly prim, a sure viciousness, an indifference to consequences to bone and muscle. If he pulled a punch it was ultimately strategic, and although he submitted to the terms of his contracts, winning or losing according to some higher plan, wrestlers hated to fight him. He hurt them even when he lost. They could not account for his steady strength. Some said he was insane, but if he was his irrationality never extended to his activities in the ring. Indeed, he seemed to have a *rational body*. His movements were so naturally deft and logical that it was impossible to imagine him ever stubbing his toe accidentally or ripping his clothes on a nail. Outside the ring, in street clothes, he was unremarkable, a tall, pale, almost gaunt man, with preternaturally black hair. He looked like a farmer, in town perhaps to visit by a bedside in a hospital. He did not speak much (you could tell that by looking at him), but he must have had an extraordinary facility with languages. Once, when I was on a card with him, I heard him explain to two Japanese Sumo wrestlers who had come over for a special exhibition what arrangements had been made for them.

116

The Sumos, delighted that they had found someone who could speak their language, tried to engage him in further conversation, but Sallow simply turned away.

It was a relief the year before when I discovered I would not have to fight him. I could abide the clowns, good guys and bad guys alike, but to have to struggle with Sallow's naked dignity, to have to believe that somehow the match really was of consequence, was something I was not eager to endure. I would have fought him if I'd had to (actually I had been scheduled to win), but not to have to was much simpler for me.

In the year I had been making my reputation, Sallow had been remaking his. I heard talk of him wherever I went. Wrestlers spoke in awe of his phenomenal strength, of his ability simply to rise under the weight and pressure of any hold. He was now wrestling constantly, wrestling everywhere, winning everywhere. It was said that suddenly he had simply refused to throw any more matches. He had never been the champion, after all; perhaps now, before his career had ended (surely it was almost over; how old *was* he? fifty? sixty? more?), he was eager at last to have the belt. At any rate he had been winning steadily.

Knowing Bogolub (who was his manager as well as my own now), I could not believe that Sallow would do anything which did not meet with Bogolub's approval, so I doubted the story that he won fights he had been meant to lose. Still, there was something odd in the persistence of the rumors, something odder in his quick, bright fame, the queer fascination of the crowds that came to watch him. They didn't like him. They never cheered his victories. Indeed, his fights were quiet, almost restrained. I had been in stadiums when he fought and there was no more noise than there would have been had the crowd never gathered, had it stayed in its individual homes, watching its individual television sets in its individual silences. They came to watch age beat youth, not to *see* it, to *watch* it, to be there when it happened if it had to happen, witnesses at some awful accident, not personal, not human, a disturbance in nature itself, some lush imbalance of nature. Even old people in the crowds watched with distaste

117

his effortless lifts of men twice his size and half his age. He was not their hope, as in the South I had been; they wanted nothing to do with his victories. They refused to be cozened with immortality. Yet, oddest of all, though they never cheered Sallow, neither did they cheer his opponents. Again, they simply watched, as one watches any inevitable struggle—a fox against a chicken, say—fascinated and a little afraid.

The papers, of course, enjoyed it all tremendously. They never let the public forget the Grim Reaper theme, equating John Sallow with death itself. "Last night, before a crowd of 7000 persons, in Tulsa's Civic Auditorium, John Sallow, the Grimmest Reaper, danced a *danse macabre* with a younger, presumably stronger man. With a slow inevitability the dark visitor"—this was the journalist's imagination; Sallow is pale—"choked all resistance from the helpless body of his opponent." They pretended fear and made John Sallow rich.

In November, 1948, however, someone actually died while fighting John Sallow. In the very beginning of the fight Sallow lifted Seldon Faye, the Olympic champion, off the ground, slammed him down and pinned him. He was declared the winner and left the ring, but Faye did not get up. If Sallow heard the mob he gave no indication, for he went down to his dressing room, showered, dressed and was out of the town before a doctor declared Faye officially dead. It turned out that Faye had a bad heart. He shouldn't have been wrestling at all, but after this "The Grim Reaper" ceased to be merely a catch phrase and took on the significance of an official title. Some zealous reporter dug up the information that a wrestler named Jack Shallow had killed another wrestler in Johannesburg, South Africa, in 1920. Were Sallow and Shallow the same person? In the myth, of course, they were.

I saw him as the crowd saw him, as the papers pretended to see him. I saw him as the Angel of Death.

Now I had to fight him. Bogolub wanted me to lose but I couldn't. Fixing beyond fixing. It would be the first honest match of my career. Well, it was back to the barroom days, one against four, the old odds, the odds

118

that make causes, that make heroes and victims out of winners and losers. That was all right. Come on, Sallow, old enemy, Boswell the Big goes against the Angel of Death to save the world. That the public would think me The Masked Playboy was fitting, too. Its heroes are never known to it, anyway. Masks beyond masks. No matter; I would save it anyway, anonymously, nom de plumely. In St. Louis I would whip old death's old ass.

Maybe others think it strange that an overgrown man like myself can believe such things. I say only this in my defense. Why not? If God, why *not* the Angel of Death? Why not ghosts and dragons? If Jesus, why not Satan? Anyway this is the *Angel of Death* I'm talking about. Ah. You don't believe in him? You think you're the one that's going to live forever? Forget it. Forget it! In the meantime don't snicker when somebody fights your battles for you.

When I arrived in St. Louis two days before the match I went to Sandusky's hotel.

"Is The Great Sandusky in?" I asked the clerk. He was the same fellow I had seen behind the desk two years before, probably the same man I had talked to on the phone. (I never forget a face either, but it constantly astonishes me when I recognize people in public places— to see the same waiter in a restaurant when I return to a city after five months, the same stewardess on two flights, the same woman who sells tickets in a movie, the same clerk at a desk. It astonishes me, but I know that these are the exceptions. The turnover in the world is terrific. Usually the waiter no longer waits for anything; the stewardess is grounded; the woman in the cashier's box files no nails; usually the clerk has checked out.)

"Who?"

"The Great San—Felix. Felix Sandusky. You don't remember me, but we're old friends. Congratulations."

"Felix Sandusky? He ain't in. He's dead."

"Don't be a wise guy," I said. I started toward the elevator.

"I told you," the clerk shouted, "he's dead."

119

"Do you want me to break your mouth?"

"Come on," the clerk said. "You better get out of here."

"*Felix* Sandusky, jerk. The *Great* Sandusky."

"Yeah. Yeah. The Great Deadbeat. He owed for two months."

"How much?"

"How much what?"

"How much did Mr. Sandusky owe you?"

The clerk went to a filing cabinet, opened it, took out a loose-leaf notebook and looked through it. *"Mr.* Sandusky owed us a hundred twenty dollars." He looked up at me.

"I saw that room," I shouted. "It was empty. It was a rathole."

"That was 416," the clerk said angrily. "That's the best view in the hotel. That's a four buck a night room, fella. Without the rate that's a four buck a night room."

I wrote a check and gave it to the clerk. I made it out for a hundred dollars. The clerk looked at it and smiled.

"He's dead, Mr. Boswell," he said.

"He's no fourflusher."

"No, sir." He looked again at the signature on the check. "Didn't you used to wrestle?"

"I'm The Masked Playboy."

"No kidding? You?"

"I said I was." I dug into my pocket and took out the pass I had meant to give Sandusky. "Here," I said, thrusting it at him.

"What's that for?"

"It's a pass. Friday's matches. You be there, you understand. You knew Sandusky—you be there. I want you to see what I do to John Sallow. You knew Sandusky."

I walked back to my hotel. I read the medallion on the building: "'Hotel Missouri—Transients." You said it, I thought. That's telling them, innkeeper. There should be signs all over—in banks, on movie seats, on beds in brothels, in churches. That would change the world. Felix Sandusky lies amoldering in his grave. Felix Sandusky lies acrumbling in his grave. Even on coffin lids: transients! Put it to them straight. No loitering! Not a command, a *warning*. Official, brass-plated Dutch unclery.

I took the key from the desk clerk and went up to my room. By some coincidence my elevator had been inspected by H. R. Fox that very day. I was safe. H. R. Fox said so. Stay in the elevator. It wasn't bad advice, but there too I was a transient. *Sic transient*.

I called room service.

"Yes, sir?"

"This is the transient in 814." (Jerk, I thought, it adds up to thirteen. How come you didn't realize that?) "Send me dinner."

"What's that, sir?"

"Send me dinner."

"What would you like, sir?"

"What difference does it make?"

I hung up.

In a moment the phone rang. It was room service, a different voice than the one I had just spoken to. Already, I thought. The turnover, the turnover. "Is this the gentleman in 814 who just called about his dinner?"

"Yes," I said. "Send it up as soon as it's ready, please."

"Would the gentleman care for some chateaubriand?"

"Is that expensive?" I asked.

"Well—" the voice said.

"Is it?"

"It's our specialty, sir."

"Fine."

"Very well then, chateaubriand. And a wine? Should you like to see our wine list?"

"No," I said. "Send up your best wine. Two bottles."

"Certainly, sir. Is the gentleman, is the gentleman—"

"Yes?"

"Is the gentleman entertaining?"

"Only himself, buddy."

"I see, sir. Very good sir."

"Oh, and, buddy?"

121

"Yes, sir?"

"You can't take it with you."

I hung up. The meal would cost a lot of money. Good, good it would cost a lot of money. Maybe it would make up for my meanness earlier. By this time the significance of Sandusky's death had gotten mixed up with the twenty dollars I had held back from the clerk at Sandusky's hotel. Suddenly my pettiness seemed as inexcusable as Sandusky's death. In a kind of way both were petty. It was for just such inexplicable actions, perhaps, that we were made to die. Our punishment fit our crimes, all right, but that didn't make me feel any better.

My dinner came and I ate it without enjoyment and drank the two bottles of wine sullenly.

I called the desk. "This is the transient in 814. That adds up to thirteen, did you know that?"

"I beg your pardon, sir?"

"I was in your elevator some while ago," I said, "looking at the control panel."

"Is something wrong, sir?"

"You can drop the sir, buddy. We're all of us transients, you know."

"Sir?"

"Have it your way," I said. "There's no thirteenth floor."

"Sir?"

"There's no thirteenth floor. There's a twelfth floor and a fourteenth floor, but there's no thirteenth floor."

"Sir," the clerk said, humoring the drunken transient from out of town, "that's standard hotel policy. Many of our guests are superstitious and feel—"

"I know all about it," I interrupted him, "but that's the most important floor of all."

The clerk smiled over the telephone.

"Get it back, do you understand?"

"I'll see about it, sir."

"Thank you," I said politely, "I thought you should know." I hung up and immediately remembered something I had forgotten. I called the desk clerk again.

"Transient in 814," I said.

"Yes sir," the clerk said. He was getting a little tired

122

of me. Fun was fun, but there was a convention in town.

"Has John Sallow checked into this hotel?"

The clerk brightened over the telephone. "Just one moment, sir, I'll check that for you."

The line went dead.

"I'm sorry, sir," the clerk said in a moment, "no such party is registered at the Missouri."

"Standard hotel policy, I suppose, like the foolishness about the thirteenth floor. Superstitious guests, I suppose."

"Shall I check my reservations, sir?" the clerk asked coldly.

"No," I said. "If he shows up, have him get in touch with the transient in 814." I hung up.

I found a Yellow Pages in the night stand by the telephone, opened it to *Hotels* and called them all alphabetically. Sallow was nowhere. Sure, I thought, what do you think, the Angel of Death needs a room? How would he sign the register? He's no transient.

I went to bed.

In the gym at eleven o'clock the next morning I went up to Lee Lee Meadows, the promoter. Lee Lee was wrapped in a big orange camel's-hair coat and was talking to a reporter. "Lee Lee, is it true you can go fourteen days without water?" the reporter was asking.

"Lee Lee," I said, "I've got to speak to you."

"I'm talking to the press here," Lee Lee said.

The reporter caught the eye of one of the wrestlers and walked over to him. Lee Lee raised his hand to object, but the reporter smiled and waved back. Lee Lee turned to me. "Yeah, well, what's so important?"

"Is Sallow in town yet? I tried all the hotels."

Lee Lee frowned. "He'll be when he'll be," he said.

"I've got to see him before the match."

Lee Lee looked at me suspiciously. "Hey, you," he said, "what's the excitement?"

"I just have to see him."

"Yeah? Bogolub called me about you. He said you ain't too anxious to fight The Reaper. That you don't want to lose."

"No," I said, "I want to fight him."

"Because I got five tankers wild to be whipped by The Reaper."

"No, no, Bogolub misunderstood," I said. "I *want* to fight him."

"The Reaper pulls here. You're nothing."

"Of course," I said. "I want to see him because I thought of a new routine."

"He'll be when he'll be."

"He's not in town?"

"How do I know where he is? He could be with a floozy on Market Street. What do I know if he's in town? That old man. That's some old man."

"Lee Lee?"

"What?"

"This shit about The Grim Reaper, what do you think about it?"

"A terrific idea. Brilliant."

"Then you don't believe any of it?"

"Come on," Lee Lee said.

"It's just a stunt," I said, "like The Masked Playboy?"

"Well, that I don't know. I'll say this. I been promoting matches in Louis since 1934. Reaper was one of my first fighters."

"That's only sixteen years," I said.

"Kid," he said. "Kid, he was an old man *then!*"

I worked out listlessly with some of the other wrestlers on Friday's card and at two o'clock I went back to my hotel.

I called all the hotels again. It took me an hour and a half. I left messages with all the clerks. Then I slept. I dreamt fitfully of John Sallow and awoke at ten with a headache. I wondered if I had been awakened by the telephone. I had to talk to him. Oddly, I realized, I was no longer worried about the fight. It was Sallow himself that interested me. I was curious about *him*. Oh, Herlitz, I thought wearily, I thought all that was over. But then I thought, no, that business wasn't behind me yet. It never would be. The Masked Playboy unmasked. It was all true

124

about me, as true as it may have been about Sallow. These things were no accidents. Gorgeous George is gorgeous. We were like movie stars playing ourselves. I was, spiritually at least, a rich man's son, a bored darling of no means, of no means at all. The last two years had been nothing more than an extended vacation from myself. But Sallow had suddenly changed all that. I was too interested in his curious achievement. I was a little ashamed, but there it was. Was I, after all, a mere seeker of the picturesque? That's what my sloppy concern with greatness boiled down to. Now my morbidness had led me back to myself. Transients within transients. Okay, I thought, here is where I live. Now just let him call.

I didn't leave my room for fear I would miss his call. Again I had room service bring my dinner. I had them send up the papers, too, and I pored hungrily over the society pages and gossip columns. Where I lived, I thought. St. Louis was an old town. It had an aristocracy. Even after two years, their names were still familiar to me. I saw a photograph of Virginia Pale Luddy, the daughter of Roger and Eleanor Pale Luddy. I called Information, but it was an unlisted number. I asked Information to speak to her supervisor. I lied, I hinted at emergencies, but she wouldn't give me the number.

"May I speak to *your* supervisor, please?" I said icily.

"I'm sorry, sir. It's after midnight. If you'll call back in the morning you can speak to Mr. Plouchett."

"How do you spell that?" I demanded.

Of course I didn't call Mr. Plouchett in the morning. It was just a threat. To get in shape. I was out of condition; all that was working for me was my will. I couldn't even generate any of my old belief that something would happen. Almost fondly I remembered that old foolishness, a faith in the thermodynamics of forever ripening conditions. But that was in another physics. Now I could not even seduce a supervisor into revealing an unlisted number. What I might have said to Virginia Pale Luddy had I actually reached her I could not even think about. That was a luxury which was beyond the hope of any merely *masked* playboy. At least, I consoled myself, I knew where I stood, and, more vaguely, what I stood for. I could take it up again soon.

I waited for The Reaper's call. It did not come. I fell asleep.

That night as I lay fully clothed upon my bed, dressed in newer versions of the clothes I had worn in the schoolyard all those years before, Herlitz appeared to me in a dream.

It was the oddest dream. I could see just his face. It never moved; it hung, suspended, on its dream horizon and I could not tell whether it was only a picture of Herlitz's face or the face itself. It did not move, but there was an astonishing depth to it. I could make out the shadowed interior of wrinkles, almost feel the oily film inside the ancient creases of the yellowing face. The expression was complex, but it seemed impatient, vaguely disappointed. Clearly it felt I was responsible for its displeasure, but when I addressed the face to plead my innocence it did not change. Suddenly I shifted. I accepted everything, all that it could possibly accuse me of had it spoken. I eagerly assented, heaping guilt upon myself as one rubs precious oils into his skin. I proposed charges and agreed to them, my remissness, my drifting, my lack of care. I promised that I would work again on my files, my journals, that I would go through them ruthlessly, excising all reference to the merely mediocre, that they would be updated. I confessed solemnly as I gazed at Herlitz through tears, as I spoke to him through a sob-choked throat, that I had been disloyal to his spirit and I promised to change. Still the face remained the same. Then I shifted a second time. I told the face to forget about me, to go about its more important business. What was I, anyway, I demanded. A mistake, an experiment gone sour—all scientists had them, I reassured it. Let it cut its losses and be at peace. It had Schmerler, the German army, the famous Harvard classes of 1937 through 1945, the man in monorails. What did it need Boswell for? I answered my own argument. It wasn't true about the one sheep out of the ninety-nine that went astray. That was lousy shepherdry, I insisted, God's awful agriculture; returns diminished, I reminded it. The face remained unchanged. It hung above me like a clouded moon, still eternal, in suggestive incoherent depths. All right, I said at last, tomorrow was Friday. I would fight the Angel of Death for it. How was that? It wasn't what we had agreed upon. I knew that, I said, but things change, conditions ripen. I hadn't forgotten that I wasn't a great man, I told it. Sandusky had taught me that much. (And, incidentally, how was Sandusky? Was he getting on? Was there a gymnasium for him, I asked slyly.) And anyway, I would probably lose. If I did lose, that would take care of the question of my greatness permanently, right? The face did not respond. Of course, I realized, it's a picture after all. How could a picture respond? Just my guilty imagination groveling before a graven image. Right? Right? God damn it, right? Well, shine on, harvest moon, I said, and go screw yourself. It was useless to plead with a madman, I told it, and resolved to wake up.

I struggled out of my sleep like a person trying to move one particular finger on a hand that has gone numb. The strings are cut, I thought. Someone's cut my strings. I looked quickly up at the face; I was positive I would catch it in a smirk. It had not changed, and I returned sadly to the job of loosening myself, and finally found myself and floated up to myself as sad in wakefulness as I had been in sleep. Instantly I knew the meaning of the dream.

Conditions do not ripen. Things do not happen. Nothing happens. We are like poor people on Sunday. We're all dressed up but we have no place to go.

I chose my clothes slowly, ceremonially, changing from one pair of seventy ninety-five slacks to another pair of seven-ninety-five slacks, like a matador into his suit of lights.

I called the desk. "Are there any messages for me?"

"Who is this, sir?"

"Boswell. Eight-fourteen."

"We would have called you if there were, sir."

"Of course," I said, "thank you."

I could not eat breakfast. I went to the gymnasium.

"Is Sallow in the city yet?" I asked Lee Lee Meadows.

"As a matter of fact, yeah," he said.

"Did you tell him I wanted to see him?"

"He said he'd see you tonight."

"Where is he staying?"

"Ah, come on, Boswell. *I* don't know. How should I know where that old man stays?"

"You knew I was looking for him," I said.

"Tonight he'll be in the Arena. Conduct your business there."

When I went back to the hotel it had begun to rain. From my room I called all the hotels again. He wasn't registered.

"That's impossible," I yelled at the desk clerk when I came to the last hotel on my list.

At five o'clock the phone rang. I grabbed it eagerly. "Sallow?" I shouted into it.

"This is the room clerk, sir. There are some people down here to see you."

"John Sallow? Is John Sallow there?"

The clerk put his hand over the mouthpiece. "No, sir," he said at last. "It's a man and a woman and a little boy."

"No," I said impatiently. "I never heard of them." I slammed the phone back.

It was six o'clock and I had not eaten. I had better eat, I told myself. I went downstairs.

I had two steaks for strength. I chewed the meat slowly, the juices and fats filming my lips. I broke the bones and gnawed at the marrow inside. The waiter watched me, his disgust insufficiently masked by a thin indifference.

When I had finished my meat he came to stand beside my plate. "Will there be anything else, sir?" he asked.

"Bring me bread," I told him.

"Bring me red tomatoes," I said when I had chewed and swallowed the bread.

"Bring me ice cream in a soup bowl," I said when I had sucked the tomatoes.

I went upstairs and lay down to wait while the food was being digested. At eight o'clock I took my white silk cape, mask, tights and shoes, wrapped them in newspaper, and went downstairs.

The doorman could not get me a cab in the rain. He held an umbrella over me and walked beside me to the corner, where I waited for a streetcar.

"I'm going to the Arena." I told the conductor.

He saw the silk cape through a rent in the newspaper and nodded indifferently. I sat on the wide, matted straw seat, my shoes damp, their thin soles in shallow, steamy dirty puddles on the floor. Useless pink streetcar transfers, their cryptic holes curiously clotted with syrupy muck, floated like suicides. Colored round bits from the conductor's punch made a dirty, cheerless confetti on the floor of the car. I read the car ads, depressed by the products of the poor, their salves for pimples, their chewing gum, their sad, lackluster wedding rings. A pale, fleshless nurse, a thick red cross exactly the color of dried blood on her cap, held up a finger in warning: "VD Can Kill!" spoke the balloon above her. To the side a legend told of cures, of four licensed doctors constantly in attendance, of convenient evening hours that enabled people not to lose a day's pay, of treatments handled in the strictest confidence. There was a phone number and an address, the numerals and letters as thick and black as a scare headline. Above the address, floating on it like a ship tossing on heavy seas, was a drawing of a low gray building which looked like nothing so much as a factory where thin, underpaid girls turned out cheap plastic toys. Across the façade was the name: The St. Louis Institute for the Research and Treatment of Social Diseases and General Skin Disorders, Licensed 1928. Though I had never seen it, the advertisement seemed wearily familiar. Soon it was as if I had never *not* seen it. I closed my eyes and saw it on my lids.

Everyone looked shabby, fatigued, their heavy florid faces empty of everything save a kind of dull ache. Those who were not returning from menial jobs were going toward them, to wash down office buildings, tend lonely warehouses, stand outside lavatories in theaters and nightclubs. Almost everyone carried some worthless thing in some unimportant package—brown paper bags which once contained cheap fruit and now held rolled-up stockings, extra rags, soiled aprons, torn trousers, stale sandwiches and waxy pints of warm milk for two-thirty in the morning. Only some teen-age boys standing at the back of the car looked as though they could still be interested in their lives, and even they seemed, despite their youth, as disreputable as the others, romanceless in their shiny jackets and billed motorcycle caps.

Outside, the rain clung listlessly to the barred windows of the streetcar. The ride was interminable. No one ever seemed to get off. The car would stop and more would climb on, crowding steamily, smelling of wet wool and poverty and dirt, into the overheated, feverish brightness of the car. They swayed dreamily against the poles and left greasy smudges on the chipped milkish porcelain.

A colored woman as big as myself sat down heavily next to me. Her knees, spread wide, bounced comfortably against my thigh. Her skirt was pulled up so high that I could see the rolled tops of her stockings, oddly light and obscenely pink against the dark insides of her legs. They looked like the massive, protective lips of some brutish sexual organ. Across the way an old man in a winter overcoat too large for him stared openly at the woman's crotch. Too large and too tired to close her legs, she sighed and turned away her enormous head, her teeth like the decayed blunt stubs in the mouth of a hippopotamus.

I had been glancing repeatedly at the conductor, as much to identify myself as a stranger and thus isolate myself as to proclaim my unfamiliarity with the route. He stared back without recognition. "The Arena," I mouthed across the colored woman's breasts. He flicked his eyes away impatiently. I closed my eyes and saw again The St. Louis Institute for the Research and Treatment of Social Diseases and General Skin Disorders. In the dark the streetcar slogged forward with a ponderous inevitability.

I thought of the fight. What was the old man's strategy? Did *I* have any strategy? Was he really the Angel of Death? Would I be able to talk to him beforehand?

An arm shook me. "You dropped your mask," someone said sullenly.

"What's that?"

"Here's your mask you dropped," the colored woman said. It seemed ridiculously white and silken in her big brown hand, like some intimate undergarment.

"Thank you," I said, embarrassed.

I glanced down at my lap. The clumsy bundle had come loose. One end of the silk cape dragged in a puddle. The old man across the aisle, leaning so far forward in his seat I thought he would fall, retrieved the cape for me.

"Thank you," I said, and looked nervously toward the conductor. He held up two fingers to indicate that it would be two more stops. I stood up. "Have a nice party," the old man said in a throaty voice. When the car stopped I got off, though I knew I had moved prematurely. "Hey," the conductor called as I stepped down. I pretended not to hear him and walked to the Arena in the rain.

In the locker room I could hear above me the thin crowd (the rain had held it down) shouting at the referee. It was an unmistakable sound; they thought they saw some infraction he had missed. A strange sound of massed outrage, insular and safe, self-conscious in its anonymity and lack of consequence. If commitment always cost so little, which of us would not be a saint?

I dressed quickly, squeezing uncomfortably and awkwardly into the damp trunks. I laced the high-top silk shoes, fit the mask securely over my head, and buckled the clasp of the heavy silk cape around my throat. Down a row of lockers a couple of college wrestlers I didn't know and who had already fought were rubbing each other with liniment. I went over to them.

"Excuse me, did you see John Sallow?" I asked.

They looked at me and then at each other.

"It's a masked man," one of them said. "Ask him what he wants, Tom."

Tom pretended to hitch up his chaps. "What do you want, masked man?"

"Do you know John Sallow? The wrestler? He's on the card tonight. Have you seen him?"

"He went thataway, masked man," the other said.

I walked away and went into the toilet and urinated. One of the college boys came in. "Hey, Tom," he called. "There's a masked man in a white cape in here peeing."

"Knock it off," I said.

"It's all so corny," the kid said.

"Knock it off," I said again.

"Okay, champ."

"Knock it off."

I went back to my locker. John Sallow was there, one gray leg up on the wooden bench.

"Bogolub tells me you may try to give me some trouble night," he said.

"This is my last match," I said. "I'm quitting after tonight." It was true. I hadn't known it was true until I said it. Too often it rained; too often I had to take the streetcar; too often I sat too close to the steamy, seedy poor. I could still see the nurse. I never forgive a face.

There were excited screams and a prolonged burst of applause above us. Sallow looked up significantly. "Upstairs," he said. "You'll be introduced first. I'm the favorite."

"Look," I said, "I wanted to talk to you."

"Upstairs," he said. "Talk upstairs."

I took my place behind two blue uniformed ushers at gate DD. Some boys just to the right of the entrance kept turning around to look at me. They laughed and pointed and whispered to each other. The ring announcer, in a tuxedo, was climbing through the ropes far in front of me. He walked importantly to the center of the ring, stopping every few steps to turn and pull a microphone wire in snappy, snaking arcs along the surface of the canvas. He tapped the microphone with his fingernail and sent a piercing metal *thunk* throughout the arena. Then, shooting his cuffs and clearing his throat, he paused

132

expectantly. The crowd watched with mild interest. "First I have some announcements," he said. He told them of future matches, reading the names of the wrestlers from a card concealed in his palm. He spoke each wrestler's name with a calm aplomb and familiarity so that their grotesque titles—The Butcher and Mad Russian and Wildman—sounded almost like real names.

Then there was a pause. Jerking more microphone cord into the ring as though he needed all he could get for what he would say next, the announcer began again. "Ladies and gentlemen—In the main event this evening . . . two tough . . . wrestlers . . . both important contenders for the heavyweight champeenship of the world. The first . . . that rich man's disguised son . . . who has danced with debutantes and who trains on champagne . . . the muscled millionaire and eligible bachelor . . . who'd rather rough and tumble than ride to the hounds . . . from Nob Hill and Back Bay . . . from Wall Street and the French Riviera . . . from Newport and the fabled courts of the eastern potentates . . . weighing two hundred thirty-five pounds without the cape but in the mask . . . the one . . . the only . . . *Masked Playboy!*"

I pushed the ushers out of the way and bounced down the long aisle toward the ring. To everyone but the kids who had spotted me earlier it must have looked as though I had run across all the turnpikes from Wall Street, over the bridge across the Mississippi, and through the town to the Arena. Modest but good-natured applause paralleled my course down the aisle, as though I were somehow tripping it off automatically as I came abreast of each row. I leaped up the three steps leading to the ring, hurled over the ropes, unclasped the cape and, arching my shoulders, let it fall behind me in a heap. Then swelling my chest and stretching my long body, I stood on the tips of my high-top silk shoes, seemingly hatched from the cape itself, now a crumpled silken eggshell. The crowd cheered. I nodded, lifted the cape with the point of one shoe, slapped it sharply across one arm and then the other, and then tossed it casually to an attendant beneath me. I grabbed the thick ropes where they angled at the ring post. Without moving my legs I

133

pushed, head down, against the ropes. Snapping my head up quickly I pulled against them. I could feel the muscles climbing my back. I looked like a man rowing in place. I let go of the ropes, dropped my weight solidly on my feet and did deep knee bends. Out of the corner of my eye I could see the ring announcer waiting a little impatiently, but the crowd applauded cheerfully. Suddenly I made a precise military right-face and sprang up onto the ropes, catching the upper rope neatly along my left thigh. I hooked my right foot under the lower rope for balance and folded my arms calmly. I looked like someone on a trapeze—or perhaps like a young, masked sales executive perched casually along the edge of his desk.

I smiled at the ring announcer and waved my arm grandly, indicating that he could continue.

He turned away from me and waited until the crowd was silent. When he began again he sounded oddly sad. "Meeting him in mortal ... physical ... one-fall ....forty-five minute-time-limit combat tonight. ... is that grim gladiator, ancient athlete, stalking spectral superman, fierce-faced fighter ... that plague prover ... that hoary horror ... that breath breaking ... hope hampering ... death dealing ... mortality making ... heart hemorrhaging ... life letting—" For the last few seconds the crowd had been applauding in time with the announcer's rhythms. In a way their applause incited him; they incited each other. Now as he paused, exhausted, there were a few last false claps and then silence.

"Widow making," someone yelled from the crowd.

"Coffin counting," someone else shouted.

"People pounding," the announcer added weakly.

I slid off the rope. "MUR ... DER ... ING," I shouted from the center of the ring. "All death is murder!"

Angrily the ring announcer motioned me to get back. By exercising the authority of his tuxedo, he seemed to have regained control. "Ladies and gentlemen," he began again more calmly, "in gray trunks, from the Lowlands, John Sallow ... The Grim Reaper."

With the rest of the crowd I glanced quickly toward the opposite entrance, but no one was standing there.

Through the entrance gate I could see the long, low concession stand and someone calmly spooning mustard onto a hot dog. Then I heard a gasp from the other end of the arena. Sallow had been spotted. I looked around just in time to see him coming in through the same gate I had used. Of course, I thought. Of course.

Sallow walked slowly. As he came down the aisle toward the ring some people, more than I would have expected, began applauding. He has his fans, I thought sadly. Most of the people, though, particularly those near the aisle, seemed to shrink back as he passed them. Recognizing someone, he suddenly stopped, put his hand on the man's shoulder and leaned down toward him, whispering something into his ear. When Sallow started again the person he had spoken to stood and left the auditorium. Sallow came up the three stairs, turned and bowed mockingly to the crowd. They looked at him; he smiled, shrugged, climbed through the ropes and walked to his corner. I tried to catch his eye, but he wouldn't look at me.

"The referee will acquaint the wrestlers with the Missouri rules," the ring announcer said.

The referee signaled for us to meet at the center of the ring. "This is a one-fall match, forty-five-minute time limit," he said. "When I signal one of you to break I want you to break clean and break quickly. Both you men have fought in Missouri before. You're both familiar with the rules in this state. I just want to remind you that if a man for any reason should be out of the ring and not return by the time I count twenty, that man forfeits the fight. Do both of you understand?"

Sallow nodded placidly. The referee looked at me. I nodded.

"All right. Are there any questions? Reaper? Playboy? Okay. Return to your corners and when the bell rings, come out to wrestle."

I had just gotten back to my corner when the bell rang. I whirled around expecting to find Sallow behind me. He was across the ring. I moved toward him aggressively and locked my arms around his neck. Already my body was wet. Sallow was completely dry.

135

"Don't you even sweat?" I whispered.

He twisted out of my neck lock and pushed me away from him.

I went toward him like a sleepwalker, inviting him to lock fingers in a test of strength. He ignored me, ducked quickly under my outstretched arms, and grabbed me around the waist. He raised me easily off the floor. It was humiliating. I felt queerly like some wooden religious idol carried in a procession. I beat at his neck and shoulders with the flats of my hands. Sallow increased the pressure of his arms around my body. Desperately I closed one hand into a fist and chopped at his ear. He squeezed me tighter. He would crack my ribs, collapse my lungs. Suddenly he dropped me. I lay on my side writhing on the canvas. I tried to get to the ropes, moving across the grainy canvas in a slow sidestroke like a swimmer lost at sea. The Reaper circled around toward my head and blocked my progress. I saw his smooth, marblish shins and tried to hook one arm around them. It was a trap; he came down quickly on my outstretched arm with all his weight.

"Please," I said. "Please, you'll break my arm."

The Reaper leaned across my body and caught me around the hips. He pressed my thighs together viciously. I could feel my balls grind together sickeningly inside my jock. Raising himself to one knee and then to the other he stood up slowly, so that I hung upside down. He worked my head between his legs. Then, without freeing my head, he moved his hands quickly to my legs and pushed them away from his body, stretching my neck. I felt my legs go flying backwards and to protect my neck tried to force them again to his body. I pedaled disgustingly in the air. He grabbed my legs again.

"Please," I screamed. "If you drop me, you'll kill me," I whined.

Again he forced my legs away from his body. Then suddenly he loosened his terrible grip on my head. I fell obscenely from between Death's legs. Insanely I jerked my head up and broke my fall with my jaw. My body collapsed heavily behind me. It was like one of those clumsy auto wrecks in wet weather when cars pile uselessly up on each other. I had to get outside the ropes. I had a headache; I could not see clearly. I was gasping for air, actually shoveling it toward my mouth with my hands. Blindly I forced my body toward where I thought the ropes must be. Sallow saw my intention, of course, and kicked at me with his foot. I could not get to my knees; my only way of moving was to roll. Helplessly I curled into a ball and rolled back and forth inside the ring. Sallow stood above me like some giant goalie, feinting with his feet and grotesquely seeming to guide my rolling. The crowd laughed. Suddenly I kicked powerfully toward the ropes. One foot became entangled in them. It was enough to make the referee come between us. He started counting slowly. I crawled painfully under the ropes and onto the ring's outer apron. "Seven," the referee intoned. "Eight." Sallow grinned and stepped toward me. He came through the ropes after me. The referee tried to pull him back, but he shrugged him off as I got to my feet. "Nine," the referee said. "Ten. One for Reaper. Eleven for Playboy. Two for Reaper. Twelve for Playboy."

The Reaper advanced toward me. I circled along the apron. He pursued me.

"Missouri rules, Missouri rules," I said plaintively.

"Natural law, natural law," he answered.

"Three for Reaper. Thirteen for Playboy."

"Not by default, you bastard," I shouted. I jumped back inside the ropes.

"Four for Reaper."

"Famine, Flood, War, Pestilence," I hissed.

He came through the ropes and the referee stood between us. When Sallow was standing inside the ring the referee clapped his hands and stepped back.

I held out my hands again. I was ready to bring them down powerfully on his neck should he try to go under them. He hesitated, looking at my long fingers.

"Games?" he said. "With me?"

Slowly he put one hand behind his back. He thrust the other toward me, the fingers spread wide as a net. He was challenging me to use both my hands against his one in a test of strength. The crowd giggled.

"Both," I said, shaking my head.

137

He slid his arm up higher behind his back. He looked like a cripple.

I shook my head again. The crowd laughed nervously.

He bent one finger.

"No," I said. "No."

He tucked his thumb into his palm.

I stepped back angrily.

He brought down another finger.

"Use both hands," I yelled. "Beat me, but don't humiliate me."

He closed a fourth finger. The crowd was silent. The single finger with which he challenged my ten pointed at me. He took a step backwards. Now he was not pointing but beckoning.

"Don't you like the odds?" someone shouted. The crowd applauded.

"You stink like shit," I yelled at The Reaper.

"Take my hand," he said quietly. "Try to force it down."

I lost control and hurled myself toward Sallow's outstretched finger. I would tear it off, I thought. He stepped back softly, like one pressing himself politely against a wall to allow someone else to pass through a door. The crowd groaned. I looked helplessly at The Reaper; his face was calm, serene, softly satisfied, like one who has spun all the combinations on a lock and can open it now at his leisure. I braced myself too late. My body, remiss, tumbled awkwardly across the ring. The Reaper had brought his fisted hand from behind his back and now smashed my unprotected ear. I fell against the rope with my mouth open. My teeth were like so many Chicklets in my mouth. I bled on the golden canvas. The Reaper stalked me. He took my head under his arm almost gently and held my bleeding ear against his chest. "I am old," he whispered, "because I am wily. Because I take absolutely nothing for granted—not the honor of others, not their determination, not even their youth and strength."

He would kill me. He had no concern for my life. It

was all true—the legends, the myths. Until that moment I hadn't really believed them. He had killed the man in South Africa—and how many others? In all those years how many had he maimed and murdered? He wrestled so that he could demonstrate his cruelty, show it in public, with the peculiarly desperate pride of one displaying his cancerous testicles in a medical amphitheater. His strength, his ancient power, was nothing supernatural. It was his indifference that killed us. And it had this advantage: it could not be shorn; he could not be talked out of it. Our pain was our argument. In his arms, my face turning and turning against the bristles in his armpit, I was one with all victims, an Everyman through loss and deprivation, knowing the soul's martial law, its sad, harsh curfew. Our pain was our argument and, like all pain, it was wasted. What was terrible was his energy. He lived arrogantly, like one who you know will not give way coming toward you down a narrow sidewalk. To live was all his thought, to proliferate his strength in endless war. The vampire was the truest symbol in the give and take of the universe.

I screamed at the referee. "Get him off."

The referee looked down at me helplessly. "It hasn't lasted long enough," he said. "You've only been at it ten minutes. You can't quit now."

"Get him off, God damn it!"

"These people paid for a main event. Give them a main event."

"Get him off. The main event is my death. He means to kill me."

"Take it easier with him, Reaper," the referee said. "Work him toward the ropes. Let him get away a minute."

"Sure," the Reaper said mildly.

"No," I shouted. "No. I quit." I tried to turn my neck toward the crowd. "He's killing me," I yelled. "They won't let me quit." They couldn't hear me above their own roar.

The Reaper gathered me toward him; he grabbed my body—I wasn't even resisting now—and raised me over his head. He pushed me away like a kind of medicine ball and I dropped leadenly at the base of the ring post.

I knew my man now. To treat flesh as though it were leather or lead was his only intention. To find the common denominator in all matter. It was scientific; he was a kind of alchemist, this fellow. Of course. Faust and Mephistopheles combined. *Fist!* I lay still.

"Fight," he demanded.

I didn't answer.

"Fight!" he said savagely.

He could win any time, but he refused. This was a main event for him, too. He had thrown me away to give me a chance to organize a new resistance.

"Will you fight?" he asked dangerously.

"Not with you," I said.

The crowd was booing me.

"All right," he said.

He backed away. I watched him. He was bouncing up and down on the balls of his feet in a queer rhythm. His shoulders raised and lowered rapidly, powerfully. His arms seemed actually to lengthen. He stooped forward and came toward me slowly, swinging his balled metallic fists inches above the canvas. It was his Reaper movement, the gesture that had given him his name. I had never seen it and I watched fascinated. The crowd had stopped booing and was screaming for me to get up. The closer he got the more rapidly his fists swept the canvas, but still his pace toward me was slow, deliberate, almost tedious. He loomed above me like some ancient farmer with an invisible scythe. Now the people in the first rows were standing. They rushed toward the ring, pleading with me to get away. At last my resolution broke. I got clumsily to my knees and stumbled away from him. It was too late; his fists were everywhere. They caught me on the legs, the stomach, the neck, the back, the head, the mouth. I felt like some tiny animal—a field mouse—in tall grass, trampled by the mower. I covered my eyes with my hands and dropped to the canvas, squeezing myself flat against it. I squealed helplessly. A fist caught me first on one temple, then on the other.

140

I heard the referee shout "That's enough" just before I lost consciousness.

I was unconscious for only a few seconds. Oddly, when I came to my head was clear. I could have gotten up; I could have caught one of those fists and pulled him off balance. But I didn't choose to; I thought of one of those phrases they use for the wars—to struggle in vain. They were always praying that battle and injury and death were not in vain—as though anything purchased at some ultimate cost ought to be worth it. It was a well-meant prayer, even a wise one, but not practical. Life was economics. To be alive was to be a consumer. They made a profit on us always. There were no bargains. I saw that to struggle in vain was stupid, to be on the losing side was stupid, but there was nothing one could do. I would not get up, I thought, I would not even let them know I was conscious. I lay there, calmer than I had ever been in my life.

"He's dead," someone screamed after a moment. "He's dead," someone else shouted. They took it up, made it a chant. "He's dead. He's dead. He's dead."

The police rushed into the ring. They made a circle around The Reaper and moved off with him through the crowd. They were protecting him, I knew. He was not being arrested. What he did in the ring was all right. He was immune to law; law itself said he was immune, like someone with diplomatic status. What did that reduce my death to, I wondered. What did that reduce my death to if my murder was not a murder, not some terrible aberration punishable by law? Missouri rules and natural law worked hand in hand in an awful negation of whatever was precious to human beings. Oh, the dirty athletics of death!

Lying there on the canvas, in the idiotic nimbus of my blood, no longer sure I feigned unconsciousness, or even whether I still lived, one thing was sure: I would not fight—ever again. It was stupid to struggle, stupider still to struggle in vain—and that's all struggle ever amounted to in a universe like ours, in bodies like our own. From now on I would be the guest. I would haunt the captain's table, sweating over an etiquette of guesthood as others did over right and wrong. Herlitz knew his man, who only gradually, and after great pain, knew himself.

If only it isn't too late, I thought; if only it isn't too late to do me any good, I thought, just before I died.

Part Two

FROM THE JOURNALS:

March 19, 1949. St. Louis.

At first the voice was simply conversational, pleasant to listen to there in the dark. I settled myself comfortably and tried to guess what the speaker was like. This mattered more than what he was saying, though it wasn't very important either. Nothing was. It probably wasn't important for the old speaker either. (I pictured him as very old.) I imagined him to be as comfortable as myself. We might have been in Purgatory together, or on some battlefield after the noise and terror of the day.

After a while the voice became a little husky. He may have been thirsty. That was too bad, I thought; he should either drink something or stop talking. The strain became more obvious, and though I could still hear him almost as clearly as before it was plain that he was making a greater effort. It occurred to me that he may have been in some peculiar position, and I thought, Why doesn't he change it if it's such an effort to talk from? As he substituted effort for momentum his speech became less objective, more urgent. I might have been able to learn something from this old man, I thought, if only he hadn't become thirsty.

"She mustn't see him," the voice was saying. "Not after what he did to her. Why do you suppose I'm here now? It was the shock. What a shock that was. Never

145

mind about that. I'll see to it that he's punished. She won't have to be there. You promise me. Promise."

He was probably right, I thought resentfully, there was no reason to expose the child. (I knew she was very young just as I knew he was very old.) But why did he have to shout? He seemed more convincing, I thought, when he simply stated his position.

"Stop that noise," another voice, deeper, surly, said. "You're unappreciative," it added unexpectedly.

"Will everyone please be quiet?" a third voice said. This last voice seemed very near and I wondered if it was me who had spoken. It seemed odd that I should have said anything. None of this had anything to do with me.

"Oh, shut up," said the second voice angrily.

"Are you talking to me?" I asked.

"Another county heard from," said the second voice.

"Look," said a fourth voice, "my head hurts very bad tonight, even worse than usual. But you never hear me complain."

"You're complaining right now," the second voice said logically. "If your head hurts so bad why don't you tell her?"

"Promise me," said the first voice. "Promise me."

"All right," the third voice said wearily, "I promise you." I listened very carefully. It wasn't I who had spoken. It was somebody older.

"I'm sorry," I said to the second voice when I realized he hadn't meant me when he had said shut up.

"Sleep," the fourth voice said, "if anybody had ever told me I'd be lying down for as long as this and not be able to sleep, I'd have said he was crazy."

So that was it, I thought. That explains the peculiar sound of the first man's voice. He was lying down. I was probably lying down also. Then I wondered why I was lying down. I wondered why it was so dark.

"Excuse me," I said, "where are we?"

"Another county heard from," said the second voice.

"He must be coming out of it. I'll bet *he* has some headache," the fourth voice said pleasantly.

"I'm James Boswell," I said. It occurred to me that

146

if I introduced myself they might tell me their names, and where we were, and why it was so dark.

"How do you do?" the third voice said.

"Charmed," the second voice said. "All right, everybody get some sleep. That's the best thing."

"Promise me. Promise me," said the first voice.

"Tell him," the third voice said.

"Buddy? Buddy?" the second voice said.

"Are you talking to me?" I said. I was the fifth voice.

The second voice ignored me. "He dropped off," he said after a while. "I'm next."

"Right," the third voice said.

No one said anything else. I wasn't tired. I hadn't been asleep and couldn't remember when I had been asleep, but I wasn't tired. It was very dark. If I hadn't been asleep I should have been able to remember how it had gotten dark.

I wondered if I could move my arms. I pushed them laterally away from my body. I was surprised how easy it was. Suddenly my hands touched something solid and metallic and cold. Bars. So that's how they do it, I thought. I tried to sit up but couldn't manage it. It was peculiar. I remembered the fourth voice had spoken of pain but I felt no pain. Probably the fourth voice didn't either. Men tended to boast about pain. Most of it was just talk.

Then, suddenly, without any effort on my part at all, I understood what had happened. I started to shout. "I'm James Boswell. I'm James Boswell. I'm James Boswell."

"Listen," I yelled, "you can ask my uncle. Ask Herlitz. There's been a mistake."

Of course, I thought. I still had the mask on; they had sealed the eyeholes. That's why it was so dark. The idiots, the lazy god-damned idiots—they had buried me as The Masked Playboy!

"I'm James Boswell," I screamed. "I'm James Boswell!"

"Now, now, now, now," a new voice, close to me, said.

"Not in a common grave," I pleaded. "For God's

sake, not in a common grave. I have a name. I'm James Boswell! Take off the mask and you'll see."

"That bandage has to stay on," the new voice said.

"Not in a common grave," I said.

"Get him out of here," the second voice said suddenly.

I was very grateful. "Thank you," I said. "I appreciate all you've done. I realize how it must be for you, but I have a name. I'm James Boswell."

"We'll put him in 508," the new voice said.

Sure, of course, I thought, thirteen.

Hands were suddenly lifting me, scooping me out of the grave.

"He weighs a ton," another voice said.

Ah, I thought sadly, *dead weight*.

They shoved me onto some sort of slab and began to wheel me through the dark. It was very pleasant. Sure, I thought. I'm James Boswell. Fair is fair.

March 20, 1949. St. Louis.

"I must have given you people some trouble last night," I said. "I'm sorry."

"It was the morphine talking," the nurse said. "You're off it now, anyhow. You have too many anxieties to take morphine."

"My pain is very bad," I said.

"We'll give you some codeine," the nurse said. "Is there anything else you need?" she asked when she had finished bathing me.

I shook my head. "Nurse," I said, "am I going to die?"

"Of what?"

"Well," I said, "my beating."

"No, of course not."

"There's no sclerotic damage?"

"Sclerotic damage?"

"Well, the bandages," I said.

"Those are for your bruises."

148

"What about a concussion?"

"The x-rays were perfectly clean. Look, Mr. Boswell, your doctor should be telling you all this."

"Was there any damage to the kidneys? To the lungs?"

"Really," she said, "you do have anxieties."

"Was there?"

"I doubt if you've even been checked for any. You haven't even any broken bones. You were just very badly beaten up."

"I'm not in any danger, then?" I said.

"Only from the nurses," she said pleasantly.

March 22, 1949. St. Louis.

"Where did you go to school, Doctor?" I asked after the nurse had left.

"The University of Chicago."

"The University of Chicago, that's one of the best in the country, isn't it?"

"Well, it's certainly a top-flight school, yes."

"This may seem too forward," I said, "but if you don't mind me saying so you strike me as being a very excellent doctor."

"Well, thank you very much."

"I'll bet you were at the very top of your class."

"I was second in my graduating class," he said.

"Second," I said.

"A young woman was first. Dr. Angela Shauffert. She became a mission doctor in Africa and was killed during one of the tribal wars. It was a terrible waste."

"Well, you're the top now," I said suddenly.

"What's that?"

"I mean if she was first and she's dead, that means you're first now. I mean, there's no *living* doctor who did better than you did in your graduating class."

"Well, I suppose that's true, though I don't see what difference it makes," the doctor said.

"You're very modest, Doctor," I said. Closing my

149

chart, he shrugged and prepared to leave. The nurse came back with a mirror and held it in front of my face.

"How many stitches did you say I had?" I asked the doctor.

"Thirty-seven."

"That must be the record," I said.

"Hardly," he said, "but it would almost make a good pair of pants."

"Will there be scars?"

"No, I don't think so. Most of them will heal very rapidly."

"I look pretty bad," I said.

"Did you know I saw the fight?" the nurse said to the doctor. "It was awful. I thought those things were fixed."

"He damn near killed me," I said. "When I collapsed in the dressing room I thought I was finished."

"Well, you'll be fighting again in no time," the nurse said.

"In no time is right," I said.

The nurse took the chart from the doctor and went out of the room. The doctor was about to follow her when I called out to him. "Oh, Doctor," I said, "one other thing."

"Really," he said, turning around, "you'll be fine."

"No," I said, "it's not about that. Have you ever had anything in the *Medical Journal?*"

"Well, I have, yes." He laughed. "You seem so interested."

"I am interested," I said. "Could you bring me a copy?"

"Of the *Medical Journal?*"

"Of your article in the *Medical Journal*. Now that my bandages are off and I can read again, I'd like to read something really worthwhile."

"But it's technical. Anyway, it has nothing to do with anything you've got, if that's what you're driving at."

"No, of course not," I said. "Please, Doctor."

He brought his article when he came to see me today. It was about how blood pressure can affect the secretion of certain glands. As he had warned, it was very technical and I had to read it through three times before I could begin to understand it. But even on first reading I realized that the doctor was right, and I started to feel very good about him, and very proud of the both of us. When I put the article down I leaned back contentedly. That man has dressed *my* wounds, I thought, taken *my* blood pressure.

Really, it is remarkable how I continue to respect the very people I take advantage of.

March 25, 1949. St Louis.

For three days now I have used my ambulatory status to explore the hospital.

I have met Mrs. Slabe. She is very important to the functioning of this place, yet she heals no one. She is, in a way, its bookkeeper. She defines its larger ends, giving it form, compass, reality. Without Mrs. Slabe the concept of "hospital" would be too abstract. In spite of her importance, however, Mrs. Slabe remains obscure; practically none of the staff know of either her existence or her work. I discovered her by accident.

In a hospital I like to visit the sick, to go into the kitchens in the basement, to see its operating theaters, its therapy rooms, even its furnaces and auxiliary power plant. I like to walk against the inclination of its concrete ramps, to sit in its emergency wards at night and watch the dependable foregathering, like some sullen reunion of a clan, of the losers of fights, the suddenly attacked, the poor, the dying. I like to step into the waiting rooms where the well keep bored vigil turning the pages of back-issue magazines and yesterday's newspapers, to stop in its corridors where people with a higher stake sit leaning forward on card chairs beyond partially closed doors, listening critically to the noises of their wounded like students in the gallery of a concert hall following a score.

I had gone into its laundry with its white, soft dunes

151

of sheets and learned the lesson there. There were sheets crusted with blood, with brown and yellowish stains, with the bright, obscene paints of the malfunctioning body. There were sheets which to the naked eye appeared white, but the machines were indifferent to these distinctions and ground democratically away at everything submitted to them, assuming filth like some first premise.

I had been on every floor, along every corridor, and yesterday came to the hospital's morgue. I might have missed it, for it is a room behind a locked, unmarked door, but as I came up two orderlies were wheeling in a dead, pale child. I followed them in.

"Hey," one of the orderlies said when he saw me, "you ain't supposed to be in here."

"I knew the boy," I said.

"That don't make no difference," the orderly said. "This ain't anything for a patient to see." He held the door open for me and I had to leave. As I was walking out he turned back to the other orderly. "That guy made me forget to pull the ticket for Mrs. Slabe."

I went to the personnel office. "Where does Mrs. Slabe work, please?" I asked the girl. She looked it up in her file and read the card to herself. She seemed puzzled.

"Did you want to see Mrs. Slabe for any special reason?" she asked.

"Yes," I said fiercely, "a special reason."

Mrs. Slabe worked on the top floor of the hospital's oldest wing in a small office that must once have been a private room. It was exactly like the room I was in three floors below. Mrs. Slabe, a plump, small woman of about fifty-five, worked at a wooden desk in which were the conventional "out" and "in" baskets, like double bunks in a child's room. There was an adding machine, and one of those long, thin spikes rising from a broad metal base that you see on the cashier's counter in restaurants where truck drivers stop.

Mrs. Slabe was holding a green slip and copying information from it into a ledger when I walked in. When she had finished she impaled the slip on the spike as if it were a restaurant check.

"Mrs. Slabe," I said briskly.

152

She seemed startled to see a patient. "What is it?" she asked a little nervously.

"Did the orderly bring you the slip on that little boy?"

"Yes," she said. "Is something wrong?"

"Let me see it, please."

She reached into the out basket.

"Your little joke, Mrs. Slabe?"

"Yes," she said guiltily.

I looked at the slip. "Then this hasn't been entered yet," I said.

"No," she said. "I was just going to do it."

"Let me see your ledger, please."

She pushed the book toward me. As I had suspected, it was a record of all the births and deaths that had occurred in the hospital. The deaths, entered in Mrs. Slabe's neat little hand, were written in red ink, the births in black. Debits and credits. There were three columns—name, date, fate.

"May I see a total?" I said.

"From the beginning or just this year?"

"Both, of course," I said.

Mrs. Slabe suddenly recovered herself. "This is restricted information," she said.

"I'm Dr. Boswell," I said.

"About the boy," she said, "has there been a mistake?"

"No, no," I said, "he's dead, all right."

"Oh," Mrs. Slabe said.

"Those totals please, Mrs. Slabe," I said sternly.

She looked into her book, punched some figures on the adding machine and then handed me the slip. I glanced at it and gave it back to her. "Interpretation, please," I said.

"From the beginning through the present, seventy-eight thousand five hundred fifty-three births, eighty-one thousand two hundred sixteen deaths. For 1949 to date, two hundred twenty-seven births, one hundred eighty-four deaths."

"Does that include the little boy?"

"Oh, I'm sorry," Mrs. Slabe said, "I forgot."

"Then that should be one hundred eighty-five deaths, is that right?"

"Yes, Doctor."

"Hmn," I said. "Hmn. It's not good, is it, Mrs. Slabe?"

"Oh, I don't know Doctor. I've been here many years doing this work, and you'd be surprised how each year the ratio of births to deaths goes up. It's the new drugs, of course, the new surgical techniques. That's what does it."

"There's something in that, Mrs. Slabe, something in that. Still, Mrs. Slabe," I said, "the books eventually balance, don't they?"

"What's that?"

"I say the books eventually balance. For every birth there's a subsequent death. The books balance. They always have."

"Why, you know," she said, "I never thought of that."

"Well, it's a technical thing, Mrs. Slabe," I said.

March 27, 1949. St. Louis.

My bruises heal. Scabs thicken over the cuts. I moult. Everything itches. I do not read. It is more interesting to contemplate the slowly freshening color of my skin—like watching a dawn that comes only in its own time. It is disgusting to know that there is nothing I can do to hasten the process. I croon like Orpheus over my damaged flesh, but nothing happens.

Being in the hospital has been a strange experience. Everything about the life here is horrible, yet it is uniquely fascinating. I have never been so interested. Just as the sea is said to stimulate others, to stir metaphysical speculations in even the sleepiest of minds, so the hospital and the notion of disease affect me.

I find that I am afraid to die.

The fear of death in a young man is usually no

154

stronger than the fear that his house may some day catch fire and burn down—it is a possibility, but hardly likely. It's fate, chance—the sort of catastrophe that happens sometimes to others. I know better. The analogy is weak. Many houses escape unscathed, but no man does. It is not something that will happen tomorrow—though it could —or in a year, or even in twenty or thirty years. But it must come. When I think that a third of my life, perhaps a half, is already gone, I think, but it was so short, it was nothing. Already, young as I am, the days seem shorter than they once did, and I wonder what the rest will be like. I do not even bother yet about the quality; I speak only of the quantity. Perhaps fear, though, is an inexact term here. I am not so much afraid to die, I think, as *sad* to die.

The deaths of others are no less terrible. On my floor there are many very sick men, men who need oxygen tents in order to breathe, or who are fed through tubes, or who pass their water through catheters—who do now under difficulty, and only with the aid of machines, what once they did with no effort and no thought. These machines are oppressive; I cannot look at them without feeling sick. And yet, how much better to take nourishment through a rubber tube, to live in an oxygen tent as in a dog's house, to pass waste through grotesque piping, than not to function at all? I see now what is bad about death. Its most terrible aspect is that it is cumulative— nails that do not grow, eyes that do not see, ears that do not hear, flesh that does not feel, brain that cannot think, blood that will not flow. It is like being strangled. I think of a small boy's panic when a companion ducks his head under the water and holds it there. Of course death makes one insensible, but surely there must be, at the moment of death itself, just this sense of impotence—only greater, much greater, and more terrible. One cannot will the simplest thing, to bend a finger, roll the eyes. There is something horrible in such nullification, to have no more significance than a grain of sand; once having mattered, to count for nothing through eternity.

So shocking is this certainty, and so profound, that

155

the merest hint of it seeping into the still living man's consciousness is enough to contaminate everything that has come before it.

There is a man in the next room who has an advanced cancer. The others in the room with him are offended by his pain and his odor, but the man himself has grown indifferent to them as one is indifferent toward one's bowels or the coarse sounds one makes in private. His family visits him—his son has come from Washington —but the man no longer cares about any of them. I learned from his son that the father was a printer, and that all his life he worked hard, making terrible sacrifices for his wife and children. By taking a second job some years ago he was able to earn enough to put his son through the university. Now the son is a lawyer and very grateful to his father, but the father is as indifferent to his son's gratitude and love as he is to his own pain, as he is even to his own old fierce love for his boy. Already he is beyond this world and functions with a different intelligence. He knows new things. He knows what animals in traps know, what stones know.

Johnson says: "Life is not long, and too much of it must not pass in idle deliberation how it shall be spent; deliberation which those who begin it by prudence and continue it with subtlety, must, after long expense of thought, conclude by chance." He means, perhaps, that everybody's happiness and unhappiness total up to the same thing finally—that the bill, when it is presented, is always the same. Perhaps. I see that no one ever really gets away with anything, that we all owe a death, but surely it is senseless to argue that some of us do not get more for our death than others. In a way, the housewife's economy is the highest wisdom. One must watch the ads, risk the crowds, know his needs.

The thing is, I see, to be *great*, to sit the world like a prince on horseback, to send out the will like a tyrant his armies, with the warning not to come back empty-handed. I need what the tyrant needs. Like him, I need plunder and booty and tribute and empire and palace and slave. I need monuments and flags and drums and trumpets. I need my photograph enlarged a thousand times in

156

the auditorium. I am not, however, a great man. I see that I will never have these things, that I must adjust to my life as I must to my death, and that finally the two adjustments are the same. But despite this, I will never do what others do. I will not write my life off or cut my losses. I will never treat with it as the man in the next room has been forced to treat with his. I see what happens to such men. Their cancers take away their histories. My cancer, when it comes, must not do that. When I am downed, when the latest drug proves useless, when the doctor, embarrassed, asks who is to be notified, when the morphine is no longer effective and pain builds on pain like one wave slapping another at the shore, when the high tide of low death is in, *I must still have my history,* and it must, somehow, *matter!*

I have conceived a plan. It is not clear in all its aspects yet, but I envisage a kind of club. It must include all the great men of my time, and I am to be the spirit behind it, mine the long table on the dais. If I cannot be great, then I can at least be a kind of Calypso. Heroes will sing in my caves, sit on my shores, seek sails on my illusory horizons.

Only the gods or death will free them.

March 28, 1949. St. Louis.

My Uncle Myles came into the hospital room. He set his umbrella against the bed and placed his derby carefully over the leather handle.

"James, I did not come before because you refused to see me when I contacted you in your hotel."

"Contacted me in my hotel? What are you talking about?"

"The evening of the fight. I called at your hotel and the room clerk rang you up."

"I don't remember that, Uncle Myles," I said. "Why would I refuse to see you? That doesn't make sense."

"Nor did it to me," my Uncle Myles said.

I tried to remember the evening my Uncle Myles

157

referred to. It was less than two weeks before, but it might have been in another life. I remembered that I had been trying to locate Sallow. "Wait a minute," I said. "I was trying to get in touch with John Sallow. The phone rang and I thought it must be him calling, but when I answered, it was the desk clerk telling me that some people wanted to see me. A man, I think, and a woman and a little boy."

"I was the man," my uncle said.

"Well, but the clerk didn't give me your name, you see. I was very preoccupied. I should have asked. I was crazy that week."

"I read of your defeat in the papers," he said. "They said you were badly beaten."

"I was," I said.

"You seem recovered now."

"I'll be getting out in three days," I said. "I could have been discharged yesterday, but my policy pays for most of this and ... well, I've no place to go now. I've quit wrestling."

He seemed to hear this. "It paid well," he said.

"Yes," I said. "I'm not rich, but I was able to save a little money."

My uncle nodded. I thought I saw what was troubling him and I said, "I won't be able to send you any more checks until money is coming in again." (I had started to send him a little money after I began to wrestle.)

"You've been very generous," he said stiffly. "I haven't always been easy to get along with."

"You've been very fine, Uncle Myles," I said.

"We don't agree about things."

"I suspect we're more alike than you think," I said. "I'm a very conservative person."

"I hope that is so," he said. He sat down and looked around the room. "You have a private room," he said after a while.

"I was in a ward at first—my policy stipulates a ward—but I couldn't stand it there and I asked to be transferred. I pay the difference."

"Of course you'll have to be careful about your money now that you aren't wrestling."

158

"Yes. I suppose I will. It was just that I didn't like being with sick people."

"With strangers," my uncle said.

"Yes, of course," I said, remembering my uncle's illness, "with strangers."

"Yes," he said. "That's very difficult. Even with people one has a feeling for. You know, James, I don't mean to offend you, but I can't say I've been unhappy about your going away. People get used to needing others. They are often surprised to learn they can do quite well without them."

I remembered he had been with others the night he had tried to see me at the hotel. "The clerk said there were a woman and a little boy with you."

"Yes."

I laughed. "Uncle Myles, you haven't gotten married, have you?"

"No."

"Are you keeping company?"

"The woman is the mother of that poor girl who had your child. The little boy is your son."

"What?"

"The woman's husband has died. They were never well off, James—you must certainly be aware of that. They took the child because you were only fifteen at the time. Now that her husband is dead she can't afford to keep the child without help. They have been staying with me until more satisfactory arrangements could be made."

"No," I said.

"They are outside, James. Please don't raise your voice. When we have concluded these other arrangements—"

"No," I said. "No arrangements."

"The boy is six years old now."

"No," I said. "No."

"You are hardly in a position to say no, James."

"Are you talking as a *lawyer* now?" I said.

"As a judge, I think, James."

"Are you talking as a lawyer now?" I asked him again.

"If you mean are you guilty of child abandonment in

159

the eyes of the law, no. The child was taken away from you and legally adopted by the grandparents, but you have a certain responsibility."

"No," I said. "No." I had begun to weep. My uncle had brought me down. I wanted to explain it to him, that I mustn't be caught just because every son of a bitch who ever lived got caught, but I was inarticulate with sorrow and rage. All I could do was shake my head and wail denials.

My Uncle Myles stood up. "I can no longer keep them with me, James. It isn't my responsibility."

"No," I shouted. "No."

"You're responsible. You feel trapped now," my uncle said. "I understand that, but when you see the lad, James—he's a nice lad—all that will change. He's outside now. I'll just get him."

"No," I yelled. "No, no, no, no."

A nurse ran into the room. "What is it?" she said.

"No," I wailed. "No, no, no."

"We can't have this," she said to my uncle. "You can't come in here and upset a patient like that."

"He stinks, your patient. He should die now."

"No! No! No! No! No!"

"You'll have to leave," she said.

"Get him out," I screamed. "Get him out. *Get him out!*"

The nurse pulled my uncle toward the door. Almost comically, smoothly, as if from some keen presence of mind, he managed to reach out and pluck the umbrella away from the bed. Even as he tugged at her he was adjusting his derby. He had begun to shake, and the nurse, mistaking his tremors for resistance, pulled him from the room fiercely. She didn't close the door and as soon as they were outside I saw a woman rush up to them and grab at my uncle. She was a woman of about fifty-five, and at first I thought it was Mrs. Slabe, but then I recognized that her face and body were aged parodies of the face I had kissed so awkwardly all those years ago, the body I had shot my death into. The nurse struggled with the woman, trying to push her away and at the same

160

time pull my uncle toward the elevator. In a moment other nurses had come up and surrounded them. I saw my uncle's hat fall from his head and one of the nurses trample it with a white, clubbed heel as she shoved against him. Slowly the nurses moved my uncle and the woman away from the door.

I couldn't move. I stared appalled at the hat, his derby that had cost him so much money, black and empty and ridiculous on the floor.

And then I saw two thin, bare legs move into position over the hat, straddling it, and a child's hand reach slowly down to pick it up. As he straightened, his eye caught mine and we looked at each other helplessly.

Then my son began to cry.

March 29, 1949. Somewhere in Kansas.

I am on a bus. I am going West. Calypso must first be Ulysses.

September 4, 1950. Dallas, Texas.

William Lome is a rich man. A rrrrrich man. As rrrittchh azz Creesusss. He has dollars and pounds and lire and pesos and rubles and drachmas and francs and kronen and Deutsche marks and rials and piastres and fils and dinars. He has sucres and quetzals and gourdes and lempiras and forints and rupees and pahlavis and sen and yen and guilders and córdobas and guaranis and sols and zlotys and leu and behts and kurus. He has monies. He has moneez. He has stocks and he has bonds, and he has securities and certificates. He has gold and he has silver. He gets di-vid-ends. He earns interest. He earns in-ter-est-ing in-ter-est.

He was once asked how much he was worth. "Practically everything there is," he said.

161

This campaign has lasted almost three months now. I must make my fortune. As in the fairy tales. And why not? Am I not the youngest son, the orphan, the kid with the squint, the limp, the blue baby? A frog isn't always what he seems, but kiss me today and I give you warts. An ugly duckling in the swimming pool of the world's fat swans—who will feed me? Everywhere there are signs, warnings, admonitions: Do not feed the ducklings.

I would share my bread with gnomes under mushrooms. I would give to testing elves, salvage the lives of bosses' daughters—I haunt the forests, the beaches—tease a belly laugh from the king's dour daughter and the joke would be on the king.

I must have money!

My way of life demands it. The savings from the wrestling days are almost gone, but there are still bus tickets to buy, meals to eat. My expenses are not great (I am easily shabby), but they exist. Need, the fleet-heeled one, will not stand still.

And what a campaign, this one! Who would have thought? Three months. The complications! Lome travels in his private plane and I follow in a bus. I must anticipate his schedule. Futile, futile. But I think I may have caught up with him. He comes in four days. I wait now.

Croesus, my would-be-father-in-law, where are your daughters?

September 5, 1950. Dallas, Texas.

Eleven dollars to the man who rents the costumes. Seven dollars to the tailor to get it to fit.

September 9, 1950. Dallas, Texas.

"You're sure now he ain't in yet?" I said to the room clerk.

"I've told you repeatedly—Mr. Lome arrives later this morning."

"You said that yesterday morning."

"He canceled out," the room clerk said. "I told you last night."

"It's just that I'm his cousin," I said.

"I understand that," the clerk said.

"I come down from Muskogee, Oklahoma."

"I know," the clerk said.

"Big-shot-millionaire-skinflint bastard," I said.

"I told you before," the clerk said, "we can't have that kind of language about our guests."

"You ever meet this fella?"

"No, of course not."

"Well, if you do you'll get an idea what I mean."

"Please," he said, "I'm very busy."

"Who do you think give him that stake those years ago? My uncle."

"Yes," the clerk said.

"My uncle give it to him."

"Yes."

"Oh, he paid it back, all right."

"Hmm," the clerk said.

"To the dollar."

"That's not—"

"The nickel."

"—any of—"

"The penny."

"—my—"

"But not a cent of interest. Well, that's all right. We're kin. Kin don't go around charging each other no interest. My uncle don't expect that."

"Please," the clerk said, "there are things I must attend—"

"Old as he is."

"Now look," the clerk said.

"Sick as he is."

"You're going to have to—"

"Poor as he is. But no thank you, even—not even a Christmas gift."

"I can understand how your uncle—"

163

"Just that old cold check in the mail when he give back the stake. Just that lonely old cold check made out to W. J. Lome and signed W. J. Lome."

"You may sit in the lobby. I've told you that."

"They got the same names even, but that man's got no family feeling. What does that kind of a W. J. Lome care about a poor old W. J. Lome who all he's got in the world's a run-down hardware store on a highway outside Muskogee, Oklahoma, selling nails to the Injuns or maybe a little bailing wire? 'Build a motel,' everybody kept telling him, but is a man supposed to be punished for the reason that he don't have it in his spirit to make blood money off a bunch of sinning traveling men and their whores? And don't keep telling me to set in your lobby. I ain't registered in this hotel and I don't mean to use none of its comforts. All I want's what's mine."

"Front," the room clerk said suddenly, slamming a little bell.

"Now stop that," I said.

"Front, boy!"

"You just cut that out," I said.

"What is it?" a bellboy said.

"Get Marvin and Frank and show this gentleman out," the room clerk said.

"All right," I said. "That's no necessary thing. I'm going."

Truthfully, the hotel was not the best place to wait. I had been coming in for two days now and they were suspicious. Actually, I was a little surprised when I saw the place. It was all right—a nineteen-twentyish sort of hotel with commercial traveler written all over it, the kind of place that would fill up during a convention—but not what I would have imagined for one of the richest men in the world. Yet his New York office had told me (I had gone all the way up to Portland, Oregon, just to make the long-distance call authentic) that this was where Mr. Lome stayed when he was in Dallas. I wrote it off as loyalty.

I took up my old position outside the drugstore two doors away from the hotel. It was very hot in the raincoat.

164

When the pharmacist saw me he came outside. "Look you," he said, "I've told you before. Clear off."

"You don't own the sidewalk," I said.

"Would you like to explain that to a policeman?" he said.

"She's gonna come, Doc," I said.

"You've been standing here two days now."

"Please, Doc. She promised. She's just so pretty, Doc. She's just so sweet."

"You've been hanging around here for two days now."

"Doc, she don't speak no English. If the pretty little thing came along and I wasn't here to meet her I don't know what would happen."

"I'm calling a cop."

"All right," I said, "all right. You've forced me to tell you the truth. She's a Mexican wet-back. The immigration authorities are looking for her. They can't have found her yet or I would have been given a signal, unless they picked up Max, too."

"Max?"

"Max the Mex," I said. "Your pharmacy is our new station on the underground railroad. Follow, follow, follow the drinking gourd."

The pharmacist stared at me for a moment and backed off. I went into the bookshop across the street. The girl looked up and frowned when she saw me.

"Did you find it yet?" I asked.

"Please," she said, "I've spoken to Mr. Melrose and he insists we've never stocked the book."

"But I saw it," I said. "I saw it right here on this counter."

"That's impossible. It's not even listed in our catalogues."

"It was published in England," I said. "Think. In a plain brown wrapper. Felix Sandusky's *Theory of Rings.*"

"No," she said.

"What about the other one then?"

"Which other one?"

I moved over to the window where I could watch the cars that pulled up to the hotel. *"Penner on Sainthood."*

"No."

"Herlitz's *Placing the Teen-Age Boy.*"

"No," she said. "Please, we don't have any of these books. My goodness, don't you ever read any novels?"

"Novels? Certainly. Murder mysteries. Like our Presidents—for relaxation. Get me John Sallow's *Kill a Million.*"

"We don't have it."

"*Vita Breve?*"

"No."

"I'll just browse," I said.

She walked away and I pretended to poke around among the publisher's remainders on a table near the window. I was beginning to think that Lome would never come. Like one of the family, I worried for his safety in the private plane. Inside the heavy rubber raincoat I was perspiring freely, but of course I couldn't take it off. It was the damned coat that called attention to me in the first place. Any coat in this heat would have been conspicuous, but not only was it not raining, Texas was in a drought.

If the cop hadn't asked to see my license I would have gotten away with it. I had been parading up and down the street with a sign on the back of my raincoat. "RUBBER PRODUCTS ARE BEST," it said, and beneath this: "RAINCOATS, TIRES, BALLS." I had been able to watch the hotel for three hours before the cop stopped me.

The girl came over again. "Have you found anything yet?" she asked.

"I—yes. Yes, I have." The limousine from the airport had pulled up to the hotel and I spotted Lome getting out of it. I took off the raincoat and tossed it to the girl. She stared at my bellboy's costume. I raced out of the door, popping the little cap on my head as I ran.

I nearly knocked Lome down in my effort to get to him before any of the other bellboys. The doorman stared at me but my uniform was authentic down to the last bit of piping. "Dallas Palace" stood out in perfect gold script on my tunic. The tailor should have been a forger.

"Mr. Lome's bags," I demanded of the driver.

"He has no bags," the driver said.

"For God's sake," I said desperately, "let me carry *something.*"

Lome was holding a briefcase. In my anxiety I pulled it from him.

"House rule, sir," I said. " 'In the Dallas Palace the Guest Doesn't Even Carry a Grudge.' "

"Hmm," Lome said, "that's a good slogan. I like that. All right."

I took Mr. Lome's arm and guided him past the doorman into the hotel.

"Hey," the doorman said, "ain't you the guy—"

"Front, boy. Front! *Front!*" I shouted. Four bellboys suddenly appeared from behind potted palms and converged on us. "Mr. Lome's key. Quickly! Quickly! Mr. Lome wants to go to his suite."

"But I haven't even checked in yet," Lome said.

"Bad flying weather over New Orleans," I said to one of the bellboys. "Air pockets like something in a mechanic's pants. Storms all over the South. Lightning crackling, thunder clapping. He'll sign the register later." I turned to another bellboy. "Get his key and bring it up to us."

I wheeled on Mr. Lome. "Come, sir. Your bath is waiting." There were three elevators and I half guided, half pushed Lome into one of these. My footwork was dazzling; I might have been doing this all my life. The doors closed.

"Aren't you waiting for the key?" Lome asked.

"They'll find us, sir," I said. I had no idea which floor he was supposed to be on. This was an oversight, like the business about the license. I stood by the control panel. "The usual floor, sir?"

"What?" Lome asked.

"Would you like to push the button? Many of our guests prefer to push the button themselves. All the fun in a self-service elevator comes from pushing the button."

"Does it?" Lome said nervously. "Yes, I suppose it does. Only I don't know what floor I'm supposed to be on. I haven't registered yet."

"Oh," I said. "Well, in that case." I hid the panel with my body and pushed number two. When the automatic doors opened I peered out. I could see no bellboy in the corridor. I pushed three.

"Must have decided to walk up," I said to Mr. Lome. The elevator stopped and again I peered out, but there was no one on three either. I pushed four. "Must have caught the one going down," I told Lome. When the elevator stopped there was no sign of a bellboy on four.

"Why does it keep stopping?" Lome asked.

"It's a safety device, sir," I said.

"Oh."

The doors slid open at the fifth floor. A bellboy holding a key was staring at me.

"Front, boy," I said. "Ah," I said, "Mr. Lome's key. Thank you very much." I pulled the key from the fellow, pushed him into the elevator and then reached inside quickly and pushed fourteen.

"Don't call me boy," the bellboy hissed as the doors closed on him.

"Ah," I said, looking at the key. "Five-twelve. Of course. Our very best."

I pulled Lome along behind me through the corridor. "Five-twelve. Five-twelve," I muttered, looking for the arrows on the wall. I turned left. When we came to the end of the corridor there were some numbers painted on the wall. "545–560. 560–590. Come, Mr. Lome, it's the other way, I think." I turned him around and we walked past the elevator again and into the opposite corridor. "Ah," I said, reading the numbers on the doors, "five-eighteen. We're on the trail now, I think, Mr. Lome. Five-sixteen. Five fourteen. Here we are. Five-twelve."

I opened the door. "One of our—" It was a tiny, shabby room. There was a commode next to the bed. "There must be some mistake, sir," I said.

"No, no, it's fine," Lome said. "Just fine. What's Hecuba to me?"

It struck me at once: he was cheap. Tight. A millionaire-skinflint bastard. It was death to my fortune. Yet again, frog beneath frog. Ugly duckling, ugly duck.

"Well," Lome said, bouncing on the bed, "thank you very much."

I saw that I would not even get a tip. "Service of the hotel, sir," I said.

"Appreciate it," Lome said.

" 'In the Palace All Guests Are Kings,' " I said.

"Service has improved then," Lome said. "Terrific."

" 'In Dallas in the *Palace* There's no *Room* for Malice,' " I said.

"That's good," Lome said. "Well, thank you again. Now if you'll just leave my key."

I had to act. The room clerk would be up in a minute. There wasn't much hope for success, but I had come this far and I couldn't back off now. I turned around suddenly, closed the door and locked it, and pulled off my bellboy's cap.

"I'm not the bellboy, sir," I said.

"You're not?" he said.

"No, sir. I'm a live—"

Someone was pounding on the door.

"—wire."

"There's someone at the door," Lome said with relief. "Perhaps we'd better see who it is."

"A go—"

"The door," Lome said.

"—getter."

"My God," the clerk was shouting outside the door, "he's probably killing him. He's his cousin from Muskogee, Oklahoma, and he bears him a terrible grudge."

" 'In Dallas in the Palace the Guest Doesn't Even Carry a Grudge,' " I said miserably.

Lome opened the door. The clerk was standing outside with a policeman and a man I had never seen, probably the house detective. Behind them the girl from the bookstore was holding my rubber raincoat over her arm.

"Ah," I said, "thank you for bringing that. I thought I must have left it someplace. There's been no rain, but—" I took it from her and started to move through the small crowd that had gathered outside Lome's door.

"Just a minute," the policeman said, "the Border Patrol wants to speak to you."

169

"Mr. Lome," I said, turning to him, "can you lend me ten thousand dollars, usual terms?"

"Well, no."

"Well, could you put up bail?" I asked.

They took me away and questioned me for five hours. Eventually, I thought, they would have to let me go. All I had done, after all, was to lie to people, and there's no law against that, is there?

It was the hotel that gave me the most trouble. They wanted to get me for impersonating one of their bellboys. Even after the man from the Border Patrol decided that he had no case and that I was harmless—that was the word he used, "harmless"—the hotel was determined to press charges. "As an example," the hotel clerk said, as though they had a lot of trouble with people impersonating their bellboys. It looked pretty serious, but that night Lome came to visit me in my cell.

"Say," he said, "those slogans you kept quoting, were those the hotel's?"

"I made them up," I said glumly.

We worked out a deal. I signed a paper saying that I had no right to the slogans and that they belonged to Mr. Lome now and forever in perpetuity—or until he decided what to do with them. In return, he promised to get the hotel to let me off; he would tell them that I had actually given pretty good service and that I had been particularly cautious in the elevator, always looking both ways at each floor.

" 'In Dallas in the *Palace* There's No *Room* for Malice,' " Lome quoted. "It would make a very snappy towel."

Inside an hour I was free to go.

September 10, 1950. Dallas, Texas.

Lome was delighted, the hotel was delighted, Dallas was delighted. When I dropped by this morning to thank the manager for not pressing charges I was told that in exchange for some slogans Lome had thought up, the

170

hotel was holding a free room for him in perpetuity (this is evidently one of Lome's favorite phrases—and there is, indeed, something awesome in it; I was reminded of those promises cemeteries make to prune graves or plant roses on them every June, through war, through peace).

The manager tells me that Lome's assured stay there is good publicity for the hotel and that now that he can stay in Dallas for nothing he'll probably come more often, which will be good for business in the city.

Only I am not delighted. I have come to make my fortune and have instead added to the fortunes of others. That's the role of most men, I suppose. However, I cannot believe that Lome's presence in Dallas can be of any long-range good to the city. I've been watching him. He is, I think, one of those absentee landlords of the spirit—a depleter of resources, leveler of forests, drainer of seas. Where he smiles, trains cannot long continue to stop.

This is nonsense. I have no real knowledge of the man. What can there be sinister in him? He is just a very successful businessman, a middleman to need. But he *knows* something, I keep thinking. He said it himself: what's Hecuba to him? Having followed him this far, I must follow him further. My fortune is in that man. Why should he yield it up without a countersign?

September 11, 1950. Dallas, Texas.

I continue to follow Lome.

I am waiting for him when he comes out of the hotel in the morning. I wave. He sees me, frowns, and walks to some appointment. I walk behind him. When he turns to see if I am following I am still there, smiling and waving. He changes his mind and urgently beckons a taxi. I am prepared for this; I have instructed a driver to follow at my pace. When he gets into his cab I get into mine.

So now I follow cabs. Making one's fortune is an intrigue, one of the great adventures.

171

September 12, 1950. Dallas, Texas.

This morning when Lome left the Palace he saw me and smiled. "How are you?" he asked.

I had not thought his capitulation would come so soon and I walked over to shake his hand. He ignored me and got into his taxi. I shook my fist at this snub and summoned the taxi that I had engaged. Lome's car waited while I got into mine, and when it pulled away from the curb it moved so slowly that my driver had to follow in first gear. After fifteen minutes Lome's cab still had not picked up any speed. I realized that we were covering the same few downtown blocks again and again. At one point Lome's driver turned a corner unexpectedly. I reasoned that he would pick up speed, but when my cab turned to follow, there was Lome's double-parked and waiting for us. Lome's cab then turned onto an expressway and drove into the country. Twelve miles from the city he turned off onto a deserted country road and picked up speed. We went deeper and deeper into the countryside, the meter registering alarmingly. At last I realized what Lome was up to. It was a warning; he was telling me that his resources were endless, that I had no chance against him in such a competition.

I told my driver to turn around and go back to the hotel.

September 13, 1950. Dallas, Texas.

When Lome came out this morning and saw me he seemed very angry. I stared at him sullenly. He surprised me by coming up to me.

"I'm leaving town today," he said. "You'd better not make any effort to follow me."

"What's to stop me?"

"You'd be arrested. The law protects people like me."

"On what charge would I be arrested?"

"On what charge were you arrested here?"

172

"I want you to help me," I said. "After all, you used my slogans."

"They're mine."

"I made them up."

"You signed a paper. Always have them sign a paper—a man's signature is his own worst enemy." He started walking, and as I fell in beside him he looked at me. "You'd better dismiss your driver," he said.

"You won't jump into a cab if I do?"

"Why should I? What's Hecuba to me?"

I paid the fare on the meter and told the driver to go.

"Please, Mr. Lome," I said, "just the name of one stock."

"Don't be ridiculous."

"An area then. What looks good? Steels? Rails? I need money."

"Compete," he said.

"All right then. Tell me a product. Give me the name of a product."

Lome laughed. "Anything," he said. "Everything."

"Please, Mr. Lome."

He stopped and turned to me. His face was angry. "All right," he said, "let's *talk* business. It's a mine. The world is a mine. It runs on the soundest of business principles. There's a law in physics which states that matter can neither be created nor destroyed. I like the sound of that. If I were asked what I believe in, I'd say I believed in that. Think of it: *nothing can be destroyed. Nothing.* How many times can an automobile be sold and resold? Four? Five? And then that one last time to the scrap man. Only it's *not* the last time—the scrap man sells it to the mill and the mill turns into fresh steel and sells it and it's a car again. Talk about life cycles, about resurrections. What's Hecuba to me? There are people who buy lint, broken toys, government surplus, smashed glass, old newspapers. Don't talk to me about priests—old men fiddling with wafers and wine like someone knotting a tie. Turn waste into profit. There's religion for you: loaves and fishes, water and wine. Christ knew."

We were passing a Woolworth's. "I have to go in here for a minute," Lome said.

We walked in and Lome went to the toy department. He looked at the toys critically, holding up one, then another, winding them, blowing his breath into the toy horns, posing the tin soldiers. "Look," he said to me, pointing to a package of clay. "How much is the clay?" he asked a salesgirl.

"Fifteen cents," she said.

He bought six packages. "Here," he said to me, "have you got sixty cents?"

"Yes," I said, a little confused.

"Give me," Lome said.

I gave him the money and he handed me three packages of clay.

"They're fifteen cents each," I said.

"I'm your supplier. I'm entitled to a profit."

"But I don't *want* the clay."

"Of course you don't. You want tips on the market, you want to ride in the country in taxicabs. Sell the clay."

"Who will I sell it to?"

"To a consumer. Find a consumer. There," he said, pointing to the street, "in the marketplace."

We went out. "Well?" Lome said.

"This is ridiculous," I said. "What am I supposed to do?"

"Sell it. Sell the clay."

"But I can't."

"You haven't tried. Try."

I went up to a woman. "Do you want to buy some clay, ma'am?" I asked her.

She looked at me as if I were crazy, and I turned to Lome helplessly.

"Here," he said disgustedly, "watch me."

He crossed the street and I followed him. As we walked Lome began to open his packages of clay. Each package contained five strips of colored clay, each strip about an inch and a half wide and perhaps a quarter of an inch thick. "I like to work with clay," he said. "It's a

174

wonderful example of what I was saying before. Clay can neither be created nor destroyed."

"I suppose so."

"Coloring it—that was a stroke of genius. Adding to it. Newton never said you couldn't add to it. That's just merchandising. I need some newspaper. There should be one in that trash basket."

He went over to it and I watched his arm disappear up to the elbow and reappear with a morning paper that looked as if it had been barely read. "Packaging and display," Lome explained, showing me the newspaper. "All right," he said, "where shall we set up shop?"

"But the police—"

"Well, we could try to get away with it, but you may be right. There are some corners which are best not cut. You stand over there by the trash basket and warn me if you see a cop."

Lome separated the strips of colored clay and arranged them according to their colors on a sheet of the newspaper which he had spread out on the sidewalk. Already a few people had stopped to watch him. He did not look at them as he prepared the clay in little balls and slabs. He worked slowly and gradually more people began to gather round him. Finally he stood up with a small chunk of clay in his hand. "Clay from the earth," he said softly. And then, louder, *"Clay from the earth!"* A few of the people closest to him edged away slightly when he began to speak. "A souvenir of the world," he called. "Ashes to ashes. Dust to dust. Clay to make feet, make men.

"Closer, Come! Gather! Yellow clay for the sun. Blue for the sea or sky. Red for the land. Ah, the red clay, the red is the saddest and best, the hardest to hold, to mold. Green clay for value, for emeralds and gems. I sell the world, the universe. White clay for the edifices and monuments of men. Not a toy, not a manufactured product. From God's hands to you. For a remembrance."

The people looked at each other and laughed and pointed their fingers at their temples. Lome saw them and

175

stopped. "What's wrong?" he demanded. "Do you think I would insult you with substitutes?" He broke off a piece from a lump he held. "Here," he said, thrusting the piece into someone's hand. "Feel it. Smell it, taste it. This is it. A chunk of the world. Real estate. You—you, sir—" He pointed to a small man at the back of the crowd. "Always go for the man at the back," he called to me. "Sell him and then work your way to the front. My assistant, ladies and gentlemen," he explained, pointing to me, "a humble clay gatherer." He moved through the crowd. "You—you, sir, may I ask you a question?"

"I suppose so," the man said, laughing nervously.

"Ah, don't be afraid. It's a personal question, of course. What's the use of any other kind, eh, brother?"

The crowd laughed. "All right, friend, what I want to know is whether you own your home or rent?"

"I rent."

"Fine. That's fine. You rent, you say."

"That's right."

"Never made it?" Lome asked suddenly, looking at the man sharply.

"What's that? What do you mean?"

"Never made it. Never broke through. Obligations kept you a tenant. No, no, don't be ashamed. Please. We understand. Here's your opportunity. Clay. Clay is land, a plot. A plot for you." Lome took another piece of clay from his pocket and molded it to the first piece. "The plot thickens," he said, and the crowd laughed again. He pulled the piece of clay apart. "Or subdivide." He held the piece of clay out to the man.

"It's just clay," the man said.

"Well, of course it is. That's what I've been telling you. But don't say it like that, brother. Don't let me hear you say, 'It's just clay.' Take that 'just' out. Be just. Say, 'Why, it's *clay*!' Because that's what it is. The emphasis is on *clay*. This is the stuff. Old Adam's in that clay. Come on, brother. A souvenir, a remembrance of the earth. And here's something else. I don't know where it's from and I don't make any claims for it—I will not misrepresent. But that clay could be Chinese clay or

176

Polish clay or Canadian or Argentine clay. Who can say who walked these old hills? Jesus Himself maybe, eh?

"All right, give me a nickel. That's my price for the earth. That's from the earth, too. We'll trade, even steven. Clay for nickel. What's Hecuba to me? Hey? And this is something you can take with you, friend—make no mistake about that. Beware of substitutes. Keep that nickel in your pants and they'll turn you upside down when you die. They'll shake you, brother. They'll shake that nickel loose. They'll never bury you with a nickel still in your pocket. But the clay stays. Ashes to ashes, pal, dust to dust. How about it? I'm waiting for your decision."

"It's worthless," the man said.

Lome turned to the crowd. "This man has resistance. I like that in a man." He turned back to the man suddenly and placed his hands on his lapels. "So you say it's worthless, do you?" he shouted. "Well, I breathed *meaning* into it? What's that worth? How much meaning you got in your life, friend, you can afford to let even five cents' worth go by without jumping at it? You're suspicious, are you? You're afraid if you give me the nickel I've taken you. Well, maybe I have. You get taken every day, pal. Renter! Tenant! Where's the gas you bought? Where are the phone calls? the electric? the food? What have you got to show me for the money you've spent? Show me something. Show me! Receipts? You hold on to that clay, you hear me? It's dirt cheap. Cheap dirt. Give me the nickel. *Give it to me!*"

Hypnotized, the man dug into his pocket and handed Lome a nickel. Turning to the others, Lome took up the clay from the newspaper and broke off pieces and handed them out as people forced their nickels on him. He laughed, taking their money, and at last held up his hands. "All gone, folks," he said. "No more clay. I thank you for your attention."

He came up to me. "How'd you make out with yours?" he asked.

"I've still go it."

"*With the great demand for clay?* It's a seller's market, friend." He took the change out of his pocket and

177

looked at it. "Not bad," he said. "I made fifteen cents on your three packages and a dollar-twenty on mine. Deducting forty-five cents for expenses, that makes a profit of ninety cents. I doubled my money."

"You were very good." I was genuinely moved.

"Pigeons," he said. "That was the lesson of the clay pigeons."

September 14, 1950. Dallas, Texas.

Last night the drought ended. There were violent, sudden storms, lightning crackling, thunder clapping, signs and portents. The people came into the street to look at the rain.

I was with Lome in the limousine when the storm broke; he had allowed me to accompany him to the airport. He stared at the heavy rain. "I've got to be in Cleveland," he said. "There's a deal."

"They'll never let you take off in this weather," I said hopefully.

"We'll see about that."

By the time we got to the airport it was raining even harder. Lome brooded about his vanishing opportunities. He went into the tower to plead his case, but it was no use. When he came down he was glum.

"I've got to be in Cleveland," he said. "It's an act of God, a damned act of God." He said this as though God might be some competitor who had to make sure that Lome didn't get to Cleveland first. "What are you grinning about?" he asked me.

"The weather works in my favor," I said. In the limousine I had been urging him to help me.

"Bull," he said. "You'll get nothing out of my prolonged stay."

We sat silently. Suddenly Lome looked up. "It has to break," he said. "It has to." He stood up.

"Where are you going?"

"To the tower. I want to look at those radar screens again."

I started to follow him. "Look," he said, "I don't need you right now."

I saw him stop to talk with one of the airport executives. I was miserable; I almost wished Lome might be allowed to take off. This was the end, I thought. My money, except for the sum I had set aside to invest on Lome's advice, was all gone, and I no longer had any hope that he would help me.

More than most men I needed to be free. My controlling vision demanded it. It was grand to be a self-made man, but bliss to be an heir, a gentleman farmer, a hereditary lord, to be fixed in some sinecure where effort bred the soul's reward. It was simple biology which finally caught up with you; it was economics that dealt the death blow. And duty was simply the food in the icebox, the roof over your head, your lousy needs, your growling upstart stomach and all the rest.

So goodbye, great men, you whose needs are met, all the folks with money in the bank and clothes in the closet, whose duty had been done, whose honorable intentions could be counted in diseases forestalled by health insurance, in down payments of one sort or another, in funds for their children's educations. They were out of my league now, out of my neighborhood, my life. They lived in drier climates where the penny for the rainy day was a superfluity. I could, of course, continue to show up at their back doors, my hand outstretched in the pauper's salute, but why should they listen any more than Lome had listened?

If I met the great now, it would have to be in the way others met them, at a humiliating second-hand, conducted into their presence by ushers with flashlights to watch their images on screens, or hear them in concert halls, or applaud them at rallies while arc lamps played across the sky, or read about them in books or hear their voices on the radio. The life I had chosen for myself—or had had thrust upon me by reasons of temperament—was over now. It had been a grand idea, a great idea, a noble idea for a life—I still insisted on that. But, like many before me, I didn't have the price.

I could still see Lome talking to the official, arguing

179

special privilege, blandishing, terrorizing in his great salesman's way. They will have to let him go, I thought. I could imagine his arguments, compelling, urgent, single-minded, and I pitied the official who did not know what I knew: that his single-mindedness, his force, his logic, were shammed, his motives all ulterior. I thought of his pitch to the crowd. He knew. He knew. He had the intimations, the hints. The ungodly voices whispered in his ear too. "Save yourself." Lome knew about death. They would not leave the nickel in his pants either. He knew that, yet he persisted. Perhaps that was it; perhaps that's what lay at the core of all greatness—a willingness not to abide by logic, to shrug it off in the soul's own optimism. He was an inspiring sight. If only I knew how to respond, if only I could learn the lesson of the clay and other pigeons that the sight of Lome, grounded in Dallas halfway to Cleaveland and death, stirred in me. He sold the clay and had accepted mere money, defying the very arguments he invented, the very truths he alone understood.

All genuinely great men were martyrs whose characters and purposes were like those double ramps in architecture which wound and climbed and never touched in a concrete illusion of strand. The rest of us climbed those ramps in the delusion that the fellow we saw across the gaping space moved on the same path. It was the barber-pole condition of life, and we assumed in good faith some ultimate matrix common to all. But *isolate, isolate*—that was the real lesson. Hecuba was nothing to any of us.

Then I saw Lome's briefcase, the one I had carried to his room. He had put it down on a counter when he was talking to the official and when they went off together —to look, I suppose, at the radar screens—he had forgotten it.

I did not hesitate. Isolate, isolate. I moved up to the counter and slid the case inside my raincoat. Inside would be the tips, the speculations, the deals, the weird money lore, the master plan. Inside would be the inside information.

With my prize I went into the man's toilet. I pushed

180

a dime into the slot, locked myself in a private booth, sat down on the toilet seat and opened the case, feeling as I did a thrill of greed. I was like some pirate before a treasure chest.

The lists and charts which tumbled out of the brief-case were like some paper abstraction of golden bracelets and jeweled crowns and ruby-mouthed statues. There were lists of holdings in foreign counties, discussions of economic prospects for various markets. These I ignored. There were plans for taking over firms, suggestions for mergers, passbooks from five dozen banks. There were lists of stocks which Lome owned, and signed proxies, and a handful of prospectuses for firms which Lome was evidently interested in. But I could make nothing out of them. Perhaps an expert, someone familiar with the language of money, might have been able to take Lome's hints, but I couldn't. Before the network of statistics and the strange bookkeeper's vocabulary I was helpless. I began to fear that I had acted in haste, and as I continued to go through the briefcase I felt increasingly frustrated. In despair I began to stuff the papers back into the briefcase and was about to zip it shut when I saw something I had overlooked before. It was written in pen on a piece of lined, yellow, legal size paper. The fact that it was on legal paper somehow gave it, even before I read it, the integrity of an official document. I felt a peculiar anticipatory excitement, and as I read over the paper it mounted steadily. Lome had written in his own hand:

The following firms will issue stock on the New York Exchange within the next six months.

There followed a list of four companies I had never heard of. The note had been dated the previous week. Lome went on:

My own plan is to purchase substantial blocks of the first two stocks and to hold them in per-petuity.

"My plan too," I said hoarsely.

Suddenly, inside the pay toilet, there came the sound of an enormous peal of thunder, growling, sustained, hoarse. For a moment the lights dimmed. The electric circuits hummed and sang and then restored themselves.

An act of God, I thought, feeling suddenly warm, befriended, destiny's child, son of Herlitz, son of fate, son of luck and chance and circumstance.

October 22, 1953. Philadelphia.

My invitation to the Irving Gibbenjoys' came today. I glanced at the envelope and called the caterer immediately for the guest list. My contact, Davis, was out, so I left word for him to call me at the hotel. Everyone has a weakness, Davis a particularly filthy one, but he can be put off easily enough. I let him watch me in my shower. It's a torment for him, more pain than pleasure. He sits on the closed toilet lid and talks shyly. He pretends, I think, that we're somewhere else, in a drawing room or a restaurant. When I turn toward him to dry myself, more often than not he looks away. Davis does not have the strength to go with his weakness. No man without character can support a vice.

Once I'm established I won't have to rely as heavily on Davis or on my other contacts. Lord, when will it happen? Of course, they're not all Davises. Beverly Brain in Chicago wants to marry me. Beverly is nice, of course, but she's insignificant. It's amazing how many of my contacts fall in love with me—Sheila Mobley in Boston, Anor Lyon in San Francisco, Jeanette Bouchard in Washington. The trick is to make yourself completely dependent on them. That's why traveling salesmen often have such good relationships with their customers. Ah, but it takes a toll. I can relax only with Nate Lace in New York. Nate is the only one of my contacts who's in on the joke of my life. I swear I wish the others were, but if I were to say to Anor, "Anor, honey, it's just supply and demand with me," she'd never do me another favor. Occupational hazard—like cave-ins for a miner. It's always what something else does to us. The fault, dear Brutus, lies in our stars that we are underlings.

Still, one has to get along with people. Live and let live. Be let to live and live. If they were all like Nate, though . . . Anyone who says I don't work hard is crazy. Look at Philadelphia, for God's sake. I was stymied in Philadelphia for years. The Main Line was busy! I saw the columnists, the society bandleaders, the golf pros. Who didn't I see! Nothing. Then I had this idea about the invitations. Idea? It was an inspiration, actually. Suddenly I remembered the prom bids from high school. They were gorgeous, I remembered: cellophane and satin, brocade and cardboard, with long silken tassels that were attached to the pegboards of the parented. The silly, romantic apotheosis of the Occasion. Each printed cardboard page vaguely visible through a covering of waxy, spidery paper, shimmering history books in raised type; the date, the name of the hotel, the band, the charity, the sponsor, the committee; a closing poem, even a page for remarks ("Willy said he loved me and squeezed me up there"). Then I thought, Where do they get that stuff? A service, of course, *a service,* and I remembered something I had once seen on a tray in a hall.

I called the Philadelphia Board of Education. "Do you give prizes for calligraphy?"

"What's that?"

"Do you give prizes for calligraphy? Handwriting."

"Just a minute, please. I'll check."

I got the names of all the prize winners from 1925 through 1951. But when I looked in the phone book I could find only a handful of names. Turnover. I called those that were listed.

"Excuse me, madam, does Gerald Vidilowski live there, please? I understand Mr. Vidilowski holds The Brotherly Love Award for Penmanship. I can use a man like that in my work."

"Mr. Vidilowski wrote a beautiful hand, but he's dead," the woman sobbed.

I called the residence of Miriam Spidota. "Excuse

183

me, ma'am, are you the Miriam Spidota who won the 1946 Brotherly Love Award for Penmanship?"

"Yes, that's right," the woman said brightly.

"Do you still wield the pen, ma'am?"

"How do you mean, 'wield the pen'?"

"I'll be direct, Miss Spidota. Are you now employed in addressing envelopes?"

"Is this Harry? Harry, is this a rib? Harry?"

"Please, Miss Spidota. I'm very serious."

"Gee," she said. "I thought you were that pimp, Harry. You a salesman? One of the boys give you my number?"

The third on the list was Davis. He told me nervously that he worked for Affairs, Inc. I arranged to meet him, and that was that. Keys to the City.

Davis called back at six. The Gibbenjoy affair sounds disappointing. Ray Pilchard will be there, of the Pilchard Hotel chain. Leroy Buff-Miner of the pharmaceutical house. Gabrielle Gal—I've heard some of her phony recordings of Greek songs. Still, she's very popular in café society. Dr. Morton Perlmutter, an archeologist. A Mr. and Mrs. Nelton Fayespringer of Pittsburgh. She's one of the Carnegies, Davis says, and he's one of the few Pennsylvania industrialists without his own town named after him. All in all, there were about three dozen names, some of which I didn't recognize at all. I'll go, of course, because it's the opening of the season, but it looks pretty grim.

October 24, 1953. New York City.

Nate's call yesterday morning caught me just as I was going out for breakfast. He couldn't talk over the phone, he said—God, how it annoys me when people call to tell you they can't talk over the phone—but something big was coming up in New York and I had better get into town immediately. I've noticed that I'm an extremely impatient person—invariably, for example, I flush the toilet before I have finished urinating—and during the hour and a half train ride from Philly to NY I could do nothing but wonder what Nate could have meant. Probably it was nothing but another party. Nate gives parties violently, and sometimes I have met middlingly important people at them. I say important rather than great because I have noticed that the great don't often go to parties—unless, of course, they are the guests of honor. At any rate, I've become disenchanted with parties (two years ago I could never have imagined myself saying this), though I never refuse an invitation. It always seems to me that the next one might change my life.

Nate wasn't in his place when I went up there, but it was already four o'clock when the train got to Penn Station and the traffic was so heavy that the bus didn't get up to Forty-seventh Street until amost five. I asked Perry whether Nate would be coming back.

"That is to speculate," Perry said coldly. Perry is one of my enemies. He doesn't approve of Nate's careless attachments to outsiders. He calls them "befriendships."

Perry is a very popular maître d' in New York, though I have never understood the reason. His dignity and aloofness seem spurious to me. I feel that they're simply tools of the trade with him, ones he uses a little squeamishly, as a professional locksmith might use dynamite. I like to picture him at home in front of the TV with his shoes off and a beer from Nate's kitchen in his hand. There are softer, sloppier Perrys inside him, I know. Even at that, talking to Perry, I always get the peculiarly grateful, slightly vicious feeling of "There but for you go I."

"I'll get him at the apartment. Thanks, Perry."

"*Messieur* Nate will have guests," Perry warned.

I looked at this maître d'hôtel, at this head waiter who got his name in the columns and was the constant *bête noir* of a government tax man who worried about his tips.

"Perry," I said affably, "you may lead them to the tables, but I, I sit down with them."

"May I show *Messieur* to a table?" Perry said viciously, knowing that without Nate there to tear up my check I could not afford even the cheapest item on Nate's menu.

"I dined on the train, Perry," I said easily. Much as I loathe myself for it, Perry is always able to force me into transparently absurd positions. As a professional mâitre d', Perry despises moochers. He once told me that I ate above my station. It is outrageous to Perry that I should even be allowed inside Nate's. It is, he thinks, like a panhandler coming to the front door of Buckingham Palace. I can see his point, of course, but that sort of demeaning introspection leads nowhere. As well for me to feel guilt because I cannot pay my checks as for a cripple to feel it because he cannot run races. We have our handicaps, the cripple and I, and a gentleman does not look too closely into them. If Perry objects that I do not meet my obligations, I can counter that there are certain obligations which I must simply be allowed to write off in order to get on with my life.

"If I should happen to miss Mr. Lace," I told Perry, "please tell him that I'm in town and that I'll get in touch with him later."

I had a hot dog and an orange drink at a Nedick's on Sixth Avenue, and walked with my valise over to a special entrance I know at the Radio City Garage which all the advertising executives and TV and radio and publishing people use when they go down to get their cars. I was a little late, but I did see Henry Luce drive off to Connecticut, and just when I was ready to leave I happened to spot Doris Day about to get into a cab. She had some packages, and I rushed up to the side of the taxi and opened the door for her.

"Good day, Miss Day," I said.

"Thank you," she said.

"Thank *you*, Miss Day," I said. "Your voice is a gift from God. Cherish it always."

"Thank you," she said, a little nervously.

I was waiting for the traffic to break. As I say, I am an impatient man. I cannot stand to sit stalled in a bus when I have somewhere to go—or even when I don't have somewhere to go. Frequently I will get out and walk, though I know I lose time this way. This habit is one of my small fictions for preserving the illusion that I am in complete control of my life. I could have gone down to Nate's on the subway, of course, but I will not travel underground. Finally at about six-fifteen I walked over and caught a Fifth Avenue bus going downtown.

Nate lives in the Village, in the Mews. The houses in the Mews are not very large, but Nate keeps a butler and a full-time maid. (Nate is a bachelor, as will be, I suspect, all my friends. I am not the sort of person wives would normally abide. Perhaps that's another reason Perry— who after all is a kind of housekeeper—finds me so distasteful.) I banged on Nate's door and the butler opened it.

"Is Mr. Lace in, Simmons?"

Unlike Perry, Simmons shows no open hostility toward me. I am not sure, however, that I fully approve of his tolerance. It too, after all, is simply a tool of his trade. I like all people to meet me unprofessionally.

"He is not, sir. I don't *know* what Mr. Lace's arrangements are this evening. He did seem to be expecting you, though, Mr. Boswell, and instructed me to invite you to stay until his return."

Nate doesn't keep a cook. There's never any food in his house; everything is brought from the restaurant. "That's very kind, Simmons," I said. "I'm a little tired though, after my trip. I think I'll just go up to my hotel and lie down. Mr. Lace can reach me there."

"Very good, sir. Should he call I shall certainly tell him that. Where shall you be this time, sir?"

"The YMCA, I think, Simmons."

"Very good, sir," he said.

I have always enjoyed my conversations with butlers, and Simmons is one of my favorites. "Yes," I said philosophically, "the International Youth Hostel is filled up this trip, Simmons. There's a convention of Children for Peace in town to picket the UN."

"Ah," Simmons said.

"And Travelers Aid is just a little weary of my tricks by now."

"Ah."

"Well, Simmons, give the master my message. I shall

187

probably be seeing you. You're looking very well, incidentally."

"Thank you, sir."

"Thank *you*, Simmons. Goodbye."

"Goodbye, sir."

He closed the door quietly behind me and I walked happily back up the frenchy cobblestoned street to the Fifth Avenue bus.

It is interesting how I got to know Nate. It was two years ago. New York is the hardest place in the world for an outsider. I had made about half a dozen trips there and was no closer to the prizes the town has to offer ("offer" is hardly the world) than I had ever been. I could see celebrities, of course, almost at will, but I could not get close to them. What was the difference between me and the teen-age autograph hounds that stalked them on the sidewalks outside their hotels? The techniques which worked in other cities were useless in New York. The great were so often there only for short intervals. Without a formal structure, without a community where the great moved always in habitual patterns, I was helpless. (It is common knowledge, for instance, that Hemingway drinks on Tuesday, Thursday and Saturday afternoons at the Floridita Bar in Havana and that Faulkner buys his tobacco at Pettigrew's Drugs in Oxford, but how many people know that Igor Stravinski borrows books religiously on the first Monday of every month from the Los Angeles County Public Library, Branch #3, or that the Oppenheimers dress for dinner every night and that Robert himself brings in the cleaning to Princeton Same Day Cleaners on Wednesday morning?) My blue suit—which I had bought when I quit wrestling—hung unused in my closet.

When I had exhausted all the techniques I could think of (at one time I was so desperate that I palmed myself off as a singer and waited six and a half hours in a cold theater to audition twenty seconds for a part before Rodgers and Hammerstein), I had my inspiration. The problem, of course, and somehow I had lost sight of it, was not to meet any particular great man—that could always be done—but to make a reliable contact. I had always been an avid reader of all the columns. It was in this way that I was able to keep track of the hundreds of celebrities who were constantly coming in and out of New York. It wasn't long before I became familiar with the name of Nate Lace, through the doors of whose restaurant celebrities of all sorts spilled in a redundancy of fame, like fruit from a cornucopia. With a contact like him, I thought—*With a contact like him*—And that was it. It was at once so simple and so profound that I could not concentrate on the details, or wait to put it to the test. My original intention had been to wait until evening, but I was so full of my plan that at two in the afternoon I could sit still no longer. I put on my blue suit and went down to Nate Lace's restaurant. I had no reservation, of course (Nate's policy is to give no strangers reservations over the telephone; somehow I had divined this), and I tried to give ten dollars to Perry, who at that time I did not know. He looked me over, laughed coldly, and handed the money back. (I thought I had done something gauche. It wasn't until months later that I discovered I simply had not offered him enough.) "That is not *nessaire*," Perry said. "As it happens there is a table."

I ordered ninety dollars' worth of Nate's most expensive food. (Nate says that his restaurant is the most expensive in the world.) I was so nervous when it came that I had difficulty eating it. (Actually, I do not really *like* good food, though Nate would be offended to learn this.) When I had finished I called the waiter. "You needn't bother with the bill," I said. "I can't pay for any of this."

The waiter went off to consult with Perry, and I cursed myself for not waiting until the evening, when Nate would certainly have been in. My only hope now was that it was too big a case for Perry and that it would have to be called to Nate's attention. I needn't have concerned myself; I should have known my man better from the columns. This was the sort of thing a man like Nate would take great satisfaction in handling personally. Perry leaned across the table familiarly and said with a nice sense of menace that Nate wasn't in the restaurant and would have to be called. Even better, I thought, by making his rage keener this works into my hands.

When Nate came in he barely nodded at Cary Grant, sitting in a booth near the window, and went directly over to Perry. He had on a heavy, fur-collared overcoat and his nose was red and dripping.

"I couldn't get a cab and had to walk from Fifty-fifth," I heard him tell Perry. "Where's the mooch?"

Perry pointed to my table, where I had been allowed to sit until Nate came. He walked over.

"You the one don't like my food?"

"It was delicious," I said.

"I see you didn't touch the Balinese wonder pudding," he said, pointing to an enormous, Victorian confection with flying buttresses of a caramelly, fruit-streaked cream which lay untasted on an ornate doily on a snow-white plate on a scalloped, thick damask napkin on a rich silver salver.

"It was a little much after the smoked whale in ambergris sauce," I said.

"Was it?"

"A *little* much," I said. Cary Grant was looking at us.

"It stays on the bill."

I couldn't imagine why he made an issue of it since I couldn't pay for any of it.

"Nate," I said. "I'm not an actor."

"What the hell do I care you're not an actor?"

"I mean to say I'm not using this incident to get a part in a picture or to obtain publicity for myself."

"Who gives a shit?"

"I know you have allowed certain of your favorite comics to run up tabs of ten thousand dollars and more."

"You ain't one of my favorite comics, buddy. What you're going to run up is a tab of thirty days or more."

"Where is your vaunted sense of humor, Nate?"

"Where's yours?" he said. "You couldn't order bear steak? You couldn't order tiger filet? Ambergris sauce! Do you know what ambergris sauce costs me? It would be cheaper to pour the most expensive Paris perfume over the god-damned whale."

190

"I'm sorry, Nate," I said. "Look, must Perry hear all this?"

"Perry's a trusted employee," Nate said. "Beat it, Perry."

I told Nate my story. At first he listened doubtfully, but then, as I told him of my past, of my desperate need for a contact in New York, he began to warm up. Soon he was picking at the Balinese wonder pudding with his fingers and I felt I had him. He seemed to find it very amusing. The more I talked the more he laughed. "Hey," he said when I had finished, "you're a character, ain't you?" He said it as though he had discovered something deep and abiding and true about the human personality.

"I guess I am," I said humbly.

"Yeah," he said, "yeah. A character."

"That's about the size of it." I said.

"Yeah," Nate said. "Hey, you want me to show you around the place? You want to see my kitchen?"

He took me with him through the restaurant. I even looked with him into the women's powder room when Estelle, the attendant, said it was all clear. In the kitchen (which was not very large and none too clean) we sat at a bucher's block drinking arctic lichen tea and laughed together over Nate's story of his troubles with the government. It seems that Nate's was a very popular place for important people to bring important clients. Of course they would then deduct the bill from their taxes as a business expense, and the government found itself in the peculiar position of buying three- and four-hundred-dollar dinners for people. They were going to refuse to allow it by declaring Nate's off limits when Nate flew to Washington and made his offer. He would rebate the government 15 per cent on everything declared a deduction in his place. The government knew itself to be on very shaky legal ground and accepted at once.

"Why did you offer fifteen per cent? Why did you offer anything if they had such a bad case?"

"Don't be a fool," Nate said. "Suppose they took it to court. Look at all the business I'd lose from people who'd be nervous the deductions wouldn't be allowed."

191

"That's right," I said, pleased as I always am when I get some insight into the mysteries of business manipulation.

"Sure," Nate said. "I would give twenty per cent." He laughed. "The suckers."

"The dumb suckers," I said.

"You know, those bozos out there"—with his thumb he indicated the main dining room—"don't know I'm helping to pick up some of their tabs?"

"The lousy bozos."

"Those bozos are my friends," Nate said severely.

"Long live them," I said. *Bon appetit* to all the millionaire bozos."

"Yeah," Nate said, laughing. "Yeah." He got up and told a waiter to get Perry. "Perry," Nate said, "bring Mr. Boswell's bill." When Perry came back he looked at it again and added up the figures.

I groaned to myself. Was it all a trick? I wondered desperately.

Nate looked up at me, smiled, and tore up my check. "With you, Jimmy," he said, "we won't even pretend there's a tab."

It was about two o'clock in the morning when someone pounded on my door.

"Who's there?" I asked, startled.

"James Boswell?"

"Yes, Who is it?"

"It's Potter, at the desk."

"Who?"

"Mr. Potter. I'm sorry to bother you at this hour, but there's a call for you downstairs, Mr. Boswell. It's a matter of life and death, I'm afraid."

"Okay," I said. "I'll be right out."

I put a pair of pants over my pajamas and followed Mr. Potter downstairs. He led me to the phone at the desk and stepped respectfully away from what he thought was my tragedy.

"Hello?"

"Jimmy, it's Nate. Sorry I missed you before."

"Yes, Nate, what is it?"

192

"Jimmy, I told you it was big. Are you ready?"

"Sure, Nate."

"Okay. Can you be at my place tomorrow night about eight?"

"Yes, Nate. I think so. What is it?"

"Jimmy, Harold Flesh is in town."

October 26, 1953. New York City.

. . . like a doctor, perhaps a surgeon, or an engineer, or someone on a committee. The important thing is his aura of conservatism—not respectability, conservatism. He seems to move in a paneled, masculine, conspicuously bookless world, to have come from rooms with bottled ships on their mantelpieces. There would be no guns on his walls though, I think, for he is no hunter. One doesn't know, finally, what he is, although I got the feeling, hearing him speak, that there is something—what? astrology? Rosicrucianism? the restoration of the Bourbons?—to which, privately, he is deeply committed. It is the measure of how little he is to be trusted that he never talks of this, whatever it is. Nevertheless, when he leaves a place there lingers the smell of something off-center, subversive, *wild*—what Bruchevsteen calls "the metallic aura of closed systems."

Flesh is not frank, and one knows instinctively—this is perhaps it—that he is constantly underrating his friends, if he has them, as well as his enemies. Patently, nothing will ever come of this, for he underrates not their talents (he moves in a world of specialists, of the delegation of authority and the division of labor), but their value as persons.

I found myself wondering about him sexually. He is not homosexual—that, at least, would take some sort of passion. I suspect that if he treats with women at all, he is most comfortable with whores. The obvious comparison is to John Sallow, yet there is something wrong here. Whatever one might think of him, Sallow is manifestly a force. Harold Flesh is too clearly only a middleman, someone high and dry within a chaos not of his own creating but which he controls with a mocking impunity and which yields to him in his perverse safety fantastic, endless profit. I was reminded rather of a scion, someone far along in the generations, whose wealth and power, great perhaps as they might be, seem out of touch with that original force which first created and wielded them. The dark-suited son of a distant king, he has hobbies, one supposes, where his fathers had causes, so that finally he seems derived, mutative, some primogenitive fact not so much of nature as of some obscure, still operative law and order.

It was surprising to me to discover how much I disliked him. So rarely do we meet someone of whom we can say positivey, "I hate him," that it is startling when it happens. In addition, I find it an extremely upsetting experience. I am nervous in the presence of my own hatred and behave stupidly.

Perhaps, though, I made him as nervous as he made me, for although there was no apparent reason, he chose to deal with me on a professional basis. He tried to corrupt me. Was I interested in being his bodyguard, he wanted to know.

I had never seen Nate so nervous. He was everywhere, directing everything. Once I saw him begin to fumble with the fastidious Perry's bow tie, only to abandon it in frustration when he realized it was already correct. To the cook he was unforgivably rude, reducing that man almost to tears and then rushing back five minutes later to offer what was transparently an insincere apology because he was afraid the cook might take it in his head to attempt some damaging revenge. He scolded the waiters for imagined offenses, and even quarreled with the Puerto Rican busboys because he felt they were making too much noise with the silver. After a while, to calm him. I suggested we have a drink together.

"What drink?" he demanded angrily. "Harold Flesh comes to the place in an hour and he tells me to get drunk."

194

"I'm not telling you to get drunk. I'm telling you to calm down."

"Mind your business," he said. "I'll throw you the hell out of here. Perry's right about you."

"Perry's a prick," I said. "Why are you so concerned about Harold Flesh? What can he do to you?"

"What, you think I'm legal? You think I'm Snow White? Jerk, you been away somewhere? You never heard the word *syndicate*? The term *Mafia* is unfamiliar to you?"

"Nate, you're raving. You're a nice man with a very expensive restaurant."

He turned on me, genuinely angry. Before, the first time I had seen him, when I had welched on the bill—that was play. This was real. "What's the matter, don't you live in the same world I do?" he said. "Are you from Mars? That's it, ain't it, you're from Mars. From never-never land, and you don't know the way we do things here. You make me sick, do you understand me? You make me absolutely sick."

"Nate, what did I do?"

"You make me sick. You do. You got no right, you got absolutely no *right* to be as big as you are and that stupid. I let you come here. You been to my parties, you meet my friends. You're a big boy, God bless you, you got an appetite like a horse. I feed you bird tongues would cost a king his fortune to eat them and you don't know a god-damn thing about me. Who I am, where I come from, how I got this place."

"You never told me."

"You never asked."

"Well, I'm asking. Tell me."

"I'll write you a letter."

"Tell me."

"I'll draw you a picture."

"Tell me."

"What'll I tell you? Perry carries a gun? Okay—Perry carries a gun. So does Simmons, did you know that? *Simmons* carries a gun."

"In the Mews?"

195

"Yes, in the Mews. *In the Mews!* Infant! Baby! There are ladies in this world would see anything. They sell the outside of their bodies. The inside—the *inside,* do you understand me? Piece by piece they sell it off, like at an auction. They do not always walk in the streets and stand under lampposts. Sometimes they sit in mahogany captain's chairs on leather seats. They eat from linen thick as carpets with forks of soft pure silver. There are toothmarks on my spoons. There are doctors who perform illegal operations. I do not speak of men with breadknives and dirty fingernails in rooms behind stores. I speak of men on Park Avenue, in hospital amphitheaters with the best equipment. There are men that push junk, that water the liquor, the gas, the milk, the currency. I do not speak of muggers in parks, of creeps at windows with their hand on their thing, or rapers and queers. There are men that cripple and others that kill, that fix fights and World Series and prices and wars. There are wheelers and there are dealers."

"If you're trying to frighten me——"

"Baby! It *doesn't* frighten you? I go to the track with these men, we sit in each other's boxes at the World Series, in Indianapolis for the Five Hundred. In Louisville for the Derby we are on the floors of each other's hotels, and *I* am frightened of them."

"Well, of course. I understand that, Nate. But why?"

"Harold Flesh."

He was in a state of active terror, abandoned to it, yet for all that still trying not so much to deal with it as to preserve it long enough to communicate it to me, his action vaguely heroic, as though I were someone sleeping in a burning house whom he must rouse before he could think of safety for himself. "Nate," I said.

"The world is not clean."

"Nate, this——"

"It is not a clean world."

"I know that. I know it's not clean. Fixing beyond fixing."

"So make sense. Be afraid in it."

"I can take care of myself."

"Good," he said. "Good news."

He took out a cigarette, something I never saw him do in the restaurant, though he smokes heavily at home. His hand shook as he lighted it.

"Nate."

"Harold Flesh is such a son of a bitch."

"Why did you want me to see him, Nate?"

"It's important," he said. "You know too many movie stars." He put out the cigarette and stood up. "Have Perry bring you something," he said and started to go.

"Nate."

"I have to see. In the kitchen, I have to see."

"Nate, please. Are you clean?"

He looked at me. "Are you?" I said.

"I'm *shmutzic*," he said.

"What can you have to do with Harold Flesh?"

"With him? Nothing. I swear it."

"But—then why do you care?"

"Because," he said. "Because I'm like you. He's a champion, ain't he? From all walks. If they're champions you tear up the check. Do you understand?"

"Nate, I don't believe you. Something is on the line."

"Ah," he said. He smiled for the first time. "You chiseler. 'Something is on the line.' All right. Good. Just one of the things on the line, just *one*, is my place. Who needs that kind of trade? Who needs it? If those guys make it a habit to come here they could ruin me. That kind of trade. Cardinals eat here, for Christ's sake." He leaned forward. "In this world there are two kinds. Those who still bother to lie and those who don't. On the average it is safer and more profitable to deal with those who still bother to lie. Perry!"

Perry came to the table. "Bring Mr. Boswell a nice pot of arctic lichen tea." He left.

I looked around the room. Across from me, in a round wide booth, the red velvet upholstery tufted and buttoned like the canopied bed of a baby prince, a handsome man toasted a lovely woman. Were they clean, I wondered. Sure they were. In a far corner two middle-aged men—they seemed as unsinister as brokers—chatted amiably. Which one pulled the trigger? I studied the well-dressed, decorous women. Which were the expensive whores? I watched the carefully polite men moving self-consciously back in their chairs as the waiters placed food in front of them. Which was Mr. Big?

I settled dreamily into a contented vision of duplicity. I saw everything twice, the chic surfaces over the dry, stale mass, the vital appearance skin-tight across the unhealthy frame. Nate was wrong, of course, but his vision was the comfortable one. It was not a worthy cynicism, only a step beyond child's play, a fantasy not of good versus evil, of good guys and bad, but the all-embracing comfort of bad guys and worse. It let one off, this view, as original sin let one off, or some sterile notion of environment. No, if anything, the world was too fine, people *too* good. Who would hold their measly temper tantrums against men who had to die?

In Nate's Place it was an understandable illusion, an honest mistake. The place was like one of those enormous night clubs in films of the thirties. One automatically dipped the side of one's jaw before one spoke. Somewhere, one was sure, a code knock would move a wall aside to reveal a casino where people in evening dress gaily gambled and talked about the DA and called their girlfriends "Sister."

I did not think I wanted to stay to meet Nate's Harold Flesh. Perhaps he was a bad man, but if he were he would be vaguely comic, too, a type who took himself too seriously or always wore a white carnation or carried a silver dollar for luck. Evil, if it exists, is as rare as virtue. No, it was in making something out of the gray, moral middle ground that greatness lay. That's why Felix Sandusky, who took flesh and spun it into muscle, was great.

So Harold Flesh, whether he was Professor Moriarty out of Boston Blackie out of Damon Runyon—whether he was, as Nate himself thought he was, the Devil himself—was not someone who could matter very much to me. Horseracing, baseball, boxing. Why, Nate's devils were boys, children.

I looked again at Nate's comical room, thinking, sadly, that perhaps it was time to write Nate off as a contact. He had said it himself: I knew too many movie stars. His people were not of that middle distance where things happen. It was too easy to hypnotize myself in my friend Nathan's nighttime world. As Perry, who only held its leaders' coats, had—as Nate had. Too easy to get caught up in its real but probably incidental melodrama. Perhaps there were the things Nate said there were in the world, perhaps it was unclean. But it was the humdrum mud in cemeteries which terrified me, not the dust indoors. How little the atrocities Nate described had to do with me anyway, I thought, whose crimes, like most people's, were merely petty, merely against myself, who picked no pocket, peddled no whore, pushed no dope, did no violence. At that moment it came to me as a revelation that I was just one more good man.

I went to the washroom. The porter did not look at me when I went in and when I left he didn't get up to brush my jacket. He knew me, knew my circumstances (which in some views are the same). He expected no tip and withheld his services, one more who would deal with me on a professional basis only.

Outside there was a pay phone. I had no change in my pockets. I went back into the toilet and washed my hands slowly in the marble basin. The attendant did not even seem curious at my quick return. He sat reading his paper in his high shoeshine chair, his feet on the brass shoe forms.

"Slow tonight?" I asked.

"Mm-hmm," he said.

"Tough."

I could see him in the mirror. He glanced at me for a moment over the top of his paper and then went back to it. Soundlessly I slipped a dime from his plate of change among the bottles of hair lotions and trays of combs and stacks of hand towels on the marble shelf above the washbasin.

"Look," I said, turning to him, "do you mind some advice?"

He put the paper down.

"Cut your overhead. A guy comes to a place like this, his shoes are already shined."

"Where would I sit?" he asked.

"Well, that's a point."

I started to leave. "Say," I said, "did you know Harold Flesh is going to be in tonight?"

He smiled. "Not bad," he said, "Not bad."

"You know him?"

"He used to pee over at Lou Mizer's old 'Monte Carlo' when I was there."

"Well, he's coming in tonight."

"Not bad," he said. I pushed the door open. "Mr. Flesh is a good tipper," he said.

"There are wheelers and there are dealers," I said and walked out.

I called Penn Station. "When's the next train to Philadelphia?"

There was one at ten o'clock. I looked at my watch. It was eight-thirty.

In the end, however, I did not go; in the end I had to stay and see him. In the end an important person is an important person.

At about eleven o'clock Perry came over to my table with a message from Nate. "He wants to see you in the private dining room. He wonders if you will take coffee with him at the table of Harold Flesh."

"Yes, Perry. Thank you." I got up to go. "Oh, Perry," I said, "Have you got your gun?"

"I lead them to the table," Perry said, "but you, *you* sit down with them!"

October 27, 1953. New York City.

Dr. Morton Perlmutter is not an archeologist. He is an anthropologist, and it was announced in Stockholm today that he has just won the Nobel Prize.

Last year I followed the campaign trains of both Eisenhower and Stevenson. I'd be there, right beneath the platform, as they came to the rear of their trains to address the crowds. (It was interesting. I used my strength to force my way through the crowds. Only the old ladies knew I wouldn't hit them, whereas such is the illusion of continued virility in man that old men thought themselves vulnerable at eighty.) My technique was always the same. I would let the candidate make his opening remarks and then, as he came to the essence of his talk, I would begin to raise and unroll a banner I carried with me on two long poles. Carefully spreading the poles I would take up the slack gently until the unfurled banner was level with and just in front of the candidate's face. The message was simple. If Eisenhower was speaking, it read "S T E V E N S O N"; if Stevenson, "E I S E N - H O W E R."

The campaign failed (I speak of my own). It cost a lot of money and a lot of time and it was silly. I had meant to gain attention with the strategy of schoolboys punching little girls on the arms. But though there were moments when I seemed to anger Eisenhower and made Stevenson wistful and perhaps a little sad, I realize now that mostly I must have appeared ridiculous to the two men. They expected such nuts and wrote us off beforehand, like a restaurant anticipating the "shrinkage" of its spoons. (I have since met Mr. Stevenson and when I reminded him of the incidents he recalled them vividly. He told me that they had seemed to him at the time symbolic, and that each time I showed up a little more energy had gone out of his campaign. He seems to think that if he could have maintained his confidence he might have gone on to win the election. Perhaps he was just being kind. I am naturally inclined toward for-want-of-a nail constructs anyway, but even if I were not I should want to believe this one. I have the hard-minded perversity of the humdrum and insist on influencing events, even if only negatively, and even—sadly—against my own and everyone else's better interests. What the hell? If that's the price, that's the price. Everybody dies.)

I am the sort of person who is good at salvaging at least *something* from bad situations. They should put me to work reclaiming fresh water from the sea. I had made a fool of myself, had spent money wastefully, had disappointed or angered everyone with whom I had come into contact. Yet I came away from that foolish campaign with something of value; I formed a new impression of the great. Since then I have had it again in all its original force.

One summer afternoon in New York I was browsing in a bookshop. I was looking through the stacks of books with a deep concentration, not even thinking of my ferocious preoccupation with the great. Yet suddenly I was aware of another presence in the shop—"presence" is the very word. It wasn't the bookseller, a typically dusty, foreign-looking man who padded back and forth between the narrow book-close aisles. It wasn't any of the two or three other browsers; it wasn't even anyone who had just entered the shop. The place had one of those bells above the door, and I had heard no ringing. I simply knew that someone great was in the shop with us, someone whom I had not seen before, who had been stooping perhaps in one of the dark corners when I entered the shop. I'm keenly sensitive to the great, of course, but I have no sixth sense; I see no visions, hear no voices. I am simply stage-struck to the point of sickness. I turned around. Behind me was Orson Welles. In other circumstances (if, for example, I had walked into the shop and come upon him) I would have invented some reason for talking to him. I admire Mr. Welles. We might even have had a successful gam. Now, however, all I did was confirm yet again the stunning validity of the impression I first had when I followed the campaign trains.

It is this. There is about great men a physical presence that always matches their symbolic one. They *look* like great men. They are like jewels set off against black velvet in a bright white light. But take away the black velvet of their deeds, the bright white light of their fame, and they are still like jewels, their worth as clear among broken bottles in an alley as in the jeweler's case. Somehow, too, they seem smaller than they really are—like small, heavy bronze reproductions of famous statues. Like the reproductions, they have the air of impressive compactness. Their faces and bodies do not bleed into the surroundings as do our own; they preserve always a nimbus of self, of opaque and valuable and hard surfaces. I cannot account for the odd discrepancy between their reduced physical size and this clear impression of *weight,* except to speculate about the notion of solidity. There is something expensive about their queer compactness, their bronzy being. It is no wonder that we speak of men of *substance.* Mr. Welles is a big man, almost as large as myself, and yet, as he shuffled through the shop in his dark blue suit, the cigar he held between his fingers long-ashed but not burning, I had the impression that I could hold him in my hand.

The faces of the great are ruddier than ours, their strange health the physical manifestation, perhaps, of their symbolic immortality. Their bodies are fit. They are better tailored than we are, but that does not explain it. Nothing explains it, but I'm glad it's so; it's a confirmation of my way of life. No one need ever be ashamed of his expensive tastes.

Busy as I was following the campaign trains, concerned as I was for the success of my bad scheme, I saw all this in Eisenhower and in Stevenson. They were like heavy bags of precious coins, like treasure in firm caskets at the bottom of the sea.

(I have just thought of something. Perhaps cause and effect are somehow mixed up here. Perhaps we pick our leaders as we pick our actors—for their looks; perhaps the great are destined by nothing so much as their physical well-being; perhaps the world *is* all appearance. Is this the meaning of life? I may have stumbled onto something. I shall have to think about it.)

I was reminded of all this again last night when I met Dr. Morton Perlmutter.

Perlmutter was not yet at the Gibbenjoys' when I arrived. When I am operating on a contraband invitation I take care to come after the other guests. In that way I am often unnoticed by the host, who, after all, doesn't usually have any idea who I am. If you have to arrive at an affair late, it is important to be precisely as drunk as the other guests by the time you get there.

The Gibbenjoys were in the hall when I presented my invitation to their butler. I didn't know they were the Gibbenjoys, of course. All I saw were some men and women in evening dress talking to each other, but I couldn't take any chances. Indeed, it's only logical that if someone is standing in the hall it's probably the host or hostess. If I walked past without acknowledging them they might have blown the whistle on me immediately.

I walked by the group slowly and gazed warmly into their faces. It was my trickiest maneuver; with it I try to make it appear that I am personally known to all the group save the individual I am immediately looking at. It requires the nerves and timing of an acrobat. I look expectantly and just a shade blankly into a face, and at precisely the instant when recognition and intelligence must dawn or be abandoned, I flash a smile of recognition and overwhelming intimacy immediately to the person's left. (Most people are right-handed so their peripheral vision is greater on their right than on their left side.) I may even wink. Frequently there is nothing to the person's left except a statue or a piece of drapery. So precise and delicately off-center is this movement that even when someone actually is there he takes my look as intended for someone to *his* right. There are variations; sometimes I have tilted my head back, smiled, opened my mouth and exhaled an inaudible "Ah, there!" to pictures on the wall just behind and above the fellow in front of me.

I peered into the faces of the small gathering, nervous, as I say, that my host and hostess might be among them. If they were, my technique would flush a nod from one of them.

"Hello there," a man said uncertainly. "Nice to see you."

"Good evening, Irving," I said without hesitation.

The man looked startled and for a moment I thought I might have made a mistake. Then he glanced in desperation toward a woman in a rose colored evening gown

204

and I knew I was all right. I turned to the woman quickly. "Eugenie," I said. "How are you, darling?" I leaned down and brushed Mrs. Gibbenjoy's confused face with a deft kiss. I turned back to Irving. "Perlmutter here yet?" I asked.

"Why no, not yet. We were waiting for him," he said.

"He told me he'd be a little late," I said, "but I thought he'd certainly be here by now."

"No," Irving Gibbenjoy said, "Not yet. We're waiting for him."

"Oh," I said. "Well, look, I'll go get a drink. When he comes in tell him Jim Boswell wants to see him."

"Yes, Yes, I will, of course," Irving brightened at once. "Oh, Mr. Boswell, forgive me for being so rude. You may not know all these other people." I blew a kiss to a waiter serving drinks in a room behind Irving Gibbenjoy's back; I waved the fingers on my left hand to an umbrella stand just as a woman walked by. She stopped, turned, and pointing to herself mouthed, "Who, me?" I looked back hastily at Irving Gibbenjoy. "Mr. and Mrs. Philo Perce," Irving Gibbenjoy said.

I bowed to Mrs. Perce, shook Mr. Perce's hand.

"General and Mrs. Bill Mānara," said Irving.

"General," I said, "I go to all your wars. *Mrs.* Manara."

"Hope Fayestringer."

"Ah," I said, "the Carnegie. How's Granddad?"

"Mr. Jim Boswell, everybody," Irving said a little uncomfortably.

"Are you a Philadelphian, Mr. Boswell?" the General asked me. Irving looked eager, thinking that now, perhaps, he might learn something about his guest.

"Not for some time, General," I said.

"Where *do* you live now, Mr. Boswell?" Mrs. Gibbenjoy wanted to know. She was a tough one, Mrs. Gibbenjoy. It did not do actually to lie to these people. One hoped that the necessity for the truth simply did not come up.

"I'm at the Love right now, Eugenie."

"The *love?*" said Hope Fayespringer.

"It's a hotel," I said.

"In Philadelphia?" the General asked.

"For some time, General."

"Is that one of yours, Pilchard?" Mr. Gibbenjoy asked a man who had just joined us.

"What's that, the Love? Lord, no, I wish it were. It's a gold mine. It's actually a kind of flophouse at the bad end of Market Street. Marvelous profits. Fresh linen just once a week. What do you pay, young man, a dollar a night?"

"One fifty."

"There, you see? An enormously successful enterprise. Fellow named Penner owns it. He buys some of his supplies from us. There's a motto on his letter head: 'For We Have the Poor Always With Us.' I tell you, Hilton and Sheraton and Pick and I are in the wrong field. A chain of flops, that's the thing. Can't you see it? 'The Bowery Pilchard.' 'Skid Row East, a Pilchard Enterprise.' It makes the mouth water. 'For We Have the Poor Always With Us.' "

Mrs. Manara and Irving Gibbenjoy looked from Pilchard to me doubtfully. General Manara smiled, and Mrs. Gibbenjoy rubbed her cheek where I had kissed her.

"Do I *know* you, Mr. Boswell? When you came in and looked at our little group I had the impression we'd met," Irving said.

"No, sir. I've never seen you before in my life."

"Is Mr. Boswell your friend, Eugenie?"

"No. He's not."

"I'm sorry, Mr. Boswell," Irving said, "this must be embarrassing for you, but may I ask how you're here?"

"I crashed."

"Do people *do* that?" Mrs. Perce asked.

"But you had an invitation," Irving said. "I saw you hand it to Miller."

"It was an invitation to a *bar mitzvah,* Irving," I said.

"Oh," Irving said.

"You've not come to rob us, have you?" Hope Fayespringer asked, touching her necklace.

"Well, of course not," I said.

"Well, you can't stay," Irving said.

"Why not?" I asked. "I probably know some of the people here."

"You do?" Mrs. Manara said.

"From other parties," I said.

"That makes no difference. You'll have to leave," Irving said.

"All right," I said. "I hope I haven't spoiled anything."

"No, of course not," Irving said. "Actually it's rather flattering of you to try to crash, but ... well, I just can't have it. I'm sorry, but there it is."

"I quite understand."

I turned to leave, then looked back. "General Manara," I said, "it's been delightful."

"Yes, it has," General Manara said.

"Mrs. Manara," I said, reaching for her hand. "And Mrs. Fayespringer. I've enjoyed meeting you. Don't you worry—Nelton will get a town one day. I have hunches about these things."

"Thank you, Mr. Boswell." She seemed to understand what I meant.

"Pilchard," I said crisply.

"Boswell," Pilchard said.

"Perce, Mrs. Perce."

"Goodbye," they said together.

"Eugenie, goodbye."

She didn't answer.

"Irving. I really am sorry about all this."

"It's all right, Boswell." He leaned forward. "You've money enough for a cab, haven't you?" he said softly.

I frowned. "Please, Irving," I said. "It's a warm, lovely night. I may walk back to the Love."

"You know best," he said.

I retrieved my hat and coat from Miller and left.

When I stepped outside the Gibbenjoys' big doors I saw that most of the party had moved outdoors. Although I had not noticed anyone when I came up the long drive, by now there were dozens of people strolling about through Gibbenjoy's gardens. I took off my coat, folded it, put it and my hat in the low branch of a tree and lost myself among the other guests.

I was astonishingly content. I had been discovered, exposed, humiliated, but one can never be wholly miserable in a tuxedo. Indeed, one cannot be miserable at all in a tuxedo. At least *I* can't. The tuxedo is a uniform, like any other. Inside one, the wearer's emotions are dictated by the game that is to be played. In the case of the tuxedo this calls for charm and a disciplined lightness of step (after all, it's the uniform of the dance). Why else had everyone been so agreeable? Gibbenjoy had thrown me out, of course, but because he had been wearing a tuxedo he threw me out with charm, with a disciplined lightness of step, with a man-of-the-worldliness which winked at the upsetting of convention. If either of us had been in a business suit we would have gotten down to business. I might have been arrested.

What is the gigolo? A manipulator, a liar, a thief, a cheat, a whore. *But in a tuxedo!* Redeemable, so long as he keeps his black pants on, his shoes shined, the velvet on his collar buffed. In a tuxedo his sins are comic, have nothing to do with the cellar, the ginny room, the unmade bed. Gibbenjoy had said, "Oh, it's all right," and the General, a man who understands uniforms, had chimed in, "It certainly is," because all the world loves a prankster, a crasher. Crash is a funny word, even. It's the word in comic books when two buffoons bang their heads together. I was a crasher. A clonker. A bang-smasher. A dealer in comical impacts. A cartoon cat who lost his fur in one reel, was whole again in the next. (A joke resurrection. No, a joke catastrophe, since all resurrections are serious, all second chances somber.)

So I walked immune, eternally young, in an oddly suspended autumn, foolish, forgiven, smiling, through the garden. I smiled at the brothers in the tuxedos and the sisters in the evening gowns on the marbled benches, and they smiled back at me. I took drinks from the trays of the servants. They were in formal dress themselves, a gay servitude. Princes, perhaps. In disguise, like myself. Masked playboys. I smiled in coded recognition.

A long-stemmed champagne glass in my hands, I

walked through the garden of the Gibbenjoys, in weather preternaturally warm for the last day of October, among trees which had lost their leaves, but which seemed in the strange warm night to have lost them prematurely, like bald twenty-year-olds whose hairlessness—like my gaucheness—was just a joke.

I sat down next to a girl on a stone bench. "Why are you crying?" I said.

"I'm not crying."

"Then why are you sitting alone?"

"I'm not doing that either," she said.

"You're tough," I said. "All I get tonight are the tough ones. Isn't anyone tender and vulnerable any more? How do you account for this warm weather? What's the word you people use—unseasonable. How do you account for this unseasonable unseasonableness? This unreasonable unseasonable unseasonableness?"

"Dry up," she said, and moved off into the trees.

A youth, I thought. You can't con youth with youth.

I strolled some more. I interrupted conversations; I started others. Almost everywhere I was welcome. Once I spotted Mrs. Gibbenjoy and ducked behind a tree until she passed by. Another time I saw Hope Fayespringer. I tried to turn away, but it was too late; she had seen me. She shook her head and made shame-shame everybody-knows-your-name with her fingers. I smiled and gave her my caught-with-my-fingers-in-the-cookie-jar special and followed it with my boys-will-be boys-bangsmasher. She sighed deeply and walked away.

At about eleven o'clock the band came out of the house and set up their stands near a fountain and played while people danced among the trees. Servants were on ladders everywhere, hurriedly stringing lights.

I had stopped drinking. I didn't want to get sick. Throwing up is amusing, too, of course, but not for the person doing it.

I went up to people. "Have you seen Perlmutter?" I asked. "Is Perlmutter here yet?" "Where's Perlmutter?"

I went up to a dark, Jewish-looking man. "Dr. Perlmutter?"

"Sorry," he said.

"Sorry," I said.

Gabrielle Gail was singing a Greek song while the band faked it. As phony as it sounded to me on records, it seemed beautiful there, and I danced in Greek on the lawn while she sang. I raised one leg and turned around slowly on my heel, digging a neat little divot in the Garden of the Gibbenjoys.

"Eureka," somebody said.

"Is good my dance? You like it?" I said. "In old countrys is used to do all nights. Is ruins grow like flowers in my countrys. Is dig hole with heel once while dance and to discover temples. Like Dr. Morton Perlmutter."

"Perlmutter's an anthropologist."

"Sure, but a terrific dancer."

Gabrielle Gail stopped singing and I stopped dancing. "Is Perlmutter here?" I asked.

"Over there," someone said, pointing to a group of people about fifty feet away. From where I stood, they looked like players in a huddle. The moonlight shone on the backs of evening dresses and dinner jackets. Strangely, the formal dress increased the impression that I was looking at some sort of a team of athletes.

"What are they doing?" I asked.

"Listening," the man said who had pointed out the group. "The little Yid is making a speech."

I walked toward them. As I got closer I saw that even more people than I thought were gathered around Perlmutter. The ones in the back were standing behind others who sat on the damp grass. I thought about the abandon of the rich, of their scorn for the indelible stains of chlorophyll. Real class, I thought. I moved closer, stalking the group from an oblique angle. (I have learned never to waste an important first view from a conventional position.) I walked past them, tracing behind their backs their semicircle on the lawn. Going by quickly, my gaze fixed on the interstices between their ears, I looked instinctively downward where Perlmutter appeared and disappeared rapidly like an object seen through the pickets in a fence. When I had twice moved past them in this way, I made a place for myself at one end of the semicircle.

My first thought was that something terrible had happened to Perlmutter and that these people had gathered around to watch while he died. He was stretched out in front of me on his belly, moving erotically up and down. In his left hand was a fistful of earth which he kneaded through his fingers.

"Like that," he said suddenly, sitting up. "None of this occidental crap about beds or anything like that. They'll screw in rivers, in fields, on the sides of mountains. I've seen them nail each other amongst a herd of their sheep, and on the day's catch from the sea. You understand? Always against some natural background. Never in a house. Now, you noticed I had some earth in my hands. That's necessary. The man holds one clod and the woman another. They smear it over each other's organs when they begin and again when they finish. It's very clear. 'Ashes to ashes, dust to dust.' "

"That's amazing," a woman said.

"What's so amazing about it, lady?" Perlmutter demanded.

"Well, it's amazing, that's all," the woman said uneasily.

"There I beg to disagree," Perlmutter said fiercely. "Where are my pills? Where are they? They must have dropped out of my pocket during the demonstration. Who has a flashlight? Darling, run get a flashlight from the house. Ask for the gardener. The gardener has to come out sometimes in the middle of the night after rainstorms to see the damage to the flowers. He'd have a flashlight."

"Here they are, Doctor," a man said, handing him a small flat box.

"Thank you." Perlmutter opened the box and took out two shiny white pills and popped them into his mouth. He waited until they dissolved before he spoke again. "Interesting about these pills," he said. "There's a direct correlation between a society and the form of its medicines. In Ur-societies—in no place in my forty-seven published works do I ever use the pejorative word 'primitive'—among people whose cultures the lady here describes as 'amazing,' the medicines are always taken in their raw states. Bark. Herbs. Grasses. Flowers. That's

211

natural, of course, but I mean they aren't even *cooked*. But wait. In cultures like Tahiti where the people have seen Europeans—let's face it, white men are Europeans —but live apart from them, they begin to prepare the medicines. The bark is scraped, the flowers are pressed for their juices. Now, in only partially industrialized societies, or in economically underprivileged areas like Poland or Nazi Spain, the medicines are almost invariably in a liquid solution. Only in technocracies do you find tablets, pills. Why? It's no cheaper to prepare a liquid solution than a pill. The only reason for this phenomenon is that a liquid solution is closer to a natural form and has a counterpart in nature—water, sap, flowing lava, et cetera. The pill, however, has no counterpart in nature and thus flourishes only in a society like ours."

"That's amazing," the same woman said.

Perlmutter glared at her. "It's obvious to me, lady, that you've had no formal intercourse either with science or with scientists. Everything *amazes* you! The world exists as a fiction for you, does it?" He put another pill in his mouth and, impatient for it to dissolve, began to speak thickly, careful not to crunch it with his teeth. He had a very strong New York accent, but pronounced his words, burdened even as they were by the pill, with a distinctness that made me believe English was a second language for him. One felt he might have learned the language and the accent at two different times; he sounded somehow like a ventriloquist who had confused his normal voice with the voice of his dummy. Even in the dim light, and though he was still sitting, I could tell that he was an extraordinarily slight man. His face was clear, and very pale. He seemed indeed a little Yid, everybody's tailor, everybody's Talmudic scholar—like someone who still took piano lessons at forty. Nevertheless, his head, brittle as it seemed in the watery light, gave the same impression of weight and value that I had observed in other great men. He had the same odd precision about his body, the same carved aspect to his features, and, despite the fact that he was the only man there not in a tuxedo, the same faint dapperness. Of course, I realized, hadn't I been thinking in terms of the ventriloquist and his dummy? Of the miniature reproductions of statues? There was something doll-like about the great. Here was a new substance, that's all, something satirical and a little vicious.

"You're a victim of a Philadelphia civilization which smothers credulity," Dr. Perlmutter said. *"That's* the difference between you and the so-called primitive—only a difference of the heart. The savage isn't shocked by the world, and you are. He can believe in appeasable rain gods, in implacable demons, and you can't. You say he's more naïve. I say he's more sophisticated. Your sophistication consists in saying 'No, no,' or, when the evidence or the authority is irrefutable, 'Amazing. Amazing,' while his sophistication, like my own, consists in a willingness to concede *everything.* Tell me, lady, when you saw the newsreels of Buchenwald did you say then, as you do to me, 'Amazing, amazing'?" He looked accusingly at the rest of us. "The Philadelphia fascist mentality makes me sick," he said. "Help me up!"

Whether by design or unconsciously, he offered his hand to the same woman he had been attacking. With a terrible self-effacement she reached down and pulled him to his feet. She was not a tall woman, but when he stood he came only to her shoulders. He pushed through the crowd. "I'm going inside," he announced.

The others made room for him. I ran after him. He was going toward the house. I couldn't risk going inside after him, so I stopped him on the lawn.

"Dr. Perlmutter," I said.

He looked around at me. "Call me Morty," he said.

"I'm James Boswell."

A little piece of Dr. Perlmutter's index finger was missing. We shook hands. "There's a little piece of my index finger missing," Dr. Perlmutter said, "but nobody ever notices it until I tell them about it."

We walked along toward the house. Morty had a slight limp. "I'll bet you don't notice my limp," he said.

"Are you limping, Morty?" I asked. His left shoulder was slightly higher than his right.

"Yes," he said. "It's my left shoulder. It's just a little

213

higher than my right. I try to have my clothes cut to compensate for it. You've got to be loyal to your own culture."

"That's right," I said.

We walked along. "You know what a lot of that Nobel Prize dough is going for?" Morty said. "Suits."

"You can get a lot of suits with all that money," I said.

"Appearance is very important in our culture," Morty said solemnly.

Walking next to him I could see that his nose had an odd down-plunging aspect to it.

"My nose was broken once in the jungle and improperly set by a medicine man. It was so long before I got back to a non-Ur civilization that the bones had already healed. I think it's too late to do anything about it. Probably people don't notice, but I'm conscious of it."

"Was your nose broken, Morty?"

"Kid," he said, "I'm a dying Jewish anthropologist."

We were on the steps of the Gibbenjoys. "Morty, don't let's go in there," I said.

"Why not? Gibbenjoy is all right."

"He called you a little Yid," I said desperately.

"*He what?*" Morty exploded. "When did he say that?"

"Before. When you were saying all those interesting things on the lawn to his guests."

"He did, did he? Let go of my arm. Let go of my arm, damn it, I need a pill." I let him put a pill in his mouth. He pushed past me.

"Where's Gibbenjoy?" he asked Miller angrily.

"I think Gibbenjoy is in the library, sir."

"Come on, Morty," I said. "Let's get out of here."

I looked at Miller nervously, but he didn't seem to remember who I was so I brushed past him and rushed after Morty. He must have been familiar with the house, for he was hurrying in what I supposed was the direction of the library. "The library's always on the ground floor in these places," he called back, stretching his neck over the shoulder that was slightly higher than the other one. "Conspicuous consumption," he explained spitefully. He pushed through a double door. We were in the dining room. "Come on," he said. I followed him into another room, a sort of office. An elderly man was kissing the young lady I had spoken to on the bench. "Where's the damn library?" Morty yelled.

"Downtown, I should think," the old man said calmly, "but it's probably closed."

"Oh, come on," Morty said impatiently.

We went up a staircase. Morty kept putting pills into his mouth. "It's even worse than I thought," he said, talking this time over the lower shoulder and appearing oddly taller, "inconspicuous conspicuous consumption. Did you know that there is no word for 'snob' in any but the Indo-European family of languages?" On the second-floor landing he chose a huge set of double doors and marched through.

There were about a half dozen men in the room. They were smoking cigars and drinking sherry. It was the first time I had ever seen anything quite like it and I was sorry that Morty was about to spoil it.

"Gibbenjoy?" Morty demanded.

By this time he had so many pills in his mouth that it was hard to understand him. "Gibbenjoy?"

"Yes?" Gibbenjoy said, breaking away from the men to whom he had been talking. "Ah, Perlmutter."

"So I'm a little Yid, am I? Evidently the Nobel committee in Stockholm takes a different view of little Yids than people in Philadelphia. I'm a little Yid with the Nobel Prize. A little Yid with four brothers, all of them brilliant psychiatrists. A little Yid who earned the only doctoral degree ever awarded by the Columbia University Night School. A little Yid who's been married six times and never had to bury a single wife and who during one of those times was married to a full-blooded black African princess six feet two inches tall. A little Yid who used to drive a taxi in the streets of New York and pulled a rickshaw for ten months in the city of Hong Kong, the only occidental ever so privileged. Also I speak fluently eight European languages, and thirty-one dialects of African and Indian tribes, including Hopi and Shawnee in this country. So that's your idea of a little Yid, is it? Well, fuck you, Gibbenjoy."

"Come on, Morty," I said.

Gibbenjoy stared open-mouthed. If I had bewildered him before, Perlmutter astonished him now. He looked from Morty to me. "What have you to do with all this?" he asked me.

I looked at Morty. He was waiting patiently for me to deliver my evidence. I looked back at Gibbenjoy, rapidly calculating which of my hopelessly severed loyalties was liable to produce the most enduring results.

"You and the whole anti-Semitic crew aren't worth the little piece of index finger Morty gave to science," I said drunkenly. "Come on, Morty, let's get away from these Nazis." I pulled him with me out of the room. Since his angry speech to Gibbenjoy he seemed calmer, almost sedate.

"You were wonderful, Morty," I said. I could believe in Morty's courage though I had no reason to believe in the need for it.

Morty shrugged carelessly. It was neither a modest gesture nor sententious self-effacement. Morty would never buff elegant fingernails down well-bred lapels. His movement seemed instead rather hopeless, and I felt a brief panic of guilt.

"I thought Hitler would have finished all that," he said quietly.

I nodded helplessly. "Well," I said, "let's get out of here." A little extravagantly, I motioned for him to precede me down the staircase.

He went down the stairs apathetically and we left the house.

"Wait a minute," I said, "I left my hat and coat in a tree. Wait right here." I ran off to get them. When I returned a minute later Morty was sitting on the wide patio steps, his elbows on his knees. His chin was in his hands.

"Are you all right, Morty?"

He looked up at me sadly and pointed to his mouth.

"Are you dissolving a pill, Morty?" He nodded. I

waited while Morty's pill dissolved. "Morty, how did you come here tonight? Did you drive?"

Morty swallowed deeply. "I drove," he said in a minute.

I looked down the long necklace of cars in Gibbenjoy's curving driveway. "Which is yours, Mort?"

He pointed listlessly down the driveway, indicating a place somewhere near the gates. "It's a Forty-seven Buick," he said softly.

"Well, come on," I said. "You'd better give me the keys." I pulled him up gently. "Come on, Morty, we can't stay here."

I led him down the drive past the shiny Cadillacs and Lincolns and Rollses. Chauffeurs in funereal livery lounged against the highly polished fenders talking quietly to each other, or sat, the driver's doors thrown widely open, staring vacantly at the tips of their boots.

We came to Morty's car, black and blocky and vaguely powerful. It was the car of a traveling salesman who did a lot of driving alone and carried his sample cases in the back seat and missed his family. I had a sudden surge of feeling for its owner when I saw it. I imagined him in some midwestern university town on a week night in the winter. He was there to give a lecture and he couldn't read the street signs very well and he moved with stiff effort inside his heavy overcoat and his thick gloves.

"Shall I drive, Morty? You seem a little tired."

"Yeah," he said, "all right. You drive." He gave me a ring of keys on a dirty bit of string. There were only a few keys on it.

I opened the door for Morty. "Well, where to?" I said when I was sitting behind the wheel.

"Listen," he said, "there's really no need for you to leave the party."

"Come on, Morty, after what I said to Gibbenjoy?"

"Yes," he said, "I suppose you're right. I hope I didn't get you into trouble with him. He's very powerful."

"That's of no importance, Morty," I said. "I wish you'd put that out of your mind. Everything's all right."

"Well," he said, "I hope so."

"How about a hamburger, Morty? I know a place on Market Street that's open all night. Cabbies and cops eat there. And truckers." I was thinking of the Maryland Café. It was across from the Love.

"All right," he said without enthusiasm.

We drove through the curving, wooded suburbs of the wealthy and into the city. Beside me Morty sat with his head resting on the back of the seat and this thin short legs stretched out. His eyes were closed. I felt very good, very powerful. I was driving through the streets of the city with the world's newest Nobel Prize winner beside me. It didn't bother me at all that I'd practically had to capture him to have him with me in this way. What would General Manara do with someone like Morty? The Mortys were his company clerks. What would Hope Fayespringer do with him? Or Gibbenjoy? He was better off with me. I smiled to myself. I was a Nobel Prize winner winner.

We went down a cobblestoned street with two sets of streetcar tracks. I skidded in one of the ruts and jolted the car in pulling it out. Morty woke up.

"Feel better, Morty?"

He took out his box and put two more pills into his mouth.

I turned onto Market Street, drove down it to the Maryland and pulled near the curb a few doors away from the restaurant. "This is it, Dr. Perlmutter," I said.

Morty revived when we walked into the café. It was a big place with wide red-plastic-covered booths along two walls. Down the center of the room was a double row of booths. A counter with stools ran along the back; behind it were grills and ice cream freezers and shelves with small boxes of Kellogg's Corn Flakes and Rice Krispies and red and white cans of Campbell's soups. The whole place was lit by strings of long fluorescent tubes that hung exposed from the ceiling.

Morty seemed pleased. "This is very nice," he said. "This is really nice."

"Yes," I said. I had picked it because it was the only place in Philadelphia I knew. I always ate there.

He went over to the cashier's glass counter and bent down to look into it. "Look," he said, "Look. 'Brach's Peppermint Curls.' 'Wrigley's Juicy Fruit.' 'Beeman's Pepsin Chewing Gum.' 'Holloway's Milk Duds.' 'Hershey's Milk Chocolate.' 'Mallen's Malties.' 'Evans' Little Licorice.' "

The cashier, sitting on a high stool behind the counter, looked down at him nervously. "Can't you make up your mind?" she said.

Morty peered up at her.

"Can't you decide what candy you want?"

"Oh," Morty said. "Certainly. Give me a package of Beeman's Pepsin Chewing Gum."

On her side of the counter the woman slid back the wooden doors and reached inside. Morty put his finger on the glass to show her where the gum was. She sighed heavily. Morty looked up at me and winked.

He stood up. "Five cents, is that right?" He had a quarter in his hand. He stooped down again, and looked inside the case. Let me have a Hershey's Milk Chocolate, too."

The woman got off her stool and bent down. "Where is it?" she asked.

"Right there," Morty said. He smiled at the woman through the glass.

"That's fifteen cents," the woman said, straightening and sitting again on her stool. "The candy is a dime."

"I think I'll take my change in a cigar," he said. "Which cigars are a dime?"

"It says on the boxes," the woman said wearily.

"Yes, of course. Do you see these wonderful cigar boxes?" he asked me.

I stooped down beside him and peered into the case.

"Look at the emblem on the Dutch Master. That's really a very fine reproduction."

"Yes," I said, "it is."

"Look at that one," Morty said. " 'That Grand Imperial. The Smoke of the Czars.' That's a dime. Do you want one?"

"No, thank you."

"I'll take a Grand Imperial," he told the woman.

"Say," she said. "Candy, cigars—how about a nice glass of milk and a bottle of beer?"

Morty stood up. He put his gum and his candy and his cigar in his pocket. "You know what's wrong with girls like you?" he said. "You're wise guys. I had my eyes right up your skirt the whole time I was looking through that glass case. You've got a run up your left stocking starting at the knee that goes up to the thigh."

"Morty!" I said.

He leaned across the counter. "My second wife was a cashier," he said to her.

The woman rolled her eyes upward in what she meant to be massive boredom.

Morty laughed. "I used to get her the same way," he said.

"Will you listen to him?" she said.

"Come on, Morty," I said, and led him to a booth. He followed, still laughing.

"This place is really nice," Morty said again when we had sat down. He seemed as lively as he had earlier in the evening. Evidently he was one of those people with an emotional second wind.

He spread out a napkin he had taken from the metal dispenser and put the candy on it, placing the wrapper so that he could read it. Then he put the gum beside it and looked from one to the other. All expression was gone from his face as he studied the wrappers. I looked at the brown and gray candy wrapper, wondering what he saw. He picked up the package of gum and holding it in front of his eyes turned it so that he could study each side. He put it down on the napkin again and sat back. Then he leaned forward, bending down slowly over the napkin. The napkin might have been a slide, the gum and candy cultures on it.

"What is it, Morty?" I asked.

He didn't answer. Suddenly he slid out of the booth and rushed back to the cashier. I saw him pointing to the glass case. He took some coins out of his pocket and looked into his palm for a moment. "Twenty cents' worth," I heard him say excitedly. *"Any* kind, that's the point." The woman gave him more candy, but instead of coming back to the booth he went to the counter at the rear of the café and leaned forward across it. In a moment he was back in the booth.

Morty put all the candy on the napkin. "See?" he said excitedly. " 'Mallen's Malties.' 'Beeman's Pepsin Chewing Gum.' 'Hershey's Chocolate.' "

"Morty," I said, suddenly frightened, "are you a diabetic?"

"Don't be ridiculous," he said. "Don't you understand?" he asked impatiently. "All the candies, all the gums have the name of the man who makes it prominently on the label. *Showing the possessive!* Hershey's. Peter Paul's. Beeman's. Curtiss'. Brach's. Wrigley's. I looked at the products behind that counter there and it's the same thing. *Campbell's* Tomato Soup. *Kellogg's* Corn Flakes. Why? It's an important question. Think of other products. Is it *Remington's* typewriter? *Chevrolet's* automobile? *Bayer's* aspirin? No! But you do find *Pond's* cold cream. Cold cream yes, but typewriters no. What an insight! There's *Welch's* Grape Juice, but it's *Schlitz* Beer! *I've explained the culture!*" Morty said, his eyes shining. "I was looking for the key. I knew there must be a key. There had to be a key. Margaret Mead said no, it was too complex to have one, but I knew she was wrong. 'Go for the belly button of the culture,' I said. 'Something that's there but no one bothers to think about.' "

"Morty, what is it?"

"All the bugs aren't out yet," he warned.

"Of course, but what is it?"

"It will have to be refined."

"I know that. Certainly, but——"

"I'll have to do a lot of legwork. Research. Dull stuff."

"Well, that's to be expected," I said.

"I'll have to get a complete list of brand names somewhere."

"Brand names?"

"Do you suppose the Department of Commerce?"

"What *is* it, Morty?"

He looked at me suspiciously. "What's your field?" he asked me suddenly.

"What?"

"What's your field?"

"Morty, I haven't got a field. I swear to you."

"What's your field?"

"Left."

"You're not an anthropologist?"

I shook my head.

"Are you in academics at all?"

"No, Morty."

"All right," he said a little uncertainly. "I suppose I can trust you. I have to tell somebody. As I say, though, it's not perfected yet. There's plenty of thinking still to be done."

I nodded.

"Well," he said, "when I first realized about the candy wrappers I thought it might have something to do with pride or craftsmanship or something. Most candy makers were probably small businessmen initially. Working in their own candy kitchens from private recipes, caramel up to their elbows. When they branched out maybe they just wanted to keep that homemade touch. So they put their signatures on the wrappers. That's the term, 'Signatures'! Maybe they thought it might even be good business. But that's crap. Who buys candy? *Kids* buy candy. What the hell does a kid care if the stuff's homemade? What does a kid know about good business? Then when I saw the cereal boxes, I realized it was bigger than that. Who eats cereal? Kids. Who eats soup? Again kids. Always kids. *Kids!* All right, let's skip to the grape juice. Who drinks grape juice? Kids, right? But who drinks *beer?* Adults! *Welch's* grape juice! *Schlitz* beer. The possessive disappears. The name is absorbed into the product, do you follow me? Pullman car, Maytag washer, Ford. It's the conspiracy of anonymity, don't you see? Just as long as Wrigley keeps that apostrophe 's' after his name, he remains an entity, a human being. We see him among the gum base, the cornstarch, the artificial fruit flavoring. But who's Morris that the Morris chair is named for? Who's Macadam of the macadam road? Can you imagine such a person? Now, why should products that relate to children have this aura of individuality, and products that relate to adults have this aura of anonymity? Why?"

"I don't know," I said. "Why?"

"I don't *know* why," Morty said, suddenly weary.

"Morty," I said.

"It's no good. I can't even state the problem."

"It *is* good, Dr. Perlmutter," I said.

"It stinks."

"Work on it, Morty."

"Do you want this candy?" Morty asked. "I break out." He shoved the candy across the table to me.

It was painful to see him subdued again. I wondered if he had a third and fourth wind. What he said about the names had excited me. After all, if I had a field that was it—brand names. The grand brands of the great. I wished Morty would go on, but I saw that he wouldn't. He was tired, bored. I decided to find out more about him.

We sat quietly for a few moments. When the waitress came over and took our orders I ordered a hamburger and potatoes. Morty wanted tea.

"Morty," I asked after a while, "was that all true what you told Gibbenjoy? About the six wives and all the rest?"

"Certainly it's true."

"You'd have to be eighty-five years old," I said admiringly.

"I'm fifty-six," he answered sadly.

I was astonished. He seemed fifteen years younger.

The waitress brought our food. I was hungry and ate my hamburger quickly. I offered Morty some French fried potatoes, but he hook his head. He played with the little tag attached by a string to the tea bag inside the pot.

"*Morton's* tea," he said, showing me the tag.

"You could still work it out."

He ignored me. "Well, maybe I saved myself in time

on that one. It's too bad it's such horseshit. You see how it is? That's the sort of thing I have to depend on. 'The key to the culture.' Right in the old home town, the old back yard, Grandma's trunk in the attic. I'm too old for anything else now."

"Too old, I said. "I thought you were about forty.

"Appearance and reality, sonny. The real key to the culture. Intrigue, secret letters, what the President really said, what really happened. Inside stuff!"

"That's true," I said. "That's very true."

"What do you know about it?"

"I believe," I said, "that certain people are in control of everything that happens, and that unless we find out about them we can't know about ourselves."

"Infant," he said, "I know about myself. I'm a dying Jewish anthropologist. Too old for the really important things in the field. It's changing. There's Coca-Cola in the jungle. It's all different now. The new stuff is about the death of the old cultures. It's a de-mystification process. There are medicine men at Oxford, chiefs in Harvard Law School. You get to a place you think is still raw and the UN has been there before you. They're singing folk songs. They're not wild. Do you understand that? They're not wild any more, all those savages. They're just like everybody else now, or soon will be."

"Is that bad?"

"It's terrible," he said. "It's awful." He closed his eyes. "There ought to be killing. There ought to be blood. Murder. Atrocity. My beauties have their violence intact. It won't be all that easy for the new men. They could have their tape recorders smashed." He laughed softly.

"You talk as though you were retiring."

"It's too hard," he said. "Tuberculosis is the anthropologist's disease, did you know that?"

"Really?"

"Sure," he said. "TB and the various jaundices. I've had them all. And six wives. Can you imagine that, a little shrimp like me? I'm a very licentious man," he said softly. "I became interested in anthropology because of the color photographs of the bare-breasted native girls in

The National Geographic." He looked at me to see if I believed him. I did.

"What the hell," he said, "it was a life. If you waste it you waste it."

"You didn't waste it. You've got the Nobel Prize."

He laughed.

"You've got the Nobel Prize, Morty."

"For work I did eighteen years ago," he said. "Anyway, what has that got to do with it? One prize. I'm a man of appetite. I need committees in all the world capitals; I need clamor." He called the waitress over. "I'll have some more tea, please, sweetheart," he said. His elbow was against her thigh. "Have you read my books?" he asked me."*The Proper Study of Mankind.* Chicago University Press. Four volumes. Six ninety-five each. The proper study of mankind. I failed, do you know that? Don't breathe a word to Stockholm. I failed. I tried to get at their savagery, their violence. Somehow it all came out sweet. The worst things sounded like the acts of naïve, unsophisticated children—like those cartoons in *The New Yorker* where the cannibals roast the missionaries in big kettles. I'm a satirist. No one understood that. Have you read my books?"

"No, Morty, I haven't yet."

"'A popularizer.' That's what the professionals call me. 'Not serious.' *The Journal of International Anthropology* said that. 'Not serious.' I'm serious, I'm serious."

"Of course," I said. "I'm serious too."

"It's the impulses," he said. "I've lost my energy in impulses, but even the impulses never interfered with my seriousness. It was what I really saw in the jungle. They could do it . . . I don't know . . . gracefully. They made impulse seem calm. Not me. I still had the other thing—the civilization, the good manners at the last minute. Still, I have leaped before I have looked. I have pounced on my life," he said bitterly. "Now I pay. I pay and pay." He groaned.

"Morty?"

"What is it?"

"What is the proper study of mankind?"

"It's man," he said. "At his worst."

"No," I said. "It's men at their best. I'm a kind of anthropologist, too. Morty, you're a great man."

"I am not finally a public person," he said.

The waitress brought our check and this time Morty didn't even look at her. He poured the last of the tea into his cup and smiled. "Look at me," he said, "I won the Nobel Prize less than a week ago and I'm sitting in a fly-specked café drinking tea with some kid I don't even know. Always I get the kids. What's your name? I don't remember your name."

"It's Boswell," I said.

" 'A popularizer.' Well, maybe so. I've always been very interested in the education of the sorority girl. Maybe all my professional life I've been writing to the chubby knees in the first row. None of my wives have been Jewish, do you know that? I mean, what the hell kind of a record is that for a man who can't hear a dialect story without getting sick? Christ, what am I doing here, Boswell? I should never have left that party."

I moved uneasily in the booth. "We had to get out of there. After what Gibbenjoy said how could you stay?"

"What Gibbenjoy said. I didn't even hear him. Impulse. Always impulse."

"Morty, he's nothing."

"What do you know about it? He's a rich, generous man."

"He called you a little Yid."

"What am I, tall?"

"Morty."

"Forget it. I'm *persona non grata* now."

I was a little alarmed. I couldn't understand why he seemed so worried about Gibbenjoy. This wasn't a third wind; it was a fresh wind in a new race. "What difference does it make?" I said.

"No difference," he said. "No difference. It's finished. Impulse. Again impulse."

He pushed the teacup away from him suddenly. A little brown tea spilled over onto the table. "What happens to my project now?" he said wearily.

"What project, Morty?"

"It was my opportunity. I won the Nobel Prize. Now I could have earned it."

"Morty, what project? What is it?"

"Gibbenjoy was going to give me thirty thousand dollars," he said.

"What? Why? What for?"

"For my project. Before it's all changed. I was going to show the UN what they were really dealing with. It's finished," he said.

I couldn't think. I had cost the man thirty thousand dollars. "The prize money," I said. "You've still got the prize money."

"Alimony," he said hopelessly, "a few lousy suits."

When we left Morty insisted on paying both checks.

November 5, 1953.—4 A.M. Philadelphia.

Yesterday and tonight, the strangest thing.

Morty called the night before last and I went with him to a party in his honor at the apartment of one of his grad students. Almost everybody except myself was from the University, and almost everybody except Morty was as young or younger than myself. Kids. Mostly grad students but some undergraduates and a handful of freshman girls.

I had the impression that none of them, though they call him Morty and not Dr. Perlmutter or Professor, really like him. They are embarrassed, I think, by his friendship, and out of some queer propriety disapprove of him both as a teacher and as a man. Morty does not deal with people professionally. After seeing him at that party I can imagine him striking up morbidly personal relationships with the very savages he had gone to study. I can hear him referring, in the manner of the very rich or the very old, to intimate situations, to his four brothers and their wives, to his days as a student, to his love affairs, using always first names, as though the natives might be expected to respond as he himself had responded. I don't know what Morty's stories would sound like in the savage

227

babble of some South Seas or African or Indian tongue but I know that he would be able to put into them all his absurd, vulnerable humanity.

"These are good friends," Morty insisted to me as we watched them dance in the dim apartment. "They're my students and my friends. I like young people."

"Do you, Morty?"

"Certainly," he said. "I like young people. I like everybody who hasn't made it."

I had told Morty my story when I went to his apartment the night after I had met him. I had wanted to tell him about the trouble I had caused him, about my lie, but he was so resigned and even pleasant about his loss that I never did. For all his volatility, Morty is apparently an optimist, with that solid, purblind sort of faith that defies all the bad breaks. One wants to shake such people, to rub their nose in their troubles. (I can barely abide so profound an advantage as my clearer vision over my friends gives me.) The temptation always is to defile, to mar sublimity with some deft slash. How many times in museums, when the guard is not looking, do we seek to touch some ancient painting, to press our thumbnail into a dry crack and shatter some vulnerable square inch of the painter's immortality? I have left my finger marks on the shellacked surfaces of masterpieces; I have unraveled the corners of priceless tapestries. It is a constant temptation to record obscenities in our neighbor's wet cement. It is the same with opposite conditions. We lie to the sick man, puff some friend's failure. We are exterior decorators.

All of us had a lot to drink. Morty, who is a slight man, does not hold his liquor well, though in many ways he is keener drunk than sober, quicker to sense offense, more concerned with people's reactions to him. He began to talk, first to individuals and then to the room at large. Morty does not have to force people to listen to him. He knows so much and despite his naïveté has experienced so much that one is eagerly a part of his audience. Only when he talks about his concern—himself—does the interest of others flag. Yet he seems to sense this, for he brings out his subject in a subtle, almost deceitful way,

228

and only after he has finished do we realize that what we had thought was a professional anecdote is really a revelation about Morty himself, a confession.

As he talked people took up casual positions around the room. Most of us continued to drink and two or three couples danced, though one of the dancers had turned down the phonograph. A few people maintained their own private conversations, but these were pitched almost subliminally beneath the level of Morty's. The result was a comfortable, almost soporific buzz which gave us all, I think, a peculiarly distant sense of *toleration*. It was as if interest persisted while wonder slowly died. I had the sense, too, that at last we had come to terms with ourselves and with each other, as though we were sitting there in the room naked, as indifferent to each other's nakedness as to our own. There was something only vaguely sexual in all this, a sense of infinite availability, as though each of us had been given a kind of promissory note. It was like bountifulness in dreams. There was so much and all time to contemplate it. Perhaps this is what Morty means when he says he likes young people, for it is chiefly among young people, I think, that this illusion of plenty is generated.

"When I was a young instructor," Morty was saying, "before I got my degree, I went out to the Midwest. Maybe you saw my book, *The Flatlands*. The title is a pun. What did I know, a punk kid from the big city? Well, I wasn't trusted. I had been hired by the University of Nebraska for a turn in summer school—I've been a teacher in fourteen state universities and seventeen private institutions, five of them abroad, where my reputation, let's face it, is greater than in this country, and I've never stayed any place more than three semesters running in my whole career—which, incidentally, is the secret of how I manage to produce so much. Stay in the night schools and the summer sessions, you young teachers, and compete for the temporary chairs here and abroad. At that time I had no record, a very scanty bibliography —I was a kid. Probably the only reason they took me on at all was that in May—it was 1933—I had come back from the Pizwall camp in Tespapas on the Upper Amazon and I had these pictures—phonies, incidentally, which I bought in Hollywood one time, stills from some *Tarzan* picture. In one shot you could barely see Elmo Lincoln's leg. Well, who needs pictures? To tell you the truth, I don't even bother with a camera any more. A tribesman, I don't care where he's from, is the craziest son of a bitch in the world if he thinks you want pictures of him. He's always got to gild. Explain to him all you want is an ordinary picture and he turns into a silly whore—pardon my French. He puts flowers where he's never put flowers in his life, or beads in his nose, or he climbs into skins or something. These pictures in the magazines give me a laugh.

"But Nebraska could get me cheap, and after all I had been with Pizwall—though frankly, at the risk of talking disrespectfully of the dead, I never cared much for his system of collecting data. Anyway, even if I was cheap, and even if I *had* been at the Tespapas digs, I was an unknown quantity and Nebraska didn't feel it could trust me. Not only was I Jewish but I was an easterner, and in those days—it's no secret—I was a Communist, too. I would be again. I was no damned nineteen-thirties liberal. I would be again if conditions changed, but what's the sense of revolution if you're not revolting against intolerable conditions? I've seen intolerable conditions, and these aren't intolerable conditions. Anyway, the kind of conditions I'm talking about have almost nothing to do with economics and never did. They have more to do with the culture itself, with national attitudes. I was in Rome once—this will illustrate what I mean, I think—and I was having lunch and wine in a sidewalk café—"

"I'm getting out of here," I heard someone say. "This is just the way he teaches, too."

"—in the Piazza del Popolo and suddenly I became conscious of this woman. A big woman carrying some sort of a bundle. At first I thought she was carrying laundry. She had the thick forearms of a laundress, broad powerful shoulders, colossal legs, but when she came close I could see she was carrying a baby all wrapped up in a kind of sheet. She was young—it's hard to tell a gypsy's age, but she looked about twenty-five and was

230

probably closer to nineteen. In the same hand that she held the baby she had a beer bottle. She had this wide rent in her dress, no underwear on at all—I could see her strong ass. I couldn't figure out the beer bottle—for a beggar, that's lousy publicity—until I saw there was a little milk in it. Now why a strapping thing like that wouldn't breast feed *I* don't know, unless it was the poor woman's concession to the rest of us, not to make a *brutta figura* by showing a tit in public. I remember it was a nice day; it had rained earlier, but now the sun was very bright and all the streets were dry. Rome and Lago Torvu in the Pacific are the only two places I know where absolutely brilliant afternoons follow cold, dreary mornings. Well, as I say, she was a beggar. The kid was a prop, of course, and could just as well have stayed home with the beer bottle and the mama's pregnant little sister, but probably the woman felt she needed it for her begging. She came up to all of us. She didn't miss a table. She'd go up to each of these fine diners sitting in the sun in the café and she'd hold out her hand. Well, they didn't even look at her. I mean, it was as if this woman *and* her baby were invisible. They looked everywhere else—out of the corner of your eye you could see them sizing up all the other people in the café—but they ignored her. I'll tell you the truth. I don't think they *saw* her. It was as if I, the only person watching her, were having some sort of a private vision. She stood there with the baby and the cruddy milk and asked for money. I mean she begged— she really *begged*, if you understand me. 'For the sake of the baby, *signore* and *signori*, five lire. Five lire.' A penny is six lire, you know. Well, it was amazing. They didn't even refuse. It was as if not only hadn't they seen her but they couldn't hear her, either. Finally she'd get tired and go to the next table. She didn't seem mad. No expression. It was as if she couldn't see them, either. It took her ten minutes before she got to me. I gave her all my money. About fifteen dollars, I think. That's shit about how they'll take it and just buy drink for the lazy gypsy fucker that lives with them. What the hell. Milk, booze—need is need. After the way those others treated her I couldn't do enough for this woman. I asked her to sit down with me and share my lunch. I couldn't eat after that anyway. She misunderstood. She thought I was trying to buy her when I gave her the money.

"'*Prego, signor,*' she tells me, 'there is the child. Here, under the table, touch my organs.'

"Look, it's no secret. I'm oversexed. And I particularly like big women. My third wife was an African princess six feet two inches tall, two hundred pounds and strong as an ox. But I didn't want a thing from this woman, you understand—for me it was just another futile gesture against an endless regime of human misery. But she couldn't understand this. She sat beside me and ate my lunch with one hand and squeezed my prick with the other. I wanted to get away, but I couldn't move. I had a hard-on that big. 'Please, *signora,* that isn't necessary.' She wouldn't stop. That hard gypsy hand was all over me. Well, it happened. I'm a man—jerk me and I come. She finished me and my lunch at the same time.

"What are you laughing at? Do you think this is a funny story? What are you laughing at?

"So she took the kid which she had put down on an empty chair beside her—she never once fed that baby a thing—and she got up to go. '*Signora,*' I said, '*please.* I've given you all my money. You've eaten my lunch. You'll have to pay the check.' Well, she didn't listen to me any more than the others had listened to her. She just got up and got the hell out of there. In the end I had to run off without paying. What are you laughing at? All right, I can see the joke, too, but please try to understand the point. Be adults, for God's sake.

"That night, without being invited by anyone, I made my first speech. In the open air, in the Piazza di Spagna. Then, the next day, I made the same speech in St. Peters'—in four languages, Italian, French, German and English. I was a guest of the government, you understand. I was there as an exchange professor at the University of Rome, and it wasn't for me, but everywhere I went until they threw me out of the country I made that speech. Later I dropped the French and German and English because I realized I wasn't there to put on a show, but to get things done. The trench coats! Everywhere you looked. I tell you, whenever I see trench coats I know that Fascism is the next step!

"My speech was as follows:

" 'My Italian friends. There is poverty in your country. That is not my concern. In all countries there is poverty. What troubles me rather is your indifference to it. I have seen beggars ignored. *Ignored.* As well to cause poverty, to bring about another's misfortune oneself, as to ignore it when it happens. You are a morally culpable people. So advanced is the brutalization in your society that the poor themselves have become brutalized. I have seen beggars ignored, but what is perhaps worse, I have seen the giver ignored by the beggar. I do not blame him—it is you who have caused this.

" 'I demand a change.

" 'You think there is safety in indifference; there is none. You think there is forgetfulness in the turned back; there is none. Or, if you are one of the few who give, you think there is remission in alms; there is none. There is none. In the altered condition only, in the revolutionized circumstance only, in the new beginning only is there the chance for grace. I address the remnant of your Catholicism—I mean to stir *that.*

" 'Revolt! Revolt!

" 'In Africa, among the Rafissi people, there is a tradition. When there is a crime, it is the chief who is punished. He is dragged from his king's hut to be humiliated and dismembered. Modern intelligences balk at this practice. How barbarous, they think! And yet I hasten to assure you that there is no lack of candidates for chieftain. There, among the Rafissi people, evil is a risk they run. Though I do not advocate *indiscriminate* violence, I see in this practice a wise deal. Who is to blame for a crime if not the father? All kings are fathers. Why, the very texture of their reign is determined by primogeniture, by the ability to make heirs. If there is crime those heirs are not well made.

" 'Italians. Throw off your chains. Begin again. *Reform! Reject! Revolt!'*

"I told them that—in St. Peter's, in my classes, everywhere. Until I was stopped.

"Well, in Nebraska, in 1933, I was worse. I was a firebrand, not a cautious person. And it didn't help that my chairman was a jealous man. We split a section. Mine had a larger enrollment than his and he found out through his network of classroom spies that I wasn't sticking to the syllabus—*his* syllabus, I might add. Well, why should I? What was anthropology in 1933? The tolerance level of an Ur-culture toward its missionaries? Artifacts? Snapshots of people with bones in their noses? How many serious people were there in the business in 1933? So, to my eternal credit, in 1933 I taught my classes what I had experienced myself about mankind and about life. *That* was the syllabus.

"Now, though I was a Communist in those days I believed in God. The God I believed in was a Jewish-Brahmin-Zen Buddhist mystic who wore a *yarmulke* and squatted in a room filled with art treasures, telling his beads. You prayed to this God and he turned a deaf ear. He was supposed to, you understand. Acceptance of fucking suffering was what he taught. He bled in four colors over the art treasures and posed crazy riddles. He answered all questions with questions. Revelation was when he said, 'The meaning of life is as follows,' and he'd pick his nose with his little finger. Profound? Bull-crap, my young friends who still believe in such a God, a tongue-tied God who is not so much indifferent as bewildered by life. Go ask him questions? Go talk to walls. You can't give in to him—give in to him and you're *dead*. I wish I had them here now, those old students from Nebraska in 1933. I would take back everything I told them. *Everything*. I would use the chairman's syllabus, rotten as it was."

In the dim light I tried to watch Morty's eyes. In the dark, smoky room they seemed singed, unable to focus. "Marry six wives," he was saying. "Take women in adultery! Spin theories! Write articles! Write books! Win through!

"I'm not like that God I told you about. I'll *tell* you what it all means. I'm fifty-six years old and I'm a dying Jewish anthropologist and the other day one of our leading philantrophists called me a little Yid and threw me out of his house and I *know* what it's all about. It's mistakes! It's learning not to accept. Accept nothing— there's no such thing as a gift. It's learning to make mistakes. Make lulus. Make lulus *only*. Don't crap around with errors, don't waste your time on *faux pas*. Go for the lulus. And if you've got to believe in God, you young people who have got to believe in God, try to picture him as some all-fucking-out lulu maker who wouldn't have your heart on a silver platter."

Suddenly Morty stopped, and rubbed his hand across his forehead. What had seemed like freckles on his thin young face appeared as liver spots on the backs of his old man's hands.

"What about the chairman of the department, Morty, and the network of spies?" someone asked.

"What about him?" Morty said, revived. "The chairman of the department hated my mystic-eastern bolshevik-Jewish guts, and his network of spies were two kids, one a moronic football player from Omaha, the other a fantastically busted coed from a farm outside Benton, Nebraska. She appears in my book, *The Flatlands,* if you care to know further what she was like. She and the football player kept a perfect stenographic record of everything I ever said in that class. As a matter of fact, they did me a favor; two thirds of my book came from those notes. The girl herself told me what they were up to when I had the class over for coffee once. I think she had fallen in love with me. I think she liked me a lot. Well, it made me sick to find out about it, just sick. What was it, Hitler Germany? Anyway, I wasn't rehired for the second term, and by the time I found out what was happening it was too late to get back into the Columbia night school, so those bastards out there cost me a half of a year. Seriously, the State of Nebraska is a very bad place."

Two of the dancers had sat down and were embracing in one corner of the room. Billie Hòlliday was singing "Sophisticated Lady." When she came to my favorite part I sang along with her softly.

I was propped against a wall, my legs out in front of

me, like someone sitting up in bed. A girl beside me kept filling my glass. My hand was in her lap, though neither of us seemed conscious of this.

"Those are stupendous lyrics," I said to the girl. "Is that what you really want?" I sang. "Stupendous." I chuckled to myself. I jiggled my behind forward a few inches and leaned back lower against the wall. Above me the last dancers moved dreamily to the music. My face was beginning to get that stunned, flushed feeling it always has when I'm drunk. As the couple danced by I could see the girl's garter straps. I watched these happily until her partner suddenly turned her and moved her back toward the other end of the room.

"This bottle is empty," the girl next to me said. "There's another in the pocket of my coat. I'll go get it."

"Sophisticated lady," I said.

The girl stood up a little clumsily and moved off toward the bedroom. I got up and followed her. She had to step carefully over and around several people lying about on the floor. She was like someone crossing a stony road barefoot, and it was very pleasant to watch the look of intense, almost deadpan concentration on her face. We went into the bedroom and she snapped on the light.

"Oh, look," she said excitedly. "Look at all the hats and overcoats on the bed. Look at them all. I think that's the most wonderful sight." Bending down she scooped them in her arms and held them against her face. She put them down very gently.

"I really think that's the most wonderful sight. Don't you?"

"Yes."

"When I was little and my parents had company, they'd put their hats and overcoats down on the bed that very way."

"Yes," I said, kissing her. "I love you."

When I let her go she looked at me curiously for a moment and shrugged. "Let's find that bottle," she said.

After she found her coat and took out the bottle we went back to the living room and took up our old positions against the wall. Morty was still talking but I had stopped listening to him, though I still heard the pleasant rumble of his earnern-Jewish-bolshevik voice. I put my hand back in the girl's lap. There was a boy sleeping somewhere near my left shoe. He sat up suddenly and turned to us. "What's he been saying?" he asked us.

The girl shrugged, and he turned to a somewhat older student who had been sitting in a deep easy chair all evening long. "What's he been saying?" he asked.

"He's been explaining how Ohio is essentially an immoral state."

"Oh, that's rich," the boy said, turning back to us. "That's really rich. He's been explaining how Ohio is essentially an immoral state. Morty's a regular moralist. He can tell you the relative moral positions of the states the way some people can name the capitals."

The kid hadn't bothered to lower his voice and Morty heard him. "I can," he said. "I can. What do you think, culture isn't reflected in morality? What would be the point? What would be the point? I'm a professional anthropologist," Morty said. "I know these things."

"He says that per capita North Dakota is the most virtuous state in the Union," my girl said.

"Not now," I whispered. "I don't care about that now."

"He says people from Connecticut are the least virtuous," the girl with garter straps said. "I'm from Connecticut," she said, lifting her dress. "Whee."

"Tell us about the Empty-Seat Principle, Morty," someone said. Most of the people in the room laughed.

"What are you laughing? Don't laugh. What are you laughing?" Morty said, smiling himself. "It's perfectly scientific." He popped some pills into his mouth. "After one ride on a rush-hour bus I can tell you the precise moral position of a culture."

"Oh, Christ," somebody said.

Silently I agreed.

"I can. I've done it. Take two cities of comparable size. Take Philadelphia and São Paolo, Brazil. Now, I tell you that Philadelphia is infinitely morla, morl moral, more *moral*—"

"Eugene Pallette," I said.

"—*more moral* than São Paolo. No, I take that back. 'Infinitely' is not a scientific term. Philadelphia is precisely five times more moral than São Paolo."

"That's ridiculous," someone said.

"Who's the anthropologist here? Who has the Nobel Prize?" Mort said angrily.

It was true; I had forgotten about that. He had begun to bore me. He lived a dangerous life full of enormous, self imposed risks. I thought of Harold Flesh, who for all the violence in his life was like a baby in a crib compared to Morty. Morty, I thought, suddenly fond of him, please be careful.

"In large cities," Morty was saying, "the buses are designed to handle rush-hour crowds. The engineers create standing room in the buses by putting in a relatively small number of seats. Now, remember the thing we're measuring is awareness of others. That's what morality is, finally. Now, in São Paolo I've noticed that during a busy hour those people who are standing do not rush to take up the vacant seats when people who have been sitting down start to get off the bus. Often I've seen a bus full of empty seats and people standing in the aisles. It's a question of scanty awareness of others. Those people who remain standing simply aren't aware of the others. Now I say that Philadelphia is five times more moral than São Paolo because the ratio of occupied to empty seats averages out to about five to one."

"Empty seats," the boy at my shoe said.

"It's a gauge. It's a gauge," Morty said. "I've checked it against police statistics. The crime rate in Philadelphia is a little less than five times what it is in São Paolo."

"That's really impressive," I said to the girl.

"Make a fist," she said.

I made a fist and my knuckles sprayed into the soft flesh of her thighs. She sighed.

"This is some way to make love," I said.

"Who's making love?" she said.

"Would you like to dance with me?" she asked after a while.

I got up and helped her to her feet. In a few

moments I had to sit down. I had become excited and I was embarrassed. I put my hand back in her lap and made a fist.

Morty came over. "Are you having a good time?" he asked.

"Yes," I said.

"Would you mind if I danced with Thelma?"

"No, of course not." I hadn't known her name until Morty said it.

I watched them dancing with a sullen jealousy. It no longer seemed, as it had before, that there was abundance and all time in which to contemplate it and choose and enjoy.

When they stopped dancing Morty pulled the girl down beside him on the couch. She made no move to return to me or even to look in my direction. From where I sat I could watch them and hear them.

"I saw her again yesterday," Morty said, "and I'm sure."

The girl nodded seriously. "Do you want to talk about it?" she said. "Here?"

"What do I care?" Morty said. "Secrets are for kids. I love her. I'm fifty-six years old and for the first time in my life I understand what real love is. Isn't that a strange thing?"

"Not so strange, Morty," the girl said.

"I've had six wives. What kind of man am I? Didn't any of those girls mean anything to me? Sex—it was just sex. I'm a licentious man."

His arm was around Thelma's shoulder. Casually he let it drop until his right hand lay lightly against her behind. "I was married one time to a full-blooded African princess who was six feet two inches tall. That was just sex. After all, what could a girl like that have in common with a Jewish guy from the Bronx? I respond to a certain wildness, I think. That's a very dangerous thing. But with Dorothy none of that enters in; Dorothy's a gentle person. She has three kids, you know. She's very mature, very ladylike."

"That's wonderful, Morty, that you should find it at last," the girl said.

"I bought her a pair of beautiful earrings. I'd like to show them to you and get your opinion before I give them to her."

"I'd like to, Morty," she said. "Do I know Dorothy?" she asked.

"It's Dorothy Spaniels," Morty said. "Professor Spaniels' wife. In History."

"My roommate has him for a class."

"Sure," Morty said. "That's the one. Listen, ask your roommate what he's like in class. You've got to know your enemy," he said with a nervous little laugh.

"I will, Morty."

"It's easy enough to imagine that he's a brute, but a lover isn't always fair."

"Does Dorothy love you, Morty?"

"We've slept with each other just once," Morty said, "and she was as shy as a little girl. I had to do everything."

"Poor Morty," the girl said.

"I fell in love with her the first time I saw her."

"Poor Morty."

"Listen, it'll work out, kid. When two people love each other the way Dorothy Spaniels and I do, nothing can keep us apart. Nothing."

"She has three kids, Morty," said the boy at my shoe.

"I love them," Morty said. "I swear it to you. If I love them there's no problem. I told Dorothy, 'I'll support them, I'll treasure them as if they were my own.'"

I stood up and started for the door. Morty saw me and ran after me. "Where are you going?" he asked.

"It's late, Morty," I said. "I've got to get back to my hotel."

"Well, listen," he said, "give me a ring in the morning. I'd like to talk to you."

"Sure, Morty."

He put his hand on my sleeve. "You think I'm a prick," he said.

"I don't know, Morty," I said. "You're not careful."

He took out his little box and started to put some

240

pills in his mouth, then checked his motion and opened his palm and stared at the pills in his hand. "These keep me alive," he said weakly.

"Then take them," I said, and left.

Then, today, the strangest thing. When I got up I had a hangover. I am a strong man and unaccustomed to illness or to feeling weak. Because of its rareness I look upon a feeling of weakness as rather an odd sensation— the way other people might react to a shot of novocain.

Despite my hangover I felt a queer relief, a sense of having done with something, of good riddance. This is my invariable reaction when people have disappointed me, as though my growth is in direct proportion to the people I can do without.

This afternoon I went to the park and sat on one of the stone benches across the street from the art museum. It was one of those intense, brightly crisp afternoons that are like certain fine mornings. Ripeness is all, I thought, and wondered what that meant. In the dazzling acetylene sun I was almost but not quite warm.

I had a pencil and some paper with me and I started to write down the names of all the great men I had ever seen. It was exhausting work and soon too much for me. It was easier to put down the names of the great men I had known, but after a while it was even more difficult to decide what I meant by "known" than what I meant by "great." It was depressing to think that Morty, although we had met less than a week ago, was the only great man I had ever *really* known. I decided I was being too restrictive, unfair to myself, and began to count the great men to whom I had spoken. There were plenty of these, but how did it mean anything if all I said was "Fine, thank you" to their mechanical "How are you?" on a receiving line? I changed my procedure again and began to write down the names of those men about whom I could say something as a result of our contact. It was soon clear that this wasn't any more satisfactory than my other attempts. My senses are extraordinarily alive when I am in the presence of a great man. Frequently what he wears or what cigarettes he smokes or whether he smokes at all has almost as much weight with me as anything that happens between us. As real evidence of our contact this is worthless; I could tell almost as much from seeing a photograph. I decided to reduce the list by including only those men I had actually *touched,* but I soon saw that this made for serious omissions. I had never touched Stevenson, for example; I had never touched Thomas Mann. In despair I was about to throw away all my lists when the solution occurred to me. I made out a list of all those who had said my name.

Although it was Sunday and the day was fine there were not many people in the park. A few women pushed strollers. Occasionally a man with a fat Sunday paper would sit down on one of the benches to read, but the sun was too bright for reading and in a little while he would get up and walk to some more shady spot. Occasionally I heard shouts, and when I looked up I would see a group of boys playing on the wide stairs of the art museum or challenging each other to cross the building's narrow marble ledges which began at the top of the stairs and framed the thin, pointless bas reliefs which ran like some dark undecipherable script around the building.

I was about to leave the park and begin the long walk back to the Love when for no particular reason I started to watch a compact little family that seemed to have just arrived in the park. There was a woman, a boy of about four, and the father (Why do I say "father"? He was a husband, too.) My attention was compelled—I don't understand why—by the father. He was about twenty-nine or thirty and he wore a brownish herringbone overcoat. He had on rimless, vaguely archaic eyeglasses. I could see that he was a good, gentle man, someone who had never been in a fight, who had missed the war, who if he didn't make much money now would one day make more. Though it was the father who had first drawn my attention, as I watched I began to feel strongly about all three of them. The father had a camera with him and was posing his family for photographs, protesting that they must not squint, that the sun had to be over his shoulder and in their eyes if the pictures were to be successful. Once he shouted impatiently at the little boy, who had moved just as he snapped the shutter. He used an old-fashioned box camera and peered seriously into the view finder fixed like a postage stamp in the upper right-hand corner of the camera. He said something I couldn't hear, and the wife laughed and hugged the little boy. What was impressive were their clothes. All three were immaculately, fashionably dressed, and I had the impression that they were wearing everything for the first time. Perhaps it was this that made me feel so strongly about them, but whatever it was, I watched them with a powerful, unfamiliar emotion.

Pretending that it was an idle, spontaneous motion I got up, stretched and walked absently toward a bench closer to them. I stared at the wife's wool suit, the soft fur collar around her neck, and at the rich, thick leather of the man's shoes. The little boy wore knickers, an Eton cap, a white, stiff collar that reflected the sun and a paisley bow tie. The man had managed to purchase for himself and for his family one good thing each of everything, as in a collection of some sort. That was it, of course. He looked after his life, his family, his wardrobe, his apartment, as if he were the curator of some minor but almost definitive collection. Perhaps one room in their home was well furnished. I could see the wall-to-wall carpet, the expensive coffee table, the costly lamp, the custom-built sofa, the richly upholstered wing chair, the single oil painting in the good frame. In the bedroom their mattress had been specially constructed and cost three hundred dollars. They had a set of Rosenthal dishes, and silverware for four, to which they would add. They had all they needed, and a list of all they wanted, and slowly, piece by piece, brand name by brand name, consumer's report by consumer's report, they would add to this, fulfilling one dream by a carefully ordered scrapping or postponement of another. They would add as they went along, their way of life a demolishment of empty space, an ethic of filled drawers, closets, rooms, houses, devoted as misers to some desperate notion of accumulation.

The wife had a sort of turban on her head, and this, together with the father's rimless glasses and the boy's knickers, lent a peculiarly 1930-ish aspect to the family. But for them there had been no Depression, no war, no

243

bereavement. Almost as if I knew their fate, I realized that the collection would never be completed, that they would grow tired of it first, that the little boy would either die or abandon them. I shuddered to see them. Their substantial laughter, their little private gestures of affection seemed hollow but tremendously brave.

The father took his son's picture and then his wife's and then the son and the wife's together. The wife took her husband's picture and then a picture of the father and the son. The father changed the film in the camera, going under a tree for the shade, and then came up to me.

"Excuse me," he said. "I wonder if I could trouble you to take a picture of all three of us?"

"I'm not a very good photographer," I said. This isn't true; I have an eye for arrangement.

"Oh, that's all right," he said. "It's just a box camera. There's not much that could go wrong."

"All right."

I asked them to stand beneath a stone lion on the steps of the art museum, the child between them. "Why don't you put the boy on the other side now, sir?" I said. "I'll take a picture of you in the center."

"Well, all right," he said.

I took the picture.

"Let's have one with Jerry on your side," the father said to the woman.

"Is it too much trouble?" the wife asked me.

"No ma'am," I said. "I'd be delighted."

I snapped the whole roll. As soon as one picture was taken I suggested a pose for another. The family, contented, let me have my way. I made them stand in certain poses, one foot on a particular step, one arm touching the other's shoulder at a precisely conceived angle. Suddenly selfless myself, suddenly concerned only to help them, to fix them in some permanently desirable position, to make them, on the steps of the museum, invulnerable as the stone lions, I caught them in all possible arrangements of their love.

Wild to stop time, I ran out of film.

I am awake now because I have been dreaming of this family. It seems the dream has lasted forever. In my dream one by one they sicken and die. Accidents happen to them and they lose their limbs, or passing each other like mechanical horses in a shipboard game, they age jerkily, irrationally, growing older or younger with no regard for the continuity of their relationship to each other. Suddenly the wife is an old woman, though the husband is as I saw him in the park. Or the son is his parents' contemporary. I see their *things* age—the husband's good belt of soft Florentine leather cracks; the boy's knickers tear; age erodes their silver. I see some new piece; a hand-carved headboard for the old bed, still in its crate. Now the family reappears; they are of drastically independent ages (though somehow all are old) and are strangely indifferent to each other.

Awake, I remember that in a few years I will be my father's age when he died.

August 19, 1954. New York City.

I've been trying to make better use of the daylight hours. Too many of my gams happen at night. People meet me then off the record, off the cuff, in a kind of democracy of evening when their time is discounted.

I've been going up and down the high-rent districts —Wall, Madison, Fifth, ducking in and out of Radio City (the scene of those old guided tours; how far I've come). I've been in the reception rooms now of many of the country's most prestigious firms, and though I do not always meet I often get a chance at least to *see* their top men. (It never fails to strike me that these magnificent lives are built on simple profit and loss.) Brashness does not work here. It's not like the movies. I must subdue myself in order to subdue others. It's the high espionage of high finance, the subversion of self. Calmness is what these babies pay for.

However, this campaign isn't organized yet. I have no really firm goals or procedures. Mostly I walk their neighborhoods like a kind of rube, my eyes on the tops of the buildings. On a hunch I pick one and go inside.

Yesterday I spotted a new one, all aluminum and glass, like some colossal upended tray of ice cubes. The impression was that the books all balanced, that I would even be allowed to examine them if I liked. The lobby was vast, a marbled, climateless hall which gave me the feeling that somewhere nearby a spectacular ice show was in progress, or a revival of *Porgy and Bess* in French, or one of those concerts for children, judiciously Negroed and Puerto Ricaned and Central Park Wested, narrated by this handsome symphony conductor who explained Wagner as though the Walkyries were a kind of baseball team in the American League. This aura had less to do with the building's architecture, perhaps, than with its state of mind. I felt that above me, in all the offices, suites, executive dining rooms and marbled toilets bright as ballrooms, were men of our time doing the work of our time. It was as if the American Can Company's vision of the world had finally won through, and that here, throughout this new, light, sleek-angled temple of new materials-through-chemistry, duty and profit mixed and were, at their highest level, one.

I gave in at once. I usually do, of course, but this time I gave in eagerly, turning over my will to the will of the place, the Anglo-Saxon genie god of Western Man who folded out, like a picture in *Life* magazine. If I had spoken just then my voice would have been low, reverential, like the voice not of the believer himself but of the visitor in an alien church who cannot keep the exaggerated respect out of his tone.

I examined the directory hastily.

There was a tremendous tier of elevators which looked like a solid wall of chrome, a huge, wide block of the stuff, in which, one day, some artist, some Western Man, would chisel the faces of the New Heroes and make of it a fresh Rushmore. Looking at the imposing set of elevators I had the feeling that somehow I would have to book passage, that there were low seasons and high, family plans and excursion tours, and perhaps, despite my feeling of being in a new and better democracy, different classes.

I went up to one of the starters. "The Complex is on what floor, please?"

He looked at me critcally. "Which office?" he asked.

"Which office?" I repeated lamely. I stared gloomily at the emblem on his tunic, a highly edited map of the world with the shapes of all the European and Western Hemisphere countries. *"Western Civilization, Inc.,"* it read.

"Press, Radio, TV, the Magazine? Which department?"

"Oh," I said. "Executive. Editorial."

"Do you have an appointment?"

"Yes. Yes I do. I have an appointment."

"With whom?"

"With—with the Chairman."

"Gordon Rail?" She looked at my clothes doubtfully, the slacks-and-sportshirt-and Toby Tylers in which I meet the world. I look not so much like Western as Bleacher Man.

"Look," I said, "I'm an ex-dope fiend."

"What?"

"A junkie. You know—pot, snow, horse, shit. They're doing a story on me, man. How I had the courage to shake the monkey. You know."

"Oh."

"Mr. Rail thinks I'll be an inspiration to all the other dope fiends. He's doing the interview himself. You know."

"Oh."

"I'm getting five thousand bucks," I said.

"Oh," the starter said. He took my arm and led me to one of the elevators. "Thirty-eighth floor, Bill," he said to the operator.

When the doors closed the world was shut out. Unfamiliar music purred. "Pretty," I said to the operator.

"It's on tape," he said. "A special composition. Lasts exactly seventy-two seconds, exactly the time it takes to get up to the thirty-eighth floor. There's a whole cycle of these compositions. They're done by a very famous composer. That's Stokowski conducting."

"Is that right?" I said. "Pretty."

"Sure," he said. "There are two hundred different

compositions. It would take hours of riding in the elevator to hear them all."

"I suppose if one had the time it would be very worthwhile," I said.

"Every elevator will have its own cycle one day, except for the lower floors maybe. You can see why it would be impractical for the lower floors."

"Sure," I said.

"Right now only thirty through sixty are installed with the service."

"It's terrific," I said.

"Mr. Rail himself commissioned it. Oh, it's very sound psychologically. You take most elevators. You get into the average elevator, you come on it's the middle of a song and usually you're out before it's over. There's a sense of incompleteness, of frustration. There's something . . . you know . . . missing. It could upset you. You'd want to hear the whole tune; you'd worry about it unconsciously."

"I know what you mean," I said.

"In a creative place like this precious man-minutes could be lost."

"Yes."

"Tum-ta-ta-tum. Tum-tum-ta-ta-tum, tum-tum. Here we are. Thirty-eight. Right on time."

"Remarkable," I said.

The doors opened and for a moment I thought I had gone blind. After the brightness of the lobby and the elevator I was unprepared for the dimness that greeted me. I seemed to be in a large room of a deep, profound brown, amid deep, profound brown walls and a deep, profound brown ceiling. My feet sank four inches into deep, deep profound brown carpet. There was no furniture in the room, just deep, profound brown space.

The very bowels of Western Man, I thought, astonished.

After a few moments I became aware that I was not in an empty room. At one end of the place, at a distance of perhaps a little less than the length of a bowling alley, there was a deep, profound brown desk, uncluttered except for a single deep, profound brown telephone. Behind it was a girl, her face washed in a nimbus of sourceless light. I went toward her, moving through layers of soft, sourceless music.

When I was closer I saw that the girl was beautiful, the most beautiful girl I had ever seen. She had a face like Laura on a train that is passing through, and even before she spoke I knew what that voice would sound like. It would be a mature blend of Bronx and London drawing room, intelligent and sexy and comfortable and a little hoarse—the voice of a girl who had quit Vassar or Smith or Radcliffe in her sophomore year, and had slept around and drunk gin neat and toured Europe on a motorcyle and been in air raids and spent evenings of the revolution in sleeping bags on mountaintops with a guerilla leader who had lost an arm. She'd had poems published and once been in love with a bald, fat sensitive little man who sold insurance door to door in Omaha, Nebraska. She had gone there to have her baby which the beaten-down brain surgeon, later a suicide in Vera Cruz, had given her. She was neurotic and sick and a black-belt judo champion who could play the guitar and the recorder and sing songs in strange, unremembered languages like Babylonian, Urdu, and Red Chinese. She had sat turning tricks in the windows of Amsterdam and been a Gray Lady in a Chicago hospital. She had been stranded during the war once in a low café in Saigon where she sat beneath a chuffing palmetto fan dealing cards to a Japanese general, all the time collecting information which would later be of use to the Allies. A beat Beatrice, she had been the lost love and inspiration of poets and philosophers and kings and to more than a few men of good will who'd had nothing before she met them but their despair. She was four hundred and thirty-seven years old but she looked twenty-six.

We looked at each other and I smiled from across years, in love, inviting her to love me, inviting her to let me screw her right there on the deep, profound brown carpet. She would have let me, I know, if only the light had been better and she could have seen my eyes and

249

realized who and what I was. (That is no argument, of course. They *all* would.)

Instead, she smiled back and said, "Yes?" It was code if ever I heard code. I understood. It was the most gracious, the wittiest thing any woman had ever said to me.

"Mr. Rail," I said right back to her. She knew what I meant.

"What is your name, please?" she asked.

"It's James Boswell. I am James Boswell," I said, getting several dozen levels of meaning into the remark.

She said something I couldn't hear, but I knew that it was my name and that she was communicating somehow with inner offices, with upper echelons, that even now the name was being spoken into machines, that cards gave it back unrecognized, professing ignorance.

In a few seconds she turned her head slghtly as if in a listening position. "I'm sorry, Mr. Boswell," she said, "you don't seem to be on the appointment schedule."

"I'm not."

"Mr. Rail won't see you," she said sympathetically. It was a kind of warning. It was enough for me that she understood.

"Come away with me," I said suddenly.

"I can't do that, Mr. Boswell," she said.

"Please," I said. "Say my name. Say 'Jim.' "

"I can't do that," she said.

"Who are you kidding?" I said roughly. I indicated the deep, profound brown space around us. "This isn't Western Civilization," I said.

"It's what we have instead of Western Civilization," she said. "You know that."

"Of course." I gazed intensely at her. "One day I'll be back," I said. "One day I'll have an appointment and be back. Perhaps then."

"Good luck," she said. "Good luck . . . Jim."

"Yes."

"Goodbye, Jim."

In the elevator, going down, I listened carefully to the seventy-two-second symphony. As long as either of us lived, I knew it would be our song.

May 12, 1955. Los Angeles.

That scheme I had for suing celebrities and settling out of court was pretty harebrained. It's different for a girl. If worse comes to worse a girl can always throw a paternity suit at a movie star, but what chance do I have? And unfortunately I'm too damn big for anybody to beat up in a night club. Suing for plagiarism might get me into the offices of one or two network presidents, but there's no future in that. Too costly. Too risky. Besides, I of all people mustn't start screwing around with the law.

I've been doing all right, I suppose, but it's slow, it's slow. I meet these guys one by one and only after fairly arduous campaigns. It's like doing piecework. One-fell-swoopism, that's *my* philosophy. Some sort of club is the only way, I know, but who's in a position? Of course I might always be able to *marry* contact the way others marry money—but then I'd have to share. These goddamned community property laws are a menace.

March 11, 1956. St. Louis.

Something has happened. My uncle Myles was buried this afternoon. Launched in his wooden box, he seemed more like some object on loan from a museum than a human being. He is low in the earth now.

I was struck, at the funeral, by how lone a figure my Uncle Myles was. There were mourners—more, I suppose, than I might have expected—but I didn't recognize many of them. It seems unlikely that this is simply a consequence of our estrangement. He had been an obscure Mason and the Masons buried him and some of them came to see the job they had done. And I recognized his doctor, a man whose presence at his patient's funeral apparently did not strike him as in the least ironic. He was as professional as ever; this might have been simply another call. Certainly, when he took me aside at the chapel, cautious to steer me wide of the trestle on which my uncle's coffin lay, to tell me that my

251

uncle had been a gravely—that was his word—ill man for whom medicine could do nothing, it might have been only another diagnostic conference beyond the patient's bedroom. I remembered these from the time when I still lived with my uncle, and I experienced again the same peculiar mixture of boredom and conspiracy. Oddly, my knowledge of my uncle's death was simply an extension of my knowledge of his illness. That he could not know of his own death seemed to deepen it somehow, as his näiveté about his sickness when he lived had made that more profound.

I was impatient with the doctor's insistence on giving me the details, though I understood that it was simply the logical consequence of his function, as though his job was finally advisory, admonitory, his position that of a man who explained death rather than of one who could cure it or hold it off.

The others at the funeral were, I supposed, fellow lawyers and one or two of my uncle's strange, pathetic clients. Perhaps some were the few mysterious friends he would visit sometimes in the evening. (I remembered, guiltily, how glad I had been to come home and find my uncle gone.) They were the raggle-taggle crew even the loneliest of us can claim, irrelevant to our existences but solidly there in our lives despite that. (I think of all the hotel clerks whose faces are familiar to me, of all the elevator operators.) They were the supernumeraries with whom finally we spend more time than with those we dream of, as though the landscape of our lives has always to be filled with people, crowds, masses, populations, the tradesman who brings the bread, perhaps, the man who waits with us each day at the bus stop, those yeasty populations of the unknown, there by accident, to whom we talk and talk and talk. They are legion. How many words, I wonder, can have passed between us? How many gestures of affection or civility?

Someone said my name. My uncle's minister was beside me. "When I've prayed, Jim, I'd like you to speak."

"I couldn't. What could I say?"

"You're his only survivor," the minister said. "Just offer a few words for the repose of his spirit."

"Wait. I wouldn't know what to say."

But the minister had already gone up to the side of the grave and opened his Bible. I barely heard his prayers; my mind was full of the things I might say. Though they all seemed hypocritical, there was something pleasant, even thrilling, in the idea of speaking there. It was like being a guest of honor, or the best witch at a birthday party. Nevertheless, I didn't know what I could say about my uncle, and I looked down before the minister could catch my eye.

"I've asked Myles' nephew, Mr. James Boswell, to address his thoughts to this sad occasion," the minister said finally.

Someone touched my arm and I moved up beside the grave. "I've been asked to speak," I said. "I didn't know this was a custom. I'm unprepared." I felt silly. Unaccustomed as I am to public speaking, I thought giddily.

They watched me. No one there, including myself, had loved my uncle; I knew this as if it had been a fact of nature. And we had been as supernumerary to him as he had been to us. It came to me that the major relationship between people was a kind of reciprocal indifference. It was comforting. I realized that no one ever had much to lose. Strangely moved, I began to speak.

"My uncle and I didn't understand each other," I said. "He'd be surprised to know that I am delivering his eulogy. We always postponed as long as we could answering each other's letters."

They looked at me stonily, but having that audience gave me a strange confidence. I might have been addressing a ship's company, or men before battle. I had a sense of heightened opportunity; it was now only a question of finding out what I needed to say.

"Well, what can I say about him?" I asked seriously. "He had very few friends," I began. "Truthfully, I don't think I recognize more than two or three of you. You couldn't have been close to him—I wasn't close to him

253

myself. Yet he's dead and we must all have felt something because we're all here to watch his funeral. Well, *I* feel something. *I* do. Jesus, I really feel something right now.

"We didn't get along. Finally I had to leave his house.

"Some of you probably knew him better than I did.

"I remember one thing. He belonged to a lot of clubs. Now maybe you think that was a defense against his loneliness, but I don't think so. He took pleasure ... Look, this is a little ridiculous, I hardly knew the man—" Suddenly I felt myself coming close to my theme. I had broken off to address the minister, warning him. He smiled and waited for me to go on. It was out of both our hands now.

"Well, he seemed to get pleasure out of certain things even if he couldn't have them himself. It was okay with him just as long as *somebody* had them, just as long as they existed to be had. I don't understand that."

I looked again at the minister and he was still smiling. Even if he weren't, it was too late; he'd had his chance. Now the power was on me. Hallelujah! I turned back to the small crowd around the grave.

"He lived a lousy life. His life was shit. Let's understand that. But he made allowances and he had his defenses, his way of dealing with it. He should have been on the other side. He was sick, even when he was a young man. He had the shakes. He stuttered. He was always poor. He should have been on the other side! His resentments should have been against the well and the strong and the rich. But they weren't—they never were. My uncle thought like a banker. His sympathies were all with influence, with prestige, and he hated men of hard luck as though they had sinned against God, as though misery were illegal.

"Jesus, he was a snob! I went to a class breakfast once, given by one of the rich girls in my high school. She lived on an estate. She was very rich. There were footmen, butlers. My uncle never tired of hearing abut it, of having me tell about it. He was proud that some people

254

still lived like that. He was proud of me for being so clever as to be invited there. It was crazy . . .

"Well, it was a comical thing, to live like that, in the ballrooms of the mind. In the heart's formal gardens . . .

"He took taxis. Sometimes he'd have the driver drop him off in front of some bank downtown. He didn't even have an account there. You know?

"But you know what was wrong with my uncle? He was a coward. All of that respectable crap, that was just fear. He didn't even have a dream—he had an outline for a dream. And all the things he did, all the notions he had, they didn't help at all. He was the sort of Peeping Tom that Power needs to have outside its windows. But what the hell, he's inside his box now. See him? So what he was a snob? I write it off. I forgive him. His death takes care of that. He just didn't go far enough." I pointed to the coffin. "Ah, sap! Ah, jerk! *CORPSE!*"

The minister cleared his throat as though he meant to interfere, but I raised my hand, silencing him. When I had started I had been speaking haltingly. Now the words poured out; I said them without having to think about them. Something was clear.

"Some of you may know about me. About my lousy life. Anyway, that's the way my uncle would tell it. I'm on the make for the great. Well, you know something? He was crazy not to understand that. *We were on the same side. We were on the same goddamn side. He should have had my anger!*" I was crying.

Something was clear. I wanted to wail, to let it out, to moan and scream, to stand there and never leave, to hold this moment of my clear, strident grief, to make it my life, grow old with it and die when it began to wane. I felt a deep relief. It was like the climax of some fierce and mounting anger, when for a moment one is freed of all thought of consequence, when for a fraction of a second one is the equal of the world and the will soars like a bird in some passionate whirling flight. It was a moment of hard and infinite ruthlessness, of triumph, in which any end at all was justified by any means at all. I floated deliciously buoyant in a sea of self, with some blank check of forgiveness, forever beyond guilt or crime or

255

folly or reality, having all future like a gift, like a prince, all choice underwritten.

Suddenly men, intruders, were holding my arms and pulling me away from my uncle's grave.

Something has happened. Something is clear. People do not change. I am no believer in epiphanies. What we are is what we come to. Lear dies passionate still. We are stuck with ourselves. Rehabilitation is when you move to a new neighborhood, but some furniture travels always with us, the familiar old sofa of self, the will's ancient wardrobe, the old old knives and spoons of the personality. Yet something has happened.

Just when I was breaking through! Recently I have had successes. Such successes! Last week I had lunch with Ezra Pound at St. Albans and with Jackson Pollack in New York. Two weeks ago I was in Albany at the governor's mansion. There have been invitations. Gams. Something is clear, something has happened. Uncle Myles has raised me. He *raises* me. I learn from death. Grist. Grist and Truth.

To hell with successes. Something is clear. Something has happened. Something is changed. *They're not enough!* I have let the great off too easily. Dinners, conversations, two hours in a bar—what is that? What am I, my uncle the corpse? I have let them off too easily. They have taken me into their parlors instead of their lives.

Something has happened. Something has changed. Something is clear.

November 29, 1957. New York City.

In Lazaar's apartment—on the desk, on the piano, on the coffee and end tables, on every surface—there are picture frames from the dime stores. Inside, behind the glass, the figures lean away from the eye, angled to the upright world like any other shadows. The thin tins of the frames are gold or silver; each has the integrity of its cheapness, like some product of our youth freshly seen. I look at one, a somewhat larger frame with wide, mirrored margins down which run extravagant, impossible flowers, lush, red, fantastic as a beanstalk in a fairy story. The pictures are of movie stars in pale, colored tints which resemble the hand-tinting of those years before color photography. The lips are pungent with pastel blood, the skin a kind of grayish pink, like the skins of people with heart disease. The faces are familiar, of course, but strike me somehow as preposterous. Suddenly I understand why. There are Robert Taylor, Gary Cooper, Gable, Barbara Stanwyck, William Powell, Deanna Durbin, Wallace Beery and Humphrey Bogart as they appeared twenty years ago. Paul Muni is a young man. Beneath each photograph is a stamped signature, a flamboyant, meaningless greeting: "Best Wishes from Hollywood, Robert Taylor"; "Musically Yours, Deanna Durbin." I am oddly moved by the pictures. They might be pictures of *things*. I ask Lazaar about it.

"The photographs came with the frames. My mother never understood that you were supposed to remove them and put in your own," he says.

He leads me into the kitchen, and makes tea while I sit on a white wooden chair beside a metal kitchen table. When he opens a cabinet and takes down a cup I catch a glimpse of a strange assortment of patterns. The dishes are familiar, too, the geometry of their designs like something remembered, known always, like a landmark or some permanent combination of old things, its impression stored on the lids of the eyes.

On the kitchen table is a glass sugar bell. Its sides are ridged; it has a chrome lid that screws on. I used to see them in restaurants.

Lazaar puts my tea in a cup and his in a glass. He takes half a shriveled lemon from the icebox and holds it above my cup and squeezes. A few cloudy drops fall into the tea. "Excuse me," he says. "I didn't even ask if you take lemon." He puts the hull in his glass.

There is an open box of Jack Frost sugar cubes on the table. Lazaar takes a cube in his fingers and puts it between his teeth. Like everything Lazaar does, this act

257

seems foreign, faintly unhygienic. I have a vision of Lazaar as a young boy. He is on the toilet. When he finishes, his mother stands over the bowl and stares down into the bowel movement he has made, examining the turds. She wipes him.

I sip my tea. Lazaar makes a slushing sound as he sucks his through the sugar. The heat and the wetness and the sweet taste are palpable for him, tactile, sensual. If I were not there he would grunt in pleasure. It comes to me again how well I understand Lazaar. For all the difference in our experience, for all our difference as persons, we might be *Doppelgängers*. Even when I am not with him I sometimes see him in some particular situation. I know how it is for Lazaar.

"Do you want more tea?" Lazaar asks. He smiles, his corrupt teeth stained, chipped, like the teeth of some careless animal.

Sweets, I think. I have a sense of all the candy, hundreds and hundreds of pounds of it, that Lazaar has eaten in his life.

"'Yes," I say, "the tea is very good."

"There's no more lemon."

"I'm indifferent to lemon," I say.

Lazaar laughs. "You're indifferent to tea," he says.

It has been so pleasant in Lazaar's apartment, I have been so content just to sit with him, that I have almost forgotten why I am there. I see that Lazaar prefers me to leave. He knows there will be trouble for me, that I will be drawn in, if he kills himself in my presence. Lazaar is considerate. He is the kindest person I have ever known. Putting the lemon in my tea without first asking if I wanted it was, for him, an almost violent breach of conduct.

"Please," I say, "I'd like some more tea. I really would."

I drink four cups, five; Lazaar prepares another pot. I have to urinate but don't dare leave him alone. Life is absurd.

"Another cup?" Lazaar asks.

"No."

He sits down across from me and stares at me. I make him uncomfortable. I am rude to be there. Good—good I make him uncomfortable; good I am rude.

"Well, then," Lazaar says finally, "let's talk, then. Let's have one of our conversations."

"Why? Why, Lazaar? Why?"

"The trouble with you is that you think only in terms of life or death," Lazaar says.

"What else is there?"

"Please. You're involved or you're not involved. I'm not involved."

"Terrific."

"Why are you angry? What do you think I ought to want?"

"Age."

"Well, that," he says mildly. "That's easy. Live in a sealed room. Eat what the dietician says. Do moderate exericse. Take all the shots."

"Sure."

"Please," he says patiently, "you're still caught up in it. Of course you don't understand."

"You need a psychiatrist."

He seems to consider this. "If I wanted to be cured," he says. "I don't need a psychiatrist any more than an arsonist needs the fire department."

"I don't understand suicide," I say.

Lazaar looks at me. For a moment he seems genuinely interested, as though I have offered some fresh philosophical position. "That's because you want to live forever," he says quietly. I am startled to see the tears in his eyes. I have ruined it; I have ruined his death. He understands that it will bring me pain, that I will not forgive him. "Boswell," he says, "please. I take no pleasure in my life. It gives me pain. If I could kill my feelings without harming myself I would settle for that. But that's impossible. To continue to live would be a disloyalty to my needs."

"I should have called the police," I say.

"That wouldn't make any difference. By the time they got to me I would have killed myself. I don't mean

259

to turn on the gas, to wait for the sink to fill with warm water. You must be made to understand there is nothing you can do to stop me."

"Then why did you tell me about it? You must want me to do something."

"That was a mistake," Lazaar says sadly. "I meant to do you a favor."

"Some favor."

"Why? You've always wanted me to share a secret with you. This is my only secret."

"That's crazy. Nobody's killing himself for me."

"Of course not."

"I'm not to blame."

"No. Of course not," Lazaar says.

"Then don't give me that stuff."

"I thought you'd be able to use it, to share it."

"What the hell do I want with your death? I can't use it. It's off the record—not for publication."

"I'm sorry," he says gently.

There is a knife in his hand. It is ridiculously small, the one he uses to cut his lemons, perhaps. It glints dully in the warm kitchen. Like the dishes and the photographs, it seems familiar. Everything in my friend's life is an old story to me.

"Maybe you'd better leave me alone now, Boswell. If something should happen, if someone were to see you, you could be accused of my murder."

I lean across the table almost lazily and strike the knife from his hands. It is as if it has never occurred to him that I would be capable of hitting him. The knife skids on the metal surface of the table. It lands against the sugar bell, clattering faintly, harmlessly. He looks at me, startled, confused; shaking his head as if to clear some false vision from it, he reaches for the knife. I slap his wrist sharply and he pulls it back as if it has been burned. His eyes go dark and suddenly he seems stupid, incapable of any perception. Again he reaches for the knife. I punch him in the stomach and he doubles over foolishly in a classic, almost comic posture. I expect him to say "ooph." I take up the knife and snap it in two. I drop the pieces on the floor. I have pulled up my chair beside him. He looks at me as if to protest; he has never been hit before. He slides off the chair onto the floor and on his knees grovels for the broken knife. I kick it from him, grazing his chin with my shoe. He falls and turns over on his back slowly. Now he has been hit and kicked for the first time in his life. He seems puzzled by it; violence is a strange food he is judiciously turning over in his mouth for the texture, the taste.

I pick up Lazaar and carry him to the telephone, and call the police.

November 30, 1957. New York City.

Lazaar is in Bellevue. They are observing him.

December 1, 1957. New York City.

Lazaar has told the doctors that he does not mean to kill himself, that he never meant to kill himself. They will give him psychiatric tests.

December 2, 1957. New York City.

Lazaar has convinced the doctors he is sane. His tests show no self-destructive tendencies.

December 3, 1957. New York City.

The doctors tell me they will have to let him go tomorrow, that they can't hold him on my charges. What do I do?

December 4, 1957. New York City.

As soon as they release him today Lazaar will kill himself. They won't let me near him. I have been told that if I try to meet him at the hospital I will be arrested. He has to be watched—someone must be there to overpower him. There is no way of saving another man's life if he really means to kill himself. Life can be spilled in a minute. With a lousy kitchen knife. With a jump from a building. Or in front of a car. Or a subway. Or by running, head down, across a room and into a wall.

Is Lazaar dead? The genius? The maker of systems? Is Lazaar dead? Has he killed himself? *And me not there to see it?*

December 5, 1957. New York City.

Lazaar does not answer his telephone.

December 6, 1957. New York City.

When the phone rang this morning I leaped toward it from my bed. (I am like that. Even in normal circumstances. A ringing telephone, a knock on the door, makes me . . . not nervous—what bad news can there be? a bachelor, an orphan, disaffiliated—so much as compulsively responsive, insanely anxious to please. Here is something I can do, some way I can be of service. It doesn't even occur to me that the call will change my life. What can change anybody's life? We're not sweepstakes winners, we're men. I cannot bring myself to disappoint strangers. I have this meaningless humility in small things.) I was hoping, of course, that the call was from Lazaar. I wanted to hear him say, "Boswell, I am alive and I am reconciled to life."

I dropped the phone onto the floor. At once I knew it could not be Lazaar. On the rug, by my bare foot, there was the sound of a girl singing love songs in the morning.

"Yes."

Music.

"Please, who is this?"

"Jimmy, did you see the *Times* yet?"

"Nate?"

"Who, then?"

"Nate, what is it?"

"Did you see the *Times?*"

"No."

"Well, there's a little item about your pal. The genius. Some genius."

"Lazaar?"

"Jimmy, the company you keep!"

"Lazaar?"

"Yeah. Him."

"Nate, what is it?"

"Wait a minute. I'll read you." He left the phone and I could hear the girl again on Nate's combination hi-fi, stereo, TV, tape recorder, AM-FM, Short Wave, Long Wave, Living Theater, Puppet Show.

"Jimmy? Wait a minute. Simmons, turn that thing down. I'm reading from the *Times* to my friend. Jimmy?"

"Come on, Nate."

"All right, don't rush me. If you took a classy paper like the *Times* you wouldn't have to depend so much on your friends. I'm beginning to read, Jimmy. 'Dr. Herman Lazaar, Lyman Professor of Philosophy at Brooklyn College, was released Tuesday from Bellevue Hospital. In the hospital for extensive psychiatric tests and observation, he had been taken to Bellevue by an unidentified companion who alleged that the Brooklyn College professor had repeatedly made attempts on his own life. Hospital officials, satisfied that Dr. Lazaar is not suicidal, have discharged him.

" 'Dr. Lazaar's work in philosophy, while comparatively unknown to the general public, is highly esteemed in professional philosophic circles. He is the founder of "Yeaism" and "Nayism," two systems of philosophic logic which, starting from identical premises, lead to exactly opposite conclusions.' How do you like that? The guy tried to kill himself. Go get a college education . . . Jimmy?"

"I'm here."

"You didn't forget the blast over at the place tomorrow night, did you?"

"No, of course not, Nate."

"Many famous chicks. Movie stars, the works. Bring your autograph book."

"Sure, Nate."

"How do you like that? An 'unidentified companion.' The creep's probably queer. Watch yourself, Jimmy."

"My eyes are open, Nate."

"Look, come over a little early. We're playing Frank's new record. A premiere."

"Thanks, Nate."

Nate said ring-a-ding-ding and I said ring-a-ding-ding yourself and we hung up.

I do not miss the significance of Nate's call. He was warning me, telling me to choose sides. He knew Lazaar was going to try to kill himself because I told him about the threats. I ran to him with them. What the hell is the matter with me? I sit with Nate and gossip about Lazaar; I sit with Lazaar and gossip about Nate. I make offerings to each of them.

Nate doesn't approve of my having friends like Lazaar. He says, "If they can't hit high C, if they don't do imitations, if they ain't actors, if they don't have prime time on a Sunday night, if they ain't SRO at the box office, if they ain't show biz, Jimmy, they're bums."

I tell him there are many great men who aren't in the business. "So let them cure cancer," Nate says. "They got to make it with the public."

When I tell Nate that I cannot come to some party of his or meet some celebrity, he is hurt. He thinks I've changed. Sometimes I see him look at me with a kind of awe. It is the way one looks at an old pal who has just announced he will take holy orders. This is touching, but Nate, who is made for awe, is nervous if it's a certain kind. Still, he will never turn on me. His is a world, finally, of permanent loyalties. A commitment once made among men who do not yield their trust easily is a commitment for life. There is something sappy in this and sentimental and incredibly noble. Nate shoud smoke cigars, heel wards, play poker with appointees on the take. He has the soul of the tinhorn; he confuses graft with friendship, conspiracy with love. Perhaps this is why he is so fond of me. I am on the take. I take Nate's meals, his introductions. I give him nothing at all in return, and this pleases him. Perhaps my gossip is an attempt at independence, an effort to even the score. I notice that Nate takes no pleasure in hearing it. He thinks I've changed, and he fears change. That is why he bothers to warn me; he is defending himself.

But I know what Nate cannot know. *I have not changed.*

Boswell is Boswell is Boswell. His truth is that the personality is simply another name for habit and that what we view as a fresh decision is only a rededication, a new way to get old things; that the evolving self is an illusion, fate just some final consequence. I have never surprised myself, come upon myself unaware. Always I know it's me.

I do not want to have to pick between Nate and Lazaar—not because I would have to betray one or the other (I talk as though Lazaar were still alive), but because I need both. I am like some small businessman enough ahead of the game to open another store. If I have a new type of man in my collection it is not because I have changed, but because the old techniques have worked.

Lazaar is an instance. It cost me almost thirty dollars in long-distance calls just to get Lazaar's name. I put in person-to-person calls to the chairman of eight Departments of Philosophy. (I will stint on lunches, wear old clothes, live in cheap, cheerless rooms, but a campaign is a campaign.) Before they came to the phone I had honed the precise edge of brassiness I wanted.

"Professor, this is Jim Boswell. I'd like to put you out on a limb for a second."

"What's that?" (Exactly. *Confusion*. Confuse and conquer!)

"Well, professor—say, what *do* I call you, sir? Professor? Doctor?"

"Either. None. Mister. It doesn't make any difference."

"How about that? Well, as I say, this is probably a toughy, and maybe you think it's a silly question, but I've got my reasons. I'm not at liberty to say what those are just now, of course."

"What is it?"

"I want to know who's the best going?"

"I am invincible. Who can stand against me? Had I sounded less stupid the man would have been more guarded. But I came at him sounding like the world—vulgar, probably powerful. None of the chairmen even asked for my credentials. My name (I never falsify *that*) couldn't have been more than a blur of sound, but it was enough. Nor did they ask my reasons. It is enough when someone who always has reasons comes at you. *The long distance,* the chairman was thinking. He was thinking endowments, chairs.

"What I want, Doctor, is the name of the king, the champ. Who's the heavyweight in your bunch? I don't know what you'd call him, the wisest man or something, but the guy who's doing the best stuff."

And Nate thinks I've changed, gone fancy. Nate is a fool. I do *my* imitations too. All time is prime time.

Almost all of them said Lazaar—and in under three minutes.

I branch out. I know more people. I use the universities extensively now. There is a big market for the famous in the universities. I add mathematicians, musicians, astronomers, biologists, historians, writers-in-residence. (See journal entries for months of February through May, 1955, for October 12, and October 23-30, 1956 and for December 2, 3, 7, 8, 1956, *et al.*)

There are ways. Oh yes, ways. A ninety-day excursion ticket takes me from the East Coast to the West Coast and back again. I know more campuses than a textbook representative. What do I need? My wardrobe serves. There's a simplicity in it. You want? Take; the world is open. The frontier is all around us. Like the sky. Don't talk to me about class, station, opportunities. Don't make excuses. Show me a door—I will knock on it for you. Lead me to a gate—I will ring the bell. Walls? Don't give away your age. There are no walls in a democracy. Something there is doesn't love a wall. Boswell doesn't love a wall, but in extremity it can be scaled. These are men, just men, even as you and I. *Only* men. *Merely* men. The ferocious declination of the infinitive to *humanity*. That's how it is; I didn't write the language. (Of course I don't say it's easy to do what I do. A few aren't made for it. The lamb will not lie down with the lion.)

I rip through their campuses, smelling of streets and streetcars, smelling of the line at the check-out counter, of the supermarketplace, of the world. These people are no match for me. What do they know? They think Red China should be admitted to the UN. They believe in fairness, civics, rights—the closed shop, the Negro vote, the happy man. Utopians! Yet there is a deep democracy in me, too. It is the democracy of giving no man quarter. I will not patronize the enemy; I will empty both barrels into him every time. I will waste advanced techniques on him in a gratuitousness of slaughter.

This year I attended some lectures by a theologian in the Harvard Divinity School. An expert on God. A very big man in the field, influential, respected by atheists. I sat in the front. (I always sit in the front; the principle of no quarter again.) I let him have the first round. Then, ten minutes before the bell was due to sound for the end of the class, as he was describing the relationship of Man to God, I began to fidget and look uneasy. I have a way of looking disturbed (it's my size) that is felt across continents. In that small room, among those rapt faces, my restlessness was like something out of the whirlwind. Nothing snotty, you understand—no vulgar mouth sounds or laughter or anything like that (though I have, on occasion, used laughter, too; one time, at the University of Chicago, I laughed like a hyena when a Nobel physicist wrote his formula on the blackboard). Just a kind of profound uneasiness as though I were wearing new underwear and hadn't taken out all the pins. People next to me frowned. Some said *shush* (though I had made no sound). At last, inevitably, there was a look of helplessness from the lecturer himself.

"Is something wrong?" he asked innocently.

"Is something *wrong?*" I exploded (as though I might yet have kept silent had he not been the one to bring it up). And then, softly, remembering where I was and who I was and who he was and who He is, "Forgive me. I'm sorry, sir. Please forgive me."

"Well," he said, "you looked so—"

"I'm sorry," I interrupted. "Please go on." I held up my pencil as though what he said next had to be a note.

The theologian began to speak once more. I waited for him to make his first point before allowing my anguish to return. By this time he was lecturing directly at me. I produced my most difficult effect. There was pain; there was mute, martyred, superior knowledge; there was fear; there was sadness; there was the young man's flushed squeamishness in the presence of senility. All this. Everything played across my face like an intricate sequence of waters in a fountain.

It was too much for him. "Please," he said. "I must insist that you reveal at once what you're objecting to. If I've made a mistake in dogma or interpretation I'd like to know about it. We're all of us students here."

"Do you *mean* that?"

"Of course. Yes."

"Well—"

"Yes?"

"Sir, if you'll permit me, it seems to me that the implicit lesson in *all* religions, the essence of the ecumenical pronouncement, is—"

The bell rang. I shrugged sadly and left the room. He wooed me. He followed me in corridors, Boswell's little lamb. He kept his office door open all day hoping for another glimpse of me. I strolled by maddeningly. He came up to me in the Yard and spoke to me; I answered politely but with reserve. We had coffee together; he bought.

Eventually he began to suspect that I was playing

with him and I moved to consolidate my position. At the beginning of the next class I asked permission to make an announcement.

"I would like to apologize for my lack of humility last time," I said softly. "It is of course unforgivable that a person like myself—I'm from the Pennsylvania coal-fields—who ought to thank God just for the privilege of hearing a wise man like the doctor here, could dare to bring even a moment's anxiety to such a saint." I watched him squirm. "Yes, a saint," I repeated. "I would be bereft of hope for my arrogant soul except for my knowledge of god's infinite mercy. Thank you."

When he began to lecture, the students couldn't keep their eyes off me. They had to see how I was taking it. I was taking it like an angel. I looked like God was scratching my back.

Finally, during a pause, I gasped. He stopped talking at once, thinking it was the old business all over again. Out of a corner of a veiled eye I could see he was angry. I gasped a second time, but it was nothing like anything I had shown them before. There was terror in it, but the terror that exists before grandeur. The man could see *he* hadn't caused it. He could see, as I meant him to see, that he was insignificant there. I pitched forward in my seat, the movement heavy, strained, as though I were being tugged by invisible hands. I trembled and there were tears in my eyes.

"What is it?" a student asked, frightened. "Is he sick?"

"Leave him alone," the Doctor of Divinity said sharply. "Don't touch him."

Then, by a supreme effort—who says the will ain't free? Free? Hell, it's absolutely loose—I managed to bring across my face, like one leading a child to a fair, an expression of absolute beatitude, of a serenity so profound it could stand before Death. My face became a crazy quilt of intelligent joy. I looked exactly like someone who could do the job, taking instructions that weren't to be questioned. I nodded gravely.

"I think he hears something," a student whispered hoarsely.

My eyes opened slowly. They rolled up into my skull and my lips parted. Then I slumped back in my chair exhausted. It was over.

I shook myself. I pulled myself together. I looked around. I smiled compassionately, bravely. I looked at the Doctor of Divinity sadly, as if I knew his fate. (I do!)

"What was it?" he said.

I stood up.

"What was it?" he asked again.

"I am not at liberty to say," I said, and left the room.

As a matter of fact, this religion thing has taken a good deal of my time lately. Just a few weeks ago I read about a miracle rabbi who lives in the orthodox Jewish community in Williamsburg, and I went to find him. It was very strange.

The lights shone redundantly from the windows of the apartment buildings even at noon, vaguely like some kind of public act, a candle-lighting ceremony in a large stadium, or perhaps some wartime measure. On one side of the street where municipal signs warned no parking was allowed on Saturdays, the curb was lined solidly with cars. Each had been ticketed. I thought of ancient taxes, old impositions. I seemed to be in a place under siege, where heroism was communal, vaguely timid. There was no life in the shops; the streets were deserted. Occasionally, in doorways, I saw clusters of old men in dark gabardine, their faces shadowed under black, wide hats. They seemed to add weight to the aura of helpless conspiracy about the place. As I went by they stopped talking to watch me. I might have been a centurion, some Roman fop. When I had passed they spoke again, talking in Yiddish. Arguing, quietly indignant with one another in the street, they had the air of persons anxious in minor causes.

In the apartment building I rang the rabbi's bell. There was no answer. When I came out a group of old men was standing about outside the building.

"Where do I find the rabbi?" I asked one.

"It's funny. To me you don't look Jewish."

270

"I'm looking for the miracle rabbi."

"Italian he looks."

"Italian looks Jewish. He don't look Jewish."

"But he looks for the rabbi."

"To hit him on the head. See his size? Since when is a big one like that friendly?"

"It couldn't happen."

"I have to see the rabbi," I said.

"Take advice. You don't appear stupid. Listen to me. Don't look for no miracle rabbis. Don't seek to know mysteries which are beyond even big-shot Talmudic scholars," said the first man.

"Do you need from a miracle rabbi in America? In America is Nature. Nature and Time. Let them take their courses."

"You couldn't go wrong."

"I called his home. He doesn't answer," I said.

"On *Shabbos* he should come to the telephone? That *would be* a miracle. Am I wrong, Traub?"

"That would *tahkee* be a miracle," Traub said.

"Tell him. Don't pull him apart," a tall od man said.

"Tell him yourself," Traub said.

"This miracle worker you mention, this Jewish magician you seek to find, he is the Rabbi Oliver Messerman? The same Rabbi Oliver Messerman who makes the old women and the young girls and the children crazy with his hocus-pocus dominocus and his chants from the Cabala?"

"The fella written up in the *World-Telegram?*" another said.

"He don't look Jewish to me, Rabbi Messerman," the first man said.

"Yes," I said. "Rabbi Messerman."

"Let me ask you a question, young man. Where would a rabbi be on the Sabbath?"

"In the temple?" I said.

"The *shul,* he says."

"Reasonable but incorrect," the tall man said.

"Where is he, then? Please, I have to find him. It's a matter of life or death." It was a strange phrase. It thrilled me to say it, as shouting "Remain calm" in a burning theater might have thrilled me. Even as I said it I thought of all the times it had been spoken to telephone operators, to policemen, to airlines reservations clerks—always somehow to strangers. It underwrote one's need. *Emergency* was a password, a universal language. Yet all those times it had been said, just as now, there was something spurious in it, as though the language of urgency undercut urgency, as though it was understood that it could never be *our* life, *our* death.

Perhaps they heard the evasion. "Life and death?" one said.

"A very important matter," Traub said.

"We are his congregation," the first man said.

"His *minyan*."

"He is our spiritual leader forward march," Traub said.

"A Messiah."

"King of the Jews."

"God's small son."

"All right," I said, "where is he?"

"In his house is where he is," the tall man said.

"You can see him through the window. He stands in a white sheet and makes prayers for the world. Go, you'll see."

"See? He'll hear."

"Three days this time."

"Messerman," Traub called, "it's enough already!"

"Where?" I asked. The man pointed to a basement window.

I went to the window. It was barred and screened, and only about a third of it was above the street. I squatted on the pavement and looked in. Through a crack I could see someone moving about. I went back to the men. "He didn't answer when I rang the buzzer before. Is it broken?"

"What broken? Can a miracle rabbi that gets pilgrims from all over afford to have a broken buzzer? If he doesn't answer it's because it's *Shabbos*."

"Listen," someone said seriously, "he's crazy. He's a very crazy person. For three days we need him for services in the *shul*."

"He knows we're here," another said. "Don't kid yourself."

"Some miracle rabbi."

"Some *rabbi,*" Traub said.

"If you ask me, Messerman don't look Jewish," the first man said.

"Why don't you get rid of him?" I asked.

"There's a law," one of them said. "A rabbi is like a captain on a ship. You can't go up to a captain on a ship and say, 'We don't like the way you're running the ship. You're not the captain no more.' This is a mutiny, you understand. You must make first a report to Cincinnati."

"Are you from Cincinnati?" one of them asked excitedly. "Maybe he's from Yeshiva in Cincinnati to question the rabbi."

"Him?"

"I'll tell you the truth I never seen him in the neighborhood."

"Excuse me but he don't look Jewish," the first man said.

"Nobody looks Jewish to you, Plotman. How is that?"

"Excuse me but that's not true," Plotman said.

"Yeah? Yeah? Name one person who looks Jewish to you. Name one."

"You look a little Jewish to me," Plotman said.

"Are you from Cincinnati?" the tall man asked me.

"No."

I moved away from the men and entered the building a second time. A card by the bell listed Messerman's name but didn't give his apartment number. I tried the hall door, knowing it was locked. I went back to the mailboxes, found the superintendent's bell and pressed it. In three minutes I went back outside. "Look," I told the men, "the super doesn't answer."

"It's *Shabbos,*" one of the men said.

"Well, is there anyone in the damn building who isn't Jewish?"

"In this neighborhood, young man, you're the only one isn't Jewish."

"There's Mrs. Helferman on six," Traub said. He

273

turned to me. "She's Jewish, but she lost her husband and her son on the same day in two different car accidents. Maybe *she* would press the buzzer."

"Yeah, yeah, Mrs. Helferman," the tall man said.

I rushed back into the building. One of the name-plates said "Marvin Helferman"; I pressed the button. The men came inside to watch. In a moment I heard a voice through the speaking tube.

"If you're look for Marvin Helferman," it said, "he's dead eight months Tuesday. His son Joe ain't alive either. This is Bess."

"I knew she would," one of the men said behind me.

"Apostate," said another.

"Bess," I said, "ring the bell. I must get inside."

"Do you mean to rob me?"

"No. Please, Bess. I'm an honest man." This is ridiculous, I thought; this is the most ridiculous thing that has ever happened to me.

"How do I know you don't mean to rape me?" Bess asked.

"Rape her?" Traub said. "She should live so long."

"I'm a widow. My husband and son, *alla sholem,* are dead. The one lays in Portland in Oregon I didn't have what to ship back his body. Robbers. Marvin came back from Chicago on the train. Did you ever hear? I didn't go to my own son's funeral." Her voice over the speaking tube was broken, her sobs lost in the brassy static.

"Bess, please. I have to get inside to see the rabbi. He won't answer the ring." I turned to the men. "Does she know any of you?"

"Sure. Marvin was a good friend."

"Bess," I said, "there are some men here who could vouch for me." I looked at the men. "Tell her it's all right."

The old men looked at each other uneasily. "It's a sin," one of them said shyly.

"I dassn't," another said.

"It's *Shabbos,*" said someone else.

"Superstitious old men," Traub said scornfully. "You expect superstitious old men to help you?" He

274

moved two or three steps closer to the speaking tube. He was still half the distance between it and the door. "I say the young man is all right," he said, raising his voice. "Traub says Bess ought to ring the bell." He was almost shouting in the small hallway.

Another came up beside Traub. "Al Frickler says so too."

"Al, do you miss Marvin?" Bess' voice said.

"Everybody misses Marvin," Frickler said. Though he was shouting he managed to make it sound kind.

The buzzer sounded brokenly, like a machine gun in the distance. I rushed to the door before it stopped.

"Which apartment number?"

The men shrugged.

I took the elevator down to the basement. When the door opened I was near the incinerator. Two day's garbage was piled high in the bin; there were empty wine bottles, chicken bones, the rinds of oranges. I moved through the corridor trying to orient myself with the window outside the building.

I knocked on a door. "Who?" someone said immediately.

The abrupt response startled me. Throughout the building people seemed not so much celebrating or observing the day as besieged by it. I could see them in their apartments, in the redundant glare of the unnecessary electric, not answering their phones, their bells, not using machinery, not resting so much as marking time until the sun went down.

"Rabbi Messerman's apartment?"

"Further down."

"To my left? My right?"

"Further down."

I continued in the direction I had been going in. I saw a *mazuzah,* the prayer cylinder, nailed to the doorway like a tin whistle. When I put my ear against the door I could hear a voice.

I knocked. "Rabbi Messerman," I called. "I'm James Boswell." The voice inside stopped. "Rabbi Messerman, let me in. I'm James Boswell and I'm here to find out the meaning of life."

The little metal loop slid aside and I saw an eye stare out at me. I had an impulse to push my finger through the hole and touch it.

"What do you want?"

"I'm James Boswell and I want to learn the meaning of life. Let me in."

The eye jiggled up and down behind the fixed peephole on the door. It was as though the pupil were somehow loose inside the eye socket.

The door was opened by a man dressed in a dirty white silk robe which hung in loose, heavy folds about his body. On his head was a white skullcap. I was startled to see that he was barefoot.

There were pictures everywhere, as in Lazaar's apartment. Faces I had never seen but which were somehow familiar stared out of ten-cent-store frames. They were the relatives that should have been behind Lazaar's frames, the cousins and fathers and uncles and brothers and mothers and aunts and grandparents and sisters, their faces stretching away in time to the very beginnings of photography. In strange ways, behind the alien fashions and notions of cosmetic, a queer resemblance emerged—as though they had all been painted by someone who had found his "style." They offered a weird, elaborate genetic testimony. A certain shadow beneath an old woman's eye would suddenly appear in some young boy, or a chin, like some flesh heirloom, made its way down the generations, sometimes recessive, sometimes dominant, as though it reflected the fortunes and attitudes of its successive owners much as a proper legacy, a house perhaps, might go through periods of repair or disrepair depending on the diligence and luck of its inhabitants. I much preferred Lazaar's pictures—movie stars, pastless, ghostless, one-shot beings who dwelled in an eternal present, like gods who sprang from some private conception of themselves. It was difficult to imagine that the rabbi and I were both men, that we were both human beings. He, so famiilied, so clearly the sum of his parts, related to the past as a model of one year's automobile is related to a model of the next. At least I was not the incarnate nose, ears, hands, mouth

276

of some primal Boswellian despot. Or at least I had been spared the knowledge. Who we didn't know didn't hurt us.

I remembered a greeting card I had once gotten from a school friend when I was still wrestling. It was one of those cards which celebrates no particular occasion but pops out at you every once in a while in the mail as a sudden windfall of contact. It was cheery, bright, the kind of card a man could decently send to another man, with a cartoon drawing of "The Thinker." Inside were big inky letters that said "JUST THINKING OF YOU," and beneath the greeting my friend had written a small note. "Caught you on TV last night in a wrestling match and couldn't help remembering those wonderful days as kids together. My best wishes to you in your new career. May good fortune and health be with you always." There was something touching in the message, but I remember feeling crowded, bullied. It was as though I were being asked to value what I had never valued. A sales technique, another piece of junk mail—you could send it without sealing the envelope and it would cost you a penny less for the stamp.

I considered what it would be like to have brothers, parents, to nuzzle in the bounty of breasts, to sit on laps, be taught to suck sugar. There were only so many ways to die. You took your choice—that was what the will was for. For some people, for myself, the past made no difference; it was beside the point, like my friend's declaration. There were some—some? we were legion—who neither made fortunes nor inherited them, congenital third sons of the woodchopper.

"Rabbi," I said, "I don't trust all this lace, that aunt's nose repeated generation after generation. What *is* your cabalistic chant, 'Auld Lang Syne'?"

"What do you want?" he asked, frightened. A loose nerve like some secretive, subterrestrial animal, slid under the surface of his skin. It was like watching the slow uncoiling of a whip. Like so many things recently, it was familiar.

"Well, I was in the neighborhood," I said.

277

He looked at me blankly.

"Well, I'm a Baptist, don't you get it? I'm making my ecumenical call."

"Please," he said.

"Oh, come on. I'm a Methodist, a Roman Catholic, a Christian Scientist. I'm Episcopalian, Lutheran, a Church of Christ man. Some of the Eastern things."

He looked at me curiously.

"It's true," I said. "I'm a converter. I join everything. Always willing to take a little instruction. Come on now, tell me, what's the meaning of life?"

"What do you want?"

"What I said. I've been becoming everything. It may be hereditary. Perhaps I got the notion from my Uncle Myles' charge accounts that he never used." I started to tell him about the time, a year before, when I had gone into one of the confessional booths in St. Patrick's Cathedral. It was outrageous.

I had gone into the confessional and pressed the buzzer for the priest. When I heard him enter through the other side and slide back the grill, something indescribable came over me. (It was this that I had forgotten, that even then the experience had been meaningful, not a prank.) When I realized that there was really a priest there, not an impostor like myself, there was nothing to do but what he expected of me. I began to tell him about my life. I had never been in a confessional before. I wasn't a Roman Catholic at the time; I knew nothing about the forms, the language.

After a while the priest interrupted me. "But what sin have you to confess?" he demanded.

"I'm telling you, Father."

"No. You must be direct. You must be honest," he said. "When did you make your last confession?"

"Well, I've never made one. I've never made a confession before. I never have."

"Are you Catholic?" he asked me angrily.

"Well, I have a soul, Father."

I thought he would melt or something at the mention of the word, but all he did was ask again if I were

Catholic. I was afraid that he would leave me there alone if I admitted I wasn't, so I lied.

"Please get on with it," he said.

"We'll be here all afternoon, Father, it looks like," I said, and I started to tell him again about my life. I told him about Herlitz and the wrestling and about Perlmutter and Lome and all the others, how I had extorted contact from them, and about the things that had happened to me. I told him about what I believed and how important it was for me not to die. At first he didn't seem very interested, but as I went on I could sense an attention even in his silence. Every once in a while when I mentioned some famous person he would say, "You know *him?*" or "Really?" and I could see that he was impressed. It was odd. I knew that for him none of this, even his hearing my confession, had anything to do with religion or with his function as a priest, whereas for me the experience was more solemn than anything that had ever happened to me. We get different things from each other.

After I had finished I asked him my question. I asked him where the sin was.

He wasn't very interested, I think, and he told me that it might be a good idea if I saw a psychiatrist.

"Come on, Father," I said, "there's a sin there someplace. Don't push me off onto a psychiatrist."

"God forgives your sins."

"Yes, I know that. But what are they? What good is it if I don't understand what God is forgiving? Shouldn't I have some idea about that?"

He thought about this for a while. I don't think he was trying to get rid of me. What he had heard must have sounded insane to him, but I think he also realized that there was something wrong somewhere, wrong in *his* sense. But he just couldn't cope with me. He'd been trained to deal with masturbators and adulterers and the profane and the various larcenies—to transmit forgiveness, not to recognize sin. What did he know about sin? He dealt with those who had yielded to temptation, who had coddled their flesh, who had been temporarily deliv-

279

ered from the deceptive needs, had fought it out on their body's battleground and lost. Finally he coughed and said something I couldn't hear.

"What was that, Father?"

"Misrepresentation," he said.

"No," I said. "I don't think so. Of course I've told many lies, but I've been more honest with others, even about myself, than most people are."

"Desire, then," he said. He was really interested now.

"Well, maybe——"

"The failure to acknowledge God," he said.

"No, Father."

"Pride."

"Father, I stink."

It went on like that, neither of us able to put our finger on it.

"Father?" I said at last.

"Yes?"

"Father, I think—this may sound crazy—"

"What is it?"

"Well, it's just an idea . . . ."

"Yes, what is it?"

"I think you better go get the Cardinal."

The rabbi stood barefoot on the uncarpeted floor glaring at me. He seemed wild and tough. I stared at his feet, pale and rough on the smooth brown wood, the toenails chipped and incredibly filthy. It was as if he had crossed deserts, knelt by streams, lived on nuts. (I thought of the old wrestling days. In his robe and skull-cap, barefoot, the rabbi might have been in disguise for a match. It might have been another identity, like The Masked Playboy or The Grim Reaper. For me there had always been something more ferociously real about those identities than false. The Wild Men *were* wild, the bad guys bad, the good guys good.)

"There are prayers," he said hoarsely.

"Come on," I said, "it's a joke. Pleased to have met you."

"There are prayers," he said again.

"Come on," I said. "For what?"

"For your sin. That the priest couldn't tell you about. There are prayers." He put his hand on my face suddenly and began to chant.

"Hey, cut it out," I said.

He was swaying in front of me now, as if I were an altarpiece.

"Now cut it out," I said again. "Just stop it."

He put his arms around me and pulled me forward and pushed me back to the rhythm of his chant. I felt tight, heavy, blocked, impossibly like some sentient trunk in an attic, filled with things no one would ever use. Suddenly he roared the word *"dibbuk"* and began to beat my breast.

"Why, you old-timey Polish man. *Dibbuks,* is it? So *that's* the meaning of life. Soul infesters, spirtual viruses, termites in the heart's old woodwork." I pulled away from him. "Enough's enough, Rabbi. Pleased to have met you." As I stepped out the door, instinctively I kissed my finger and touched it to the *mazuzah* in exactly the way I had read somewhere that Jews do.

My techniques grow increasingly desperate and bizarre. What is it? Why? I begin to break through. I begin to know the famous. I begin to see them a second time, a third. I am young; I am a young man. How many young men have the lists I have? Yet I become extravagant, bolder, wilder, as though I were without the glands of shame. I am driven to outrages of the spirit. I plunder. I rape. A barbarian of the better neighborhoods, somehow my own victim, too. There is in me a kind of prurience—not sexual, a misappropriated lust, misinformed. I am at large, a subversive in the suburbs. It is startling that I have not been arrested, that I do not languish in jail, that civilization has not brought charges.

Sometimes, when I pass policemen, I feel like dropping little notes in crayon saying, "Catch me before it's too late!"

Lano's incredible sources of supply continue to amaze me. Today a plane with Polish markings landed at the airstrip here. The Chinese pilot had a Maori, a Greek, two Canadians, an Egyptian, a Sherpa and a Pakistani with him.

Lano greeted the others warmly but was furious when he saw the Pakistani. "This man weighs only eight stone," he shouted. "He weighs only eight stone. Where's my Turk? I was promised a Turk. How can I make an international revolution if I have no Turk?" He turned to me. "In his country is the famine so to here he comes. Already I feed nine Pakistanis. To make a revolution with so much Pakistanis is very bad." He turned to the Chinese pilot. "Where is my Turk?"

Although he had been flying a DC-6, the man wore enormous pilot's goggles over his eyes. The lenses were faintly steamy and behind them his pupils looked like some weird seafood. He stared at Lano sadly.

"Get him to say," Lano demanded of Dr. Mud.

Dr. Mud said something to the pilot in Chinese.

"This is unnecessary," the pilot suddenly replied in English. "No Turk could be found. Perhaps next trip. There is a Turk in London who has expressed interest."

Lano sighed wearily. "I go in the plane," he said. He climbed into the DC-6 and we heard him moving around inside, shoving aside the heavy wooden crates. "Machine guns," he shouted. "Hands gren*ades*. Revolvers. Where are my automatic rifles? Never mind, I see them." He stood in the doorway. "Where are the magazines?"

"With the rifles," the Chinese pilot said.

"Not *those* magazines. The *magazines*. The press."

"There's just this," the pilot said. From his flying jacket he produced a copy of *Time* and handed it up. Lano took it eagerly and sat down in the cabin of the plane and began to thumb through it very rapidly. "Two paragraphs," he said dejectedly and stood up. "Here," he said, "Boswell, from your native land." He threw the magazine to me.

Tonight, in my tent, I have been reading it. It is the issue of May fifteenth, but I've been in the mountains since early April. As I read each of the departments—*The Nation, The Hemisphere, The World, People*—I began to compose a letter to the editor:

Sir:

We here at The Revolution don't get much chance to hear about what's happening to People back in The Nation. We're kept pretty busy making over The World. Then, too, we don't often have the opportunity to see The Press, and so miss out on the latest developments in Art, Books, Cinema, Education, Medicine, Religion, Science, Sport and Milestones. So, believe me, when even an old copy of *TIME* comes through it's pretty well thumbed, believe me . . .

I was having a pretty good time. Toward the back, in *U.S. Business,* there was a picture of William Lome, and I started to read the story. It spoke of Lome glowingly, recounting anecdotes which, despite their familiarity, were interesting, but somehow I couldn't see the point of the article. It was only after I had almost finished it that I realized that it was an obituary and that William Lome is dead.

Uncle Myles. Lome. Lazaar. Turnover, turnover. Herlitz. Turnover. My parents. *Turnover. Turnover. Turnover.*

July 5, 1958. Los Farronentes, Q. R.

Yesterday I got another chance to speak with Lano.

Rohnspeece came into the tent excited. "It's Fourth of July," he told me. "The General is going to give all us Americans a special toast. You better hurry." He flashed a rag across his boots and raced out. "He's taking us through the gate himself," he called back to me.

I wasn't going. I had been disenchanted for weeks.

283

Jesus, I thought, how do I get involved in these things? There were enough great men around without going into the jungles to look for them. I had made a mistake. It was the thought of being in on something big from the beginning that did it. When I'd first heard about the revolution it was still only a rumor, something plotted in a tavern. Not all the people were even out of jail yet.

Now I wait for one of three things to happen: Lano to win the war; Lano to lose the war; Lano to get me out through one of his complicated channels. "Only the deep wounded can go," Lano says, and adds, "when there is time." And ought to add, "And when there are wounded." There are no wounded, no dead, no missing. We might be in the Catskills waiting out the summer. We sit encamped in these damn mountains and Lano makes his revolution over the radio, sending out phony communiqués about towns taken, bridges blown, labor unions out on sympathy strikes, leaders of the regime committing suicide. He makes up a terrific revolution, Lano. Privately he explains that this is the "Valley Forge phase" of his revolution and that Los Farronentes is our chrysalis. A classicist, Lano.

Dr. Mud came in. "God's first attribute is His eye," he said. "Lano will perhaps note the American's absence."

"He doesn't need me. I'm not one of his soldiers."

Mud shrugged and gave me his mysterious smile.

Dr. Mud is the only genuinely sinister man I have ever met. I'm always looking for the fez which ought to be on his head, the Palm Beach yellow-white suit on his back. I had coffee with him in his tent one night and automatically I found myself switching our paper cups. As far as I can make out he represents "certain foreign interests."

He shaded his eyes (it is dark in the tent, but whenever he looks at you Dr. Mud shades his eyes) and told me in his amused, Cauco-Asiatic voice, using the upper register tones this time, that it would be better not to anger Lano.

"The shell of the young turtle is hard," he said, "but exceeding brittle." (Mud uses a lot of sinister Eastern

284

sayings. I think he makes them up. I have taken to answering him in kind and have gotten pretty good at it.)

"The east wind never blows without first consulting the west wind," I said.

"Ah," said Mud, "every ocean climbs mountains to the shore."

"Your ad," I said.

When Mud left the tent I decided I'd better go to Lano.

I went out. The east wind tells the west wind when to blow, I thought, polishing as I passed Dr. Mud. He was by the Lister bag. It made me a little nervous to see him near our drinking water. "Ah, Mud," I said, "the thirsty man drinks deepest."

"A hungry man is no judge of food," he said back, quick as a shot.

Sinister bastard, I thought.

Outside Lano's compound one of his supernumerary Pakistanis stood guard. He carried no rifle but in each hand he held a grenade from which the pin had already been pulled. His famine-thin thumbs strained against the safety device to depress it.

"I'm invited," I said.

He shook his head and looked troubled.

"I'm American. I go inside, yes? The Generalissimo Lano awaits."

He didn't understand.

"A hungry man is no judge of food. North wind blows south wind," I told him Easternly.

He looked helplessly at the grenades in his hands. He was, I knew, ordered to throw them at anyone who tried to get past the gate.

I whistled "Yankee Doodle" and he smiled suddenly in recognition. "Foh Jul," he said happily, "Foh Jul." He motioned me inside.

"Jesus Christ," I said, "don't wave."

I had never been inside before (none of us had) and did not see immediately where I was supposed to go. From outside Lano's electrified fence the compound looks pretty much like the one I am in myself, but once inside I noticed some subtle differences. For one thing, there were flowers. Not the exotic man-eaters that grew in such abundance elsewhere in this steamy jungle, but gentle, familiar ones, homey ones. They grew along both sides of a tree-lined path that wound up the mountain. I climbed the path for about a quarter of a mile and then heard voices. I knew I must be going in the right direction and walked faster. Suddenly the path leveled off and I came into a clearing. About fifteen yards away were the thirty-three other Americans in Lano's army.

Lano, on a high platform exactly like the one at the drill field where the men did their calisthenics each morning, saw me and waved.

"What's happening?" I asked a thin soldier in a shabby Class A American uniform.

"We're celebrating the Fourth," he answered glumly. "Only he does all the drinking."

"Attention," Lano called out through a megaphone and raised a canteen cup. "Attention there! I propose a very important, very special sentimental toasts to the memory of the great General Washington. Proclaim liberty throughout the land." He leaned forward and drank. "Happy Fourth July to all," he said, smiling. He put down the cup and placed his hands on the railing. "Celebration over. Back to your stations at once," he shouted abruptly. "And don't forget," he said, pointing to a tent just below and to the side of the platform, "you saw yourselves how your General Lano shares with you disfortune and hardship, as he will share with you the prizes of the victory. Tell the others. Dismissed!" The soldiers turned and began to walk off uncertainly. "Go back the way you came," Lano roared from the platform. "Follow the flowers down."

I was walking beside Rohnspeece when I heard my name shouted in Lano's deep voice through the megaphone. "Boswells," he called again. I looked back at him over my shoulder. "I dismissed only the soldiers. My aides cannot yet go," he said. Rohnspeece looked at me admiringly as I walked back toward the platform.

Lano rested his arms along the railing and leaned down toward me, smiling. He seemed very pleased. Raising his megaphone again he spoke into it in a normal voice. "What's the matter," he said, "don't you want to be my aide no more?"

"I want to go back."

"Only deep wounded can be moved. My planes bring in equipment, take out deep wounded heroes." He laughed. "Relax," he said, "it's not a bad war. I fight for freedom. You free man yourself, you understand good cause." He climbed down from the platform. "Hey, Boswells, when I win, you fix me up with big-shot pals?"

"Lano, I told you. I only said that to get you to take me in. I don't know any big shots."

"Sure you do. You know me. I make world's first international revolution. Everybody come." He slapped me across the shoulders. "Hey," he said, "I show you my operation here."

"I've seen it," I said.

"No, no, not that. Something special. My *operation*. Big military secret. Come on. Special day, Fourth July. Sentimental occasion for Lano. Live Wilmington, Delaware, three year. Seen Du Pont firework display. Beautiful, beautiful. See that, think, America the beautiful. Some day Lano make international revolution, Du Pont do the firework."

With his arm across my shoulders he led me off across the field and into the woods. In a few minutes we struck another path and started to climb again. "You don't know what Lano got back here," he whispered. "Only Dr. Mud see this. Now you. Special. Very sentimental."

I had come a long way in my life. There had been a time when I had responded to the bizarre without understanding it, feeling only the need to be curious, to remember it, as though anything truly outlandish were a kind of signpost, an indication of a sort of clumsy, cloudy truth. I can remember as a kid in school during the war being visited by a private named Pressman. He came to us several times. Needing a platform, he used our classroom and told us endlessly of his pathetic life in the army, apologizing, laughing at the jokes the other soldiers played on him, losing the thread of his story in his own roared laughter, shouting above it like some comedian who has lost control of his audience, "But wait a minute, wait a minute," taking it or some new shame up again, recounting humiliation like a braggart in reverse, but mixing it all up somehow with a kind of civics and endorsing everything, everything—the Pledge of Allegiance, our penny milk program, the Second Front, casualty lists— insisting in a crazy, personal grammar on the fitness of everything that happened in the world. Pressman was insane. His desperation, his clumsy, Jewish being, his self-hatred had brought him finally into a mad agreement with everything that forced him down. Forever short-sheeted, a man with frogs in his beds, he came to accept all insults, to convert them into proofs of justice and the wisdom of power.

I used to stare fondly at the Pressmans of the world, primitives holding their insanity as a sign from God. Now I know better. Pressman's nuttiness was just the self trying to get out. Death gives us nerve. I am calmer now; I see pain everywhere.

"Not far now," Lano said. "What a surprise for you. There. Look!"

I looked in the direction Lano was pointing and saw—a ranch house. A ranch house! There, high on a mountain, hidden by the pines, in still unmapped Los Farronentes, Q. R., two miles from the tents, the quiescent bivouac of the world's first international revolution, a ranch house. Landscaped with a patio, a barbecue pit, picture windows. *A carport, for Christ's sake!* I could not have been more surprised if he'd shown me a full-scale replica of the Taj Mahal and informed me that he used it as an outhouse. What simple things were at the core of our revolutions, finally! What little content to our discontent! And how unmysterious the world mysteriously was! Dr. Mud sinsister? Don't make me laugh.

"Lano," I said, "I want to get out of here. Tomorrow. Tonight. Now. The next plane, Lano, the next plane. Lano, do you hear me? The next plane."

"How about that?" he asked, excited. "Beautiful. Like in Wilmington, Delaware. I had it built to specification. Everything to specification. Four bedroom. Sunken living

288

room, three bathroom, full basement. Half bath downstair off pine-paneled rumpus room."

"The next plane, Lano. Do you hear me?"

"Very special. Sentimental. Beautiful. In capital, when I win war, I make another. Better than this one even. Come on, I show you."

He started to run toward his house and I ran after him. I caught him by the fake gas lamp.

"Wait a minute," I yelled, holding him. "I want to get out. Lano, you're crazy. I want to go back to the real Wilmington, Delaware, and I want to go back now."

He looked confused for a moment and then began to struggle to free himself. I shoved him down on the lawn. "Give me an answer, Lano. I'm warning you."

"Ony the deep wounded," he said.

"Goddamn it," I shouted, "there *are* no deep wounded. And even if there were, do you think I'd let myself get shot?"

"There will *be* deep wounded, don't worry about that," he answered as though that were the point.

"Stop it, Lano. I'm warning you. If you don't get me out of here I'll break your face. I'll tear you up, Lano, I promise."

"Counterrevolution," he screamed suddenly.

"Give the orders, Lano. Give the orders."

"Counterrevolution!"

"What are you talking about? Goddamn it, don't you hear me?"

"Counterrevolution! Go ahead. Be ridiculous. Hit me, kill me. Counterrevolution! Revolution in infancy. At delicate stage. Anyone who punches Lano in face be its new leader. You want that?"

"What are you talking about?"

"Seven hundred forty-one men. From all over world. Hundreds of thousands of dollars equipment. You want that? You want that responsibility? You hurt me you make successful counterrevolution. You the *new* leader. Move into the ranch house. You want that? You ready for that? You have to want a thing like that. Where you stand on certain issues? You got five-year plan? You got even lousy three-year plan? No—you don't even have fucking ten-*minute* plan! What you think of agrarian reform? Compulsory education? Shit, what you think of *freedom?*"

"You're crazy."

"Yeah, yeah. Go on, you hot to make revolution, hit me. You be new leader. No, you don't want? Then you go when I say. Go on, get off my lawn. Doesn't mean a damn no more if you tell troops what I got here. In two days we attack!"

July 8, 1958. Los Farronentes, Q. R.

Lano started moving the men out at two in the morning. He had trucks for only half of them; the rest went on foot. Corbonzelos is a nineteen-mile march.

Rohnspeece couldn't understand why I was staying behind. The Eskimo was drunk and Rohnspeece got to drive his truck. He was very pleased.

Before Lano gave the command to move out he had the men gather in the training compound in order to address them. I had dissociated myself and remained in the tent. Some men came to move it. They said it was equipment earmarked for the trucks and I told them, fuck that, it was staying put, I was in essence a prisoner of war and entitled to be housed as such. I cited a Geneva convention which I made up on the spot and got a young Persian lieutenant to agree with me. They let me alone finally.

A quarter of a mile away I could hear Lano haranguing the men in several broken languages. Then, after the men did the Chant of the Revolution and the War Scream, they re-formed into their units and went away.

At about three that afternoon I heard the abrupt dull pops of distant explosions. I walked higher up the mountain, into Lano's abandoned compound, and followed the flowers to the scene of the celebration and crossed the field and went into the woods and made my way up to the ranch house. I broke in. Through the big picture windows I could see flames, smoke rising.

It was crazy. Lano's argument had been enough to destroy whatever ideas I had of doing something about my situation. He was right: to act against Lano was to make a counterrevolution, to drag others into it behind me. A strong man travels very light. Unless I murdered him—and I am no murderer—and hid his body, I couldn't get away.

At seven Lano came racing back in a jeep. Dr. Mud was with him. He pulled the jeep into the carport and they got out. When he saw me in his house he didn't even seem surprised.

"Many deep wounded," he said. "Terrible."

"The flame that cools one burns another," Dr. Mud said.

"Heavy resistance. Terrible. It was better over the radio," Lano said.

"So," I said, "you lost. The revolution's over. Now I can go."

"We *won*, Boswells," Lano said. "My grief special, sentimental grief of all generals. On the other hand, victory glorious, brilliant! I blow up whole town entire!"

That night I stole Lano's jeep.

Down the mountain, on the plain, I saw the fires. Corbonzelos was burning, and I turned the jeep in that direction.

There was death. There was turnover.

People were burning. Lano's soldiers moved leadenly among the corpses and survivors. It was awful.

It was not entirely unpleasant.

"Okay," I shouted when I brought the jeep back. "Mud can't help you. He's unconscious. Hey, Dr. Mud," I screamed toward his collapsed, Boswell-clobbered body, "heal thyself."

"Get back to your tent. You're a prisoner of the revolution," Lano said.

"Balls," I said. "When does a plane go out? Come on, come on. I'll stick dynamite up you, blow up whole ass entire. Get on your radio. Give orders. Get a plane."

"Take the jeep."

"I'd get pretty far in your jeep, wouldn't I? Come on, come on."

"Counterrevolution."

"Lano, don't start with me, Lano."

"Counterrevolution."

"All right, then. Your way. Counterrevolution. Okay. Counterrevolution. I'm ready. Yesterday no, today yes. Counterrevolution. I've got a five-year plan now . . . ten years . . . twenty . . . a million: Live forever, live forever! Where's a knife? A gun? Give me bombs! Lano, you bastard, I'll kill you. I'll kill you!"

Lano backed away from me. "All right," he said quietly, "in a few days. A ship. From Texas. It brings mercenaries, supplies. You'll get out. I promise. I promise you." His face was white. "Please," he said, "don't kill me."

March 3, 1959. Chicago.

A man came out of a shop on Michigan Avenue that made shirts. His chauffeur opened the door for him and he stepped into a Cadillac. They drove off and I stared after the big car. It occurred to me with the force of that vision in which we suddenly see familiar things for the first time—a postage stamp, a pattern in the wallpaper, the shape of our own hand—that I had never ridden in a Cadillac. It was astonishing: I had never ridden in a Cadillac. I had never sailed a boat or been on a yacht. I had never screwed a belly dancer or an acrobat or a contortionist or a movie star. I had never paid fifty dollars for a meal or had a suite in a hotel. I had never owned a self-winding watch or gone Pullman. I had never flown a plane or bought property. I had never been dressed by a valet or made a recording. I had never acted in a movie or performed surgery or climbed a mountain for fun. I had never ridden a horse or played golf or been a member of a country club. I had never played in an orchestra. I could not speak French or German or Italian.

I had never been elected to public office or seen my name in a book. I had never had an unlisted phone number. I had never gone fox-hunting or deep-sea fishing or on a safari. I had never had a suit made or my own mixture of pipe tobacco. I had never taken out a patent, written a song, made a will, danced till dawn, bought a painting, eaten snails, drunk Pernod, been to Europe, shot a gun, played a piano, bought perfume, given a speech, made a touchdown, owned a tux, a par of skis, learned to waltz, worn a vest, a top hat, a ring, a monogrammed shirt, bet on a horse, been to an opera, a coronation, a costume ball. I had never broken the bank at Monte Carlo!

It was a formidable list of experiences not to have had.

What was happening? As I watched the Cadillac disappear, I saw clearly and with a sudden sense of massive, infinite privation, that I would never do or have most of these things—further, I should have to do without. Even if I started now, rolled up my sleeves, tightened my belt, went to work, pitched in, buckled down, hoed the row, held the line, went the distance, I could not hope to make more than a dent in those glittering abundances. It was like trying to tunnel through to China: it was like the feeling you got sometimes in museums—angry that you didn't own anything there. I felt overmatched. My three-score-and-ten, even if I could be sure of them, seemed as paltry as loose change. And how many of those years had I already used up? How many were left which could be enjoyed in health? Already the pains began, the summer colds, the mysterious backaches, the malaise in parts that yesterday gave no trouble; already the hair began to catch in the comb, the food in the throat; already there was aspirin in the toilet kit, a prescription I carried in my wallet. Even giving myself the best of it, granting health (as if it were some premise I could demolish later in the argument), granting more—granting luck—how much could a man hold in his hands anyway, how much could he grab? How much could he touch, smell, taste, see, hear? And of what use was it? How much could he keep? That was the important thing; was it possible to keep anything? Was it possible to keep one single solitary thing? Never mind the money in the bank, the good looks, the health—*could you keep your finger-nails?*

Suddenly everything I saw was the enemy. The silk scarves, the smooth-handled canes, the expensive umbrellas in the warm window. The tall buildings named for a single man. The cars that passed in the dusk, their dashboards glowing like Christmas lights. The girls who went by me in the street. I felt a quick powerful stirring of lust, greater than any I had ever known. I stared at the girls ravenously, so frankly that they looked away. I saw their legs shiny in the nylons. I saw the behinds, the cunts, the breasts, the ears, the nostrils, the mouths, all cleavages, all openings. I stood in the street like a rapist. Under my coat I held myself. I knew the rapist's desperation, his singleness beyond mere loneliness, his massive urgency greater than any legitimate need, greater even than the convention and morality and law that forbade its satisfaction. It was a confirmation of what I already knew about the uselessness of the senses. It was as if I had already abandoned them and was pressing, like some mute seeking his voice, toward a sixth sense, as yet unevolved; of containment, possession, the ability to know final things finally.

I stopped behind a girl who had paused to look in a window. It was a travel agency, and the whole window had been made over into a kind of crêche. Whoever had designed it had been very clever; it was very real. Oddly mature dolls lolled on some sunny, idyllic shore. In a toy sea, blue as ink, small boats bobbed. The sand around the edges of the sea was as white and fine as powdered sugar. Close to the shore tiny waves lapped perpetually at the knees of bending bathers. On the shore the dolls lay on colored pocket handkerchiefs while little white-coated waiters leaned over them with trays of drinks. Inside the miniature glasses the liquid shone like colored apothecary waters. Cabañas of vaguely biblical fabrics, like the thick-striped garments of Old Testament heroes, dotted the beach. In the background a model of a hotel, white and smooth as a pebble, shaped like some cement scroll, rose over the frontier of beach like a monument. No advertisement intruded; the place was not identified. It was Nassau, South America, Miami, Puerto Rico, one of the Rivieras. It was elsewhere and it was very real. It was only here that was not anywhere.

By watching the girl's reflection in the glass I could see that she was having my insight—or at least part of it, a fraction of an inch of it. As she stared at the scene the corners of her mouth edged down in an unconscious, piecemeal bitterness and her nostrils flared in a brief flutter of desire. She turned away from the window protectively, as if she might escape the implications of what she had learned.

"It's a big boulevard, miss," I said. "There are windows everywhere."

She moved by me cautiously, downlooking. It was all I could do to keep from grabbing her, taking her to my hotel, holding her prisoner there.

It was true. Here *wasn't* anywhere. Sunk in my finite body, things were helplessly reversed for me. I might have been a stone at the bottom of a well, dust in the corner of some closet. A cat who could look at a king. Big deal!

It was doom to know so much. As if I had just been told by some doctor who was never wrong that I had so many days to live. I knew what men rarely knew: the exact dimensions of the insuperable odds against them. Nor did this make me brave, as hopelessness sometimes does. It was disastrous. Now I would have to live always as though in the presence of some overwhelming fact of nature, like some primitive on the edge of the jungle, the vast desert.

Suddenly, however, as quickly as it had come, my lust began to subside. The knowledge that had caused it remained, but I could no longer see it in detail. All that was left was all that was ever left: a renewed desire, a controlled lust, a heightened hope. I continued down the boulevard, past the expensive shops, against the grain of the evening traffic, lascivious, dangerous, capable of heroic crime.

"We are the jet set," Angel Farouk, the filling-station heiress, announced to the waiter.

"Ready, jet set, go," Astarte Morgan, the central-heating heiress, said.

"Whee-ee-ee," said Angus Sinclair, the contour-chair scion.

"Whee-ee-ee the people," said Wylia De Costa, the miracle-drug widow.

"Let 'em eat cake," said Rudy Lip, the international playboy and rat.

"Nobody knows the truffles I've seen," Buster Bird, the white-paint tycoon, sang softly. "Nobody knows the truffles."

"I say," the general said, "I'm hungry."

Angus Sinclair clapped his hands. "Caviar. Caviar for the general."

The waiter presented a bottle smartly to Marvin Rilroyl, the wax-paper magnate. "Thirty-eight," Marvin Rilroyl said. "A very good year."

"The Nazis were in the Sudetenland," the general said wistfully.

"I don't know," Astarte Morgan said, "Rome's changed."

"My God, what hasn't?" asked Rudy Lip.

"Africa's not the same," Buster Bird said. "When I was on safari there last, I thought I was in some kind of zoo. They've spoiled Africa."

"The Côte d'Azur isn't azur any more," Angus Sinclair put in.

"They've spoiled the world," Angel Farouk said. "It's not like it was in Grandad's time."

"Her granddad was a baron," Angus Sinclair explained. "A robber baron."

"I think I've planned my last campaign," the general said.

"Ars longa, dolce vita breve," said Wylia De Costa.

K.O. Bellavista, the movie starlet, turned to Marvin Rilroyl. "How much are you worth, Marvin?" she asked.

"Depends upon the market," Marvin said. "My cotton is down, my land is up. My steels are mixed, my utilities off. My glamour stocks, of course—"

"Kiss me, darling," K.O. said, "your glamour stocks are glamorous."

"I know," Astarte Morgan said, "let's fly to Bombay."

"Bombay Away," the general said, and chuckled.

"People don't talk like this," I said.

"The best people do," Angel Farouk said.

"Well, the *best* people," I said.

"He's cute," Rudy Lip said unpleasantly. "Wherever did you find him?"

"Oh, he's not *mine,* Rudy, but I found him in Washington, at the Vice-President's party. He's a kind of gate crasher, but it's all absolutely high art with him. Boswell is devoted aren't you, Boswell?"

"I'm very pure," I said.

"He's an absolute pauper," Wylia went on, "but he knows more people than I do. Tell them the people you know, Boswell."

"Alphabetically by country?" I said.

"Whatever's convenient," Rudy Lip said, giving me some.

"The Archbishops of Aden, Australia and Austria. A big shot in the Bahamas. A bananaman from Brazil. A—"

"That's marvelous," Marvin Rilroyl said. "Rouse the Principessa."

"Principessa, Principessa," Buster Bird said, shaking a woman at the other end of the table who had laid her head on her arms and gone to sleep. "Principessa, you must hear this."

"Please stop that screaming," the Principessa said. "I need my rest. Too much depends upon my longevity. Shut the windows. I feel a draft. Throw someone on the fire."

"It is too sad," Bizarrio said to me. "Such a lovely young woman and she goes on like that." He shook his head.

"I heard what Bizarrio told you," she said. "What

297

would a clown and fop know about it? I am thirteen hundred years old, the last of my race."

"Cheery beery be, Principessa, old pat," I said. "Every cloud has a silver lining."

"Who, I wonder," she said, "is your jeweler, young man?"

April 5, 1960. Rome.

She came to my *pensione* and we made love.

"What are you a Principessa of?" I asked afterwards, looking down at her.

"Mmrrhhghh," she said comfortably.

"What are you a Principessa of?" I asked again.

"Of all the Italies," she said. "I am Principessa of all the Italies."

I rolled over on my side. "You're very beautiful."

"Molte sano," she said, "like a classy whore."

"What's wrong?"

She sat up swiftly. "Hasn't it registered with you yet just who you've got in your bed? I'm Margaret dei Medici. A Medici. The Last of the Medicis."

I put my arms around her. "Medici," I said, "Medici. Poisoners and conspirators, weren't they?"

"You're thinking of the Borgias," she said. "The Borgias were a bad lot. 'The bad Borgias,' we used to call them. What are you, Guelph or Ghibelline?"

"I beg you pardon?"

"Guelph or Ghibelline? Who do you root for?"

"Which is the home team?"

"Oh, Guelph," she said.

I put my hand lightly against her face. "Are you really a Principessa?" I said.

"What is more to the point, are you really a commoner?"

"Common as clay."

"You're quite sure that gypsies didn't steal you at birth?"

298

"No," I said seriously, "as a matter of fact, I'm not."

She smiled.

"I might yet turn out to be a Princippe or something," I said. "I may just be in reduced circumstances."

"Who isn't?" she said.

"Principessa?"

"Who isn't?" she said again.

"Principessa?"

"Oh, shut up," she said. "Stop calling me that, will you! It sounds as if I'm supposed to precede you out of bed or something."

"Will I see you again?" I asked.

"It's not much as personal tragedies go, is it? Selfish, isn't it, to be concerned about being bored? Why, it's trite. A bored princess! But you see, that's all made up. I'm the only bored princess I know. The others keep saying they are, but it's just talk with them. Well, I'm sorry. I'm not poor or crippled or anything like that, but unhappiness is unhappiness, isn't it? It's fatuous to quibble about degrees of unhappiness."

"Will I see you again?"

"Do you know the Pitti Palace in Florence? The Uffizi Gallery? My people gave them."

"Will I see you again, Margaret?"

"Principessa."

"Will I see you again?"

"No. You can't come to the castle." She giggled.

"Please."

"No playing in the palace."

"Margaret, I think I love you."

"Heavy, heavy lies the head that wears the crown, did you know that?" She moved away from me and sat up on the edge of the bed. "Well," she said, "is it all over?"

"What do you mean?"

"The lovemaking. It is all over? Was that all there was to it? I'll be damned. And I thought you commoners were supposed to have such extraordinary sexual powers."

Angus Sinclair called to say that he and Buster Bird and Rudy Lip were on their way over to the Hassler to have dinner and catch Mussolini's son, who plays piano there.

"A lot of the boys will be there. You come too."

It occurred to me that being alive was beginning to seem like being off on a convention somewhere. "I don't think so, Angus," I said. "I've been trying to get in touch with someone all day."

"Principessa Poison? The Royal Welcome Wagon?"

"Hey, listen," I said.

"Not so edgy. She's the ignoblest Roman of them all. Common knowledge. Public domain. Come hear Mussolini's son. I'll introduce you as one of the Allies. No kidding, wait till you hear him. Great jazz style. Does a riff on 'Deutschland, Deutschland Über Alles' makes strong men weep."

I decided to go. Angus might be able to tell me something about the Principessa. Only after I began to walk to the hotel did my indifference about meeting another celebrity strike me as peculiar. Was this a stiffening of character on my part? Probably I had simply made a choice. Between the son of a dead, discredited Duce and the daughter of a once great family, I had chosen the daughter. Boswell, you old fraud, I thought, you family man.

I asked Astarte Morgan about the Principessa.

"Oh, Boswell," she said, "you aren't falling in love with her, are you?"

"Oh, love," I said. (This is my new style in conversation. People say something to me and I choose one of their words and repeat it back to them. It's very sophisticated and Henry Jamesish and sounds as if it might mean something.)

"Because it seems such a touristy thing to do," Astarte Morgan said, "like seeing the Colosseum by moonlight or attending Mass in St. Peter's."

"I'd hardly say that wanting to be with the Principessa is anything like attending Mass in St. Peter's," Buster Bird said.

"Well, is there anything wrong with her?" I asked.

"She's a character," Buster Bird said.

"She's middle class," Astarte said firmly.

"That's ridiculous, Astarte," I said.

"She is—she's middle class. You'd think all those centuries would have bred something into her. Not Margaret. I tell you she's as surprised to find herself a Principessa as my char would be."

"That's just her enthusiasm," I said.

"Enthusiasm, indeed. It's all she talks about. She's always going around giving the secret handshake," Astarte said.

"She carries herself like a queen," I said.

"That's difficult to bring off with your head on the table."

"Well, that's just a remark, Astarte," I said.

"Is it? You were there. You saw her that night. No, Boswell, forgive me, but she drinks."

"Oh, drinks," I said.

"And she screws," Buster Bird said.

"Oh, screws."

April 17, 1960. Rome.

I borrowed Mussolini's kid's car. It's something called a Rameses X-900. I couldn't find first gear.

"Are you sure you can handle this?" Mussolini's kid asked me.

"Well," I said, "if you'd just show me low."

"It's very simple," he said. "You just make a trapezium."

"Oh," I said. "In the States you only have to make an H."

"America is so innocent," he said.

He drew a trapezium for me and I drove off toward the Appia Antica, bouncing over the old Roman stones black and shiny as lumps of giant coal. On either side along the narrow road were ancient tumuli, crypts, broken statues, their noses flat as boxers', the wrecked monuments of Romans dead two thousand years. Spaced every thirty or forty feet were Italians incongruously having picnics, their Fiat 500's and 600's pulled up on the grass, their picinic hampers balanced carefully on the tomb-tables. Except for the cars and their clothes they might have been people who had assured themselves of a good view of a triumphal procession by taking up their positions before the others got there. They waited good-naturedly and passed their time by posing each other for photographs beside the ancient monuments. Inside hollowed-out tumuli or in niches from which statues had been removed I could see young lovers hugging and kissing each other. As I drove along several people noticed my super car and waved; I waved back. Some of the younger ones amiably made obscene gestures; I amiably made obscene gestures back.

I came to the Principessa's villa. It was surrounded by a high stone wall. I stopped the car just outside the gates and honked the horn of the Rameses X-900. It sounded the opening notes of the "Triumphal March" from *Aïda*. No one came to the gate, and I got out of the car. I was feeling pretty good. Further down the road I saw an old woman in a black cloth coat who stood weeping beside an ancient crypt. I laughed and climbed back into the car.

An old man in a peaked cap came up to the gate on the other side, stared at the car and then said something in Italian.

"Permesso," I yelled, trying a word I had heard people use when they wanted to get by me on the crowded bus.

He shook his head.

"Scende," I said, using another word I had heard on the bus. He shook his head sadly.

I pounded the horn. "Ta ta ta ta-ta-ta-ta ta-ta," I sang. He turned away. "Hey, wait," I called after him.

"Get the Princess. The Principessa." He looked at me curiously for a moment and waved me away with his arm. *"Io"*—I pointed to myself—*"volere la Principessa."* I speak only in infinitives. It gives my Italian an air of command and a certain good-natured sinister quality, like a Mexican bandit in the movies. The old man answered in Italian. My difficulty with a foreign language is that given time I can usually frame what I want to say, but I can never understand the replies. Perhaps if everyone always spoke only in infinitives, as I do, there would be universal peace and understanding. It would be the dawn of a new era. *If everybody to speak as I to do, to be peace, to be dawn of new era. Lions to lie down with lambs.*

The fellow started away again, and I got out of the car and rushed up to the gate. "To want to get to see Principessa," I called.

"———," he said in Italian.

"To need to talk to marry," I said.

"———," he said.

I got back in the car and blew a few more bars of *Aïda,* but my heart had gone out of it. I was studying Mussolini's kid's diagram of the trapezium in order to figure out where reverse was when the old fellow reappeared. He had someone with him, another old man, in a chauffeur's uniform.

I leaned out the window. "To open the gate," I said.

"You to speak English?" the new old man asked.

"To do," I said excitedly.

He looked at me curiously.

"I mean I do," I said.

"What you to wish?" he asked.

"I want to see your mistress," I said.

He blushed. My God, I thought, him too? This was some Principessa!

"I want to see the Principessa. I'm a friend of hers."

"To say your name if you please," he said.

"Boswell. James Boswell, King of Pennsylvania, Prince of Indiana, Duke of the Republican Party."

"I to announce you," he said quietly, and added, *"Mister* Boswell."

"To hurry," I said.

He went into a little sentry booth I hadn't noticed before and evidently called the house. In a moment he had reappeared.

"Not to home," he said.

"Of course she's home," I protested. "You're her chauffeur and *you're* home."

"Please to clear drive," he said.

"No. I want to see her."

"To do," he shouted. There was a gun in his hand.

I got back in the car and drove away.

That night I returned to storm the wall. Mussolini's kid wanted the Rameses X-900 back, so I had to catch a ride on the rear of a motor-scooter. Going over those stones on the scooter wasn't as gentle as in the Rameses X-900, which had been rather like being drawn down the Nile in a basket, but I have not entirely lost the common touch. After the fellow let me off in front of the villa he wanted to hang around to see what I was going to do. He pointed to the wall. "Principessa Medici," he said, and clicked his tongue.

"To appreciate it," I said, "to beat it, please." He bounced on his scooter a few times to start it and zoomed off.

I reconnoitered. Finally I chose a spot near the house and began to scale the wall. When I got on top, pressing myself tightly against the narrow surface so as not to be seen, I was seen. Three men were waiting for me. "James Boswell, requesting permission to come aboard," I said. They jumped toward the wall. Before I could let myself back down the other side two of the men had reached up, grabbed me by the ankles and pulled me toward them. The Palace Guard, I thought as I tumbled through the air. I was going to tear them apart as soon as I had recovered myself, but the new old man from that afternoon was standing over me with his gun.

"To rise," he said in English.

"To stop to point that at me," I said in Italian.

"To rise," he said in English.

"To don't rush me," I said in Italian. Experience

304

teaches me one thing anyway, I thought. Infinitives will not bring peace to the world.

They took me to the Principessa. When she saw who it was she told them they could go, but asked the new old man to wait outside in case she needed him. She took his gun and held it in her lap.

"My God, Principessa," I said. "We've slept with each other."

"Don't be vulgar," she said, "and don't presume on old favors. You'll never receive them again."

"Doesn't it mean anything to you?"

"Does it to you?"

Of course it does. Indeed, I have become embarrassed in the presence of divorced persons just imagining their memories of each other. I have always been unable to understand some people's casual acceptance of intimacy. It amounts, in effect, to an indifference, and yet I have noticed that those people who are the most casual about sexual experience are frequently the most avid in seeking it. Once a man has made love to a woman he is marked for life—they both are. Of course I have not been very successful sexually, and perhaps this is because of my attitude, but I carry what experiences I have had— mostly, sadly, with whores—indelibly. I will see a whore I have been with only once, and it is anguish that she does not remember me.

Once at a party I was in a room with two women with whom I'd had what they would have considered minor affairs. Of course neither knew that I had slept with the other—nor would they have cared much had they known. They might have regarded me with the same interest they would have taken in some mutual hairdresser. Nevertheless I remember being paralyzed with fear, as convention-stricken as a kid. I would always love both of them, I told myself, and our relationships began to seem tragic as I recaptured them. That nothing final had come of them was somehow my responsibility. We should have had children together, sat in hospital corridors during one another's illnesses, shared cemetery lots. That this was impossible never even occurred to me; I understood only that it was tragic that emotions play out, that feelings lose

305

their edge and in time become meaningless. Perhaps I have too much respect for the gift and for its giver. My mistake, if I make one, is that, like all people on a dole, I have never understood that the giver can usually afford his gift.

"Of course it means something to me," I told the Principessa.

She laughed. "They told me you came by this afternoon in that foolish car. Wherever did you get it?"

"It's not mine."

"Well, thank God for that," she said. "What do you want, anyway?"

"Just to be with you," I said.

"Well, you're with me," she said. She put the gun down beside her and laughed.

Then she grinned. Then she smiled. And then she looked at me.

April 18, 1960. Rome.

I shall try to describe my love's person.

So lucky am I, I think. For example, I am thirty-two years old (My God, am I thirty-two years old already?) and Margaret is thirty. A man should be older than a woman. He should be taller, heavier, stronger, coarser. (I don't approve of these mixed marriages.) He should be knowing and she innocent. It is all right if he breaks wind, but she must not even hiccup modestly. He can be plagued by beard, but her hair must be of a fixed and permanent length on her head. What, follicles in my love? Glands? My love has no follicles, no glands. That moisture on her body after exercise isn't sweat. Perhaps it's dew. Yes, dew. Her body is mysterious, its ways fixed— unlike my own—like some planet in its orbit, performing its rounds unconsciously, with no surprises, like a law in physics. To think of her as subject to the queer nether turmoil of the flesh is monstrous, disloyal, a lover's sedition. She could not have had childhood's disfiguring diseases, your poxes, your measles, your mumps; she could never have made its disfiguring sounds, your whooping coughs, your diarrhetic groans and sighs. Indeed, it is difficult to think of her as a child at all, as one subject to anything as vulgar as growth. Yet of course she has a body, and that is what is so mysterious: she ought not to have one at all. But she is so clever about it that she has somehow marvelously arranged it. It is as if she pulls it out of the wall only when it's needed, like a Murphy bed. And indeed there *is* something of fake bookcasery about her, of hollow woodwork, unseen passageways, secret staircases, hidden crypts—something plotted, designed, carefully contrived for contingency. She is absolutely Tudor, Renaissance, manorial.

She is of medium height. Admittedly I was piqued by that at first. What, medium height? Average? Do you say "average"? But then I saw the artful subtlety of it—to work only with the given. How clever of Margaret, really! (She has the air of being responsible for her entire being, the curve of her ears, the shape of her hands—everything.) To avoid an ungainly tallness (women do not know how to handle height; it is above them) and yet to finesse a coy compression. Women do not know how to handle depth either.

Her hair, the color of ancient coins, is a lushness beneath lushness, as though spilled from a cornucopia of hair, from the very source of hair, her sweet hirsute hair source. It is a Niagara of hair which tumbles from hidden bluffs of scalp. (I have seen this scalp. It is *so* pale. I have touched—the wondrous whiteness, thin, I'm sure, as paper—my tongue to it, its very center, the point where it begins its slow careful spiral, more complex than a thumbprint.) It frames her face and lends to it the aspect of a tan gift on some golden platter. Max Factor, you are no factor here.

Her nose is a propriety. An attribute. Her mouth ... How I love to gaze into the marvelous machinery of her mouth, to watch the tongue as it scales the walls of teeth, to spy on it as it makes its mysterious, wondrous noises. I do not even listen to the words. I don't even hear them. One listens as one listens to a song, ignoring the words. It is strange to think that they are formed by a

307

brain, that they demonstrate a will. (Away from her I can sometimes think of her as a human being, but when I am with her, never. Even her name, Margaret dei Medici, with its alliterative melody, seems something improbable and anthropomorphic gotten up for children, so that I find I must patronize her, pretend that she is as real as I am, talk of her to herself as one talks of Donald Duck or Mickey Mouse to a child.) How bright of her, I think, to make speech, show anger. It must be just some clever parlor trick performed for company. I should like to see her dance, hear her sing, recite. It is comical that she should wear a dress, jewelry, stockings, complicated underwear, that she should take food and need sleep.

She has eyes. I presume they see. They are green. How remarkable!

How much does she weigh, I wonder. I shall have to lift her.

I have seen the pulse in her neck. It starts my own.

I have seen her legs. Don't speak of them; they will break your heart.

I have seen her breasts. Enough. You will go mad.

April 22, 1960. Rome.

Rudy Lip said that Margaret is the whore of the world. I knocked him down.

Rudy stared up at me from the floor. "This won't get around, you know. I'll never say you hit me defending Margaret's honor. I'll say you hit me as a professional warning from one international gigolo to another. Well, it's too late. You should have hit me years ago."

April 25, 1960. Rome.

I was with Margaret at the cocktail party at the Embassy. She had seen Rudy Lip and he'd told her I had hit him.

308

"Why did you do such a stupid thing?" she asked me.

"He's a son of a bitch."

"We don't slam people around for that, do we?"

"He said some things," I said.

"Ah," she said. "About me."

"No, of course not. Why should he say anything about you?"

"Why not? He told you he made love to me."

"I'd never believe anything like that," I said.

"Why not? It's true. Rudy is an attractive man."

"Oh, Margaret."

"Don't look so tragic. You know all about me. You won't reform my character."

I told her that character had nothing to do with it, that I was worried about her.

"Why?"

"Damn it, Margaret, what if you had a child?"

"I won't."

"Why not?" I said gloomily. "You didn't let *me* use anything."

She laughed and said who did I think I was dealing with, anyway? She was a Principessa, a Medici. She had status. She was one of five unmarried women in Roman Catholic Italy fitted for her own diaphragm.

April 30, 1960. Rome.

The Principessa had gone to a concert at the Teatro d'Opera.

I bought a ticket. "Near the Principessa dei Medici's box, please," I told the girl.

"Oh, sir," she said, "the Principessa has a season box. I am not sure where it is. Perhaps the flunky would be able to show it to you." She indicated a big, distinguished-looking old man in elegant livery. So, I thought, they're really called flunkies. "He does not speak English, however."

"I'll make out," I said.

I went up to the fellow. *"Dove Principessa Medici?"*
I said.

He looked at my clothes. *"Non lo so,"* he
said.

"Come, come," I said. *"Venire, venire. Sono Principe Boswell il Eccentrico. Dove Principessa Medici?"*

"No lo so."

"Sono Mister Boswell, il ricce Americano, molti dollars, molti macchinas, lotsa lire. Dove Principessa Medici?"

"No lo so."

"Sono Boswell the lovesick. Dove Principessa?"

"No lo so."

"Flunky!" I said to the flunky and walked off.

I rented a pair of opera glasses and scanned the boxes. It was half an hour before I located Margaret. I waved to her but she did not respond. During the intermission I went to her box. She didn't seem very surprised to see me. "Look," she said, "there are sixty-three princesses in Europe—sixty-four if you count Anastasia. Twenty-six of those girls are the real thing. Perhaps eight of them will one day succeed to a throne. Why don't you bother one of them?"

"Oh, Margaret," I said.

"Just thinking of your career," Margaret said lightly.

"Margaret, I am not Rudy Lip."

"Don't be so self-righteous," Margaret said. "Mr. Lip serves a worthwhile purpose. Mr. Lip is a craftsman, like a leather worker or a blacksmith. You ought to feel sorry for him—and for me too. We're both in danger of technological unemployment."

"Margaret," I pleaded, "talk seriously with me."

"How can I when you wave those ridiculous opera glasses at me? Besides," she said, "you are not a serious person."

"I am so."

"No," she said. "You're not. You are not serious. You're only obsessed." *She* was serious.

"By love," I said lightly.

"Maybe," she said. "Oh, I don't know."

"I'm taller than you are," I said absently.

"What?"

"I'm stronger."

"Don't show off," she said.

"I'm older and heavier. Oh, Margaret, we're perfect for each other."

"Don't be ridiculous."

"It's because I'm a commoner."

"Oh, honestly, Boswell," she said impatiently, "would you want your sister to marry one of them?"

The music began and she had nothing more to say to me.

This conversation with Margaret has illustrated an important principle to me. It was something I was aware of before, of course, but it was only our exchange and something that happened earlier in the week that brought it home to me so forcefully. I had gone to one of those movie houses here in Rome where there is a variety show after the film. They are sort of haphazard and just barely professional, and I find they relax me. When the lights came on after the picture and I looked around to see who was in the house, I noticed two men coming down the aisle toward me. As usual, I was sitting in the front row in order to see into the wings, and when the men passed I saw they carried instruments. The piano player and the drummer were already set up in the pit. The men with the instruments still had their coats on. There was no way of getting into the pit unless they climbed over the railing. It was a little awkward with the instruments, and the piano player reached up and took their cases from the two men and then offered his arm to steady them as they climbed into the pit.

Once he was in the pit the taller of the two men picked up his instrument case and took out a saxophone. He was fitting the pieces together when the piano player came up and started to talk to him. By the earnest expression on both their faces I could almost guess what they were saying.

The piano player was saying, "Henry, it'll depend upon the timing. If it looks like we're going to be pressed

311

we'll just have to forget it, but if I nod after the seals I want you to go into your solo on number 14. It may work out. Douglas was telling me that the trailers will be very short tonight, but the time saved there may be lost during the collection for Victims of Earthquake Relief."

The sax man nodded and said, "My lip's a little thick anyway. I was doing a wedding until two this morning."

"Well, we'll just have to see," the piano player said. Then he twirled around on his stool and leaning slightly forward began to address the others. "Listen," he probably said, "take Rose's number pianissimo. She was complaining last time that the audience couldn't hear the taps."

"There's a crack in my drum," the drummer probably said.

"Bass or snare?"

"Bass."

"Why didn't you get it skinned?"

"Walter the Skinner is down with flu," the drummer probably said.

"Oh," the piano player probably said. "Well, just hit it very lightly. That'll work out all right in Rose's number anyway."

"I use the snare in Rose's number," the drummer probably said.

"Okay," the piano player probably said. "Are we all straight?" He looked at the other musicians.

The other musicians nodded that they were all straight, and indeed they were. It was this which my life lacked. I had never had a conversation like this. I mean, this is the way people talk to each other. This is the way things get done. One man asks another man where Taylor Street is, or what train his wife is coming in on, or how many beds are set up in the hospital for the casualties, and the other man tells him. There's no hanky-panky. It's very professional. Serious! Scientific! There are no conversational flights soaring toward planes where life is not lived, no badinage, no repartee. What a calm, silent, serene world, I think.

The Principessa sensed this about me at once. She
312

cannot love me because she thinks she cannot talk seriously to me. She is afraid of me, as one is always a little afraid of anyone who one suspects is not entirely serious. From time to time I have even felt this myself. Why else do I always have so much to say to elevator operators, to clerks, to officials? It's as though I deliberately seek them out to practice some foreign language on them. But I haven't the art of it, really. Even with them I am soon involved in conversational maneuvers. I fall back on my English, as it were, and instantly we are into a routine, like two people at some college reunion with nothing in common but their briefly mutual past. If I am ever to be successful in my campaign with the Principessa I must remember what I learned from the musicians. I will be ruthlessly clinical; I will introduce shop talk into love.

"Look, Principessa," I will say, "the angle hasn't been right. Slip this pillow beneath your buttocks. Let's try for fifteen minutes of pre-play tonight. Of course, we'll have to see how the time is. I haven't had an orgasm in three weeks and I may not be able to control it. But let's see how it works out. Are you ready? All right, begin!"

May 4, 1960. Rome.

I told Margaret that I meant to have all the experiences and she said she had already had them and couldn't we do something else, and I told her very frankly, I said, "Listen, Principessa, Margaret—dear—this is *my* love affair and we'll do it my way. It's not my fault you're a depraved sybarite and come to me deflowered and spoiled and idly rich and all."

"Well," she asked, "what *are* all the experiences?"

"Actually," I said, "I was hoping you could help me. After all, this is rather outside my usual line."

"Well, what did you have in mind? Something flashy and expensive?"

"No, no," I said. "I think not. Why not utilize the resources at hand?"

313

"Like Audrey Hepburn and Gregory Peck in *Roman Holiday?*"

"That's it, that's it," I said. "You can pretend you're just an ordinary shopgirl and I'll be an ordinary shopper. Cinderella in reverse, you see. Young love at its simplest and most innocent, with all the anxiety about screwing and everything left in. I'm thirty-two years old but I think I could handle it."

"Well," she said doubtfully.

"Please," I said. "You'll see."

"What could we do? The things I can think of don't seem like much fun."

"Say what you're thinking."

"We could go to the Colosseum by moonlight," she said doubtfully.

"Excellent," I said. "We'll do that. For a starter we'll go to the Colosseum by moonlight."

We went to the Colosseum by moonlight, but we had to wait two days because it was raining. On the morning of the third day I called Margaret and told her that the paper said fair, and we promised to meet that night.

"I'll pick you up at the *pensione,*" Margaret said.

"No, no," I said. "I mustn't see your car. Come in by bus."

"Don't be ridiculous," Margaret said. "No buses come this far out the Appia Antica that time of night."

"All right," I said, "but don't pick me up. Park your car on a side street and I'll meet you in front of the place."

"Aren't you afraid I'll be raped?"

"Are you kidding? The whore of the world?" This was our little joke.

I met Margaret at the main entrance to the Colosseum.

"It's locked," she said.

"Why? What could anyone take?"

"It's locked," she said. "Try it yourself."

I went up to the big iron gate that had been set across the main arch. It was sealed only by a small Yale lock. I'll break it, I decided, queerly pleased that I was

314

still something of an outsider, that some violations were still a matter of strength.

For some reason I did not want Margaret to watch me. "I think I might be able to pick the lock," I said. "You stand over there and warn me if anyone comes."

I turned back to the lock. I spat on my hands. Tugging at the lock experimentally, I saw that I wouldn't be able to twist the metal. It was sturdier than I had thought. If I were to break it I would have to pull the bolt loose in exactly the same way that I would if I'd had a key. Gripping the torso of the lock in my palm I pulled heavily against the bolt. It didn't move. What's this? I thought testily. What's this? I put both hands around the lock, working my finger through the steel arch. I set my feet carefully into position, like an athlete seeking leverage and strained against the lock mightily. I heard the gate itself creak as it bulged petulantly on its hinges, but the lock remained intact. I could almost see the thick, brutish overbite of the jagged metal inside the lock.

"Hurry," Margaret said, thirty feet away.

Shut up, I thought. Leave me alone.

"In a minute, Margaret," I said. "This is delicate work."

All right, I thought. Now! I folded both hands about the lock, lacing my fingers. I invoked Sandusky. It was an intrusion. I thought of myself alone in the gymnasium, in the jockstrap, under the weights, the tons of metal on my back. I heaved against the lock. "Because," I murmured, "because my heart is pure." It didn't budge. "Because, because," I insisted, "because my fucking heart is pure!" I broke my heart against that lock. It wouldn't give. My strength is gone, I thought. And in an Olympic year. It was important. Panic filled me like something sour. I was out of condition and the condition was singleness, and my strength—any I'd ever had—had been in that. You were not in it for the money, I thought. You were *not*. I had been shorn. Had I touched my head I would have felt scalp. Hairless as Samson, like some gross fairy, I sweated outside the Colosseum in the moonlight, in the soft air. In rain I might have broken it, I thought. In rougher

315

weather. The condition was singleness, and I was out of it. Aloneness. My strength was in solitude. In being a stranger in town, in lies, in indifference. In the heart's decision to go it alone, in its conviction that it could hold out against the world's ponderous siege. For months, for years, guaranteed for life like an expensive watch. Oh Christ, I thought, it isn't fair, to be burdened like that, to *have* to be a hero. Who needs it? To have always to reject and refuse and negate like some saint in reverse. Not to give quarter, that was simply good generalship, but not to *accept* it, that was insanity.

"All right," I confessed. *"I'm in it for the money. Margaret is nothing to me!"*

I fell to the ground, but the lock—the lock was in my hand.

"What happened?" Margaret asked, rushing up.

"Just fell for you, Principessa," I said.

"Oh, get up," she said.

"The Rape of the Lock," I said, showing Margaret the lock.

We went inside. "Oh," Margaret said. "Oh! Oh! Let's go up."

With only the light of the moon to guide us we went through the dark passages and up the ancient, dangerous steps. At the second landing Margaret paused for breath. I kissed her.

"Come on," I said. "I've just begun to climb."

We went to the very top. Here the Emperors had sat. I looked out over the broken stones below; they resembled some harrowed cemetery in the moonlight.

"I could have been a gladiator," I said. "If I'd lived in those days I could have been a gladiator."

"Not a Christian?"

"The gladiator had a better chance than the Christian."

"I could have been a Roman," Margaret said.

"It's funny," I said, "I never thought of being a Roman."

"Poor Boswell."

"Well, maybe a freed slave," I said.

I clapped my hands imperially. I turned my thumb

down. I lifted it high. "Which is the real me, Principessa?" I asked.

"Oh, the thumb up," she said.

"Up it is," I said. "All the way."

I put my hand in my pocket.

"What's wrong?" Margaret asked after a moment. "Isn't it working out? Isn't this what you had in mind?"

"Oh, it is," I said. "Exactly."

"What shall we do now?" Margaret said.

"The Spanish Steps," I said quickly.

"By moonlight," she said.

"Moonlight it is," I said.

I let her drive me in the car. "Come on," I said once we were there, "let's go up."

"But it's so high. Must we?"

"Of course," I said, starting up. Margaret came along behind me. "Come on. Two, four at a time. Rome, Margaret," I said, calling over my shoulder in the manner of one explaining an important principle on the run, "is a test of strength."

May 6, 1960. Rome.

We were in the Piazza di Spagna yesterday afternoon by the Bernini the Elder fountain and it was two o'clock and the shops were all closed and there wasn't much traffic in the street and a horse carriage went by. "Say," I said to the Principessa, "that looks romantic. Is it expensive?"

"What's expensive?" the Principessa of All the Italies said.

"Listen," I said, "I think we ought to try it. You translate for me and say everything I tell you."

"But we were going to lunch."

"We will," I said. "We will. I'll just call the next one over."

I raised my hand as an old man in a long brown smock was guiding his carriage past the fountain. "Horseman," I called, "I say, horseman!"

317

"Sair?" he said, drawing up the reins.

"He must be made to think he's dealing with Italians." I whispered to Margaret. "Tell him that I mean to engage him, but that first certain arrangements must be made."

"Oh, Boswell, he has a meter."

"Never mind that. Tell him 'certain arrangements must be made.' Can you say that in Italian—'certain arrangements'?"

The Principessa said something to the horseman and he said something back.

"What's he say?" I asked.

"He wants to know what you mean, 'certain arrangements'?"

"Tell him that when I say 'certain arrangements' I am speaking in reference to the fact that he has nothing to pull that cab but a single horse, that this is an age of mechanization—of horsepower, that is true, but of horsepower in concert, as it were. Tell him that this is the horsepower age and that it would hardly be fair for him to expect people to pay a man with only one horse the same rate they would pay a man with thirty-five or forty horses. Tell him also that a motor-driven taxi can cover a given distance in a fraction of the time a single-horse-drawn carriage can cover it."

"Oh, Boswell," Margaret said.

"You are a Principessa," I said. "I am a lousy commoner. I have to think about these things. Tell him."

She told him. He looked from Margaret to me, staring at me curiously, but not without a certain admiration. He hesitated for a moment and then said something to Margaret.

"What's he say?"

"He says that all that has been taken into account by the people who make the meters, but that you have to expect to pay a little something extra for the romance."

"Tell him that I do expect to pay a little something extra for the romance, but that it must be held to a minimum, that one is always paying a little something extra for the romance, and that one expects service rendered too."

318

She told him.

"What's he say?"

"He says what do you mean?"

"Tell him I mean that I see he has a kilometer gauge in the cab. Tell him that I will undertake to engage him and the horse if he will accept payment for distance delivered plus one hundred lire for the romance."

Margaret told him.

"What's he say?" I asked.

"He says all right, where do you want to go?"

"Tell him around and around the fountain."

"Around the fountain?" Margaret said. "Just around the fountain?"

"*Around and around* the fountain. Tell him."

She told him. "He says get in," she said.

We got in and we drove around and around the fountain. After about three circumnavigations the people sitting on the Spanish Steps waiting for American Express and Keats' house to open began to watch us with interest. Every once in a while one would point. The horseman muttered something, but I didn't ask Margaret to translate. Soon there was a crowd, and in a little while people began to call things to us. The horseman growled and said something to Margaret.

"What's he say?" I asked.

"He says this is crazy."

"Tell him he wants romance I'll give him romance and a deal's a deal. Can you say that in Italian?"

Margaret said it in Italian.

Now there was a big crowd watching us; people were standing in the street. As they pushed forward the traffic had to slow down to avoid hitting them. Many of the drivers craned their necks out of their car windows to discover what the crowd was looking at. When they noticed our slow pace around and around the fountain they were as interested as the others. Some of them turned off their ignitions and waited to see what was going to happen.

"Wave," I said to Margaret.

Margaret waved.

"Tell *him*," I said.

She did, but he wouldn't wave. There were too many cars piled up and he had to use both hands in order to maneuver the horse around them. We had barely made another circuit around the fountain when the cars, now bumper to bumper, almost stopped our progress altogether. The horseman applied the whip ruthlessly and tried to force the big carriage through narrow and narrower spaces. He drove valiantly. He used the whip with an almost arch indifference. He swore at the stalled drivers. But none of it was of any use; we could not go another ninety degrees. We were stuck tight in a solid sea of metal.

From our greater height we stared impassively down on the shiny roofs.

"Well, then," I said after sitting amiably, arms folded across my chest, for about ten minutes, "I think we'll get out here. Tell him."

Margaret told him. Tears came to his eyes.

"I notice on his kilometer gauge that we have gone less than one kilometer. Tell him."

Margaret told him.

I paid the old man for distance delivered, plus one hundred lire for the romance, and Margaret and I stepped down from the carriage.

May 7, 1960. Rome.

"But I can get a pass to the studio," Margaret said.

"I never bring my own bottle and I never use a pass, Principessa."

"But it would be so easy. Fellini and Antonioni are friends of mine."

"We must do it my way," I said. "A man moves in more mysterious ways than a woman."

"Well, I'll be recognized anyway," Margaret said. "There will be no trouble at the gate."

"There *must* be trouble at the gate," I said. "There's always trouble at the gate. How could you respect me if there were no trouble at the gate? How could I show you what I do? But that's a point about your being recognized. Perhaps you'd better not come."

"But it's *my* courtship," Margaret said.

"Yes, there's that."

Margaret wanted to use the Maserati but I told her that she would certainly be recognized if we did, and so we took the streetcar out to Cinecittà. We got off one stop before the movie studio.

"But it's five streets further," Margaret said.

"Never mind," I said. "We have to get off here."

We got down and I went into the men's room in a gas station. I took off my shirt. "Here," I said to Margaret, who was standing just outside the door, and I handed it to her. Then I took my jar of Vicks VapoRub and began to pat the stuff over my arms and chest and back and neck and face. I am not the kind of person who tans, but I am darkish, and the Vicks, thick as butter on my body, gave my skin the fine, high gloss I wanted. I felt like sixteen cartons of burning Kool cigarettes and smelled like something in a sickroom, but the visual effect was startling. The Vicks added a sweaty, faintly greasy definition to each muscle, so that I looked, even at rest, like someone hard at some powerful labor.

It was wonderful, I thought. I had used to think that something always turned up. It was true, of course, but inadequate, and as an only partially optimistic vision of the world it was a little vague. It was no philosophy to live by unless one enjoyed long waiting. I know now that although something will always turn up, one needn't wait. Any position, any action, however absurd, produces consequences. The wilder the action the more desirable the consequences. Everything works; anything works. Chewing gum will plug a dike. One must remember that, as *all* aggressors are fond of saying about their enemies, the world is decadent. It won't fight. So right away I have the advantage of surprise, the high ground of the insane gesture. A steady hand and a poker face are all one needs. Only be bold—brazen it out and the day is yours. Therefore have *chutzaph!*

Listen, one man with a cap gun and the proper

attitude can take the Bank of England. If there's little comfort in this, all right. If you think, What can I do with the Bank of England, you're right—but that's another story. What can you do with victory itself? We winners know, yes? But rich or poor rich is better, and give or take take is nicer. Are you with me?

With the rest of the Vicks Margaret got the spots I had missed and we walked the five blocks up to the gate. She was a little nervous, I think, but outside the gates is familiar territory for me. It's my home town, so to speak.

"Hi, Pop," I said to the policeman behind the gate. "It's a line I learned from the movies," I told Margaret. I turned back to the policeman. *"Parle Inglese?"*

The policeman shook his head.

"Sono Boswell," I said. *"Capito?"*

The man said something which of course I didn't understand. Margaret opened her mouth to translate and I interrupted her. "Don't speak," I said, "don't say a word." I put my hand on the gate to push it open and the policeman moved stubbornly in front of it. He asked me something.

"Sono Boswell," I said again. *"Capito?"*

He looked at me a little uncertainly, trying to decide whether he had ever seen me before. He examined my shiny, shirtless torso as if, after all, it was not such a very unusual sight. *"Sono* Boswell. *Boswell,"* I said. *"Capito?"* I said very softly.

He was going to say something, but before he could open his mouth I spoke again. *"Sono* Boswell. *Capito? Capito?"*

He shook his head, deciding he did not know me, but a ltttle unsure of it.

I said it slowly, sounding a little exasperated this time. *"Sono* Boswell. *Capito?"*

Now he was very unsteady. I gave him another one. *"Sono* Boswell. *So-no* Bos-well. Bozzz-well. *Ca-pi-to?"*

He said something in a very rapid Italian. "Tch-tch-tch," I said. *"Sono Americano. No parle Italiano."*

He repeated whatever he had said more slowly.

"Americano," I said when he was through, smiling widely, innocently. I shrugged a little stupidly and smiled

322

even more broadly. Then I turned to Margaret and spoke very quickly in English. For his benefit I tried to make it sound as if I were saying, My my what are we to do now here it is already such and such o'clock and we're late for our appointment and all of us will lose our jobs if we don't get inside. I said, "Don't look so nervous, Margaret. We're almost through. I recognize the third degree of self-doubt on his face. I want you to say something in English now. Anything—it doesn't make any difference. Make it sould like a suggestion."

Margaret hesitated.

"Go ahead," I said. "Say something. Anything at all. It ought to sound as if you're giving me an idea."

"I might be able to live with you," Margaret said.

"Ah," I said, "ah." I turned back to the policeman.

"*Sono* Boswell, *capito?*" I said. I flexed my muscles. I held up my left arm and made the biceps jump around on it. I did some of Sandusky's best stuff. I pointed to the high gloss on my body. All the while I repeated the simple formula. "*Sono* Boswell. *Capito? Capito?*"

The policeman began to nod in faint recognition. The more I asked him if he understood, the surer he became. I smiled, nodding vigorously, repeating my name. Boswell, smile, vigorous nodding, muscle spasm. Boswell, smile, vigorous nodding, astonishing sudden appearance of hidden muscle like a submarine surfacing. Boswell, smile, vigorous nodding, delighted pointing to some intricate maneuver under the skin.

"*Capito,*" he said at last. "*Capito. Samson!*"

"*Capito?*" I said.

"*Si, capito, capito,*" he said. "Bosswail." He pulled the gate open wide and beckoned us inside. We walked past him beaming and smiling. He waved and I waved.

"Ooo kay," he said. "Ooo kay."

"*Capito?*" I said.

"*Si, si,*" he said, "*capito.*"

Margaret said now what, and I said we're inside aren't we, and wasn't that enough for one day, and she said but what was the point, and I said the point was that we got away with it. Margaret didn't reply to that.

I felt a little badly about Margaret's question. What *did* we do now? I had no follow through, no real style; it was all the flashy stuff. Sure, how many people could get inside, but then how many people would want *just* to get inside? Wouldn't they have ulterior motives? My flaw was I had none. I had only means, no cause to put them to. I was up to here with means; I had means enough for a regiment, but I was at a loss for ends.

When in Los Farronentes with Lano I had bunked with a kid from Milwaukee named Rohnspeece. He wasn't very bright, I'm afraid, and he must have been very poor, for he used to annoy me with the great pleasure he got from the small comforts. If there were cookies for dessert, before he ate them Rohnspeece would fondle each one as if it were some rare coin. He was also an admirer of Jello, of all flavors of ice cream, and of the dark meat. But the thing he loved most in this world was the blanket on his cot. There were two kinds of blankets; one was contraband from the Argentine army and the other was a stolen shipment of U.S. Army blankets. The U.S. Army blanket was a little thicker than the Argentine one and Rhonspeece, to his unfailing amazement, had been issued one of the former. Sometimes, on the colder nights, he would suddenly become conscience-stricken by his good fortune and would wake me up. "It's cold again tonight," he would say. "It isn't fair that I should always have the U.S. Army blanket. Would you like to trade?"

"No," I would say. "Go to sleep."

"Look," he would say, "I'm from Milwaukee. It gets pretty cold up there sometimes. I'm used to the cold weather. I don't need this U.S. Army blanket."

"Rohnspeece, roll yourself up in your god-damned U.S. Army blanket and go to sleep," I would say.

It was only because he annoyed me so much that I didn't take his blanket. I knew that by refusing it I was forcing him to lie awake all night with his guilt and his pathetic metaphysical speculations about why some men always seemed to get extra large portions of vanilla ice cream and U.S. Army blankets, while others were issued blankets from Argentina and had to take a banana when the ice cream ran out.

Once while we were eating chicken Rohnspeece gave one of his heart-rending sighs and said something I shall never forget. "Gee," he said, "I got the thigh again. I had it last time, too." For him it was the capstone of his good fortune.

When Lano blew up Corbonzelos a piece of a building caught Rohnspeece in the stomach, and as he lay dying he told me that he had heard one time that if you had to get it it was best to get it in the stomach because it didn't hurt so much when it was in the stomach, it only made you a little thirsty.

"Is it true, Rohnspeece?" I asked him.

"You know," he said, surprised and pleased, "it is," and he died wondering about his good fortune.

I had never realized it before, but Rohnspeece and I were a lot alike. We both had that surprising humility of expectation that arises, I think, from profound discontent. To be inside when it was raining, warm when it was cold, to be able to sleep, to move your bowels regularly, to throw peanut butter sandwiches at your hunger—this was living. I shuddered, but there is nothing one can do about one's character except avenge it, and I am always thinking of ways.

Margaret and I walked through the busy lot, strolling past the fantastic sets laid down in a weird contiguity of geography and time, turning from a toy Roman street corner into a jungle, going from the jungle into the courtyard of a medieval palace where we could see a messenger on his knees before a king. He had run from the direction of a small sea, where miniature destroyers and cruisers and battleships pitched eight feet off shore. We crossed the border into Palestine and Margaret pointed out to me the papier-mâché temple which some humiliated Samson would pull down one afternoon.

"Here's where the policeman thought you belonged," Margaret said.

"Oh, belonged," I said.

We crossed a slum where people pretended to be unhappy, a mock Riviera where they pretended to be gay.

"It's like a big park," Margaret said. "I've never seen it this way."

I was thinking about Rohnspeece and I didn't answer her.

"Did you hear what I said before, Boswell?" she asked after a while.

"That you'd never seen it this way," I said.

"No," she said, "earlier. When you were talking to that policeman and I said I might be able to live with you."

"Oh," I said, "live."

August 4, 1960. Rome.

We were married in the Palace of the Cavalieri di Malta by the Grand Master of the Order.

The Italian Premier was there and the Agnellis of Fiat and Enrico Mattei, the oil man. The Colonnas came. The Borgheses did. There were four Cardinals from the Curia, one of them the Pope's special representative. There were film directors and the owners of ski resorts and chairmen of boards and directors of banks. There were ambassadors who had to find seats in the back. There was some royalty, and society so high it made me dizzy.

One old man who came by himself and whom I never got a chance to meet was said to have been the developer of the Bay of Naples, an artist with TNT.

Three prima donnas and four male leads from La Scala sang in the choir.

Inexplicably, though many of the others seemed to know him, Harold Flesh was there. Ah, I thought, the Mafia! The bride's side!

Someone who said he was Cholly Knickerbocker came up to me and said, "At last we meet."

I heard a German countess say to an English lord, "Europe needed a wedding like this."

I had sent invitations to all the famous people I could think of, but only Penner, who was in Europe buying up youth hostels, could come. Finally I'd phoned Nate Lace in New York and asked him to get up a party. He brought a dozen of his actors and comics and recording stars, and though they looked something like a lost troupe of USO performers, they behaved very well really, and were such a hit with the Europeans that I was proud of them. It was sad, though, to think that after thirteen or fourteen years in the business of meeting people these were all I could muster for my wedding. Where were Stravinski and Adlai Stevenson and the Vice-President? Where were Perlmutter and Gordon Rail and Rockefeller and Faulkner and Bellow and Hemingway? Where was Dr. Salk? Where was Lano? Where were the scientists and governors and university professors? Where were the Gibbenjoys? Where, for that matter, was John Sallow?

After the ceremony we strolled among the guests in the gardens of the Maltese Order.

I introduced Nate to Margaret. "Princess," he said, and dipped his head smartly, as if all his friends had titles. And so they had, of course: Heavyweight, Batting Champion, Leading Ground Gainer.

When Margaret left us to speak with some of her friends I remained standing with Nate. "Happy, kid?" he said.

"Oh boy," I said. "Oh boy oh boy."

"Well, I wish you all the luck," he said. "All of it. All the luck."

"Thanks, Nate."

"And Perry thought you were such a wash-out."

"Perry's a prick, Nate."

"You always felt that," he said philosophically. "She's really a princess," he said.

"A Medici, Nate. A Medici. She's the whore of the world but she's very sweet."

Nate seemd a little shocked. "Say, have you had anything to drink?" he asked.

"A little, Nate, I've had a little."

"Well, where did you get it? I didn't want to say anything but there's no liquor."

"Well, it's religious, Nate. That's a religious thing. This is a Jesuit palace. The man who married us is the

327

Grand Master himself. The GM. And you know what they say, Nate—what's good for the GM is good for the Catholic Church."

"You're not Catholic," Nate said. "I never knew you were Catholic."

"Sure, I'm Catholic, Nate. I'm very flexible religiouswise." I winked. "Would I let a little thing like God interfere with this wedding?"

"Say," Nate said, "that's really something. Not even Catholic and married by a high priest like that."

"Oh, the highest, Nate. The highest." I lowered my voice. "They call him the Black Pope. He tells the White Pope what to do."

Nate shook his head, amazed.

"Did I ever tell you how we got engaged?" I said. "No, of course not. Well, we were sitting in the Tre Scalini in the Piazza Navona. Margaret was having a little drink and I was eating the tartufo. That's a world famous ice cream, Nate, and you know how I am."

Nate looked puzzled.

"Come on, Nate. Toledo blades. Irish linen. Your own arctic lichen tea. Tartufo ice cream. I steer by Betelgeuse and the larger stars. Landmarks, Nate. Milestones. Beware of imitations. The best is barely good enough. Here is not anywhere. (Later, Baron, I'm talking to my friend, Nate Lace.) So there we were. I was eating the world famous tartufo ice cream in full view of the statues by Bernini the Younger, sitting with the last of the Medicis, and—well, it was very heady, Nate, very heady."

Nate was embarrassed. He would have walked away if I had given him the chance.

"So I figured to msyelf, 'Boswell, don't be a fool. It could always be this way. The girl loves you.' Oh, Nate, I had given her the business; I was at the top of my form. Wildness. Self-destructiveness. The works, Nate, the very romantic works. I even faked a tic in my left cheek."

"Hey, hey, hey, hey," Nate said soothingly.

"No, no, listen to this. Social history. I had taken that girl for the ride of her life. Listen, it wasn't easy. You think this was some bobby-soxer? This was one of the most sophisticated women in Europe. I mean, there was real unhappiness there. I mean, at first it was the other way around. I was actually convinced I loved her."

Nate was astonished.

"Whoops," I said. "Whoops, whoops. If you drink, don't drive, hey, Nate? A slip of the lip can sink the ship. Well, no matter, right? *Entre nous,* no?"

I knew, of course, that I was doing irreparable damage, setting a course which it would be impossible to check later. Already it was impossible to check. No selfish man ever kids himself. No *really* selfish man ever bothers to kid others. The surprising thing was that I wasn't even that drunk; I'd taken only intermittent sips from the flask in the pocket of my morning coat. "My missal," I had said to the Grand Master, explaining the slight bulge. " 'The Good Book,' as we Americans say." It was my triumph that I was high on, the impossibly glorious conjunction of myself with grand people and great events.

Texture is a quality of the experience of the single man. It is no accident, for example, that I have never worn glasses, or that I am uncomfortable in gloves. Nor was it an accident that I could speak this way to Nate. Loneliness is sentimental. It slaps back and prolongs the handshake and weeps easily, for it always imagines— though it knows it can't be so—that the sense of juxta-position is universally felt. Even when I was wrestling, and used to sit in the strange hotel lobbies with the other wrestlers, men with whom I had shared a card in Kansas City or in Maine, I could hardly restrain myself from clapping them on the back and saying, "Well, old horse, we meet again, hey? Here we are in a hotel lobby in Cheyenne, Wyoming, among the ferns and spurs." Often my companion would look bewildered. He could hardly have known what I meant. Why shouldn't two men in the same profession, traveling in the same circuit, meet again and again? What was strange? The world, the world itself, the world was strange; recognizing another face was strange; being alive was wondrous strange. But the others had families, pictures in their wallets, letters to write. You had to go it alone for it to mean anything. To share experience with so much as one other person was immediately to halve it. To divide it among three of you was to reduce what was left to yourself by two thirds. It was mathematical. All we could ever get from others, really, was comfort. In the long run it was the deepest wisdom to be a pirate, to plot among the survivors on the beach to kill off the other survivors, and then to scheme how to dispose of whoever remained.

I had regard for Margaret, certainly. I was even fond of her. But love of another always involved at least a small betrayal of the self. It was not impossible to love; the temptation was always there, to give comfort like a small sleep, a sweet forgetting. Too often I had read in books that such and such a person was unable to love. It always came out as if something was wrong with one of his organs—as though a kidney were functioning improperly or a hand couldn't clench into a fist. It was the cliché of our time. One heard it on buses. I was not incapable of love; no one is. I think I could love anyone. But it has never been enough. It provides only a kind of emotional illusion, as community singing, raising your voice to the bouncing ball, provides the emotional illusion of good fellowship.

"So," I told Nate, "I asked her. And as you saw for yourself, they were married. I made a match, Nate, I made a match."

"Well," Nate said uncomfortably, "I wish you all the luck. She's beautiful."

"What am I, Nate, chopped liver?"

"All the luck."

"Thank you, Nate." I had no desire to make him any more uncomfortable. "Listen," I said, "I'd better go find Margaret."

"Sure."

I walked away, nodding happily to all the guests— my guests, I thought, *my* guests. Margaret had dowered me handsomely. It was a different feeling, I saw, to give the party, even if I was giving only nominally.

As I passed the USO troupe I heard Nate say, "It's an international incident."

"What I want to know is who gave him the two bucks for the Cardinal?" one of his comics said.

"Margaret," I said.

"No offense," he said shamefacedly.

"None taken," I said.

I continued my happy walks through the gardens, nodding and smiling to everyone. I had a greeting for everybody. "Baron," I said. "Countess." I went through the clipped arch of an enormous hedge. "General," I said. "Premier." I strolled past a fountain where a group of distinguished-looking people stood somewhat protectively around an infirm old man. "King," I said, "how are you?"

It was wonderful. I felt the special immunity of my elation. I was a genuinely charming man. I oozed not sophistication so much as a sort of genial novelty. Men could restore themselves in my presence. I went among them like someone bearing a gift; it was life itself I was prepared to show them. I could join any of these people. I had things to tell them all. I could speak to the point about triumphs and about times I thought the game was up; I could bring them my life as a happy lesson in persistence, turning it before them like some bright crystal to catch the sun. Perhaps Margaret even got as good as she gave. It was only a pity that I was taking her away to America before I had the opportunity to prove it. I was the incarnate American-con-artist-adventurer-rustler-Mississippi-river-boat-gambler, a sort of Medici in my own right, or what narrowly passed for right among the breed. Add to this the fact that I was an understander, going the merely compassionate one better, and Margaret came out almost ahead.

Was this what they meant by happiness? Why, it was wonderful to be happy. I would have tried it years ago had I known. Suddenly I felt I had to sit down to think about it. Very carefully I held the crease in my morning trousers and sat down beneath a tree. I placed my top hat beside me.

Margaret came up. "You'll stain your clothes," she said.

331

"Margaret," I said, "until ten minutes ago I never felt cute. Now I feel it. I feel waves of cuteness. Am I cute, Margaret? I mean really *cute?* It's very important."

"Well, you're more curious than cute," she said. She stepped back happily to appraise me. "You know, I never noticed before, but you don't wear clothes very well. Boswell, you're a little slobby."

"But am I *cute?*"

"No," she said seriously. "Your real charm is your despair. I married you for it."

"It's left me, Margaret," I said. "I don't feel it any more."

"It will come back."

"I hope so, Margaret."

"It will come back," she said. "Just think of death." I had told Margaret about death.

I contemplated death for a while. At first it seemed difficult, far-fetched among these lovely people in this lovely garden, but by degrees it began to take on its old validity. I pretended it was two years hence. Already the garden seemed not so crowded, a little desolate even, the voices more subdued. The infirm old king was gone, and two or three of the other old people. I projected five years into the future. There was not much change. Some of the younger people had come into their prime and many of the old ones still hung on. I increased the tempo, stepping up the future by ten years, fifteen. Now you could see the difference. The place was half empty. If you didn't know better you might have thought there had been a war. Nate Lace was gone. Penner, that old saint, had been gathered to his reward I pushed time ahead another two years. It was child's play now; I need only leap ahead by months, even by weeks, to empty the garden. In another year Margaret herself would be gone. And I wasn't feeling too good either.

It was my statistic trick and it always worked. Whenever things got to looking up, whenever the sense of fate seemed to leave me, the old confidence in withering catastrophe, I would think of the future in order to restore order to my life. It's amazing. You're sitting in a crowded theater and you think, One of these people will die in an automobile accident this year, eleven will have heart attacks, seven will be stricken by cancer, two will be shot, one will commit suicide, four will die of blood diseases, three of wounds that will not heal. And so on. And so forth.

"You'll really have to get up," Margaret said.

"I was getting up," I said.

"The Grand Master wants to see you. He sent me to look for you."

"Why?"

"Well, to talk to you. He's a little angry, I think."

"Why?"

"I told him about the settlement I made on you," Margaret said.

"It's not his business," I said. "He can tell the White Pope, but he can't tell me."

"Of course he can't, darling, and I'm sure he won't say very much, but he wants you to explain it."

At the palace the Grand Master was in his study, a young priest told me. He took me to the huge double doors and knocked for me. A voice answered, and the priest nodded and left me. I pushed the heavy doors and entered a remarkable room. I had expected books, rich carpets, a fat, illuminated globe, but it was empty except for a crucifix and a very long table. The table was familiar from the movies: people drank mead at it. I expected to see it bruised from so many heavy mugs having been thumped against it. There were high casement windows all the way around the room; the effect was somehow like being in a cloister. The shutters on all but one of the windows had been pulled and light came into the room queerly angled through this single window as though it were a gangplank fixed to a ship, or, perhaps purposefully, some oddly illuminated tunnel that led to heaven. The table had been placed along the wall opposite the door, as if it had been set there to make room for dancing. The arrangement unbalanced the huge room and I didn't seem to walk so much as pitch forward into it. Ah, the Jesuitical intelligence, I thought.

The Grand Master had placed himself in silhouette in front of the open window at the far side of the long

333

table. He had removed his ceremonial vestments and was dressed now in the plain suit of the ordinary priest. As I stepped toward him I felt like someone in a black and white film. The bright gardens behind him seemed part of a different world.

Despite my boasts to Nate, I had taken the Grand Master for granted. Margaret had explained the tradition of his marrying all the Medicis. It went back five centuries. Until now it hadn't puzzled me that I had become involved with something that had gone on for five centuries. Well, so what? Nobody ever said man's traditions were mortal.

Though he had spoken in a firm, clear voice a moment ago, the Grand Master now seemed to be asleep. He was an old man, as old as Herlitz had been. His face, as difficult to see in that dark room as if it had been in a painting in a church, seemed even in repose faintly cruel, used to power. It was no different from the Renaissance faces I had seen in portraits in the Uffizi when I had gone with Margaret to Florence. (Margaret still had rooms there—that was part of the five centuries, too—though her family had given the palace to the state long ago.) It was a pale face with a surprising patch of red on each cheek, faintly like the high spoiled blush painted on dolls. It was undeniably handsome, though drained by its long familiarity with power, as though power were a sort of bad habit like alcohol or narcotics that ultimately ravaged the features. Its expression was what people euphemistically called "aristocratic," and was at least one part a faint fear and two parts a boredom with the stupidity of others' responses. Clearly, the Grand Master loved a mystery. To give myself the advantage I tried to imagine him naked, on the toilet, dead. I couldn't; he had a tenacious dignity and I began, despite myself, to admire him.

"You are not what is called 'a good Catholic,' are you?" the old man asked suddenly.

Surprise me no surprises, I thought, "I try to be," I said.

"Do you?" he said. "I watched you before. You fumbled with the rituals."

"I'm a convert, Grand Master. It's still somewhat new to me."

"I hope there has been no mistake in making this marriage."

"Because I didn't make the sign of the Cross smoothly?"

"You made it very smoothly," he said.

Runs deep, I thought. Familiar type. Recognize him from literature. Marvelous when you meet him in life. Grand Master, Grand Inquisitor. Grand. Lee J. Cobb plays him in the picture. Good guy or bad? Hard to tell. But, I thought, that's it. To be like that. That's the ideal. Cryptic wisdom. Talk like a double acrostic. Never raise your voice when you shout. Spiritual politics. Run scared. Every day a new election. Move! Manipulate! Mold! Power the still center at the core of motion. That's it. That's it. Seen everything, been there before; nothing new under the sun. Past so long you're already immortal. Never sick a day in your life but always in pain. Anguish in the smell of a rose. Heart, strategies, philosophy. Wisdom, the black art!

So much for you. It boils down to death, statistics. Everybody dies. Death is my argument. Leave me alone.

"My wife"—he would understand the thrust—"My wife has told me that you are angry about the settlement. I'll try to explain it to you."

"The settlement is a matter of indifference to me," the Grand Master said.

"Of course," I said. "I understand that. She has made me a wealthy man. That part was her idea, anyway. I know you don't object to that—you don't care who has the wealth as long as someone has it. I think perhaps it's The Club you're interested in."

I began to explain about The Club.

Part Three

I

The truth is we haven't caught on. We are so lonely.
Margaret asks, Are we happy, and the question makes me
furious and sad. I put her off with a joke. I read our
bank balance. I point to the carpet and indicate its thickness with my forefinger and thumb. I bring her to the
kitchen and show her our meats.

I tell Margaret that she is my war bride. The fact is
she seemed actually to diminish when we went through
customs. The man asked if we had anything to declare
and Margaret stared at him as if she didn't understand
the question. When he asked again she looked at me and
I thought she would cry.

"No, nothing," I said. "We have nothing to declare."
You know how it is when you make a mistake.

I can't explain it. We are out of touch. Not with
each other, but mutually, with everything.

Hawthorne tells a story about a man named Wake-
field who left his home one evening and didn't return for
twenty years. His act was a whim, unpremeditated, but it
made no difference; if he had come back a week later it
would already have been too late. One must never break
the rhythm of his life. You stay in lockstep or you suffer.
Every vacation is an upheaval. I have seen men at the
seashore whose free time is the most grotesque of bur-
dens. They are haunted by the idea of things going on
without them, of someone at the office doing their job,
opening their mail, answering their phone. It's an intima-

tion of death. You have to make a life, however grab-bag or eccentric; there has to be routine, pattern. I've failed there. Something about my life gives my life away, something improvised and sad. At my dinner parties there are mismatched dishes, chairs, plastic spoons. I was better off alone, I think. There was desperation to keep me going. It's all what you're used to. For me running scared is the only way to travel. Poor is what I know best, and there are times when I can almost taste the old degradation of the bones—ten minutes for a rest stop, pee, spit, and regret, talking to the driver beside the big open underbelly of the bus where the cardboard suitcase goes, the box tied up with string.

I'll tell you what's wrong with me. I don't know what to tip. A grown man!

There are "executive flights" now and I am on them and there is always monogrammed linen and the best booze in my attaché case, but the truth is I was never less attaché. I have heard the stewardesses singing each to each, I do not think that they will sing to me.

Well, the grass is never greener, I always say. The course of true life never did run smooth.

When as a child I was home ill everything was fine until the others came back and I heard their voices and laughter outside. Then something would happen inside me, in my heart, and I'd have to get up and shut the window. To this day the most awful sound for me is a conversation overheard, people talking to each other in a restaurant at the next table, behind me on a bus. I swear, sometimes I feel already like a ghost.

For me envy isn't a sin, it seems, but a fact. I need it to live, like air. Sometimes I think, If I'd lived more to the purpose . . . Crap! Who has lived more to the purpose than myself? No; disappointment, like rotten fruit, is always the last thing left in the larder. Things pall. The world's appalling. A'palling. It goes like a song.

Each day the conviction grows. I'm going to die. *I'm going to die*. I'll tell you how far it's gone: I've stopped smoking; there are seatbelts in my automobiles; I will not have phosphorescent dials on my clocks; I watch my cholesterol; I am wary of air-conditioning. All that can be done I do. It means nothing. *Nothing.*

For a year we lived like tourists in our own city. We went to all the shows, the movies, the museums, the public buildings. Three times we went on the boat around Manhattan island, five times to the top of the Empire State Building. For a sense of belonging we took out library cards. We joined the clubs that send you merchandise or books. Making our fastidious choices provided us with the illusion of will. Margaret learned to cook. I learned nothing.

I sent money to my son's grandmother, enclosing with the checks long letters. I wanted my boy, I said, and outlined the advantages I could bestow upon him now. When she opposed my plans I was glad, for that allowed me to continue to compose the letters. Like the book clubs, these gave me the illusion of somehow shaping a domesticity. Something ritualistic had been absent from my life always, I recognized, was absent still. I made a conscious effort to live as others lived, but I noticed that whenever I did the things other people did, I felt strangely incognito—as if, like all orphans, I was ultimately at home only in the homes of others. It cannot be good for me to have an address, my own phone number. I have been too long bizarre. Domestic *dibbuks* have claimed me. Ah, I think, reality flattens everything, despite its being good for us. (One must come to grips, they say. If they mean I must embrace pain, that's redundant. What the hell *isn't* reality; who doesn't face up to it?)

I had my ruses; they were legion. Sometimes I read the obituaries in newspapers for the opportunity they gave me of further rituals. In my files there is an example. From the *Times* of October 19, 1960:

ELWORTHAM. On October 18, 1960, peacefully, in his sleep, at his home, 143 Bell Avenue, Brooklyn, Edward J. Elwortham, aged 59. Beloved husband of Frances, dear father of Robert. Funeral service 11:30 A.M., Friday, October 20, 1960. Phizer's Chapel, 71 Avenue C, Brooklyn, N.Y. No flowers.

The feeling with which I wrote Mrs. Elwortham was not faked. It was almost as though I had indeed known him as I said. I even signed my name.

I wrote:

Dear Mrs. Elwortham,
Words cannot express the deep sense of shock I experienced when I read Thursday of Edward's death. We haven't met, Mrs. Elwortham. Of recent years Edward and I had drifted apart, as even best friends do, and we saw each other only infrequently, but Edward was a friend of my youth, and I have thought of him often over the years. No words of mine can ease the grief I know you must be experiencing now. Edward was a good man. His absence will be keenly felt by all who knew him. I can only pray that time, that old healer, will do its job to assuage your and Robert's pain.

    I notice that the paper mentions the family's desire to omit flowers. I do not know what Edward's favorite charity was, Mrs. Elwortham, but perhaps it would be all right if I made a contribution in Edward's name to the Red Cross. In the meanwhile if there is anything I can do, please don't hesitate to call on me. With all sympathy, I am . . .

Writing the check to the Red Cross and entering the figure on the stub was enormously satisfying to me. That's the sort of thing I mean. Once I wrote a letter to the president of General Electric complaining about a refrigerator. I told him it wouldn't make ice cubes and that butter melted in the tray.

Although these masquerades calmed me I saw that to continue with them would make me sick.

Late in that first year of our marriage, my son's grandmother died. I talked my decision over with Margaret, though this was simply a courtesy. I am not one of your typical rich women's husbands, always sneaking

342

around the corners of his intentions. We have an understanding, Margaret and I, which is that under no circumstances am I ever to feel obligation. I consider taking things for granted part of the marriage agreement, a piece of the dowry. So a year after we were married, when I was thirty-three and he was eighteen, I sent for my son.

Whatever else may be wrong with me I am essentially a civilized man, and as such I enjoy my little scene now and then. I arranged this one with all the old style. I wired the boy a ticket on an executive flight. I sent him money and the address of the best tailor in St. Louis. A car met him at the airport. For the occasion I wore a smoking jacket for the first time in my life.

"Boswell, you're crazy," Margaret said.

"How is that, my dear? As yet no real link has been established between smoking jackets and cancer."

I also wore an ascot, flannel trousers, black silk hose and carpet slippers. I made Margaret put on a green taffeta dressing gown. The rustle was deafening, but we looked wonderful.

When the boy arrived I shook his hand and offered to make him a drunk. "How are you, David?" I said. "Margaret, this is my son David."

Margaret shook David's hand. She has a strong, horsewoman's handshake which would be advantageous to me in my business, if I had a business.

I stepped brightly to the bar whistling Noel Coward, and mixed drinks for us all. "Water, David? Soda?"

"That's all right," David said. "Whichever is easier."

"Well, neither is terribly difficult, David."

"Well, whichever is easier," David said politely.

The problem had never occurred to me. "I think water is easier," I said from behind the bar. "All you do is turn the tap."

"Water is fine, thank you. I don't want to put you to any trouble," David said.

I wondered if my boy was capable of irony and watched him as I mixed the drinks.

I brought the drinks out with a flourish and stepped

343

between Margaret and my son. I put my arms around their shoulders. "My big family," I said expansively, looking from one to the other.

David smiled and raised his glass to his lips. It was the first time I had ever seen anyone swallow while smiling. Of course he was uneasy but I began to see that my son was one of those people who were constantly apologizing for their presence, treating themselves like an untidy bedroom through which a housewife reluctantly shows a guest to the toilet. Standing there before me, he seemed to be attempting to hide. There was something maidenly about him, as though he might be trying to cover his privates. David, I saw sadly, was not an ironist but a jerk. It was all my big family needed. I mean, it's all well and good to play Noel Coward, and considered in one kind of light a sophisticated father and a dopey son have certain comic possibilities, but the fact is David was a disappointment. I had been hoping—illogically perhaps, considering my past treatment of him—for a different type, someone's roommate at a good prep school, with trees in his past and summer places and a few years in a classy hotel off Central Park, a deep-chested lad who had been to Europe and spoke French and could get down a mountain on a pair of skis and didn't smile when he swallowed. But the truth was David was scared stiff and looked a little Jewish.

"The trip was—"   "Well, David, how was—"
"I'm sorry," David said.
"No, no, go ahead."
"No, please. You," David said.
"Well, how was the trip?"
"The trip was very interesting," David said.
"I see."
"It was *very* interesting," he said again, tentatively forceful.

I wondered what was so interesting about it. Probably the little paper sack, or the funny cellophane packages of butter and silverware, or the brochures, or the instructions for ditching at sea.

"They let you read magazines," he said. *"Fortune,*

344

U.S. News and World Report, everything. I don't often get a chance to see those books."

Why did things always turn out this way? There was something careless about people's lives, something spontaneous in existence which spoiled it.

I had prepared a speech to make to David. It would have been a silly speech under the circumstances; now it was ridiculous. He wouldn't know that, I thought, but Margaret would. I decided to give it anyway. Like most people it is impossible for me to change my plans. We are able to forgive and forget the past, able even to ignore the future, but let him beware who treads on our present.

"Now look here, David," I began and immediately saw my mistake. Thinking I was about to reprimand him, David had jumped back. He looked guiltily down at the carpet, perhaps to see whether he had spilled any of his drink.

"No, no," I said. "Look, David. I mean, listen, David, why don't you sit down and relax?"

"It's all right," he said, "I can stand. I like to stand."

"No, sit down," I said.

"Well, I don't want to make any trouble for you," he said.

"Well, it's not making any trouble for us if you sit down," I said.

"If you're sure it's all right?" he said.

"Margaret, it's all right if David sits down, isn't it?"

"Just this once," Margaret said.

David, who was wearing a sort of a grayish suit, chose a sort of grayish chair. He had a habit of putting his hands out of sight, like a nun. Once he was invisible I began again.

"What I want to say, David, is by way of apology and explanation." At the word "apology" David moved his lips to make one. I rushed on, feeling lost and more sad in the presence of the real David than ever I had in dealing with the harmed, sensitive, prep school David of my imagination. "There's too much talk about fathers

345

and sons," I said. "David, I don't understand other people very well. The integrity of someone else's identity is a mystery to me. I'm astonished by other people's lives, David. For me, every human being is somehow like a man under arms, a good soldier. He seems so sure of his cause that I wonder if it ever occurs to him that he might have to die for it. What I respect in other people, I suppose, is their capacity for victory, their confidence that it will come. I know *I* wouldn't want to go up against most of them. You've seen men. You've seen them coming at you down the sidewalk, taking up your space. You know what they're like. There's a lot of nonsense talked about human beings. If you believe it you might think the least little thing is capable of breaking people down. My God, David, that can't be true. Do you think those guys on the executive flight are made of glass? Yet one hears every day of lives ruined by unhappy childhoods, broken homes, nervousness about the bomb, bad marriages, unrequited love. Those things are nothing, David.

"You probably feel you've been mistreated by me, denied a birthright. You—"

"No," David protested. "It's all right. I don't mind."

"Jesus," Margaret said, "the man abandoned you, sonny."

"I didn't *abandon* David, Margaret."

Margaret laughed.

"I didn't," I said again.

"It's all right," David said. "I don't—"

"You don't mind, I know," I said angrily. "Look, maybe all I'm saying is that men can take care of themselves. Certainly that's what I did. The thing is to forget grief, David. If I've harmed you by not providing you with myself, then I'm sorry, but you're mistaken to be harmed."

"I see," David said.

"We want you to live with us. I've talked this over with Margaret and she agrees," I said. "You wouldn't be putting us to any trouble," I added hastily. Suddenly I foresaw all the objections he would raise, the soft demurs and small effacements that would have to be answered one by one, point by point, until it was obvious to anyone

346

that David did in fact put people to trouble. He surprised me, however.

"I don't think I could come until June," he said.

"Why?"

"I'm supposed to be in school until then," he said apologetically.

I began to see that my son had the beggar's trick of spurious withdrawal so that all you finally saw was the hand. His very grammar was deceptively soft. He didn't *think* he could come, he was *supposed* to be in school, as though the world were always arranging itself independently of his will. There was toughness in his style too, I saw, and if I didn't approve of his methods I did begin to like him a little more. It has always been reassuring to me to have it confirmed that others are as selfish as myself.

"Well, if you can't come till June you can't come till June," I said. "The fact is, David, that your grandmother was never very committal with us where you were concerned. I didn't even know you were going to school."

"I go to hairdresser's school," David said very softly.

"Hairdresser's school? You're a beautician?"

"Yes, sir," David said sadly. For a moment he allowed us to see his hands.

"Is that what you *want?*"

"In high school the placement counselor thought it might be something I would be able to do."

"Cut that out," I said impatiently.

I saw him grin briefly despite himself. "It might be better if I stayed just where I am," he said.

"Why?"

"You might change your mind about me. Then where would I be?"

"We could give you a check right now," I said. "That would protect you."

"I don't think I'd better," David said.

"Suit yourself."

"My teachers think I ought to come to New York after I graduate."

"Don't you ever say *you* want anything?"

"I'm sorry," David said. He shifted slightly in his

347

seat, somehow giving the impression that his back was to us.

"David," I said. "You won't be any trouble to us, and if your business forces you to be in New York I see no reason why you shouldn't stay with us. As you see, there's plenty of room here. I have a great deal to make up to you for, of course, so I would consider it a favor to me if you would stay with us and allow me to force certain advantages on you that I am now in a better position to give."

"That's very nice of you both," David said slyly. "If you're absolutely sure I won't be in the way."

"Of course not," I said. "Will he, Margaret?"

Margaret laughed.

Then I made a test. I said something under my breath so that David couldn't quite hear it.

"I beg your pardon?" David said.

"Don't you ever just say '*what*,' David?" I asked.

II

Despite what I may have told David about there being too muck talk of fathers and sons, I find that in one respect I was mistaken. Relationship—blood—is a peculiar business. I don't care how close a friendship is, you can always pull back at the last moment. There's the possibility of betrayal. The same thing in a family is a higher treason. Somehow one is closer to a first cousin than he is to a wife, for it isn't merely an alliance of choice, of the will. I've spoken to Morty about this and he says I've stumbled on an anthropological truth. He points out that all tribes, no matter how primitive, have ceremonies of divorce, but that no ceremony exists anywhere for the undoing of a relationship between kinsmen. My first cousin is my first cousin, no matter how much we may come to hate each other. It's nature, a fact the way a stone is a fact. How much more interesting, then, is the bond between a father and a son. I never imagined it. I wouldn't look at him twice in the street perhaps, but he is my son and that makes the difference.

Because David is mine I try to change him. I come into a room where he is deferentially dematerialized against a wall (his old habit of blending with furniture of any style is still unbroken; indeed, I suspect he deliberately dresses for rooms he knows he will inhabit), and I call in a loud voice, "David, where are you, son?" It embarrasses him to be flushed out this way, but he does not yield: next time it is the same. The boy's will is like iron.

349

Margaret is left out of this; she understands that David is not her son. We have been trying to have children together. She wants them badly, but mine is the more urgent need. I *must* have them! We are neither of us ardent but we have used no devices since David came to live with us. We make love with an extraordinary frequency and there is a sense of emergency about our throes. In a way that I do not understand, I see that if I have a destiny at all it is to be a father. It's not that I am putting aside for that rainy day when there will be no more Boswells. I am not concerned with perpetuating my name; that kind of immortality has nothing to do with me. But were I a king whose succession depended upon getting sons I could not be more concerned. (I perceive that as I grow older I become *more* obsessive rather than less. If one day this leads me into a park where I will sit, my fingers inside my corrupt overcoat fondling my erection, waiting for the lunchtime passage of one particular small schoolgirl, that's just too bad. There are only two kinds of intelligences, the obsessive and the perspectual. All dirty old men come from the former and all happy men from the latter, but I wouldn't trade places. In this life frustration is the Promethean symbol of effort.) Fatherhood, I think, *fatherhood!* I lust for sons and daughters, but nothing happens. The more I pump Margaret the less good it seems to do. I asked her if there was something wrong.

"Wrong, what do you mean wrong?"

"In the old days in Italy, did you ever have an abortion?"

She was very angry and for several days wouldn't allow me in her bed. My God, how those days were torture. I had never felt so strong, my seed so ripe, never experienced greather impatience, the sense of time so uselessly destroyed. I realized that I could not risk offending her that way again and I became conciliatory, fatuous in the pains I took with her. Yet the question, which I had not meant to ask, had implications. I had never really minded Margaret's promiscuity, nor had I any reason to suspect that after we were married she was unfaithful. Before David came I might have forgiven an

350

infidelity with a wave of the hand, but now I had a horror of raising another man's son. After I had apologized, I immediately re-risked everything by telling Margaret that if I ever discovered she had gone to bed with another man I would kill them both.

I made her go to a gynecologist. She had all the tests. Her womb was not tipped, her tubes not stopped. She produced eggs like a million hens. "Then why aren't you pregnant?" I demanded.

She shrugged. "The doctor says I can have children," she said. "He thinks you ought to be examined."

"Did you explain that I have already proved myself?"

But of course I went. I made an appointment with a Dr. Green, whom the Doctor's Exchange listed as a specialist in these things.

"Your wife has been examined, I assume," the doctor said.

"Yes. She's all right." I was looking at the certificate on the wall, from a medical school I had never heard of. Why did it have to be a school I never heard of?

"Yes, the husband's always the last partner to be examined. That's masculine vanity for you, isn't it? And I suppose you thought it out of the question that a strapping fellow like yourself could be the sterile one."

"That's what I'm here to find out."

"Well, let's go down to it then, shall we? We're not here for recriminations or to fix blame, but out of scientific interest, am I right? Now I don't know what I'm going to find in your case, but I don't want you to worry. If we should discover that you're infertile there may be some things we can do to build you up. If that fails there's the possibility of adoption, isn't there? So don't look so nervous. As it happens, I handle a lot of adoptions and you don't even have to wait as you would if you worked through an agency. It's all legal, brother. I don't want to hear any uninformed talk about a black market. It's expensive, I won't crap you, but how are you going to fix a price on human life, do you see? I mean it *ought* to be expensive."

"I'm not interested in adopting children."

351

"Now look here, son, I can see what you're thinking. I'm way ahead of you in that respect. You're thinking, 'Why, he's a quack.' "

"Something like that."

"Sure you are. Well, it's not true. I'll tell you the truth—there's a lot of prejudice in this business. Very few men are as honest as you evidently are and will even come in for an examination like this. The adoptions? That's something I do just to keep my experimental work going. Because you see I *haven't* put all my cards on the table for you. How'd you get my name?"

"Through the Doctor's Exchange."

"That's what I thought. That's just what I thought. Well, I'll take care of you. Nobody could do it better. But do you know what we do here? It's a fertility clinic. This is a donor station. I'm talking about artificial insemination. I only accept the very highest type of donor: intellectual, slightly left-wing Jewish medical students. How'd you like a son by one of those fellers? A very popular number right now. Well, we get them all. Artists from the Village, writers. All very good-looking as well as smart. It's the surest way I know of to raise a family. Takes all the risk right out. It's the genes—the genes are everything. Some of my patients come back two, three, four times. You'd be astonished to learn just how many of Dr. Green's kids are the leaders of their communities today."

"Are you a donor?"

"No. Oh God, no. In the early days when it was slow I won't say I didn't try to cut expenses by putting something in the bottle now and then, but that's water under the bridge. Well, images change. Taste changes. This I promise, my young doctors are the higest example of the current image. To get on my list they take vows of celibacy. That keeps the stock up, you see. It's a kind of quality control."

"But let's suppose, for argument's sake, you don't *like* the current image. Well then, pick any type you do like. If you don't see what you want, just ask for it. If I haven't got him now I know where I can get him. This I promise—the biggest depth in the City of New York.

What do you want? An actor? A politician? I've even got scions of famous families who have to be specially solicited. Now for obvious reasons the donors have to remain anonymous, but if you want I could show you my library. It's a file, you see, with the biography of the donor. What the father did, the mother, personality traits, IQ's, medical histories—the works. You'd be surprised at the famous men represented in that library. They're not all active donors now, of course, but when they were young they might have needed a little extra dough. You could get men just like them today. Every type, any type.

"Now this is all probably very premature. I'm not saying you're going to need these services. I don't know what I'll find until I look through that microscope, but I just want you to keep it in mind if the news turns out to be bad. And this I promise, it's perfectly painless. As a matter of fact, I'll tell you the truth, many women enjoy it. Just a little injection into your wife and that's all there is to it. We even mix a little of your own stuff in with it so you can't ever be completely sure the kid isn't actually yours—well, he *is* yours, of course, but you know what I mean. Incidentally, that's a new wrinkle. The profits from some of those adoptions you scorn paid for that. Very tricky scientific problem to work out. To develop the seminal host so that the donor's and the husband's sperm can live together without eating each other up. What a contribution to the field *that's* been, I don't mind telling you! What solace it's provided even prouder men than yourself! And no charge until conception. I don't care how many injections it takes."

"It's not what I had in mind."

"All right. All right. I'm not trying to sell it to you. I'm just telling you what the alternatives are in case the news isn't what either of us wants to hear. That's okay, isn't it?"

"Yes."

"All right," Dr. Green said. "Let's see it."

At first I didn't understand. Then I showed him.

He looked at it thoughtfully. "May I?" He said.

"Of course."

He held my penis in his palm for a moment and then

353

flipped it casually to the other hand. "Not bad," he said at last. "Nothing mechanically wrong anyway but you can't judge a book by its cover. I'll need a specimen. Now you've got a choice here. I can exercise the prostate and I can get enough that way to tell all we need to know, but its painful and frequently embarrassing to many men. The other thing is you can go into the lab—the same one the donors use—and bring something back in this bottle."

"The lab," I said.

"Through there," said Dr. Green. He pointed to a doorway hung with a curtain, vaguely like the fitting room in a cheap department store.

"Turn on the light," Dr. Green called. "There's a switch on your left."

"It can be done in the dark," I said.

"You're my patient," Dr. Green said, "your vanity means nothing to me. The cure's the thing."

Oh, go away, I thought.

The doctor must have read my thoughts, for in a moment I could hear him padding about the office, opening drawers, tapping his pockets, like one making preparations to go out. "I need some cigarettes," he announced. "I'll just go down and get them. I'll lock you in so you won't be disturbed. Okay?"

"Okay," I muttered.

"Okay?"

"Yes, yes. Fine."

"Take your time. Turn on the light." I heard him close the office door and lock it.

It was impossible; I felt ridiculous. For a moment I thought of escaping, but then it occurred to me that what was happening to me was a rare thing indeed. Masturbating for science. In a lab, for God's sake. Sanctioned by society! Juvenile fantasies in a good cause! I thought, Why waste it? Still, I had never been less stirred. I removed my pants and underwear. Despite my sense of freedom I felt foolish and a little cold. For five minutes I stood there, idly manipulating myself, distracted. It occurred to me that the practical difficulties were insurmountable. Then I realized what it was: it was the bottle;

354

I had to put the bottle down. I decided to turn on the lights so that I could find it easily when I needed it.

What I saw when I had switched on the light took away my breath. What Dr. Green had called a lab was really a kind of closet. Around the three walls were unevenly spaced shelves, on each of which had been placed some object obviously meant by Dr. Green to inspire lust. There were those tiny models of women one sees in those drug stores where they sell trusses. The women, otherwise naked, were intricately and suggestively taped, their bandages oddly emphasizing their nakedness. There were rubbery, life-sized breasts removed from some medical school lecture room, the nipples spread and torn by cancer. There were posture charts ripped from old textbooks, the girls in profile, anonymous, one square-shouldered, straight-assed, the next round-shouldered, the pelvis somehow fallen, the behind dragging sluggishly. There was a 1944 wall calendar from a garage in Pittsburgh. There was a model of a plastic, transparent woman, the organs like tainted meat inside her, vaguely suggesting one of those heavy globes portraying some cozy winter scene. I had the impression that if I turned it upside down and shook it, her insides would glow with impossibly slow-falling snow. Everywhere there were plaster of Paris breasts, torsos, behinds, vaginas like halved fruit. In one corner of the closet was a bald life-size department store manikin, completely nude. She had movable arms and legs and these had been arranged in an obscene pose by Dr. Green or one of the donors. The profits from some of those adoptions I scorn paid for this, I thought.

I thought, Oh God, I'm getting out of here, but I made no effort to move. I told myself that it was my fascination with the act of fatherhood that kept me there, but against my will, or rather without it, I began slowly to respond. Quickly my fantasies began to multiply, proliferating wildly so that it was impossible to concentrate on any one of them. One after another, insane images leaped into my head. It was like being on a magic-carpet ride or on one of those subterranean tours of the world.

Suddenly my hands were everywhere, touching, fondling, torturing. I put my palms over the rubber breasts and squeezed, the hard doll cancer-ridden nipples pressing unpleasantly into my flesh. I nuzzled my head between the manikin's breasts; I arranged her hands caressingly and rubbed against them. Just before the orgasm I leaned back heavily against a shelf. The uneven wooden edge put a splinter into my back, but I nearly swooned. I forgot the bottle and only at the last moment managed clumsily to catch the dregs. Sperm was everywhere. Weakened, I knelt to scoop it into the bottle with my cupped palm.

Suddenly Dr. Green pulled back the curtains.

"Forget it, dear boy," he said. "The woman cleans it up."

"I thought you were out getting cigarettes."

"Cigarettes cause cancer. I'm a medical man. I don't smoke." He smiled. "That's mine, I think," he said, taking the bottle from my hand. "I don't mean to rush you, but I have to make the test while the stuff's fresh. You'd be surprised how quickly it dies in the open air." He took the bottle to a microscope and poured a little onto a slide. The outside of the bottle was smeared with sperm and a little got on Dr. Green's fingers. I stared at them. "Don't worry," he said. "I'm used to it. Go get dressed. This won't take long." I had forgotten that I was still naked.

"I'm sorry," I said.

"Don't worry about it. You're a very vigorous man."

In the closet I pulled the curtain and put on my clothes quickly, averting my eyes from Dr. Green's collection. When I came out the doctor was sitting behind his desk. For the first time since I had seen him he inspired a kind of confidence. That he achieved this at the expense of my own barely occurred to me.

"Well," he said expansively, "the count's a little low—what I call 'the lower limits of normal.' But you're not sterile."

"What's wrong, then?"

"Well, your sperm count is only seven million per square inch, plus there's too high a proportion of long-tails and short-tails."

"Seven million sounds like a lot to me."

"You laymen give me a laugh," he said. "Of course it only takes one to make a life. It only takes one."

"Then it's all right."

"Well, it's a tricky problem," he said. "We don't understand it. Somehow the more a man has going for him the better his chances are. You hear seven million and you think you could be the father of your country, but that's not the way it works. The average man has about sixty million per square inch, did you know that?"

I shook my head.

"The goddamn sperm are incompetent. They don't know what the hell they're doing. They'll swim backwards, get lost, drown, anything to keep from getting the job done." He frowned. "Oh, it's a tragic thing when a couple wants children and can't have them."

"But you said I wasn't sterile."

"Well, technically you're not. You're not. But it's going to be harder for you. Listen. There's a terrific emotional thing here too that goes on. Don't leave that out. Your count is low to begin with and you get anxious about conception and that doesn't help anything. When you make love you got to put all that out of your mind. It's like what they say about rape. You've just got to lie back and enjoy it."

"Crap," I said.

"Look, you want some advice? Listen to me. The thing for you is to adopt a kid. Once you do that the edge'll be off. You'd be surprised how often one of my couples conceives after they've adopted. People who've been childless twenty years."

"It doesn't make sense," I said. "The fact is that when I was fifteen years old, on my first try, *on my first try,* I made a girl pregnant."

Dr. Green looked dubious.

"I did," I said.

"Who?"

"What does it matter? A girl."

"Your girlfriend? A virgin?"

"Yes. No. I don't know."

"There, you see?" the doctor said.

357

"Do I see what?"

"Well, sonny, you may have been taken for a ride, that's all. Did you marry the girl?"

"No."

"Good for you. Good for you. Sure, that's what it was, you were taken for a ride. Oh, sure, the sperm count could go down over the years, but it's an unlikely thing. The first time out? Seven million? Such a high proportion of short-tails and long-tails? It's hardly likely, and that's my professional opinion."

"What do I owe you?"

"Hey, are you sore?"

"What do I owe you?"

"Come on, don't get sore."

"What do I owe you?"

"You are sore."

"He lives with me," I said.

"Oh," the doctor said.

"He's my son."

"Well, he probably is. It could happen. Sure he is. Certainly."

"He's my son!"

"I'm certain of it," the doctor said. "The father would know a thing like that."

"What do I owe you?"

"Fifty dollars," Dr. Green said.

I put the money on the desk and got up to go. When I walked out of his office Dr. Green followed me. "Listen," he said, "the next time you make love to your wife, relax." I pressed the button for the elevator. "Your sperm are a little sluggish. Copulate only once a week. Have her use a pillow under her ass—it makes for a better angle. Make sure the room is warm but not overheated. Cut out fatty foods. Meat is very important."

I started to walk down the stairs. The doctor stood at the top and called after me. "Try wheat germ. Get in shape. Don't be anxious."

"He's my son," I repeated to myself. "*My* son."

I didn't want to go home; I didn't want to see David until I had figured it all out. I went to a bar, and as I drank I thought about Dr. Green. I was a little surprised that I wasn't really angry. He's my son, I thought. I began to giggle. Seven million, I thought. Father of my country. I laughed. Short-tails, I thought. Long-tails. I told the barman to leave the bottle. Only one will get through, men, but I'm asking for seven million volunteers. Who swims? Not you, short-tail. Not you, long-tail. I went into the men's room to pee. You worthless prick, I thought. I went back to my stool at the bar. We're dead a long time, I thought. How rare a thing it is to be alive, I thought. I told the barman about it. He shrugged. "You laymen give me a laugh," I said. But really, I thought, how rare a thing it *is* to be alive, how really rare. It was almost clever of us to manage it. Everything was against it: a hostile solar system, booby sperm, short-tails, long-tails, fatty foods, the wrong angle, cold rooms, overheated rooms. Finally, ultimately, death itself was against it. I felt liberated, almost gay. It wasn't unlike that sensation one has of self-congratualtion at the death of a friend. What did it matter not to have sons? "All the better to hoard one's life, my dear."

I went home improved, buoyed by an unfamiliar illusion of well-being. Margaret assumed I had been given a clean bill of health by the doctor, and I didn't tell her otherwise. But it didn't last, of course; these visions never do. Moments of truth are only *moments* of truth.

A week later I made love to Margaret as in a dream. We were alone in the house and I practically seduced her. I played the phonograph and used strategic lighting; I offered her cocktails; I rubbed her neck and read poetry. I felt myself softened, like one who has just stepped out of a warm bath. I was incredibly gentle. We might have been nymphs, shepherd and shepherdess. I spoke to her in promises, in the language of vows. In bed, I fitted a pillow tenderly beneath her, preparing her as slaves prepare a bath the caliph will enter. Then at the last minute I shouted to the escaping sperm, "Now, conceive. Damn you, *conceive!*"

III

For a time at least I was like anybody else. I had become someone to whom several things could happen at once. It was a shock to realize that the willingness to live complexly—doubly, trebly—to throw open one's windows to all weathers, was the ordinary experience of most men.

Yielding to one human ritual is yielding to all. It is like being a sharecropper come North. We fanatics are simple men, unused to toilets, traffic. I had slums in me. Behind my life now, in its nooks and crannies and unseen corners, was a texture of domesticity, thick as atmosphere, as complexly *there* as government—its highways, national parks, armies—implicit in a postage stamp.

One night—we had made the book club selections for August; had decided not to take a phonograph recording that month; had chosen an alternate musical for Show-of-the-Month—I suddenly noticed that Margaret spoke with an accent. It was odd that I had never heard it before, and then I realized, Why of course, *it's new*—as if in marrying me she had disfigured herself, had actually canted her tongue or ruined her mouth so that the sounds came out off-center, muffled, and with some eccentric emphasis. It suddenly struck me that Margaret was lonely —not lonely as we were both lonely together, playing our meaningless house by choosing books, recordings, restaurants and plays as others might figure a budget or decide what model car to buy, but lonely in a way that had nothing to do with me. It was frightening to be suddenly confronted with the tight, closed system of another human being; it was like watching someone asleep, mysterious, seductive as a frontier.

I began to wonder why Margaret had married me. Obliged, once I recognized her condition, to respond to it, I responded with anger.

"You don't enjoy this," I said, accusing her. I meant our marriage, being alive together, the peculiar primacy of her own unhappiness, but she thought I was speaking about our absurd household game. I needed time; I didn't correct her.

"You think it's unmanly." I was really angry. My causes multiplied. I would never get them sorted.

"It's all right," she said softly. She said "olright." It was not all right.

"I don't know how to be married," I said, stalling her.

"My life is therapeutic," I said. "My life is a cure for my life." She let me go on.

A strange lassitude had come over me. Though I still thought about The Club, though it was still urgent—indeed, the idea kept percolating in my mind—there had been in my life a sort of substitution of intensities, as when one playing with a shaped balloon absently shifts volumes of air from one of its sections to another. It was difficult for me to do so many things at once.

In August we went with the Holiday-of-the-Month Club on a weekend trip. Gathered with forty-five other couples at the Port Authority Bus Terminal, we looked, with our overnight cases and our name plates, like so many kids going off to summer camp. All the women except Margaret were wearing slacks or Bermuda shorts. The men in their Bermuda shorts and knee-length stockings (I wore trousers) recalled to me city people I had seen out West in starched, fresh bluejeans, as though summer, like a distant state, were something in which they would forever be dudes. The members milled about casually, introducing themselves to us unself-consciously.

361

"We're waiting for Mr. and Mrs. Jerry Cohen of Queens," said Eddie, the tourmaster.

"Where we going this time, Eddie?" asked Dodo Shivitz of Great Neck, Long Isalnd.

"Dodo baby, I'm surprised at you," Eddie said, grinning.

"It's a regular military secret," Lorraine Land said.

"Come on, Eddie," Dodo said. "Don't be like that." She turned to Margaret. "In May Eddie flew us to Miami. None of us had swim suits or anything. It was terrible."

"Sealed orders are sealed orders," Eddie said, and walked off to another group.

Al Medler, a fat man from Queens, said, "I'm not too crazy about surprises. There's too much of a strain on the heart."

"Your first time? I don't think I've had the pleasure," said a small dark man whose card identified him only as Harris. He shook my hand.

"We just joined," I said.

"Oh, yes."

"All you people seem to know each other," Margaret said.

"We know each other all right," Harris said. "That's crap about the Jerry Cohens. They won't show up. Mister is still sore from June."

"What happened in June?" Margaret asked.

"Grossinger's," Harris said darkly.

"Oh."

"Look a' Eddie, look a' Eddie," Mrs. Sylvia Fend said. "He's whispering to Gloria."

"It's not right," Mrs. Land said.

"Live and let live," Al Medler said. "It's less strain on the heart."

"She's a w-h-o-r-e," Harris said.

"She is?"

"Of course," Harris said expertly. "I've studied the economics of this thing. Your average trip is ninety-five miles."

"Miami?"

"Once a year there's a big trip. You don't know

362

when it's coming up, though you can count on its being off-season."

"What's that got to do with Gloria?" Mrs. Sylvia Fend asked.

"Well, you got to figure it costs the company with food and lodging and travel twenty-five cents a mile. That's $23.75 per person per trip. They usually get about sixty couples each trip, but summer is the slow season because the members go on their own vacations with the kids. So Eddie has to call out Gloria to make up the difference."

"You seem to know a lot about it," Dodo Shivitz said.

"I'm an actuary. I got to keep up," Harris said.

"I can't get nobody to write me a policy," Al Medler said.

"You're too fat, Al," Harris said.

I drew Margaret aside. "Margaret, this isn't for us."

"Why? It's more fun than Book-of-the-Month," Margaret said.

"All aboard," Eddie shouted from the bottom step of the bus.

"Where's Jerry Cohen, Eddie?" demanded Harris.

"All aboard."

"What about Jerry Cohen?"

"Jerry's a god-damned puritan sorehead," Eddie said.

Everybody laughed.

"All right," Eddie said. "All right. All aboard for Mysteryville. What's it going to be this time, folks? North, east, south, west? Where she stops nobody knows. The management is not responsible for stolen or misplaced property. Keep your eye on your own wife."

"Whooopee," everybody said.

"S-e-x," Harris said.

Margaret and I weren't allowed to sit with each other on the bus. As soon as we stepped aboard Margaret was commandeered by a tall, good-looking man named Marvin Taylor. Mrs. Taylor, a small, pretty woman of about thirty-five, sat down beside me.

363

"Your lovely wife and yourself aren't Jewish, if I may ask, are you"—she leaned across my chest and read my card—"Mr. Boswell?"

"No, we're not, Mrs. Taylor."

"If I may say so without giving offense, we Jews are usually better sports than you gentiles. Do you play badminton, sir?"

"No."

"It's not important," she said. Sighing, she settled back into the deep seat.

"It's just that a nice game of mixed doubles helps to break the ice," she said suddenly. She laughed and turned around to address the couple behind us. "I was just telling Mr. Boswell here that a nice game of mixed doubles helps to break the ice. Pass it on." She turned back to me. "Your wife is very lovely. I noticed it. You two must be very happy. But tell me, she isn't native-born, is she?"

"She is the former Principessa Margaret dei Medici of Italy," I said.

"That's very funny," she said. "That's really very funny." Then she startled me by reaching over and taking my hand. "I like *goyim*," she said, leaning back against the seat dreamily.

"Some of my best friends are Jews," I offered gallantly.

We had come out of the tunnel and were driving down the New Jersey Turnpike through country that looked like a huge, well-kept golf course. Mrs. Taylor had fallen asleep holding my hand and I took it back as gently as I could. Behind and around me I could hear the mixed doubles speculating about our destination. There seemed to be a strong feeling that we were going to Washington, D.C. Sylvia Fend didn't believe this. "Washington in the summer?" she kept saying. "Are you kidding? The heat is terrific." In two hours we had crossed into Pennsylvania and in another half hour the bus had left the turnpike. After a while the driver pulled off onto the side of the road and Eddie, who had been sitting in the back with Gloria, went up to speak to him. As he passed through the bus he was booed. He held up his hands good-naturedly.

"We're lost," Al Medler said. "The thing to do is keep calm."

"It's a rest stop," J. Y. Krull said. "Come on, Gloria, it's a rest stop." Everybody laughed. Gloria thumbed her nose at J. Y. Krull. "Gloria!" he said.

"Well, come on then," she said and stood up and stepped into the aisle. J. Y. Krull bolted out of his seat and everyone laughed.

"Oh, sit down," Emma Lewen said, pulling at J. Y. Krull's arm.

Mrs. Taylor had awakened and was rubbing her eyes. "Why've we stopped?" she asked. "Are we there?"

"Al Medler says we're lost," I said.

"What a way to run a railroad," Mrs. Taylor said.

The bus turned around ponderously; apparently the driver had made a wrong turn ten miles back. Harris leaned across the aisle toward me. "Eddie's sore," he said. "The company lost about five bucks because of that mistake."

"Really?" I said.

"Figure it out," he said.

In another hour the bus turned into a twisting, pot-holed, narrow trail. After about twenty yards it was clear that the driver would not be able to go further.

"We'll have to walk the rest of the way," Eddie announced. "It's not far."

No one knew where we were, but clearly we were in the country. In the wooded foothills of something. Eddie made an announcement: "The Holiday-of-the-Month Club has brought you all for an unforgettable August weekend to beautiful Camp Starglow, just outside Windsor, Pennsylvania." He explained that it was a kids' summer camp but that we'd have it all to ourselves because the first session had just ended and the second wouldn't begin until the middle of the next week. "Be careful what you leave lying around, won't you?" he said. Everybody laughed.

Mrs. Taylor turned to me happily. "Did you bring your camping equipment?" she said.

"Mrs. Taylor," I said, "despite my hearty good

looks, I have a low sperm count and am a troubled man and a lousy sport."

"You *goyim*," she said, crinkling her nose.

"Just warn your husband," I said calmly, "that if he so much as shakes hands with my wife I will break his legs for him."

Mrs. Taylor stopped smiling. I could see I had disappointed her. She was not, after all, a bad woman; perhaps she was not even as silly as she seemed to be. Maybe this was just a routine—probably it was. At any rate, as she squeezed by me I felt I ought to make it up to her in some way. I pinched her behind. She turned on me furiously.

"It's all talk, you," she said in a low, dark voice. "That's all it is," she hissed. She began to cry.

"Look," I said. "I'm sorry."

The people filing past stopped to look at us. Spotting his wife, Taylor moved up the aisle through the crowd. "Here, what is this?" he demanded.

"Nothing," I said. "It's a mistake."

"Marvin, be careful," Mrs. Taylor sobbed.

"What is this?" Marvin said uncertainly.

"He'll hurt you," she said.

"Nobody's going to hurt me," Marvin said. His knees, below his Bermuda shorts, were shaking. I felt sorry for him.

"I'm sorry," I said. "I just told your wife a filthy story and she took it the wrong way."

"Oh," he said, clearly relieved. "Is that all it is?" He lowered his voice and put his arm around his wife's shoulders. "Honey," he said, "you've got to be a sport about these things." He winked at me.

"What's going on?" Eddie said. He looked at Mrs. Taylor. "Hey, now," he said, "the Holiday-of-the-Month Club is supposed to build up confidence. Otherwise what's the good?"

"My fault," I said.

I pushed past the people shuffling off the bus and caught up with Margaret. "Margaret, it's a mistake," I said. "Let's pay the driver to take us back to the city."

"Oh, Boswell," Margaret said, "you've lost your

366

sense of humor. My God, *I know!* You're jealous of Marvin Taylor."

"Nonsense," I said, "it's all t-a-l-k."

The Taylors passed us. "See you later," Marvin said significantly. He touched Margaret's shoulder.

"I'm not a jealous man," I said. "You have reason to know that. But I won't raise another man's child."

"That's ridiculous," she said. "You're ridiculous."

"Accidents happen."

"Do you actually think I'd sleep with Marvin Taylor?"

"Look, let's not talk about it. You know how I feel."

We followed Eddie to the guest lodge, and each couple was assigned a room. "Look," Eddie said, "there's something else. There are some cabins—not enough to go around or there wouldn't be any problem, but I've got thirty keys. Who doesn't think he'll be wanting one?" Everbody groaned. "What a bunch," Eddie said. "I never saw such a bunch. You ought to be ashamed of yourselves." They laughed. "No volunteers, hey? No good sports in the crowd? Well, all right, all right. We'll auction them off. Proceeds to charity."

"Crap," Harris whispered to me. "He'd put the money in his pocket."

Eddie help up a key and asked for a bid. The men laughed, but no one offered him anything for it. "All right," he said at last, "I'll throw them up in the air and you stallions can fight for them." He flung the keys as high as he could and they came clattering down on the wooden floor of the lodge. Everyone scrambled for the loose keys. Eddie stood on the stairs and laughed. "What a bunch," he said. "Oh, well."

In our room Margaret and I were changing into our bathing suits when someone tapped on the door. "Who is it?" Margaret asked.

"Oh, I'm sorry. I thought this was Mrs. Schmidt's room." It was Mrs. Taylor's voice.

"That was your friend," Margaret said.

I looked at her helplessly. "It's pretty shabby, isn't it?" I said.

"What's shabby? This? This isn't anything."

"Our needs," I said.

"Fuck it," Margaret said.

I wondered again why she had married me. I suspected that when I finally knew the reason would be dark, damaging. I wondered if I could ever be insane again, if I would ever recover my mad, unconfused Boswellian purposes.

"Let's go down," she said sadly.

That afternoon we swam and played basketball and threw softballs to each other. I am a good athlete, and though I had not done anything in a long time I moved with more certainty than any of the other men. I knew the women were watching me, and this was not unpleasant, but somehow I manipulated my body almost absently, with the peculiar preoccupation of someone in pain. Later we ate the sandwiches and drank the beer Eddie had brought from the town. That night, in slacks and heavy sweaters, we sat around the campfire which Eddie made and toasted marshmallows and drank bourbon. We sang "Going Home, Going Home" and "Swing Low, Sweet Chariot" and "The Battle Hymn of the Republic." That is, the others sang and I listened; I do not know the words to songs.

We lay stretched out on blankets ripped from our cots. I gazed at the stars and into the orange fire. In the dark I could see shapes moving, people changing blankets and going around the campfire like ghosts. Gradually the voices flagged. Couples lay locked in each other's arms.

Eddie shouted suddenly. "Come on, wake up, wake up. Let's dance. There's a wind-up phonograph in the theater and some records. Hey, Boswell, you're just with your own wife, so I won't be disturbing you. Come on, give me a hand with them."

"That stupid bastard," I said.

"Oh, go ahead," Margaret said. "Help him."

"He's a jerk."

"Help him with the machine," Margaret said.

I got up reluctantly and walked over toward Eddie. He was grinning foolishly and looked rather like a very stupid devil in the glare of the fire. "No offense, right?" Eddie said.

"None taken," I said.

"Good. Good. Here's the key. The stuff's on the stage."

"Aren't you coming with me?"

"What, and let the fire go out? Mrs. Taylor here will go with you," Eddie said slyly.

"Look, what's the matter with you?" I asked him.

"Hey, hey, easy," he said "What's wrong? You got our literature. Didn't you read between the lines?"

As a matter of fact I hadn't even seen their literature. It was Margaret who had told me about the club. Mrs. Taylor moved up beside me and took my arm. "I've got a present for you," she said as we moved off. She was drunk. "I mean it. Because you were so nice to Marvin before."

"I thought I had made a mistake."

"No," she said. "No." It was like a sad, escaping sigh.

"I've been wondering."

"Life," she said with weary significance. It might have been an epigram in French.

"Oh, come on, Mrs. Taylor, let's get the damned phonograph."

"Don't you want your present?"

All right, I thought, if she kisses me, she kisses me.

"Give it to me," I said.

She put a key into my hand. "It's Marvin's," she giggled. "I took it out of his pants. He was so proud of getting one."

"Oh, Jesus," I said.

"Don't you like a good time?"

Even the rhetoric of her sin was off-center. I thought of the men in their Bermuda shorts. For a moment I thought I was going to laugh.

"Don't you like a good time?" she repeated.

"You don't know what you're talking about," I said.

369

"I do," she said. "I do. I'm talking about a good time. I'm talking about being with people. How many years do you think we have?" she said. She didn't sound drunk.

"That's ridiculous."

"I'm no Gloria," she said suddenly.

"It doesn't make any difference," I said.

"I'm a mother. I have a kid in camp."

I did laugh.

"Yes," she said giggling, "I see the joke, too. All the same, what does it mean? People have to be with people."

"Is that what screwing is all about? People being with people?"

We went into the big wooden room the kids used as a theater. "Ooh," Mrs. Taylor said, "there are always bats in these places. I was in a camp play when I was a kid—say, that wasn't so long ago either—and there were bats above the stage in the what do you call it, eaves. If they get in your hair it's a real mess."

"Well, let's just get the machine and the records and get out." I switched on the lights.

"You're terribly romantic," Mrs. Taylor said. "Terribly."

The machine was on the stage, the records beside it. "If you take these I'll bring the phonograph." I handed her some old 78's.

"Why, they're camp songs," Mrs. Taylor said without looking at them. "Why bother? They can grind this stuff out for themselves. He wouldn't want these."

"What does he want?" I asked.

"He wants people to be happy," Mrs. Taylor said. "You don't understand anything."

"I certainly don't understand this place."

"Didn't you read the literature?"

"That's the second time I've been asked that. I'm beginning to wonder how they send it through the mails."

"Oh, he made a joke," Mrs. Taylor said.

"Come on," I said. "My wife is waiting."

She hoisted herself onto the stage. "I doubt it," she said.

"Cut it out," I said. "What I said about Marvin's legs still goes."

"I don't like to hear talk like that," she said seriously. She had a way of drifting in and out of drunkenness.

"Mrs. Taylor," I said. "Mother, I think we can go back now." When she reached down for me to help her off the stage I put the key in her hand.

Walking back we could hear the voices of the club members raised in some soft, sad song. Perhaps it was just our distance from them but the voices seemed thinner now. "That herd's been cut," I said.

"You really don't want to sleep with me, do you?" she asked.

"No."

"Is it me? I'm too pushy, I think."

"Not at all," I said. "You're as demure as someone in a nursery rhyme."

"This little piggy went to market," Mrs. Taylor intoned forlornly.

We were walking back through the trees toward the distant fire. "Oh, that song is so sad," she said. "Camp songs make me cry. They don't make you cry, do they?"

"I'm a very callous person, Mrs. Taylor."

"No," she said. "I'll bet you're not. Not deep down inside yourself."

"Oh, Jesus," I said. I was anxious to get back and find Margaret and break Marvin's legs.

"This will be the last time you come on one of these weekends, I guess. I'll bet she really was some kind of princess or whatever. You both have a lot of style."

"When you're the King of France," I sad, "it shows."

"Yeah, you," she said. She poked me playfully. "You know," she said, "it may sound funny, but this club saved our marriage, mine and Marvin's."

"That does sound funny."

"No. I really mean it. Oh, I don't suppose we would have broken up or anything, but it . . . well, gave us an interest."

"You've got to have an interest."

She went on without hearing me. The truth, finally,

371

was what I had begun to suspect. I was far more interested in her, in her motives, in what she had to say, than she was in me. "You know what it is?" she asked. "It's not the pleasure. What's that, two minutes? I don't give a damn for the pleasure. That's just a mechanical, chemical thing that doesn't have anything to do with us. I'll tell you the truth, you would probably have been disappointed in me after all my talk. I'm not very good at it. And it's not what you could call *love*. It's just the idea that somebody wants you—all right, your body, but you are your body. Just to lay like that in somebody's arms, knowing you're the only thing just then that he's thinking of. You know something? I think that if the house were to catch fire just then, or if there was a tiger, he'd save you. No matter what it meant. The same guy that might run right over you in a burning theater, he'd save you. It's funny. Being like that with somebody softens you. Even fat old Medler. He's who I was with last time."

"Medler?"

"What's wrong with him? He's alive. I'll say." She laughed. "It's just being with somebody. Loneliness is the most awful thing in the world."

"Loneliness is nothing," I said.

We came back to the group and I looked for Margaret. The blanket we had been sitting on was gone, and so was Marvin.

I rushed up to Eddie. "Where's my wife?"

"Well, how should I know?" he said.

"Look," I said, "tourmaster, pimp, where's my wife? I'm asking for the last time." The others had stopped singing and were listening to me.

"We don't need members like you," Eddie shouted. "Tough guy. I'm tearing up your membership card. Don't worry, don't worry, you'll get your lousy money back. What I want to know is if you don't like people why'd you join a club like this in the first place?"

"That's enough. Where's Taylor? Where's Taylor?" I shouted.

I saw someone get off a blanket. "I'm here," Taylor said weakly. "What do you want?" The woman he was with wasn't Margaret.

"Nothing," I said. "I'm sorry."

"Some guy," Eddie said.

"Telling off a member like that, that'll cost the company," Harris said.

"If it was out of my own pocket," Eddie said, "I wouldn't care. The guy's a jealous jerk. What'd he come here for anyway? Storm trooper!"

"Eddie'll have a heart attack," Al Medler said.

"Hey, Medler, your girlfriend's waiting for you," I said.

"Okay, all right," Medler said, getting to his knees, "a fat man's got to move slowly in affairs of the heart. Pass it on."

"You're degenerates," I shouted.

"Let's lift our voices in song," I heard a woman call. It was Mrs. Taylor. "Everybody. Everybody."

She started to sing. " 'Keep the home fires burning,' " she sang in a thin, reedy voice, and slowly the others joined her. As I walked toward the lodge they began other songs, going quickly after a few bars from one to the next. They sang of wars they had never fought, of losses they had never sustained. They were gathered on a darkling Pennsylvania plain, far behind the lines, singing, forgetting the words, appropriating the harmony for themselves, convinced of a heroic desolation, toasting their sadness in the big campfire like another marshmallow. " 'It's a long way,' " they sang, " 'to Tipperary.' " It is indeed, I thought.

The light in our room shone beneath the door like a bright brass threshold. Margaret was in bed, reading.

"Margaret," I said, "why did you marry me?"

She pretended not to look startled. It was a princessly gesture but it did not come off. "I had my reasons," she said at last.

"I'll bet you did," I said. It had actually crossed my mind that I might have been a front man in some international plot. "What were they?"

"Why?"

"Because I must understand how I'm being used."

"You'll never understand that."

"Ah," I said.

"Did you enjoy your walk with Mrs. Taylor?"

"I didn't touch Mrs. Taylor."

"I know that," she said.

"You don't seem very grateful for my fidelity."

"You have no fidelity," she said.

I was enjoying the conversation. People with unnamable sorrows touch and awe me. Margaret now struck me as one of these. It was very adult talk, I thought. I had the impression that our voices had actually changed—that my flat, midwestern vowels had rounded and that Margaret's faint, Italianate English had become somehow Middle-European, the sound of a queen rather than a princess.

"Why did you marry me?" I repeated.

"Oh," she said, "love."

Outside the voices swelled. " 'Oh, bury me not,' " they sang, " 'on the lone prair-ee.' "

I waited for her to go on. She sat up in bed, and the sheet fell away from the royal breasts.

" 'Where the coyotes howl,' " they sang, " 'and the wind is free.' "

"A famous American folk song," I said. "Jesus, these people feel sorry for themselves."

Margaret was staring at me.

"Let me understand you," I said. "Did you love me?"

"I've just told you."

"But what was the mystery?"

"That's the mystery."

"Just that?"

"Yes."

"Only that?"

"Yes." She turned away.

"Well, that ties it," I said, suddenly exploding. "That really does. That ties it. You're the one who should have gone walking with Mrs. Taylor."

"You're insane."

"I'm harmless." I giggled. "Like everyone else."

"What is it you want?" she shouted suddenly.

"What everybody wants," I said calmly. "What you want, what Mrs. Marvin Taylor wants."

374

"Happiness," Margaret said contemptuously.

"Screw happiness. Immorality."

It was odd, finally, to be in a position to say no, to deny others with a clear, free conscience. It came with age, I supposed. But really there was nothing to it. It was just an illusion of power. No one had any real power. No one did except maybe suicides in the brief moment between their self-violence and their deaths.

"Well," I said, "cheer up, Principessa. And move over."

"I don't want to make love," she said.

I shrugged.

"There are other people alive," Margaret said after a while.

"Millions," I said. "Zillions. That's my point. It would be pretty silly to try to care for all of them."

"I wasn't suggesting that you care for all of them."

"Oh," I said. "I see. One for one. Double up. Like the buddy system." I sat down on the edge of the bed.

"I don't want to make love, I tell you," Margaret said.

"In that case, pass the brochure. I want to read the literature."

IV

Finally I understood what the trouble was. I had been confused by alternatives, overwhelmed by the extraordinary complications of ordinary life. Some men—and I was one—could function only under a pressure, a deadline, a doom. One hones himself against his needs, so he had better understand what those are.

But maybe, too, there had been a certain good husbandry in my bad marriage. There were, after all, natural laws—who knew it better?—and perhaps men, like farms, like phoenixes, had to lie low once in a while. Like Lome's scrap iron and lint, nothing was ever a total loss; everything went on working for one, counting for something better than it seemed to. There was just so much faith that one could put in serendipity, however, and I decided that it was time to make a change in my life.

Compromises and disguises were out. The King of England walking Harlem in a zoot suit is only a white man in funny clothes. His Highness knows where his Highness' bread is buttered. The secret agents, with guns, with transistor equipment, are right behind him. There has to be a deep amnesia of the soul. Indigence is the one thing you can't fake. Low birth is all some of us have.

Still, the solution wasn't to leave Margaret, only to get away from her. Divorce or separation would just have been a further complication. I had to get outside again, to enter the world like a nun in reverse. I recognized the difficulties. They talk about the *nouveaux riches,* and one knows what to expect, what to avoid, but who ever heard of the nouveaux poor, the nouveaux stricken?

One afternoon I told Margaret I felt guilty about my life.

"You're just bored," she said.

"No," I said, "it would be wrong for me to be bored. I don't *do* anything. I make no contribution. For the first time in my life I'm uneasy about people less fortunate than myself." It was true in a way; at least it would have been if such people existed. I told her I had volunteered my services in the Police Athletic League and that I would be teaching Puerto Ricans body-building in a gym on the East Side. I don't think she believed me. It was not a very inspired lie, but even its baldness served because it announced to Margaret that I was up to *something,* that I did not want to be disturbed.

The next day I took a room in a boarding house off Fifty-eighth Street and went to a pawnship on Eight Avenue to lay in a wardrobe. I told the pawnbroker that I was an actor, that I needed a certain kind of clothes for the part I was playing, not seedy so much as shabby, and not shabby so much as tasteless, and not tasteless so much as anonymous.

"I see him as a guy in the bleachers," I said. "He drinks beer. You know? Probably he's not really from New York at all. Probably he's originally from Gary, Indiana. He wears black shoes and powder-blue socks."

"A hayseed," the pawnbroker said.

"Well, yes and no," I said. "My conception is more of a guy used to hard work in a factory, or somebody who wraps packages in a stockroom. He likes to watch people bowl. He likes to be comfortable. He wears windbreakers. His pants turn over his belt."

"Yeah," the pawnbroker said, interested. "I think I see what you're getting at. He could probably afford better but he's ignorant."

"That's it."

"He's got underwear with big red ants painted on it," the pawnbroker said.

"He wears wide ties."

"There's a loud pattern on his socks," the pawnbroker said.

"Oh, an awful one," I said.

"Yeah," the pawnbroker said. "Yeah."

"His wife is a waitress," I said.

"Sure," the pawnbroker said, "and now he drives a bus because he strained his back in the factory."

"His sister's married to an enlisted man stationed in West Germany," I said.

The pawnbroker stroked his long jaw. "That's a tall order," he said. He came from behind the counter and studied me. "You got some size on you, God bless you."

"It would be all right if the clothes were a little small," I said. "That would heighten the effect, you see."

"Maybe I got something in the back," the pawnbroker said.

"Go see."

He brought out exactly what I needed. It was as though the twelve men we had been describing had died back there. "See if these work," he said, handing me some clothing.

"Have you been in show business too?" I asked.

"I've just got an interest," he said shyly.

I tried on the clothes and the pawnbroker leaned back against the counter and admired me. "You look like a different person," he said.

I laughed. "That's very funny," I said.

"To tell you the truth," he said after I had decided which clothes I would take, "I don't know what to charge for this stuff. On the one hand it's all old, unclaimed, but on the other hand it's a very good costume. What the hell, three pants, shoes, all those stockings, a jacket—say fifteen bucks."

My hand was reaching for my wallet when I stopped myself. "Listen," I said, "fifteen bucks is very fair. As you say, these aren't old clothes, but a very artistic costume. If that's your price I'll pay it. But I just thought. You say you're interested in the theater."

"I don't want no passes," the pawnbroker said, suspicious.

"No, of course not," I said. "Of course not. I just had an idea. Listen, let me give you your fifteen dollars." I reached into my wallet and took out the money and extended it, but the pawnbroker hesitated.

"What was your idea?" he asked.

"Well," I said, "you know the *Playbill* they give out?"

He nodded.

"Well, did you ever notice the credits? I mean where it says 'Furs by Fendrich,' 'Jewelry by Tiffany'? Look, I'm no businessman, but I happen to know that that sort of thing is the most prestigious advertising space anybody can get." I lowered my voice. "It's payola."

"I've wondered about those credits," the pawnbroker said.

"Well, of course," I said. "Now suppose we put it in that Al's clothes—that's the character's name that I'm portraying—were donated by"—I looked through the pile of second-hand cameras and radios and musical instruments to the name inverted on the window—"Charley's Pawn Shop."

"My clientele don't go much to the theater," the pawnbroker said.

"That's not the point. For one thing it would be a gag. On the other hand it would polish the image of the profession."

He thought about it for a while. "What's the name of your show?" he said finally.

"*The Dying Gladiator.*"

"It's not very catchy," he said.

"Those things are worked out in New Haven." I held out the money again. The pawnbroker looked at it for a second and then waved it away. "What the hell," he said, "it'll be a good joke."

"It will," I said. "It is."

I went back to my room with the old clothes. Already I felt better. There are certain people who are not happy unless they get something wholesale; others, like myself, do not possess a thing unless they have had it for nothing. It was the old water into wine principle, a little harmless miracle-making. That afternoon I felt as if I were making a comeback.

Each morning I kissed Margaret like someone going away to the office and walked the few blocks to my shabby rented room. In my old clothes I was a new man. In a week I was ready.

I went into a restaurant and strolled by a table the waitress had not yet cleared. I picked up her tip for courage, for luck. Using the dime I had stolen, I went into the phone booth and called the Ford Foundation.

When I gave a secretary my name and asked to be put through to the director she hesitated, so I gave her a little razzle-dazzle. "This is Detroit calling, baby," I said. "Get it? *De*-troit!"

She said she'd try to connect me; she must have been a new girl. Years before I had discovered the uses of the big Foundations. We were on good terms. I had suggested projects to them and they regarded me as an interested amateur. I was on their mailing lists. I knew, for example, where all the young poets were, the novelists. At one time I used to keep a map with little pins in it, like something in a War Room. I could put my finger on any of those fellows, any time I wanted.

"Harley," I said, "it's Jimmy Boswell. I'm sorry I had to scare the little girl, but it was urgent. I've had a scheme, Harley, which you people might be interested in. My word of honor, Harley, I haven't gone to The Guggenheim with this yet."

I told him about The Club. He was very interested, but vague when I tried to pin him down.

"Could I get a commitment on this right away, Harley? Twenty-five thousand a year is all it would take."

"It's cheap, Boswell," Harley admitted, "but you must appreciate how the Foundation works."

"My God, Harley, I'm only talking about twenty-five thousand dollars a year. You could take it out of the stamp fund."

"Well, it's not that, Boswell."

"Bring three poets back from Yucatán," I said.

380

"Call off two musicologists. You don't really believe there's a future in that electronic stuff, do you?"

"Boswell, believe me, it isn't the money."

"Well," I said a little more softly, "the truth is I've never known you people to be mean. What is it, Harley? Is the plan no good? I'd like a straight answer on this."

"Boswell, the idea *is* good—it's sound. But don't you think it's a little, well, *snobbish?*"

"Ah," I said. I was grinning.

"Well, after all," Harley said.

"The Rockefeller may not be so fastidious, Harley," I warned.

"Now, Boswell . . ." Harley said.

"The Guggenheim and The Carnegie may have different views."

"Boswell . . ." Harley said.

"The Fund for the Republic people may think along other lines."

"Please . . ." Harley said.

"Well, dammit, Harley, if it's not too snobbish for The Fund for the Republic people, I don't see what you have to be so squeamish about." My grin had folded into an open smile; I couldn't keep a straight face; I almost doubled up; my nose was running. Here I was in a phone booth in the Columbus Circle subway station, with the little rubber-bladed fan whirling merrily away, and the light going on and off as I opened and shut the door not fifty feet away from the mad faggot in the stall in the men's toilet peeping through a hole at the businessmen standing before the urinals; here I was, James Boswell, orphan. Herlitz-placed, Mr. America in second-hand pants, lawful husband of the Principessa Margaret dei Medici of All the Italies, being apologized to by the director of The Ford Foundation.

"Why are you laughing?" Harley asked.

"What's that? Excuse me?"

"What are you laughing at?"

"Well, you'll forgive me, Harley, but your remark about snobbishness strikes me as just a little absurd."

"Does it?" Harley said coolly.

"Well, figure it out," I said. "You and I are both

dedicated to a kind of talent elite. Anyway, Princeton and Palo Alto have been doing this sort of thing, only on a bigger scale, for years."

Harley thought about that awhile and I thought, It's grand to swing, it is grand to be a swinger. If it were ever my fate to be executed for something I would hope they would hang me. Fitting—a broken neck and a hard-on. What more could anybody get from life?

"I'm sorry, Boswell," Harley said at last. "I'll certainly take it under advisement, but I can't hold out any more hope than that at this time."

"Harley," I said, "you leave me no alternative. I'm going to The Lace."

"What's The Lace? I don't think I've ever heard of The Lace."

"Now who's being a snob, Harley?" I said, and hung up.

My conversation with Harley, like my conversation with the pawnbroker, made me feel marvelous. My year of relative retirement had changed me, made me stronger. I could put people off now. It was odd; taking them in and putting them off came finally to the same thing. There was freedom in it. I gazed happily at my shiny, unpressed pants, my windbreaker's broken zipper. The abuses, I thought proudly, the abuses of adversity. So be it. Amen. If I could not do anything about death I could at least do something about something else, do something about men. Let me at them! I could con the fat cats of the world, the wizards and counselors and generals and poets, the people with power or ideas who lived, I saw, with a terrible unconsciousness, like sleek, expensive, ticking bombs. The progress of a hero worshiper was inexorable. The Italian cynic, Neal Admirari, was right. No man is a hero to anyone he's been introduced to. I had lived my life as a kind of Irishman, in forests of imagination searching under mushrooms for elves and leprechauns. Now I was entitled to shout that that they didn't exist. I had earned disbelief. Whee, I thought. Here comes Boswell!

I would have to see Nate, but first I went back to my

room. So long as my plan was still unrealized I needed time to relish and contemplate each step. That night I didn't go back to Margaret. I lay on the bed in my room and listened to a man shout at a woman down the hall. I heard him hit her; I heard her scream. I lay there testing my loneliness, feeling my singleness as one might cautiously put pressure on a sprained ankle. I needed to forget not that I knew Margaret and David and that I had lived with them, but that they had known and lived with me. I had to imagine myself forgotten, dead, someone who had lived seven hundred years before in a country that had kept no records. I had to imagine myself not born yet.

I waited two more days. I took my meals in the Automat during the busy hours and sat next to others who spooned their soup and chewed their sandwiches as if I were invisible. You've got to get used to it. You're a long time dead.

On Thursday afternoon I went to Nate's. When he saw me in my old clothes he broke into a broad smile. "Margaret's left him," he said to Perry. "Margaret's left you," he said.

"No," I said. "Pick up my tabs, Nate."

"Jimmy, you're a rich man. What are you talking about?"

"Nate it kills me. It stifles my creativity." I told him about the room I had rented. He laughed.

"Pick up my tabs again, Nate." I had discovered the secret of Nate's indifference to me since I had married Margaret. Anyone who is around the successful too much develops a passion for the occasional failure. Now I was no longer of any use to him.

"It wouldn't be the same thing, Jimmy. You don't need it any more."

"I need it."

"Well, a cup of the arctic lichen," he told Perry, "for Jimmy and me. For auld lang syne, Jimmy."

Perry muttered something I couldn't hear and signaled to a waiter standing by an enormous gilt samovar.

383

"Nate," I said when Perry had poured our tea, "I've got a terrific proposition for you. What did I cost you in the old days? Five hundred, six hundred a year?"

Nate sipped his tea. I picked up my cup and drank from it quickly; it was as awful as I had remembered it.

"Some years a little more, maybe. But that's a fair average, I'd say."

"Okay," I said. "Peanuts."

"Wait a minute," Nate said.

"Peanuts, Nate. I've got a bank account of my own now. Peanuts are peanuts. I have an idea, Nate, that could cost you twenty-five thousand dollars a year at the very least."

"Hey, wait a minute," Nate said.

"Nate, forgive me, you're a fool."

"Hey, wait a minute."

"A fool," I said. "Short-sighted. You do not see even the topmost E on the eye charts. That E is for eternity, Nate! Where will you spend eternity? Nate? Where will you spend eternity?"

"Hey, wait a minute."

"What have you got here? A fancy clip-joint. Five forks and spoons in the Michelin Guide. Dorothy Kilgallen puts your name in the papers. The movie stars come after the world premieres. Signed pictures on the wall— Nate with Shirley Temple, Nate with Robert Mitchum, Nate with Jimmy Stewart."

"Nate with Senator McCarthy," Nate said. "Nate with John Foster Dulles."

"Republicans, Nate, Republicans. Where will you spend *eternity*? It's nothing. You're living on borrowed time, do you know that? What do you think history will have to say? That Dag Hammarskjöld once had lunch here? That you turned out the only decent ground-reindeer-horn cakes in New York?"

"What are you talking about?"

"I am talking about history, Nate. I'm talking about history, tomorrow and tomorrow and tomorrow. Do you *even* have sons? Do you even have *sons*? Who gets this place when you die? Perry? You won't be cold six months when somebody'll whisper in his ear: 'Perry's Place.' Perry's Place. It has a nice ring, he thinks; Nate's dead, I'm alive, he thinks. Perry's Place. *Perry's Place.* Two weeks later your sign comes down and a new one goes up. PERRY'S PLACE. With, if you're lucky, a footnote: 'Formerly Nate's.' *Formerly Nate's!* What the hell kind of write-up is that? I'm talking about history. Do you think that as of today you're history? Do you think it is even peeping at you as it scans Forty-seventh Street? Don't kid yourself."

"I don't know what you want me to do," Nate said.

"Nate, have you ever heard of the Algonquin Round Table?"

"Are you nuts? Sure I heard of it. Dorothy Parker, F. P. Adams, Woollcott—that crowd. Sure I heard of it."

"It was nothing," I said. "Nothing. Journalists. They had a better press than you. It was in the family. But what I'm talking about is history."

"History," Nate said.

"A Club."

"A club," Nate said.

"*The Club!* I could go to the Foundations with this thing, Nate. They'd back it in a minute. But what would happen? The Hilton Chain would do the catering. Pasty little sandwiches for the gullets of the great. It isn't to be thought of. I owe it to you—you owe it to yourself. And if not to yourself, then what about Perry? What do you think history would do with someone like Perry? He'd be sensational. He'd be magnificent, the sullen little bastard. They'd call him 'Perry.' Just like that, his first name. Whole generations would come to know his picturesque, miserable ways. And if they'd do that for Perry, what wouldn't they do for *you?* I'm giving you a chance to be respectable, Nate. The Algonquin Round Table was nothing compared to this. Think of it, Nate. Your place. Your place in history. Once a month, through your doors—" I pointed to the doors. "Through your doors would pour the cream of the scientific, political and intellectual worlds. That crowd. To sit at your tables." I pointed to the tables. "I'm talking history to you, Nate."

385

"You're crazy."

"They'd have to work the Presidential Inauguration around our schedule."

"You're nuts."

"Stockholm would have to be advised of our meeting dates so as not to interfere with the Awards."

"Insane."

"The universities would have to agree to set some fixed date for their June graduation in order to get our speakers."

"Have some more arctic lichen," Nate said.

"Wars would be declared only on days we weren't meeting. Once a month the world would go to bed secure, knowing the bombs couldn't fall that night."

"Perry, bring us an orchid salad."

"The TV people would probably want to block off the street."

"Perry, two whooping crane steaks. Rare."

"We wouldn't allow anyone to take pictures inside the place. Like Parliament. Like Congress."

"Balinese wonder pudding, Perry."

"We might have to set up a special table for the Secret Service men. Some of these babies can't go anywhere without them."

"And—and—and ice water!" Nate cried, ecstatic.

"The Russians would send spies."

"It's marvelous. Marvelous."

"Once a year we'd pose for an official portrait. We might even authorize some candid shots of the members. Yes! They'd turn up years later in attics. Skira would collect them and publish them in a book."

"Eat. Eat your orchid," Nate said happily.

I stuffed a purple petal into my mouth. "Nate," I said, "do you trust me? Let me work out the arrangements. I promse you a Club. I'll get the biggest people, the biggest. The first meeting in two months. We'll turn this place into a pantheon of the famous."

"It's marvelous, Jimmy," Nate said. He was chewing the tough flowers fiercely. A bit of bluish bloom stuck to his chin.

"I've got to get started," I told him and got up.

"But your dinner," Nate said. "The whooping crane. The Balinese wonder pudding."

"Later, Nate. There are too many things to do. The orchid salad was actually very filling."

On the way out I brushed past Perry in his white dinner jacket with its subtle bulge. "Everything to your taste, sir?" he asked, grimly smiling.

"Excellent, Perry, excellent. My compliments to the gardener!"

V

Now it came to pass that in those days a call went out ... Tee hee hee.

If you get a one per cent return on junk mail you're doing well. Starting cold I couldn't hope even for that. Was I Sears Roebuck announcing a January White Sale? I was a stranger inviting presidents and kings to my party.

The problems were staggering. In comparison a bride puzzling how to distribute thirty-five or fifty invitations among relatives and friends numbering in the hundreds had as little to do as a ranch cook ringing a bell to call hired hands to supper. There was a plethora of exceptional people in the world. In the old days you had a king, a half dozen nobles, a few ministers of state—maybe a handful of others, a poet laureate, perhaps, a court architect, a genius working in a basement. But today! A world where people could seek their own level worked against me. There were sixteen thousand, four hundred fifty-three people listed in the current *Who's Who*—and that just took in America. Nate could accommodate two hundred. Which two hundred?

Ruthlessly I hacked away at those parts of my plan which I saw were impracticable. Although I originally hoped for The Club to be genuinely international in character, once I got down to it I realized that the problems of transportation and expense to foreign members were prohibitive. They might come once. (This raised the problem, too, of monthly meetings; it was too much. We could meet quarterly, perhaps.) So now I figured on only token foreign representation, ten places to revolve among important non-nationals. Admittedly this made The Club one-sided, like calling seven games between two American baseball teams a *World* Series, or naming the winner in a competition that never attracted entries from more than four countries the World Heavyweight Champion. But what could I do?

Next, how could I be sure that the most important people would, in combination, be good mixers? A minor point, or course—what counted was that they come, not that they enjoy themselves. Also, great men are not notably gregarious. I'd have to impress upon them the exclusivity of the project, the summit conference tone of the thing.

The problems of organization were appalling. Like many obsessed men, however, I am like a scientist when it comes to working out the technical obstacles to my obsession. I classified and sub-classified like a biologist. I made experiments. Once I wrote down the names of a dozen men in a particular field and discovered from this single list an invaluable lesson: There are essentially two kinds of men, the practitioner and the theoretician, and although the theoretician is often the weightier in history's scales, it is the practitioner to whom the glamour attaches. To strike a balance it was necessary that both classes be represented. Delicate proportions had to be established, for I saw that this problem was inextricably linked to the problem of the selection of categories. Who was to say that a zoölogist did not do more finally to change the world than a surgeon, or that a writer of popular songs didn't have a greater effect than either?

Now I was involved in the very heart of my problem, for I was beginning to consider the issue of fame and power. Was I after something that was ultimately quantitative or qualitative? In whom was I actually interested, the guy on stage or the fellow in the wings? This was not an organizational so much as a metaphysical issue, and I saw I was dealing with nothing less than the old business of appearance and reality. What, I had to ask myself, were my aims? My character gave me the answer: I had none. In the final analysis I was involved in creating an effect, merely an effect. If I concerned myself with these issues it was only to the extent that they reflected on that effect. I saw myself again as someone without collective or contiguous purpose in the world—as someone, finally, without community or continuity. What I cared about, I discovered, was The Club, not the people who would be in it. Like any zealot I thought not in terms of ends, but at once and at last of the old ineluctable self. *That,* it turned out, was the principle of the thing. Hey, I thought, you've the makings of a leader yourself. The stuff of greatness is in you. With that established, all my finicky concern to strike a balance became irrelevant. I had unnecessarily confused myself. Now I saw that I had to be arbitrary, artistic rather than thorough, theatrical rather than scientific.

A gathering of zoölogists and lapidaries and musicologists was too tame; it was beside the point. I needed doers, not dons. One had to go, then, not where the power was, but where it seemed to be. So in the end I had to look no further than the newspapers or any other mirror of popular opinion. I threw away my *Who's Who* and took up my *Time*—the categorical techniques of which nicely fitted my scheme, incidentally. By poring over the last two years' back issues and collating the most frequently alluded to names I soon had a practical, workable list of potential members.

To my shock, however, I discovered that while I had some tenuous access (through friends, through friends' friends) to many of the people on my list, I had nothing like the first-hand knowledge of them I needed. I had thought I had done better than that, and I saw that I was dependent on The Club to complete the circle of my intimacies. Of the two hundred people I picked as first choices, I knew only nine well (that, is, only nine knew me) and had been introduced to only fifty-seven others. How I would get the remaining hundred and thirty-four to come to The Club I didn't know, but at last, starting with my basic nine, I hit upon the idea of an elaborate series of chain letters. (It seemed far-fetched until I remembered that Christ Himself had started with only twelve apostles.) Thus, Nate could be responsible for Frank Sinatra, Sinatra for Darryl Zanuck, and so on. From my reading and personal knowledge I worked out detailed charts demonstrating the overlapping of thousands of relationships, like some cosmic genealogist showing the real though attenuated connections between apparent strangers. Incest, I saw, was a real principle at work in the world.

I was still faced with the problem of reserves, of creating alternates for first choices who would not or could not attend. Now my problem was the reverse of what it had been in the beginning. Then I had been overwhelmed by the apparent superfluity of the eminent; now I was aware that any substitution was bound to be unsatisfactory.

It was the creation of the second team, however, that ultimately brought out my most exquisite sense of nuance and that made the fiercest demands on my artistic imagination. Again I created not power itself but the illusion of power and glamour in depth. A Magi done with mirrors, as it were. In a way I was almost sorry when later I had to scratch off each alternate candidate as first choices made their decisions to come. (It would have been one more thing I had gotten away with.)

Once my lists were prepared the real work began. There were instructions to give the basic nine, schedules and suggestions for follow-ups. All this took time and I saw that the first meeting would have to be pushed back another two months. It was necessary, too, to guarantee the loyalty of my nine workers. Margaret and Nate were easy, of course, but many of the others I had not seen in years. I set aside three weeks for winning them over, and began by trying to revive their interest in the old flamboyant Boswell.

DR. MORTON PERLMUTTER. INSTITUTE OF MAN. UNIVERSITY OF ILLINOIS. CHAMPAIGN, ILLINOIS. I AM BEHIND CONVOCATION OF CAPTAINS OF INDUSTRY, ARTS, MANKIND, RELIGION AND WHAT HAVE YOU. FANTASTIC OPPORTUNITY TO STUDY LIFE AS IT IS LIVED AT THE TOP. MORE

FUN THAN A FIELD TRIP TO PAPUA. FREE EATS.
FREE SPEECH. FREE LOVE. NATE'S PLACE.
NEW YORK. DETAILS FOLLOW.

My Dear Rabbi Messerman, *Shalom:*

Your presence is respectfully requested at
the charter meeting of a new spiritual organization whose membership will be made up of the
world community's leading religious and secular authorities. Although I will not burden you
now with the full details we are hoping to at-
tract some of the Yeshiva people in Cincinnati,
as well as several of the more important
goyim.

When further details and the reservation
blank arrive, please indicate whether you prefer
fish or fowl.

Field Marshal Augustus Lano,
Presidential Ranch House,
Los Farronentes, QR.

I am sending you this through one of my
contacts in the International Red Cross in the
hopes that it reaches you in time.

There is about to be established in New
York a new secret organization whose purpose,
the *vis-a-vis* confrontation of world leaders in
an atmosphere of peaceful cordiality, is one
which I am sure you must endorse.

It will be necessary for you to come to
America for this. Because of the willful perversity of an unfortunate official policy toward you
your current status is one of *persona non grata,*
and it may be more convenient if you could
arrange to come up by two-man submarine
through the St. Lawrence Seaway. You could
swim to Cleveland and make it from there to
the Turnpike and New York. However I leave
these details to you. More follows.

Today Los Farronentes, Q.R. Tomorrow
the world, eh, Lano? P.S. How's the crabgrass?

Dear Harold Flesh,

Some of the boys thought Nate's. Hush hush. Q.T. S.S. N.K.V.D.

These I followed with other letters—matey, detailed, sincere. I sent brochures, gifts, reply-prepaid telegrams. With some of these men I had, in our mutual past, already vaguely alluded to a Club, for this was not a new idea with me. Many were used to doing me favors, but I let them see that no favor they had ever done me was quite complete without this one; I played on their sense of being allowed to participate in a human continuum outside their own, generating in them not duty, not love, but the high privilege of knowing some human fact in perspective—a small immortality. No one knew as well as I the irresistible appeal of the words "for old time's sake." Ultimately, of course, they had to come round.

Then I set to work on the other fifty-seven. Again I wrote letters, feeling something already historical and marked about the very pen that inscribed *"Mon cher Picasso,"* "Dear Oppenheimer," "Exquisite Miss Taylor," and taking an almost physical pleasure just in folding the paper and addressing and sealing the envelopes. It was as though, stamped, these already enjoyed the status of official documents, artifacts, the thin, blue, barber-pole-edged airmail envelopes like a kind of money. I sent the letters special delivery; it was satisfying to know that they would have to be signed for, that whoever got my letter would see *my* name, *my* handwriting, handle something *I* had handled. It was only the spurious tactility of the famous, the special sense that they alone could give of possessing an almost healing power in their touch. It was only the barbarous, talismanic power of the autograph book, and I should have known better, but for the time I was caught up.

On a chart I devised I kept a strict accounting of when and to whom a letter had been sent. I allowed three days and then followed up the letter with a person-to-person phone call from the booth in the Columbus Circle subway station. It was perhaps the most intensely active period of my life. I didn't spare myself for a moment. My room on Fifty-eighth Street became my office; stationary, stamps, rough drafts of letters, charts, lists and telegram blanks were everywhere. I felt like Marx loose in the Bronx. Late into every night I wrote, rendered, revised, polished, aiming in these letters to the fifty-seven for the fat, safe, exactly perfect pitch of ultimate respectability.

It was spring and warm for that ime of year in New York. I worked away with the windows flung wide, unconscious of hunger, discomfort, heat, weariness, time. It must have been then that I caught the draft.

VI

The cough was dry, hard, a sustained and piercing howl from the chest. I could bring nothing up with it. Worse during the day, it seemed to have something to do with the light itself, with the very sunshine. It didn't seem to have any connection with my body. My throat did not tickle; my chest, when I blew out long, deep experimental exhalations, seemed clear. But every so often the rhythm of my existence was broken by a sudden, irrelevant explosion, strident as a signal.

In a few days I began to notice after each seizure a light residual sensitivity low on my left side—not an *ache*, rather a kind of flesh memory of contact, as after a handshake, or a pressure, not in itself unpleasant, like the thin sensation that you are still wearing your hat just after you have taken it off. Gradually, however, and almost in direct proportion to the subsidence of the cough, this pressure developed from increasingly less vague sensations into an intense and unbearable pain. I had the impression when I moved my hand inside my pants to touch the area that it actually glowed with a special localized heat. "I'm in trouble, I'm in trouble," I groaned. Nor did it ease my fear when just two aspirin killed my pain. I'd been had. What, I thought, two aspirin– For this? For what *I've* got? I felt that my body was playing with me, teasing me into a phony confidence.

It was clear that something strange and bad had happened to me. My malaise, spontaneous as a sneeze, had been generated full-blown, complete, with no sympton less intense than any other. After a week it became apparent that whatever had struck me had done so with a peculiarly adaptive kind of cunning, with an almost biological sense of justice. By keeping careful track of what was happening to me I soon noticed that no two symptoms ever occurred simultaneously. It was as if what had been true of my life was true now of my chemistry—that not even my body was capable of doing two things at once. As the cough subsided the pain grew. As the pain subsided something else took its place and kept it only until some other threat presented itself. Those who live by the sword die by the sword.

There was something else. Besides this waxing and waning, this sweeping of my body's circuits by progressive symptoms—a kind of vulgar, physical absurdity, almost like one of those garish movie marquees which operate according to some fixed mechanical cycle, one light popping on only after another has blinked off—there was a weird inconsequentialness to these tokens. The unproductive cough, the pain in the left side, too low to be connected with my heart, on the wrong side for appendicitis, bespoke a kind of triviality that belied the cruel realness of their presence. The other symptoms (I had accepted from the beginning that these were *symptoms,* that not even disease could present itself without a mask) seemed just as far-fetched, almost comic. For several days I seemed to be possessed in turn by all the basic drives. During one period I was always hungry, and no matter what or how much I ate I failed to satisfy myself. The hunger was as intense as the pain in my side had been—what one imagines starving men feel. In the next phase I was constantly cold; I had to get my winter sweaters and overcoat from our apartment and went out dressed as I might be in the depth of a cold winter, despite the unseasonable April heat. After that I felt an almost overwhelming sexuality. I brought magazines to my room on Fifty-eighth Street and pored lasciviously over the pictures of the girls, as susceptible as a pubescent boy to the silly accompanying text. Almost any casual contact with a woman—a clerk in a store, a girl beside me on a bus—was enough to set me off. Once, after staying up late writing my letters, I went to an all-night cafeteria for some coffee at about three A.M. A charwoman, middle-aged and fat, was on her hands and knees scrubbing the floor beside my table, and it was all I could do to stop myself from climbing on top of her.

Endlessly symptom followed sympton. My urine seemed thick. I was conscious of a hypersensitivity of my hair ends; it was torture to put a comb to my head. My hands fell asleep; my skin burned; my gums swelled. My heart tumbled heavily in my chest, like one casket loose in the hold of a ship.

My sleep during all this had never been so profound, yet I was as tired during the day as an insomniac. I awoke each morning to some new outrage, sudden, unanticipated, yet somehow already familiar, sadly certain and permanent as a doom. I might have been a city held in patient siege by wily, dangerous enemies. One morning I realized, with the queer rush of relief familiar to one who has at last learned some unpleasant rumor about himself, that I was going to die. I knew this. I was, simply, *going to die*. That's what it would come to. I was incurable.

Much as I had thought of death I had given almost no thought at all to ill health. Now I perceived that death was a consequence of something that happened to your body, and this obvious truth struck me with a force that I would not have imagined. I understood that what I had thought of as oblivion, annihilation, was rooted in a bedrock of matter—that, as was now being demonstrated to me, a thousand things could go wrong, a million; that there were no guarantees that life would or needed or even wanted to go on; that whatever chemical experience meant when we said *life* was as consequential and in effect as accidental as the arrangement of fallen leaves on a lawn; that anything could happen; that one thin tissue bruised in a trip on the stairs could pollute others; that fatality was a chain reaction, death some ubiquitous thing on springs inside us, neither waiting nor ready to pounce, but set to go off at the merest untoward, uncircumspect jostle. I saw my body as something volatile as a bomb. Hypochondria was deep wisdom and ludicrous folly; there was nothing that we could do.

Thinking this—seeing myself not as someone who would one day die, but as one who was already dying, who even as he lived broke down whatever odds there were in his favor, who against his will recklessly used up his single provision, his small store of time—I began to feel a tremendous, almost heroic power. In the streets I sensed a strange, previously unknown force within me, as if I were in possession of some dread, terrible secret, which, were I to disclose it, would permanently affect the lives of others. Living, I was simply one among others; dying, I was above them, imprudent and colossal as some lame-duck hero. Although in one sense The Club had never seemed so important, it was irrelevant compared to this new thing. I saw again, but in a fresh, totally unexpected way, that I had not been prepared to die, that I had only been prepared to dread and hate death. While this was unchanged—while, indeed, I saw my death as the greatest of tragedies—my new reaction was neither tragic nor sad. Instead, I felt a weird giddiness, a strange lightness of heart and mind. I did not want to die, but the sense of rude power I experienced when I knew that I was dying was the most stimulating thing that had ever happened to me.

It was in this mood and to test this power that I began my series of death experiments.

Fully clothed I lay down on my bed. Placing my arms full length, unnaturally stiff, beside me, I arranged myself as in a coffin and closed my eyes. I tried to put all thought out of my mind, but the effort of keeping my body rigid produced a constant strain on my consciousness. It was unsatisfactory, and after a few minutes I gave it up; shockingly, whatever else it was, death was not uncomfortable.

I got on a Broadway bus. As inconspicuously as possible I slumped in my seat. I closed my eyes; I took small, imperceptible sips of breath; I stiffened; I allowed my body to pitch, as volitionlessly as a stone, with the momentum of the bus. In a few minutes someone sat down beside me. The rustle of a newspaper indicated that my seat mate was as yet unaware of me. Once the bus stopped abruptly and I fell stiffly against my companion; then we turned a corner and I was buffeted away from him, against the window. My feet shot out in compensation and I could feel our shoes touching. I could no longer hear the rustling of the newspaper, and I knew that whoever sat next to me was studying me. I could feel the power of my corpse slowly collecting, accumulating. The temptation to open my eyes was almost irresistible. Gradually the soft, random chatter of those around me began to subside. The silence pulled out behind me like a rug unrolling. Soon the only sound was the bus itself and the noises of traffic. Now I felt the full weight of everyone's curiosity, the contagious, rubbery-necked swoosh of their attention, their startled, disturbed dread. They were like creatures arrested by some unaccustomed noise in a forest. I felt my death ooze out to them; I felt their almost adrenal response. It was as if some powerful taboo had been violated. I ached to stare back at them.

When the bus swung around another corner I collapsed ruthlessly against the person next to me. He gasped and recoiled as if struck by something profoundly unclean.

Someone rushed up. "Is he all right?" a voice said.

"I don't know. I can't tell," said the man next to me, shoved now into a kind of action. He leaned forward and shook me cautiously.

I looked up at once. "What is it?" I said, a little angrily.

"I thought . . ." he stumbled. "We thought something was wrong. That you were sick. Dead."

"I must have fallen asleep," I said. "Is it Fourteenth Street yet?"

"Blocks back," said the man who had come up the aisle.

The bus stopped and I got up quickly.

"Excuse me," the man next to me said as I moved past him, "but you sleep like a dead man."

"Excuse *me*," I said, "but I need the practice."

I went up on the roof of a ten-story building and climbed onto the ledge.

A crowd gathered and someone below ran off to get the police. I was too high to see their expressions, but I can imagine that they were seeing me as if I had been an ominous sky they scanned for warnings of a storm.

As I waved once and screamed and jumped backwards out of sight onto the tar and gravel rooftop, I could sense their shocked, massed inward suck of air. Never mind what you read about crowds at a motor race or a prizefight; people do not want people to die.

I took an elevator back down to the ground floor and went out into the streets to join the crowd.

"What's happened?" I asked someone.

"Some guy was trying to kill himself. He fell backwards and probably knocked himself out. A cop's gone up to get him."

"They'll put *him* away," I said. "Suicide's a serious crime."

I went down into a subway station and boarded a train for the first time in my life. My hands cautiously in my lap, I sat on the wide wicker seat that ran along the length of the carriage and rode out to somewhere in Brooklyn. I got off the train, crossed the platform and got on another train going back. I sat next to a young girl about thirteen years old. She carried one of those little brass and plastic suitcases kids pack their leotards and ballet slippers in when they're going for a lesson, and she was reading *Mademoiselle*. As the train tunneled under the river I pitched forward suddenly and groaned. I grabbed my chest and rocked it, frantic as a mother with a dead infant. I leaned heavily against the child. "Today's the day," I gasped, "a man died in your arms on the subway."

On Fifth Avenue I saw a very well-dressed man carrying an expensive briefcase.

"Please," I said, rushing up to him, "I've just swallowed cyanide. I was trying to kill myself but I've changed my mind."

"Oh, my God," the man said. "Oh, Jesus. Quick, let's get a cab. Taxi," he called. "Taxi! Here, take my arm. Taxi. God damn it, *taxi*. How much did you take? Where's a hospital? The driver would know. Taxi! *Taxi!*" He waved his briefcase like a leather flag. "TAXI!" he screamed.

"In New York there must be fifty thousand cabs," I said, "but do you think you can get one when you really need it?" I pulled away from him and disappeared around a corner.

I went up to the Bronx and walked around until I came to a park. I was wearing good clothes—I didn't want anyone to think I was a bum sleeping one off. I found a deserted gravel path and stretched myself out face down across it. Soon I heard someone coming up the walk; from the squeaky crunchy sounds it must have been either a housemaid pushing a perambulator or a kid on a tricycle. Then I heard someone cooing as if to a child, and I knew that it was a housemaid. She didn't see me until she was almost on top of me; then she screamed. I thought she would run away, but she came up to me and turned me over.

"Mister," she called. "Mister. Please. Oh," she yelled, turning away from me, "there's been a murder. Help! Help!" Leaving the baby carriage, she ran off to get help.

When I could no longer hear her cries I rose, brushed myself off and walked away.

I was sitting in a cafeteria on Seventh Avenue when a woman came in leading an old man. She brought him to a table next to mine, pulled the chair out for him, and took his hand and guided it carefully to its wooden back. "It's just behind you," she said very softly.

The old man lowered himself tenderly into the seat as if he were tentatively sitting down in a tub of hot water. He might have been an old man at the beach, with his back to the waves, sitting in the sea.

The woman leaned over him. "What do you feel like having, Papa?" she asked gently.

401

"I think an egg salad sandwich," he said. "Tomato soup. Do they have pie? Pie. Coffee."

"I'll bring it right back for you," she said.

When she left him to go through the line, the blind man pulled himself closer to the table with great care. He put his hands out experimentally, feeling for the salt, the pepper, the bottles of ketchup and mustard and sugar. He frowned as if he might have forgotten to tell the woman something, and then sighed resignedly. I had the impression that his blindness was fairly recent. He took off his hat and set it down too close to the edge of the table. In one of his clumsy motions of orientation he brushed it off and it fell to the floor.

The woman came back with the food and set it down in front of him. She picked up the hat and put it back on the table without saying anything. "Do you think you'll be all right?" she asked as she hovered over him. "I have to see Sybil before she leaves the office."

"I'll be fine," he said. "What am I, an old blind man?"

She put a tablespoon in his hand and moved the soup in front of him. "I won't be long," she said. "Her office is in this block."

"I'll be fine," he said.

"Well then, twenty minutes." She took a cigar out of her purse and put it in his breast pocket. "There's a cigar for you when you're through."

When she had been gone for about five minutes I looked hastily around the cafeteria. We were almost alone. I waited for another minute and then leaned toward the old man and slammed a chair down violently. The blind man was startled and turned his head uselessly toward the sound. I bent down quickly beside him at a level with his stomach and grunted twice. I stamped my heels clumsily on the tile floor.

"Is anything wrong?" the old man asked. "Is anything wrong? Ruth?" A little tomato soup had spilled from the spoon in his shaking hand onto his vest.

I drew back soundlessly as the old man called again. When there was no answer he shook his head and

402

scowled in frustration. He pushed the soup away from him, splashing some onto his sandwich, where it soaked into the bread like blood. He fumbled for the sandwich, found it, and pulled it without appetite toward his mouth. I waited until he had finished half of it and then rose from my seat quietly and went around behind his chair.

"I'm a detective," I said. "My credentials."

"What is it?" he asked nervously.

"It's none of my business, of course, but I don't see how you can just go on eating. Well, maybe you're used to it. Fourteen years on the force and I'm not." I turned away for a moment and lowered my voice. "Better call the morgue, Harry. This is their baby."

"What is it?" the old man said again.

"I'll have to ask you a few questions," I said. "You're our only witness."

"What is it?"

"Did it seem to you that the deceased acted peculiar in any way? I mean, did the deceased do anything that may have looked funny to you?"

"Is someone dead?" he asked, frightened. "I don't see," he said. "I heard a noise. What was it?"

"You're blind?"

"Yes. Yes. Who is it? Is it a woman?"

I hesitated. "No," I said finally. "A man. About thirty-three, thirty-four. A big fellow, strongly built."

"Oh, that's terrible," the old man said. "That's terrible."

"That his wallet, Harry? Yeah, give it to me. Let's see who he was."

"That's terrible," the old man said softly. He realized suddenly that he was still holding his sandwich, and he dropped it as though it were something foul.

"Boswell," I said. "His name was James Boswell."

"Oh, what a terrible thing," the man said. "A young man. That's a very awful thing."

"I'm sorry," I said.

He said my name to himself over and over again, as though he were trying to imagine from the sound of it what its owner could have been like.

"Well—" I said.

"It was kind of you to try to do something for him," the old man said.

"That's my job."

"Is he from here?" he asked.

"What?"

"Is he from this city?"

"No," I said harshly. "He's from out of town. From somewhere else. He's a foreigner."

"It's a terrible thing," the old man said. "Maybe he was on holiday. On business."

"A tourist," I said.

"Poor man," he said. "I wish I had had my sight. Maybe he gave a signal . . . I might have helped."

"No," I said. "Nobody could have done anything."

Oh, what a thing it is to be settled by our past—to be no better, finally, than our toilet training, than domestic arrangements we don't even understand at the time. The symptoms for the day are a virulent disgust, advanced abhorrence, endemic loathing, mortal destestation, inoperable repugnance.

He died such a healthy fella, and everybody—*everybody*—was very kind.

VII

At first the doorman did not recognize me. He moved with a faint threatening motion to block my way and slipped his whistle out of his breast pocket.

"What's the matter with you?" I said. "I live here."

The doorman stared. "Oh, excuse me, sir," he said at last. "I didn't know you. Your clothes . . . Are you feeling all right sir?"

"I'm sick. I'm having a little trouble with my breathing. With my heart. All my glands are oozing."

"I'll help you up to your apartment," he said.

"No." The whistle was still in his hand. "Just pipe me aboard," I said. The doorman held the door for me and I moved through it almost drunkenly. A woman coming out as I entered looked at me curiously.

"We're taking over," I said. "The neighborhood's changing." I backed into the elevator giggling.

For a moment I couldn't remember my floor. I pressed the button and felt the elevator lift me by pushing at my shoes and had an impression, brief but terrifying, that it would move me upwards through the roof, the clouds, space, past the stars.

I stumbled out at my floor, but when I felt in my pockets for the key I did not have it. I could not remember now if I had ever had a key to the apartment. When I rang the bell the chimes inside (Gift-of-the-Month Club) sounded a fragment from some hymn. There were no other sounds. I pressed the bell again; I knocked on the door. It hurt my fists to tap even lightly upon it and I stopped a man walking down the hall toward the elevator.

"Excuse me, neighbor, but I am neurasthenic and it is acute agony for me to rap upon this door. I wonder if you would do it for me."

"Why don't you ring the bell?"

"I have, sir. No one comes."

"Then it won't do you any good to knock on the door, will it?" the man said, and continued down the hall.

I looked helplessly at the door and taking the knob in my hands began to shake it. "Open up," I yelled. "Make my bed soon, Mother, for I am sick to the heart and fain would lie down."

I moved on to the next apartment and pressed the buzzer. A woman I did not recognize opened the door almost immediately. I had not shaved for several days and now, a huge reprobate presence in old clothes, I stood leaning clumsily against her doorway. She gasped and tried to shut the door.

"Just a minute."

"I'm sorry," she said. "The lady of the house is not at home."

I put my arm on the closing door and pushed against it with all my remaining strength. "All right," I said, shoving a finger into my pocket and pointing it as her as if it were a gun, "this is a stickup."

The woman stepped back. "What do you want?"

"Is that the kitchen?" I asked in a low voice, jerking my head around to the right.

"Yes," she answered weakly.

"Then you better gimme—gimme—gimme a glass of milk!" I laughed. "No. I live next door. I forgot my key and no one's home. I'm sick. Get the doorman. He's got a passkey. Call him, lady—please."

She didn't move.

"I'm James Boswell," I said. "From next door. I'm in the book. Look, in time to come we'll laugh about this. See, it was just my finger. I fooled you." I saw the speaking tube on the wall just inside the door. "May I?" I asked, already pressing the button. I put my lips next to the mouthpiece, receiving it as I would a kiss. "Who's there? Who's there? Operator! Operator!"

"You've got your finger on the button," the woman said.

I took it away and a voice, tinny as the sound of a ventriloquist's dummy came out of the small speaker. "Yes?"

"It's Boswell. Get up here. I'm with the good woman next door. I've got no key, no one's home. I'm sick. Hurry! Hurry!"

In a few minutes the doorman had let me into the apartment.

"It's disgraceful," I said. "Having to be let into my own place like this. Humiliating."

"Do you want me to call a doctor, sir?"

"Get Dr. Green," I said. "On Twelfth Street. Old family physician. Knows me inside out, upside down. Get him. I want Green. Call Green."

"Yes, sir." The doorman started to leave.

"Where's my wife?"

"I haven't seen Mrs. Boswell, sir."

"The kid—David."

"I haven't seen him either, sir."

"Fine way to treat a dying man."

The doorman left. The woman in whose doorway I had stood now stood in mine. "Is there something I can do?" she asked.

"The lady of the house is not at home," I said. I went into our bedroom and lay down. "Close the goddamn hall door," I shouted. "There's a draft."

The door slammed.

"Snug as a bug in a rug," I said. "Spry as a fly in an eye." I rolled over, scraping my shoes across the satin bedspread. "Oh, Jesus," I said, "what a way to die." I placed my hand gently on my heart. "Help," I said very softly. I made a song out of it, singing "Help Help Help Help Help Help Help Help" as if they were notes in the scale.

I closed my eyes and fell asleep and when I opened them Dr. Green was standing over my bed watching me.

"What interesting things do you keep in your bag, Doctor? I asked, looking at his satchel.

"I'm a scientist," the doctor said. "I don't make house calls. You sick?"

"Oh Jesus, what a way to die."

"What is it with you? You sick? What did you call me for? Where's your wife? I brought a little stuff with me on dry ice. Even so, you can't keep it too long. It melts like ice cream." He leaned down over me. "Say," he said, "I won't crap you. I know how particular you are. Guess who I got in the syringe."

"O Jesus, did I call for you?"

"Where's your wife? What is this? The guy called and said it was an emergency. I don't make house calls, but I remembered you and I looked upon it as a professional challenge. Jesus, the way you messed my place up!"

"Are you really a doctor? What's wrong with me?"

"I'm very impressed," Dr. Green said. "Your footman brought me up and let me in. This is a nice place. I like to see the stuff gets a good home." He tapped the bag. "I'm not at liberty to disclose names," he said, "but I got a cabinet minister in here. A president. A king!"

"Help Help Help Help Help Help Help Help," I sang down the scale.

"Come on, where is she?"

"It's a mistake. Go away."

"What do you mean a mistake? I don't make house calls. What do you mean a mistake?"

"Please," I said. "Please. If you're a doctor you must have taken an oath to help the sick. Go away."

"Seventy-five bucks," the doctor said.

"Bill me," I yelled at him. The shout raised devils in my chest.

"Well, make up your mind, will you?" Dr. Green said.

"Get out. Now. Get out!" I moved to get up and the doctor backed out quickly.

"Frail as a snail in a pail," I said when I was alone again. I felt very cold and I got up to pull back the spread. It was April and there was only one thin blanket

408

on the bed. I went to the closet to look for others but couldn't find any. At the back of the closet, high on a shelf, was a box under some suitcases where some blankets might be, but I hadn't the strength to move the suitcases. I pulled some of Margaret's and my clothes off the rod and staggered with them back to bed. I arranged the blanket and bedspread and clothes on top of me, but when I tried to sleep again I was conscious of the smell of cleaning fluid on the clothes. This grew stronger until it filled my nostrils, my head, my throat. At last I could stand it no longer; I knew I was going to vomit, and I tried to push back the heavy clothing. But the weight was enormous, and I threw up on the bed.

I shuddered. "I'm sick. I'm really sick." At first this seemed genuinely strange to me, but as I thought about it I began to cherish it as a justification. It was as if this one sickness, this one real thing in my life—the smell of the vomit, the quick, cold ache that floated transitionlessly through my body as something blown by the wind—were all that I needed to underwrite my behavior. My body, frailer now than it had ever been, was my credential, my card of identity, my alibi. At last I had a legitimate need. It filled me up; for the first time in my life I began to feel outrage, the ferocious satisfaction of the injured, the framed, the damned. The feeling was at once unfamiliar and conventional, as exquisite as the slaking of a thirst.

Where were Margaret and David? Their absence was only what I should have expected, perhaps, but somehow I hadn't expected it. Margaret's insistence that she loved me had been true enough, but no train waited forever. What I might have loved was the train that did. And I understood, too, the David whose pleasure in me derived from a kind of humility used as keenly as a weapon.

Their hatred of me now—that was what their absence must mean—was wrong. What I had suspected about myself never seemed so true. In a way, my hands were as clean as many men's, cleaner than most men's. I had done nothing to foster death, nothing to encourage it. Though I had never loved anyone, neither had I hated. I was a genuinely amiable man who recognized something

409

clear, who believed from the first what others were afraid to believe—that it was the nature of love to be forever misplaced. Love was the country bumpkin of virtues. All I had ever wanted was to live forever, without pain.

I was terrified. Now my body was my enemy. If I, like other men, had not escaped pain, at least my pains had seemed—even as I suffered them, when the imagination and the foresight were most dulled—explicable, temporary, almost secular. This was something else, different in kind. My body was pitted, gutted, oozing the fumes of decay. I was on fire.

Where *were* Margaret and David? I was square with them both now. If their desertion was hard for me it wasn't because of love, but because they might have done something, fetched a bedpan, changed my linen, brought me drugs. Well, it was true. One's chickens went away to roost.

I tried to think about it rationally. That Margaret had not taken her clothes meant nothing. She was a Principessa—money *was* no object. I thought bitterly of how I had failed to scold her for this. For then the presence of her clothes might have meant something; I could imagine her leaving them behind as a gesture. She could be back in Italy now, arranging with the Black Pope himself a decree, a special dispensation. Fixing beyond fixing. People could not make other people happy, I thought, and love was no debt. Yet my wife and son, with their moral U.O.Me's, would never understand this. They had meant to bring me down with guilt, tirelessly focusing their unspoken accusations like children flashing the sun in your eyes with a hand mirror. Screw guilt. Men died. It was physics, not metaphysics.

I hauled myself out of bed, the vomit suspended in slimy strings from my mouth, and went to the bathroom. It might kill me to shower now, but I couldn't stand my stink. I undressed clumsily and stood, weaving and ridiculous, before the full-length mirror. I turned on the shower taps full blast; the water felt like heavy knives. Drying myself, I remembered how I had felt fifteen years before in the gymnasium—powerful, and despite my size, almost light. David could beat me now.

I didn't want to go back into our bedroom; instead I staggered into David's room and lay on the narrow bed. Margaret had decorated the room. There was simply no sign of him; it might have been a room in a hotel. What it must have cost David, I thought, to have suppressed his sense of beauty, the single coruscation of personality he had allowed himself. How vindictive he was really; how angry he was. Then I thought, I am a man rankled by human waste, put off by the deflection of self as other men are by high treason. I wondered that David could have misunderstood so much.

I looked sadly out at the dusk gathering like a fog on the windows and fell fitfully into a doze. In my sleep—which was not free of pain—I had the impression that I was being moved through time, past landmarks of evening and night and morning and afternoon, leaving time behind as one left behind the farmhouses one saw through the window of a moving train. But when I woke the dusk was the shade I had remembered it and I wondered whether I had slept at all. I thought I should be hungry; I tried to remember when I had last eaten. It was in the cafeteria when I had pointlessly humiliated the blind man. That was at least two days before, or, if I had slept around the clock, three. I had spent a day in my room on Fifty-eighth Street, and there had suffered the attack.

What a fool, I thought. It was the business of my life to keep on living. I was getting no treatment, no medicines. If what had happened to me was, as I suspected, a heart attack, I wondered why I had not called a doctor earlier, why I had given Green's name when the doorman asked me if I needed help. The pains were still with me and I wondered what the world's record was for a heart attack.

I picked up the phone beside David's bed, but when the girl at the desk asked what number I wanted I realized that I knew no number, that though I could give her the unlisted phone numbers of half the celebrities in New York, I didn't even know the name of a good doctor.

"Get me the doorman."

"Roger?"

411

"Yes. Please. Get me Roger."

The operator connected me.

"Roger, this is Mr. Boswell."

"Yes, sir. Feeling better, sir?"

"Not so you'd notice, Roger."

"That's too bad, sir."

"Roger, I need a good doctor. Who do the tenants use?"

"That would be Dr. Mefwiss, sir."

"Is he a good man, Roger?"

"Yes, sir. He's a very big man."

"Far?"

"No, sir, he's right in this building."

"Well, would you see that he comes up here, Roger?"

"Dr. Mefwiss doesn't like to make house calls, sir."

"Goddamn it, Roger, it's his own house. I'm too sick to move. Who knows what it's costing me just to speak to you on the telephone? Get Dr. Mefwiss. Get him. I want Mefwiss."

"I'll get him, sir. I'll get him right away."

"Yes," I said. "Oh, Roger? When did you let me in?"

"Yes, sir, that's right."

"No, no. When? When did I come home?"

"That would be this morning, sir."

"Oh," I said, "only this morning." I was disappointed that I had not slept around the clock. Was it possible that Margaret and David were just out for the day?

"Thank you, Roger."

"I'll get Dr. Mefwiss, sir."

"Yes. Thank you."

When I put down the phone I thought of something else Roger might do for me and I picked it up again. "What's Roger's extension?" I asked the operator. "I might be needing it."

She rang, but there was no answer. Roger must have gone for Dr. Mefwiss. "Just let it ring," I told the girl.

In a few minutes Roger answered.

"What did Dr. Mefwiss say, Roger?"

412

"Is that you, Mr. Boswell? He said he'd come right up, sir."

"Fine," I said. "Thank you, Roger. You may just have saved my life."

"You're not to worry, sir. You'll be all right."

"Thank you, Roger. Nice of you to say so. Roger, I want you to go to the desk and find out if my rent's been paid for next month."

"Your rent, sir?"

"It's after the twenty-fifth, isn't it?"

"It's the twenty-seventh, sir."

"Our rent is due on the twenty-fifth," I said. "My wife usually takes care of it. Look, Roger, I'll level with you. I'm trying to figure out if my wife has left me. I can't call the desk myself—they'd get too suspicious. I haven't got a dime of my own, you know. She's the Principessa, you understand. I didn't marry her for her money exactly, but let's not kid ourselves, she pays the bills. You see, if she hasn't paid up that could mean she doesn't intend to come back. If the desk found that out they'd try to evict me. I'm in a tough spot—if I'm as sick as I think, I might have to use this place for a while."

"I see," Roger said, astonished.

"I thought you might help me." I lowered my voice. "I haven't got a dime. I'm this—you know—stud."

"Really?"

"Oh, sure," I said. "I wouldn't be surprised if that wasn't why I was sick now. The demands that women made! Anyway, I thought you might help me. You won't make a nickel out of it, but you wouldn't have to call me Mister Boswell."

"I see," Roger said.

"We'd be in it together. You and me against the syndicate that runs this place." There was a pause as Roger thought about this. "I could tell you stories about those guys that would curl your ears. Tie-ups with gangsters, the fire chief, the unions. Fixing beyond fixing. Deals in flawed cement, watered steel. Stand clear of the building, Roger, when you blow your whistle for a cab."

"Really, sir?"

413

"Jim."

"I beg your pardon?"

"You said 'Really, sir?' Call me Jim."

"Jim," Roger said experimentally.

"A deal's a deal," I said. "Look, someone's at the door. Probably that doctor. Find out about the rent."

I shouted that I was alone and too sick to move and told the doctor to go down to the desk for a passkey. In a few minutes he returned and let himself in. I told him about my symptoms in detail, explaining about the cough that brought nothing up and the pain in my side and the hunger and the flashes of prurience and the thickness of my urine and the hypersensitivity of my hair ends and finally about the pains I had been having in my chest for the past two days. I tried to tell him about this sense I had of moving through time, but by then the doctor had placed his stethoscope to my chest and was listening to my heart. I waited impatiently for him to finish and then told him again about my disoriented sense of time.

"Hmn," he said, "*Angst*. Classical."

Hmn, I thought. *Angst*. Popular.

"Frankly, Mr. Boswell, I find nothing the matter with you," the doctor said. He was one of those men who, thirty years after the fact, still have the air about them of the Middle-European refugee. "Your heart seems quite sound," he added.

Dr. Mefwiss told me that examinations in the home were by their very nature superficial and that if the pains did not go away then by all means I must come in for additonal tests, but that in the meanwhile he didn't think there was much to worry about, that I seemed to him somewhat tired and that these symptoms might very well be my body's way of warning me that it was time to slow down. Here was an opportunity to get some rest, he said, and that if I thought it would help he could leave me some prescriptions for that purpose—tranquilizers, a mild sleeping pill, something for my pain.

"Leave them with the doorman," I said.

"Yes," Dr. Mefwiss said. He snapped his case shut and stood up.

"I threw up," I told him hopefully.

414

Dr. Mefwiss shrugged.

"Well, thank you very much, Doctor. You can let yourself out, I think, and please don't forget to return that passkey to the desk."

When he left I picked up the telephone. "Roger? Jim."

"Yes, Jim," Roger said. "How did it go?"

"He doesn't think I ought to be moved at this time, so he's not hospitalizing me just now, Roger. He'll give you some prescriptions for me, I'd like you get them filled right away."

"Yes, of course," Roger said worriedly.

"What about the rent?" I asked.

Roger hesitated.

"Come on, what happened?"

"She didn't pay it, Jim."

"Ah."

"Maybe she just forgot."

"Mind like a trap, Roger. Seven languages. Photographic memory."

"Well, it's only two days late. The office didn't think anything of it."

"The doctor said I had to rest," I said wearily. "It's tiring me to talk."

"I understand," Roger said.

"Get the prescriptions filled," I said. I replaced the phone and then called him back immediately.

"Roger? There's something else. That doctor . . . I don't know. Ask around; something may be fishy. See what you can find out. I don't have to tell you to be discreet." I hung up.

Lying there, I had the sense that something which I had not wanted to happen was already beginning. At last I knew what it was. At any time during the past fifteen years someone could have asked me, "What's troubling you, Boswell?" and I could have answered, "The three-hundred-pound bench press," "John Sallow," "A contact in New York," "The Great," "The Club," "Death." My life had been without real complexity. It had had the classic simplicity of an obstacle course, the routine excitement of anticipated emergencies. I had lived peculiarly untouched by what men call fate, and if I had sometimes missed complexity I had usually been able to see it as a proliferation of passions, something I was unqualified for. If I had ever regarded myself sentimentally, it was as a kind of hero *manqué*. No one could long grieve for what one was unsuited for by condition and will. No one could cry over unpoured milk. I lived untouched by fate still, but the other thing—complexity—was being gradually forced upon me, and only now was it clear that what I called "complexity" was not so much a proliferation of passions as a diminishment of them, a chipping away at whatever passion one could call his own. It was indeed a heart attack I had suffered, no matter what the doctor said. Real life, if not knowing where one stood *were* real life, was simply a question of subterranean manipulations, of contrivings, a robbing of Peter to pay Paul. The great thing was to be obsessed, to maintain one's certainty, to be able to know arrogantly.

Something had gone wrong. Still, I knew that if I had been betrayed it had been by my own hand; the doctor had as much as told me so. If the symptoms I felt, the disturbances of my peace like the violences of terrorists, were psychosomatic, as the doctor had more than hinted, then it could only mean that I had mislived my life, that all the time I had thought I was doing otherwise I had been working overtly against my own silent nature. At my age this was unthinkable; that only now my nature, whatever oriental a thing it might turn out to be, was taking its revenge, was outrageous. It was like being damned without warning, like being condemned to Hell because one was an ignorant pagan. Why didn't you tell me, I felt like demanding of my nature. Why were you so silent, so demurring all these years? Evading with no comment and sometimes even with approval all those things you privately condemned? You were my God, I thought, I had no other. Why didn't you love me?

Now it was simply too late; I would not reform. This *was* the record for a heart attack and there was no cure. I would have to sing the tune the way I had learned it. If one of us had to give in, it would have to be my nature, my self-righteously taciturn and conspiratorial true self. Had ever a true self been less true?

If I had no genuine disease now, why, one day I would. One day I could bring the doctors a real cancer, a recognizably diseased heart. I warned my pain that I could live with it, my nature that although I would never understand its treachery, I could live with it as well. My pain had confused me, but now that I knew the awful thing it stood for I could resist it. In three days, I told myself, I would be better. I closed my eyes and slept better than I had in days.

The phone rang. "It's Roger. Did you get the medicine? I let myself in and put it by your bed. You were sleeping."

"Yes, Roger. I see it. Thank you."

"You know," he said, "you were right."

"Was I?" I asked sleepily.

"You certainly were. I can't say very much about it now, but it looks as though you were right about him."

"Was I? About whom?"

"That doctor—Mefwiss. I asked the doorman at Number 36. Mefwiss used to have his office there. He's mixed up in some stuff. There's talk of a malpractice suit over his head in another state."

"Fixing beyond fixing."

"He sure fooled me," Roger said. "All his talk about virus going round, cigarettes and cancer, men with heart conditions leading normal lives—just a front."

"Fixing beyond fixing."

"You really spotted that guy."

"Fixing beyond fixing. Thank you, Roger."

I leaned back. The pains in my chest were just as severe as ever, but I was untroubled. Roger had helped me. Another doorman in my life, I thought, another gatekeeper. There was something Elizabethan about it. The old democracy between king and fool. But I knew pleasantly that if I were inside the walls now it was in body only—not spirit, thank you. There was still something in myself reprobate and unreconstructed. If it was not, as I had just learned, my soul, then it was something better than my soul—my will perhaps, the glands of my

417

need. Fixing beyond fixing, even within myself. Here I was in civil but civilized war with my own nature, the two factions outwardly like gentlemen who still behaved courteously toward one another, but deeper and more importantly, wheelers and dealers who cynically kept the trade routes open.

Later I called Roger and asked him to bring the newspapers.

"Which ones?"

"What difference does it make? Fixing beyond fixing, eh, Roger? Scratch a hero and what have you got left?"

"Nothing," Roger said.

"Right. Men are hollow. It's easier to keep the trade routes open that way."

"You can't trust anybody," Roger said.

"The truth shall make you free," I said.

"So long as it doesn't make too free with you, eh, Jim?"

"Jackanapes!" I roared when I replaced the phone. "Man in motley! Clown!"

I wondered where Margaret was.

Toward evening the telephone in our room rang (to make David feel more at home we had given him his own telephone) and I got out of bed to answer it. It could have been Margaret. People rarely called us; mostly we used the phone to call each other. When I picked up the receiver the person on the other end of the line listened to my voice without answering. "Margaret?" I said. "Is that you? I'm a sick man, Margaret. What have you been doing with yourself, kid?" I hung up.

Back in David's room it occurred to me to call my son. I dialed the Fifth Avenue salon where David worked. "May I speak with Mr. David, please?"

"Who is this, please?"

I experimented. "A friend. He'll know."

"Mr. David is *very* busy."

"*Bitch,*" I said.

"Look, if this is the party that's been bothering him, he's asked me to tell you that he's very upset and that you're not to call any more."

418

"Get him. It's his father. Get him," I shouted.

David came to the phone. I could imagine its being thrust into his hand and him taking it as though it were a microphone into which he was expected to sing while people fled a burning theater. He would be turning his head now, looking around him with that special, sly confusion he affected. "Yes?" he said uncertainly.

"David, it's Papa."

"Oh," David said. "Oh. How are you?"

"Why do you spite me, David?"

"Is something wrong? I'm sorry, is something wrong?"

"Forget about it, David. Cut your losses and try to live. Where are you?"

"I'm working."

"Where are you? I'm home for a few days. I haven't seen you."

"Oh," David said. I knew what he was going to say next and when he actually said it there was nothing more I could do for him. "You were gone so much," David said, "I thought it might be because of me. I didn't want to put you to any trouble. That's why I left." Then he added, "I'm in the Village—with a friend."

"Look, Telemachus, you'll never catch me. Give it up. Do something you're good at. I didn't know it was going to be you when I screwed your mother. Forget about it. Look at it this way, what happens when I die? You'll just be left holding your lousy bag of spite."

David didn't answer. I sighed. "Where's Margaret?" I asked finally.

"Isn't she with you?" he asked happily.

"You're a rotten kid, sonny. I disinherit you for the second and last time. Goodbye."

That was the way to do it, I thought. The cutting of one's losses was an art form. I had never allowed David to drain much of my spirit, but it was useless to pretend he hadn't gotten something. He wasn't entitled to it, but what he got away with he got away with. Already I felt a little stronger.

I called Roger and asked him to pick up some things for me in the room on Fifty-eighth Street. I had been neglecting The Club. The strength I had won back from David I would put into the arrangements that had still to be made.

Now that was the way to live, I thought. Simply. Why, the world was a Walden if you knew how to look at it. Madness and method were the strengths of the true champion. For the first time in many days I forced myself to think of the great. For the first time in my life I allowed myself to say "we."

VIII

April 30, 1962. New York City.

I dreamt of The Club.

I had a new symptom: I could see only in lurid shades of red. It was not unpleasant, and I strolled about the room almost merrily, making sure that everyone was happy and had what he wanted. I had never been so content. I had the comfortable sense that all time was before us, that it had been frozen forever at Saturday night.

I was the Host. "Oh, Boswell can be the Host," people called when I walked in, and the Queen ran up and slipped the mantle of Host around my neck. "The amiable man," she said.

"I am not genuinely fond of people," I replied modestly and they all applauded. "As you were," I said and they returned to their conversations.

I continued my tour of the room, the merry old uncle of Scrooge's early Christmases, long hose over my plump, pinkish, hairless calves, fat as jolly roasts. They had dressed me in silks, and I walked among them wide-behinded, hearty as a father of the bride, moving people under the mistletoe, proposing toasts, drinking all men's healths, shoving money into the fiddler's hands. People smiled at me and begged me to stay, but I remembered my obligations and shook my head. Frequently I wrote out checks and folded them into their parting handshakes.

Nate's was as lush as a tropic. Now that I was an

intimate of the place, it struck me as it never had when I was an outsider. My dancing slippers glided silkenly over the soft fur carpets. The linen, thick as blankets on the tables, looked like the cloths that set off precious stones in jeweler's trays; indeed, I could just perceive the repressed gleam of gold and silver beneath the rosy haze of the cutlery. The knives and forks and goblets and dishes seemed expensive precision tools, like the studded, complicated brass of band instruments.

As I walked about the room, nodding happily to the lovely women, the handsome men, sound as athletes in their evening dress, I had a vision. Through the windows of Nate's Place, past the crowds outside, I could see the Times Building, and moving across the dream-restored electric-bulbed banner in letters of fire: SURVIVAL OF THE FITTEST. Of course, I thought. It was good to know. I remembered films I had seen where the end of the world was portrayed. The Bomb had fallen and the survivors were always a cross section, a tiny representative handful of men, cozy as people in an elevator together—a laborer, a businessman, a young officer, an old lady, a Negro, an ingénue, a bum. But it wouldn't be like that at all—it would be like this. The last men and women on earth would be in evening clothes, as we were. We were vulnerable, perhaps, but were were less vulnerable. I began to congratulate the people around me as I greeted them, to love them for their safety. We were like finalists in some cosmic beauty contest—mutually gorgeous.

I felt a new elation, a new freedom, and I moved now with that special, just controlled wildness of the exceptionally happy. I became more interested in what people were saying, realizing just in time that it would be important. I didn't want to miss any of it, but I saw that I couldn't be everywhere at once. Had it not seemed ungracious I would have demanded the silence of all groups until I could join them. Things were being said, I knew, that I was missing—intimate shop talk of the Great, as sweet to me as the songs and voices of the Sirens. Two hundred was too unwieldy a number, I realized, and I had a sense of imperfection like the awareness of a stain on my trousers. It was no longer enough simply to live forever. It was no longer enough to be just one single man. I wanted to be everyone in this room and all the people in the crowds outside and all people everywhere who had ever lived. What did it mean to be just Boswell, to have only Boswell's experience?

I walked faster. Soon I was running around the room from group to group, but I saw that this was no better and I resumed my normal pace, a long, impatient stalk like an angry cat's.

At one table where Morty Perlmutter and Dr. Green, the noted gynecologist, were among the group, I made up my mind to stop. "Gentlemen," I said, nodding to both. I sat down and a famous senator handed me a drink. I did not know the senator personally and Dr. Green introduced him to me as his son. Gordon Rail, the communications tycoon, whispered in my ear. "Our next President," he said. "The man to watch. He has the support of all seven hundred and forty-three of my morning newspapers and of five of my TV and radio networks. Three hundred and twelve of my evening papers will say they're against him, but that's only to make it look good, you understand."

"Fixing beyond fixing," I said.

"What did you expect?" he asked.

"Dr. Green was just telling us something very interesting when you stopped by, Boswell," Morty Perlmutter said. I glanced at Dr. Green, who seemed a little uneasy.

"Go on, Doctor," I said.

"Well, it's not really very much."

"No, no, please go on," I said. "I shall feel I'm intruding otherwise."

"It's just something about the Profession," he said.

"Yes?" I said, waiting.

"Well, it's rather personal, when you come right down to it."

"Yes?"

"Well," he said at last, "you know how we gynecologists are supposed to be able to look on the female anatomy just as if it were some kind of machine?"

"Yes."

423

"Well, it's just that I never could."

"I see."

"I get nervous," he explained. "It's damned hard to have to examine some of these girls. It drives me crazy."

"I should have thought you'd be used to it by this time, Green," Gordon Rail said.

"Not at all," Morty said. "It's our culture. It's only where the weaving trade flourishes that you have prurience. Paris and Rome and New York are world centers of the garment indstury. That's why there's so much emphasis on sex in those cities."

"I never realized that," the senator said.

"Well, of course," Morty said. "Why do you think my tribes are so underpopulated? Where you have nakedness you don't have much of your copulation."

"That would suggest an interesting new interpretation of the Fall," the Black Pope said.

"To this day I can enjoy making love to my wife only if she has a sheet over her head," Dr. Green said glumly. His son the senator looked down shyly. "Once she almost smothered," Dr. Green said.

"On the Isle of Pica the unmarried virgins all go around nude except for this bandage on their left knee," Morty Perlmutter said. "It used to madden me to think about what was under that bandage. I mean, for God's sake, I had the example of the right knee, but it didn't make any difference."

"It embarrasses me even to look at the equipment," Dr. Green said. "'I'm a fetishist about gynecological supplies. I talk this way only because we're behind closed doors." He lowered his voice. "It's good to be able to get it off my chest, but I don't really deserve to be among you men at all."

The other men demurred politely. "We're all of of us corrupt, Green," Gordon Rail said with kindness.

"Have any of you boys ever had a tube of vaginal jelly in your hands?" Dr. Green asked ardently.

"What do you think about the dissemination of birth-control information, Green?" Gordon Rail asked. "As a newspaperman I'd like to know."

"Well, it's good for business, of course," Dr. Green said. "Excuse me, Your Reverence," he said to the Black Pope. "Say," he said to the rest of us, "how would you fellows like to hear an amusing story? Of course it's off the record."

"Well, of course," Morty said.

"Naturally," Gordon Rail said. He looked at the rest of us and we all agreed.

"It goes back to the day when I finished my internship. There was this guy I had gone through med school with, another gynecologist. A stiff bastard—he never saw the humor in what we were doing. Nothing ever bothered him. He was made out of stone, I think."

"The Party Whip is like that," the senator said.

"Really?" Gordon Rail said.

"Oh yes," the senator said. "Thinks he's a regular goddamn Thomas Jefferson. I never saw anyone like him for passing laws. No sense of humor at all."

"When we finished our internship we both set up practices in the same city. Any of you boys ever see a gynecologist's office?" Dr. Green asked.

"I have," Morty said. "I've seen everything."

"Then you know there are a lot of screens around, and sheets and special tables. We have to make it as impersonal as we can. We deal only with the specific thing, you see. Like a bank teller who only gets to know a depositor's hand as he pushes the passbook under the cage.

"So anyway, this time I'm talking about I had a date to have dinner with my friend and I went over to pick him up at his office. He told me he'd be all through but there was still one woman waiting to see him when I got there. Well, she must have been very nervous because when my friend came out and indicated that he was ready for her, and said to me, 'Hello there, Green, I have one more appointment,' and went back into his office, this woman just got up and went out the door. I looked at her, but she was tongue-tied with embarrassment—this happens sometimes—and just got the hell out of there as fast as she could. So I went on in to pick up my friend and tell him he'd just lost his patient, but his back was to

425

me and he was stooped over examining some records. Before I could even open my mouth he said, 'Go behind the screen and get undressed, Mrs. Davis.' Well, when I saw all this equipment and everything, I figured here was a good chance to shake this bastard up for once, so I went back there and took off all my clothes. All the time he kept talking to me and reassuring me. 'Well,' he said, 'when you're ready what I want to establish in this preliminary examination is your general condition. Just get on the table, please, and cover everything but your legs with the sheet.' So I did. I got on the table and pulled the sheet over my head, and this guy asked me if I was ready, and I grunted, and he started around behind the screen. 'I just want to see what your trouble is, Mrs. Davis,' he says. 'Oh my God,' he says, 'Mrs. Davis!' "

"Say, that's very amusing," Gordon Rail said.

"A little irresponsible, I think," the Black Pope said.

"Well, isn't that exactly what's so amusing about it?" I asked.

"Gordon Rail's right," the senator said. "We're all corrupt."

"Of course it wouldn't do for them to find out," Gordon Rail said. He pointed to the crowds still gathering outside the window.

"We're behind closed doors," Dr. Green said.

"Maybe you'd better pull the drapes as well, Boswell," the Black Pope said.

"Yes," I said, "I've been thinking about that." It was a good chance to get away. I hadn't forgotten that there were others to visit. I stood up and began again my counter-clockwise promenade about the room. It was Market Day, the opening of the Fair, the Easter Parade.

I still felt uneasy about not being everywhere and everyone at once. It was no longer, I think, that I feared to miss them doing their turns, seeing them at their most expansive and best. Almost without my being aware of it a new weight of maturity had settled upon me like dust, the old-shoe ease of compromise. I felt older, and I knew that I would have been content to share their boredom or know their bleakness—to have been, so to speak, a crumpled handkerchief in the torn pocket of their gray bathrobes. As I reflected on this I realized that I knew nothing of human beings really, nothing of their characters, nothing even of their experience. The desire to know what people thought was a torment, like gazing at heights in the night sky and wondering if there could be life on other planets and what it would be like if there were, always knowing that you would never know, that some day others might, but you, never. The weight of one's solitary existence was overwhelming; one was pinned by it, caged by it like an animal. (Surely, I thought, love is only the effort weak men put forth to compromise their solitariness.) One could not be sure of others; one could not be sure they didn't lie when they said they were solitary too. I was Moses brought so far and no further, my single knowledge the knowledge of the margin that separated me from all I had ever hoped for, that margin another desert, another complicated wilderness. To be teased with sight and hearing and speech and to have seen and heard only oneself, held conversation with only oneself—this was the sad extravagance of life. Sure, I was less badly off than many men—I was not a little blind boy, I was no one who was starving, I was not someone with a wife in the hospital or a man with no legs—but trouble was trouble.

I nodded to Robert Frost. "Provide, provide," I said.

I saluted the Cabinet. "Who's minding the store?" I said.

I spotted Harold Flesh by himself in a corner. "Stick 'em up, Harold," I said.

"Mr. Boswell," someone called. "Mr. Boswell." It was W.H. Lome, Jr. He stuck out his hand.

"How are you?" I asked.

"I just thought of something," he said. "If a man owned a tavern his friends would have to buy their liquor when they came to see him." It was his way of greeting anyone who had known his father.

"The rich get richer," I said, and nodded to a tall old man standing by the sweets table.

"Ah, Boswell," he said.

"M'lord," I said.

Nate was at the *table d'afrique.* "It's marvelous," he said. "It's costing me a fortune but it's marvelous."

"Two hundred is too unwieldy a number," I said. "They don't even know each other."

"No, it's marvelous. I want to thank you for doing this for me."

"Dope," I said. Something occurred to me. "Here," I said, taking off the mantle of Host the Queen had hung around my neck and handing it to him. "It's restricting my progress."

"No, I couldn't," Nate said.

"You will."

"No, I really couldn't."

"Damn it, I said you will." I grabbed him and held him with one arm while I slipped the mantle over his head.

"No, it's yours," he said shyly. "Really, Boswell."

I twisted the mantle tightly and holding both reins pulled up on them sharply. Nate fell against me as I choked him. "We'll hear no more about it," I said. "You're the Host."

"Well, then," he said, "thank you. I want to show Perry. Where's Perry? He'll have to see this."

I felt a little better after strangling Nate. It was still necessary, however, to organize the two hundred—at least necessary to start with them if I ever hoped to do anything about the others outside, and the others else-where, all the people behind the Iron Curtain and the people in the Andes and Tierra del Fuego and the Australian outback and the handful in the Antarctic and people on tiny islands in the Pacific, and the populations of Europe and Asia and Africa. A general call would have to go out in a language they all could understand. Of course there would be problems, but first things first.

I clapped my hands. With the shock of my palms coming together my vision darkened. The reds went deep-er. It was as if I were lookinp now through blood, but I also felt a kind of boozy randiness. I clapped my hands again; four or five people looked around and grinned.

I clapped my hands a third time. "Your attention. Your attention, please," I called.

"Shh. It's the Host," someone said.

"You'd better get up on something if you want them to hear you. Two hundred is an unwieldy number," said General Manara. He had won two additional stars since I had first met him in the Gibbenjoy home in Philadelphia. One was his Korean Star and the other was for Miscellaneous Small Wars.

"Of course," I said. I cleared away some of the food from the *table d'afrique:* a small zebra fillet (I was surprised to see that the stripes were carried through into the meat itself—Of course, I thought, light meat and dark meat) and a platter of lion livers. Climbing onto the table, I clapped my hands a final time.

"Ladies and gentlemen," I called. Nate looked embarrassed. "For History," I whispered hoarsely. I spotted Margaret across the room with Harold Flesh. "Where the hell have you been?" I yelled, but I was careful not to yell in exactly her direction so that no one else could hear me. I didn't wait for her answer.

"Mr. President, Queen, Warlords, Chairmen of Boards, Leaders, Owners, Guests and Friends—Ladies and Gentlemen. May I have your attention for a moment?" Gradually people began to look up at me. With their eyes on me I noticed that I felt a little warm; excited as I was I made a mental note of this. (I had never before been aware of the sheer physical heat generated by attention.) I waited until they finished coughing. "All right," I said, "now look. Two hundred is too unwieldy a number to work with if we're going to get anything out of this. Now I'll be perfectly frank with you. I don't personally give a good goddamn if the rest of you get anything out of it at all. That's your lookout. But I'm here for a good time. Let me hear it if you feel that way about it too." They applauded brightly. They were a surprisingly tractable group to work with, I thought. It would probably be harder when I got everybody together. Already I was thinking tentatively of a suitable site, the Sahara perhaps, or a huge platform built out over the Atlantic. "All right then," I said sharply, "let's get organized. I want all of you Nobel Prize winners to stand up and go over to that wall." I pointed to the small table of space foods Nate had set up. "That's right, Morty, by the space pastes." Morty was the only one who had moved. "Come on now, the rest of you as well. Follow Dr. Perlmutter, please." I indicated the South American poet. *"Señor,"* I said, *"por favor,* if you please." He smiled shyly but stayed where he was. "To get the hell to where I told you," I shouted. "All right," I said when he had started, "now Dr. Green."

"I didn't know Green had a Nobel Prize," someone whispered.

"Peace Prize," his son the senator said, giggling.

"Now where's that team from Cal Tech?" I spotted two Chinese lounging near Harold and Margaret. They grinned good-naturedly and set off to join the others. "They go everywhere together," I told the crowd. "Ying and Yang." I looked around the room. "Where's my chemist?" I demanded. "Where's my authority on International Law?" I prodded the remaining Nobel Prize winners, and soon they made a sizable group by the table. I carefully arranged the rest of them around the room and smiled down at the group approvingly.

"Are we all here?" I asked. "Who's minding the world?" I motioned for silence.

"Okay," I said, "the way I see it is this. There's a symbol involved. We're behind closed doors, as Green says, but in a deeper sense we've always been behind closed doors, if you see what I mean. Well now, I don't think that's a very satisfactory way to have to live. Personally I think I'm missing a lot that I might otherwise be getting out of life. Incidentally, I want you to notice that I'm addressing you in clichés. That's the deliberate oratorical style I've adopted in order to reach the greatest possible number with the least possible misunderstanding. It's going to be my *lingua franca* with you. I tell you this because my cards are on the table and I don't intend to pull the wool over anybody's eyes. I'm not that kind of person. As a matter of fact I have absolutely nothing to

430

hide. Indeed, I never had. But the rest of you—*my God!* Ask anybody here if Boswell hasn't always been open and aboveboard in his dealings. I think you'll find that if the truth were known I certainly have.

"Now you ask what my purpose is and I tell you it's simply this. I can't stand the idea of your knowing something I don't know. Now I know why that is. I haven't lived this long in the world for nothing. It's just that you people have to die. I understand that. If you people lived forever you'd be better people than you people are. But you don't live forever so you become all shut up inside and you rush around hither and yon from pillar to post, keeping your own counsel, living your own lives, with no regard for me and what I might require of you. I know, I know—it's a rat race. But I'm of the opinion that it doesn't have to be that way, that if we just use a little common sense and try a little harder to help the other fellow we can change all that. Just as an example, look what we have not fifty feet away from us right out there on Broadway. Open the drapes please, Nate."

Nate pulled back the drapes and we could see the crowds outside surge forward, swinging their heads around each other's necks to get a better look at us.

"Okay, Nate, you can close them now. You see? That's what I mean. You create this wake of curiosity wherever you go. Now these are just little people and you might think they don't count for much and I grant you that, but the principle is unchanged.

"All right. What I'm asking you to do is to forget your own deaths for a minute and think about mine. That isn't selfish or unreasonable of me as it might sound. I mean, when you come right down to it I never had anything very much to do with death, and the same can't be said for a lot of you people. As a matter of fact, some of you folks have been making a pretty good profit out of it for years. Don't get the wrong idea—I'm not condemning you. You have to make a buck, a name, wherever you can; I appreciate that. General Manara here, for example, has four stars on each shoulder of each suit in his closet. Now just as an approximation, General, how many lives do you suppose each of those stars represents? Just as an approximation, now."

The general blushed and looked away.

"Just so," I said. "And it's pretty much the same story with most of you. Perlmutter here deals in dying cultures. He won't touch them unless they're unspoiled. Well, how many of you have ever stopped to consider what an unspoiled culture actually is? It's one without proper facilities for sanitation, without electricity, without hospitals or a balanced diet or a vaccination program. Anything, in fact, which might extend longevity by a single day may be said to contribute to culture spoilage.

"But I don't mean to bring this down to a personal level. What's true of General Manara and Morty here is just as true of a lot of others. Quick, Black Pope, how does a Christian get into your Heaven?"

"He must first die," the Black Pope said.

"There—you see? And that's not all. Some of you who are doctors, haven't you sometimes sent a bill to the next of kin after you've already lost the patient? There are lawyers among us, prosecuting attorneys." I pointed to a famous district attorney.

"Hey, wait a minute," he said. "I'm not even in favor of capital punishment."

"There is no other kind, sir," I said. "But that's not the point. As I said before, I'm not attacking anybody. It's just that I'm trying to get across to you that I come to you with my hands clean, a veritable Switzerland among men."

I paused while they nodded to each other like people who find themselves in agreement about a good pianist. Some of them even winked. I could see that I had impressed them; even Lano was concentrating intently upon me. Only Morty, that egoist, seemed a little bored; I saw him pop a pill onto his tongue. It seemed to me he frowned but of course it may just have been the bitter taste of the dissolving chemicals. Which was an example of what I meant: it was impossible to know what was really happening to someone else.

"Now in a kind of way," I went on, "all I mean to

get across to you in this little talk is that I exist. I don't really think you've been as cognizant of that fact in the past as you might have been. No, don't protest—I think that if you'll just look into your hearts you'll see that what I've said is quite true."

I gave them time to consider this. "He's right, you know," I heard the President of the United States say. "I haven't been as cognizant of him as I might have been."

The Party Whip patted his arm reassuringly. "You can't keep every campaign promise. No one expects you to."

"Now let me emphasize again, I'm not attacking you," I said. "You've had your reasons, little as I might think of them, and I'm perfectly willing to let bygones be bygones." I held out my hands as if to bless them. "Let us look upon this night as a new dawn, my friends—the dawn of a fresh start, a second chance." Disappointingly, they did not applaud here, and I rushed on. "I speak from this platform to you world leaders—and later, I trust, from a still wider platform to a still more inclusive group —of a second chance." I lowered my voice. "But let no man here think that this is my only object," I warned. "Indeed, I would be less than honest with you if I left you with the impression that this was all I expected."

"It's quite the most remarkable speech I've ever heard," someone said. "What do you think, Perlmutter?"

"It's atavistic, archetypal," Morty said offhandedly. "I've heard it all before."

"The fact is," I said, "I am quite as much aware of your own existences as I have asked you to be of mine. Had I the time I should ask you to listen as I revealed to you every thought I have ever had, each variegated personal impression, intuition, in the wide, but alas not wide enough, kaleidoscope of my consciousness. I should urge upon you in detail the panorama of James Boswell's experiential life. But"—here I shrugged—"I haven't the time, and surely this is all our loss, for what splendid release there would be for you in knowing *in toto* another's experience, another's vision! No savior could do more! Nor would *that* be all, for then I should require of you each in turn to reveal yourselves in just such a way to me,

433

and I should give, step by step, my reactions to your own and ask of you yours to mine and then offer to you mine to yours to mine, and so on and so forth. Nor would that even *then* be all. I would not be content that this should be done only here where the fire laws allow the seating of a mere two hundred people. We would gather on a great plain where all might come, black and white, gentile and Jew, rich and poor, believer and Turk, young and old, quick and dead, without regard to race, creed or color. There, all would partake of the gentle communion I speak of. Then might we *know one another* indeed, and begin to dissipate the unwholesome—I say *unwholesome* —mystery which hangs—now like a miasma about each separate, solitary life!"

"Quite remarkable," the man who had spoken before said.

"Ho hum," Morty said. "Archetypal. Ontogeny recapitulates phylogeny."

"It does not," I yelled. "Hear me out," I demanded.

"Hear, hear," the Queen of England said. Others took the cry up and Morty, looking amused and superior, shrugged.

"Give the man a chance, there," Harold Flesh shouted after everyone had quieted down, his timing a little off.

"All right," I said, "all right. There *isn't* time. I wasn't born yesterday. I know there isn't time—there isn't that much time in the world. Only I think it very peculiar that a certain party could already have forgotten what the proper study of mankind finally is. I won't go into that— this isn't the time and place for indulging in personalities. I am content that you all know who I mean.

"All right, then. What I'm getting at is this. Since there isn't time for the other thing, we're going to have to find a kind of shorthand for it, and it's occurred to me that one way we might do that is by looking upon each other as metaphors. That's right. I've been working on this for some time now and I think it's a breakthrough. Do you follow me here? It would be like a morality play. You know. Only much more sophisticated. We'd be using metaphors to reveal ourselves to each other.

"Now it's not for me to say what metaphor each of you is. It's a free country and of course I have my opinions, based on sensitive, scientific observation, but admittedly one has to allow a certain margin for error. It's that margin, ladies and gentlemen, which I hate! Which of us can afford to be wrong about which of us? Do you see what I mean? Do you see how important this is? As I see it there's only one alternative, the one I've just suggested. Every man his own anthropologist! That would be our cry. Do away with the middleman entirely. Okay. Don't speak out at once. Consider your essences, your basic properties as men, the individual quality of your lives, before you make your metaphorical reductions. Let no secret be sacred, no area of your soul undefiled. The watchword is Trespass! Trespass, gentlemen, trespass!

"Now synchronize your watches. Begin!"

I was sweating as I waited for one of them to make a start. I searched their red faces for a sign. I had touched them, I knew that. They were silent, concentrating. A red smile played unconsciously across several mouths, perhaps touched off by some memory of what they were or had once been. In a few eyes red tears appeared and flowed like blood down the burning cheeks. Only Morty's face seemed clear, unconcerned, with that nauseating look of self-containment I had come to despise in men.

I waited, giving them as much time as I could. At last I saw that though many of them had found the metaphor that would express themselves—their very faces shone with their solutions—each was reluctant to be the first. Or perhaps that was giving them the benefit of the doubt. I had put them in touch with something valuable they had been unaware of, had indicated to them where a treasure lay buried, and now they stood before me stiff with greed.

Pretending that I misunderstood I resumed my speech. "Come, come," I said, "it isn't that hard. As thus: 'As egocentric as Harold Flesh.' Or in another vein, 'As egocentric as Morty Perlmutter.'" Here Morty put another pill into his mouth. "I feel absolutely seized with inspiration," I confessed. "Here's another one: 'As ego-centric as James Boswell.' That might be even further compressed. 'As egocentric as Boswell.' 'Egocentric as Boswell.' These are only rough approximations—I'm not a poet, you understand. They need polishing, of course, and I've no doubt that many of you can do as well if not better than that, but it's the sort of thing I mean. How's this one—'As self-centered as Jim Boswell'? Well?"

They seemed to admire my analogies, and I thought that perhaps I had misjudged them; perhaps they had merely been struck dumb by the aptness of my thought, the happiness of my language, and were reluctant to compete with me on that basis. At any rate, I saw that I would have to be patient. "All right," I said, "this isn't the last time we'll be getting together. I expect you to do your homework and be prepared to recite your metaphors when we meet again."

I looked around. They seemed relieved that I had left them off so easily. Only Morty's expression had not changed. I owe you one, I thought, as I looked at him.

"Well then," I said, "we've been pretty serious to-night. I've made some rather heavy demands on you, I think, and it occurs to me that one reason may be that my speech has been without much humor. Most public speakers like to sprinkle a few jokes into their talks. Usually those jokes come at the beginning, but to dem-onstrate that I'm not atavistic and that ontogeny doesn't always recapitulate phylogeny—*and never has in my own case*—I'd like to reverse the usual order and tell you one right here at the end."

They were smiling, already prepared to like my story, but I ignored them and looked directly at Morty. "There was this *Jewish* lady," I began, "whose husband died and left her a lot of money. So one day she got into this huge Cadillac convertible and drove down to Miami Beach to the biggest, flashiest hotel they had there."

Morty glowered at me and put out his tongue to receive another pill.

"When she pulled up in front of the hotel she leaned on the horn until a bellboy came around to open the door for her."

The color had begun to drain from his face.

" 'Look here,' she says in a loud voice, 'I'm Mrs. Ginsberg, and I've reserved the biggest suite in the hotel. You'll carry up my bags to it, yeah? And you shouldn't forget the *MINK COAT* in dee-t-r-ronk!' "

Watching me, Morty was now desperately putting one pill after another into his mouth.

"So the woman rides up in the elevator to her penthouse suite and waits for the bellboy to come up with her bags."

Now Morty's was the only face that was not red. He had taken the bottle of pills from his pocket and unscrewed the cap. Raising the bottle to his mouth he began to pour the pills directly onto his tongue. He chewed obscenely, his pale jaws working automatically, rapid and clumsy as an infant seeking a breast.

"In a little while the bellboy comes up loaded down with so many suitcases you can't even see his face. He puts them down and the woman starts to take a dime out of her purse to give it to him, but all of a sudden she stops. 'Vere's de boy?' she asks.

"Well, the guy looks at her, not understanding. 'I beg your pardon,' he pants. 'Where's what boy?'

" 'De boy,' she says, *'de boy.'*

" 'Do you mean that grown man I saw in the back seat?' he asks.

" 'Yeah, him,' she says. 'My son, in de beck. Vat's de matter you didn' carry him up too?'

" 'Oh, I'm sorry,' the bellboy says, 'I didn't realize he couldn't walk.'

" 'He cen valk, he cen valk,' she says. 'Tenk God he doesn't have to.' "

Morty was gasping for breath. He had run out of pills and was clutching at his chest as if to stop blood that might be flowing from it. The rest of the people in the room hadn't seen him and were still laughing. I pointed to Morty, who was on his knees now, pulling in terror at his collar.

"Dr. Perlmutter doesn't get it," I said calmly.

They stared at him and one by one raised their hands to their faces, to stop their laughter as they would a sneeze. They spread away from him evenly, creating around him an island of space.

On his back now, Morty looked up at me helplessly. Already his deah had settled and he had begun to shrink. It was very interesting. His white face was a stain in the room. Gradually, as it had when I had cut myself off from my son, my body began to strengthen. Morty's vitality flowed into me. I felt myself grow taller. My vision cleared. As he continued to shrink I continued to grow. I was becoming a giant. I filled the room, forcing the others to flee into corners, pressing them hopeelssly against the walls, jamming them with my expanding body into tiny *cul-de-sacs* of space, smashed shards of dimension. As they suffocated and died they began to shrink also and so made more room. Others rushed into the space they made only to crash against my irresistible growth, nudged murderously by my expanding shins and enlarging thighs. They too died and shrank, feeding me freedom, precious room, which I needed now as ohers need air. I was filling out like a balloon—only not hollow. Solid, with a beautiful, felt solidity. I was greater than the room now and expanding into the street itself, where the crowds fell back from me as they would from a tidal wave. There was no place for them to go, and soon I had taken their space as I had taken the others' before. And still I continued to grow. Whole populations were plunged into a stifling darkness in the shadow of my calves. Races divided into my pockets and no sooner had found room there than my thighs, swelling, smothered them against the lining. Gradually the cries of the stricken began to subside, their great grief silent only when there were no more mourners.

"Ah," I said, my voice like thunder in the surrounding silence, "a way had to be found, and a way *was* found."

IX

Roger brought up the tuxedo I had rented, and waited while I dressed.

"Do you like a cummerbund, sir?" he asked.

He had started to call me sir again when he found out I was involved with The Club. The columnists had been talking about it for weeks, publishing the names of everyone who would be there and somehow making it sound like a journey of Magi. Some papers, taking note in their editorial columns of the diversity of the guests, had indicated a possible conspiracy of the important, a first move of the famous toward some still unstated end. Reading as news of something which had originated with me (though I was mentioned only as someone who would be there), I sometimes found it difficult to believe that I had had anything to do with The Club at all. I was very nervous.

Roger went to the window again and looked out.

"Still raining?"

"Very nasty, sir. A cloudburst."

I struggled with my tie.

"I'd better go down and get you a taxi, sir. Do you have money?"

"Yes."

"Better not take too long, sir. They won't wait on a night like this."

It was almost eight o'clock. The people had probably been arriving for an hour now.

"Roger, can you fix this damn thing?"

He made a deft bow, a knot hard and round as a black button. "Don't forget your raincoat, sir, or you'll be drenched just getting into your taxi."

He left me and I went to the closet. I felt terrible. After a month I was still troubled by my dream. My raincoat was the one I had used when I had been with Lano in the mountains, a great stiff brown canvas coat from some earlier war. I put it on over my evening clothes and shoved the hinged, rusted fasteners through the holes. Going out, I saw myself in the mirror. Years ago in a school play, just before the curtain had gone up, I had felt like this. I had asked myself what the hell I was doing there and had wanted to run.

The phone rang.

"Yes?"

"It's me," Margaret said.

"Yes, Margaret?"

"I've been staying in a hotel."

"Yes, Margaret?"

"Well, how are you?"

"I've been sick," I said. "I'm still quite weak."

"David told me. I called him."

"I see."

"He was beaten up very bady by a queer. Did you know that?"

"No."

"Yes, well he was. He's better, but I gather he's living alone now."

"We all are, aren't we?"

In the mirror, in the enormous baggage of the rough coat, I looked like a defector, someone running for his life.

"Boswell? Are you still there?"

"Yes. I'm here."

"Do you want me to come back?"

"Nah," I said, and hung up.

Roger had not found a cab for me. "It's the rain," he said. "If you'll wait here, sir, I'll go around to the avenue again and try to get one."

"I'm late," I said. "I'd better start walking."

"You'll ruin your clothes."

"No, it's letting up." When I walked out from under the striped canopy, the rain *had* let up. Even if I saw a cab I would not want it now.

I walked toward Nate's. I was a little calmer but still depressed. I came out on Broadway into the light, within easy range of the exploding signs, the excitement of neon like a kind of war. As I continued toward Nate's I became aware of the crowds almost congealing round me, seemingly increased at every side street and doorway. We moved slowly, thickly, in a single direction. I had caused this, I thought; I had invented The Club and caused this.

Across Broadway Nate's red sign flared like the name of a boat above the heads of people looking up at it from a pier. I tried to move faster, using the last of the old great strength, pushing past people who looked up at me resentfully. "Excuse me," I said. "Will you please get out of my way?" I said.

I made my way toward the curb. There were yellow barricades lining my side of the street; the other side had been roped off and it was clear except for photographers, doormen and police. On this side policemen on horseback patrolled the curbs. Other policemen leaned back into the crowds.

I was surrounded by a sort of incredible democracy. There were lovers, tourists, children, salesmen down from their hotel rooms, students, old people; there were adolescents, strangely brutalized, already unrespectable (I wondered if the boys carried knives, if the girls laid). All of them, jammed together in an anonymous intimacy, glared with a kind of solemn envy into every car that pulled up. Their feelings mixed, their faces showed the surprise and controlled resentment of people watching something which had nothing to do with themselves.

"There's one," a man next to me said.

"Can you see who it is?" another asked.

"Some movie star, I think. Jesus, look at all them jewels."

"A studio paste job," someone else said expertly.

"That's the Secretary of State getting out of that limousine," a man said.

441

"Where? No, that isn't him."

"It is so. That's the Secretary of State."

"Look at Nate Lace. He doesn't know who to shake hands with first. Hi ya, Nate."

"I never got my invitation," a large young man said.

"Why's that?"

"I'm incognito," he said.

People laughed.

"Listen, plenty will be happening in there tonight. Don't kid yourself."

"There's the millionaire, whatsisname. Look at that Rolls he's in."

"It's like a goddamn housing project."

"That's the Governor with him."

"Something's up," a woman said. "I don't like it."

"Nah, they're just going to get each other's autographs and go home."

"Excuse me," I said, "I've got to get through."

"Don't shove, will you. We're all trying to see."

"Let me by, I've got to get over there."

"He's representing the old soldiers," someone said.

"Get out of my way."

I was about to step between two barricades when a policeman pushed me back. "It's blocked off, Charley," he said. "The big shots are throwing a party."

"I've got to get through."

"Not here you don't."

"Look," I said, "this is ridiculous. I'm supposed to be over there."

"Oh, you are, are you?" he said. "Who in hell do you think you are?"

"I started it all," I said.

"He's Adam," said the young man who had told us he was incognito.

"There's one in every crowd," the policeman said good naturedly. "I've been working these affairs fifteen years and there's one in every crowd. Gate crashers! If it's a parade there's always some nut who thinks he ought to be marching."

I tugged at my raincoat to show him the dinner

442

jacket beneath it. "There," I said, "does this look as if I didn't belong there?"

Clearly I had surprised him. "Well, I don't know," he said, rubbing his jaw. "Who are you?"

It was like old times. Only the doormen were backed up now by cops with guns. It made it a contest. I felt giddy. "You wouldn't know my name," I said.

The policeman grinned. "Nice try, Charley, you had me there for a minute."

"I'm a gentleman of the press."

"Take my picture," he said.

"I'm the caterer."

"Give me a sandwich," he said.

"I'm the entertainer."

"Sing me a song," he said.

"You don't believe I belong over there, do you?" I said.

"No, sir, I don't. Now quiet down. These folks are trying to get a look at the big shots."

"So you don't think I'm a big shot?"

"All men were created equal, fella. Just quiet down, now."

"You're an idiot," I said. In a minute I could tell him who I was and it would be all over.

"What's that?"

In a minute I could tell him who I was, but I felt a weird pressure, as though at last I was about to do something infinitely mad, press a claim infinitely untenable. "I said you're an idiot," I said.

The policeman turned away. "I'm having trouble with a guy," he said to another policeman. "Signal the wagon."

"You still don't know who I am?" I said.

"I only know what you are," he said.

"Then look!" I shouted. I thrust my face to within inches of his own, holding it like a fist before his eyes.

He backed off uncertainly, startled. "Listen," he said uneasily, "if you really are with that crowd, why don't you just tell me who you are and we can check? Then I'll guide you personally across the street."

I turned to the people around me and winked. "He

wants to know who I am. Fifteen years he's been working these affairs and he wants to know who I am."

They laughed, in, they thought, on the gag. "Shall I tell him, sir?" the young man asked.

"Not yet," I said. "Give him another chance." I turned back to the policeman and stared at him. I would do it with my eyes, I thought; I would use my vision as a battering ram. In the gym, in the old days, it had been a mistake to lift bar bells, pull against heavy springs. People need people to work out against. I held my face in front of him, balancing it as steady as a weapon.

"Look," he said nervously, "let's stop all this. Just tell me your name."

Across the street cars continued to discharge the famous onto the sidewalk in front of Nate's, the men and women like secular gods—imperious, flattered, giving nothing. All that stood beween us was my name. It was incredible that anyone should ever get what he wanted, and I experienced, sharp as pain, deep as rage, a massive greed, a new knowledge that it was not enough, that nothing was ever enough, that we couldn't know what was enough or want what was enough. It wasn't even a question of deserts. Everybody deserved everything.

I had been working these affairs for fifteen years myself, I thought. In all that time I never once used a false name. It had been an incredible burden, a useless loyalty.

Now I used one. It came out of my mouth like the words of a song, like a poem, like a beautiful, triumphant idea, a piece of the truth. I said it recklessly, like someone stepping from behind his shield to throw a spear. I felt light, relieved, free.

The policeman shrugged helplessly. "Do you have any identification?" he asked.

"Not with me," I said arrogantly.

He looked at the other policeman. "We'd have to see some identification," the second policeman said.

"I don't have any."

"That's just what I thought," the first policeman said. "Now come on, stand back. The joke's over." He turned his back to me.

I nodded indifferently and made a face behind the policeman's back. I grinned and the people in the crowd clapped me on the shoulder.

"There's a cardinal getting out of that car," someone said.

"Look who just pulled up in that Cadillac."

"Now that's the Secretary of State!"

"Yes," a man said, "you're right."

So I watched. Peacefully, with the others. The self at rest, the ego sleeping, death unremembered for once.

I had lived my life like someone bereaved, keeping over it always a sort of deathwatch. And why not? I was always dying. I had a disease. It was neither metaphysical nor psychosomatic, and it was less immoral, finally, then simply unhygienic, pathological. It was a disease, this gluttony of the ego—a lifelong feast on the heart, wounding, tearing, devouring, leaving it in a ruin, disgusting as the scraps, the indigestible bones and fats that smeared the plate. That baffled our chances and wasted our hope and used up our lives.

But what's this, what's this? What was I thinking of? The ego, the ego. *Sleeping?* Say, I thought, who was I kidding? Why, I was like Nate's zebra fillets. With me, too, the stripes went all the way through, all the way down. They were my longitudes and my latitudes. I know where I'm going. *Nowhere I'm going!* I *made* The Club. I know about creation. Everybody dies, et cetera. Well, not yet, not just yet. Rise and shine, I thought. Rise and shine, old sleepy slugabed of a self.

"Hey," I called from the barricades. "Hey," I called across the wide street to the Secretary of state. "Hey, hey, down with The Club. Down with The Club. *Down with The Club!*"

THE BEST OF BESTSELLERS
FROM WARNER BOOKS

A BAD MAN
by Stanley Elkin   (95-539, $2.75)

Leo Feldman is A BAD MAN. In the basement of his department store he provides abortions, drugs, prostitutes, advice on procuring all manner of illicit wish fulfillments. Leo Feldman is an evil joke and he is condemned to prison. It is, he soon realizes, a no-exit purgatory in which he is doomed to die. "No serious funny writer in this country can match him," writes the *New York Times Book Review. The Saturday Review* writes that A BAD MAN "is a very funny book . . . The prose, dialogue and imagery are brilliant . . . The laughs alternate with the philosophy and sometimes merge with it."

BOSWELL
by Stanley Elkin   (95-538, $2.75)

Boswell wrestled with the Angel of Death and suddenly realized that everybody dies. With that realization he begins an odyssey of the ego, searching out VIP's and prostrating himself before them. He seeks out the world's richest man, history's first international revolutionist, a Nobel prize-winning anthropologist, an Italian *principessa.* Although he has embarked upon a journey that cannot help but disillusion, it is his destiny! BOSWELL "crackles with gusto and imaginative fertility."
—*Book Week*

CONFESSIONS OF A MEDICAL HERETIC
by Robert S. Mendelsohn   (95-544, $2.75)

In *Confessions of a Medical Heretic,* Dr. Robert S. Mendelsohn tells you why. The effects of the exam may well be detrimental to your health, and the diagnosis, even if confirmed by lab tests could very well be erroneous; in a recent nationwide examination of "high standard" laboratories, fifty percent failed. Dr. Mendelsohn argues cogently that drugs are now being so over-prescribed that more illnesses are being caused by their side effects than are being cured. "A hard-hitting eye-opener . . . fascinating."
—*United Press International*

PROVOCATIVE READING
FROM WARNER BOOKS

THE DICK GIBSON SHOW
by Stanley Elkin

(95-540, $2.75)

Like *The Great Gatsby*, he wants life to live up to myth. An itinerant early media man, he travels across the country working for dozens of small-town radio stations. He is the perpetual apprentice, whetting his skills and adopting names and accents to suit geography. Stanley Elkin captures the essence of the man and the time. His "prose is alive, with its wealth of detail and specifically American metaphors," says *The Library Journal*, "and the surreal elements are tightly controlled," with "brilliant sequences . . . compulsively readable and exhilarating."

THE LIVING END
by Stanley Elkin

(92-537, $2.25)

Whoever thought the holdup of a liquor store in Minnesota would lead to all this? Not Ellerbee, good sport and wine and spirits merchant. Not Jay Ladlehaus, who robbed and helped kill him. Not Quiz, the dieting groundskeeper who hates dead people. Not Flanoy, the little boy who plays Suzuki violin for the Queen of Heaven. Maybe not even God the Father—who, here, is called upon to explain his ways.

CRIERS AND KIBITZERS, KIBITZERS AND CRIERS
by Stanley Elkin

(91-543, $2.50)

"An air of mysterious joy hangs over these stories," says *Life* magazine. Yet the *New York Times Review of Books* reports that, "Bedeviling with his witchcraft the poor souls he has conjured and set into action, Stanley Elkin involves his spirits sometimes in the dread machineries of allegory and fantasy." Stanley Elkin deals in contradictions. He is a master limner of "joy" and "dread." CRIERS AND KIBITZERS, KIBITZERS AND CRIERS proves the inadequacy of a simplistic response to life. "This book," *The New York Herald-Tribune* had said, "reveals Mr. Elkin as a writer of conspicuous intellect, talent and imagination."

OUTSTANDING READING FROM
WARNER BOOKS